"A moving, enchanting story of love and loss. Amanda Wen takes readers on an adventure that weaves past and present together in a beautiful tapestry of skillful storytelling. I was blown away by this book and its timeless message."

HEIDI CHIAVAROLI, Carol Award–winning author of
*Freedom's Ring* and *The Tea Chest*

"Amanda Wen seamlessly blends the historical and the contemporary in this lyrical debut. From Annabelle, a courageous young woman building a life on the Kansas frontier, to Sloane, a museum curator searching for answers within the pages of a diary penned over one hundred years ago, *Roots of Wood and Stone* spans generations in a brilliantly rendered narrative that explores the heart behind the places we call home."

AMANDA BARRATT, author of *The White Rose Resists* and
*My Dearest Dietrich*

"Compelling. Rich. Winding through past and present and linking them in surprising ways, Wen's debut novel captures the legacy of a historic farmhouse and all the people who've made their lives there. I was rooting for Sloane out of the gate, and my heart went up and down with her story until the well-drawn conclusion. Wen writes with warmth and a delightful voice about heritage, family, and the nature of what's truly important."

JOANNA DAVIDSON POLITANO, author of *The Love Note*

"Now and then I am fortunate enough to read a book that so thoroughly captures me that I forget I'm reading. It's rare, but when it happens it feels a whole lot like magic. Amanda Wen has written such a novel. In *Roots of Wood and Stone*, Wen invites readers in, introduces them to characters who feel like dear friends, and gives them the gift of a tale well told. And in the telling, Wen reminds us of the beauty of friendship, love, and finding out the fullest meaning of home."

SUSIE FINKBEINER, author of *Stories That Bind Us* and the
Pearl Spence novels

# ROOTS
*of*
# WOOD
*and*
# STONE

# ROOTS of WOOD and STONE

## Sedgwick County Chronicles

### AMANDA WEN

KREGEL
PUBLICATIONS

**Library of Congress Cataloging-in-Publishing Data**
Names: Wen, Amanda, 1979- author.
Title: Roots of wood and stone / Amanda Wen.
Description: Grand Rapids, MI : Kregel Publications, [2021]
Identifiers: LCCN 2020034239 (print) | LCCN 2020034240 (ebook) | ISBN 9780825446689 (print) | ISBN 9780825477188 (epub) | ISBN 9780825468698 (kindle edition)
Subjects: GSAFD: Christian fiction.
Classification: LCC PS3623.E524 R66 2021 (print) | LCC PS3623.E524 (ebook) | DDC 813/.6--dc23
LC record available at https://lccn.loc.gov/2020034239
LC ebook record available at https://lccn.loc.gov/2020034240

ISBN 978-0-8254-4668-9, print
ISBN 978-0-8254-7718-8, epub

Printed in the United States of America
21 22 23 24 25 26 27 28 29 30 / 5 4 3 2 1

To the glory of God, in honor of my mother, Deanna
Peterson, whose passion for our family, past and
present, brought this book to life.

# CHAPTER ONE

SLOANE KELLEY STOOD in the lobby of the Sedgwick County Museum of History, the thick buffalo robe hanging warm and heavy on her arms. A line of first graders filed past to stroke the robe's coarse brown fur. But no matter how many little hands poked and prodded that robe, it held up. It was resilient.

Just like the pioneers who'd worn it.

The last child, a girl with wide brown eyes and a riot of red curls, trailed her hand over the robe. "It's softer than I thought it'd be."

"That's a great observation." Sloane loved those light-bulb moments when history came to life.

"That *is* a great observation, Josie." Mrs. McPherson, the dark-haired teacher charged with controlling the chaos, rewarded her student with a warm smile.

But Josie looked instead to a beaming, T-shirt-clad woman at the back of the room. Same brown eyes, same coppery curls.

Mother and daughter, no doubt.

Jaw tight, Sloane turned to hang the robe on its wooden rack. She scanned the placard beside it, covered with facts she'd researched. Facts to fill gaps in people's knowledge.

A semi-successful cover for the utter lack of facts about her own past.

"Okay, class." Mrs. McPherson's voice rose above the din. "What do we tell Miss Kelley?"

"Thaaaaaaaank yoooooooooouuuu."

Sloane both smiled and winced as the childish chorus bounced off the lobby's ornate tile walls at earsplitting volume.

"You're welcome. Thank you all so much for coming."

"Now, friends, the bus is waiting. We're going to *walk*, please. It's pouring, and the steps might be slick." Mrs. McPherson nodded to the red-haired chaperone, who leaned into the handle of the beveled glass door. Outside, a large yellow school bus idled at a low growl, and rain sheeted from a leaden April sky.

As the kids hurried to the bus, laughing and shrieking in the deluge, Sloane breathed a sigh of relief. She enjoyed field-trip kids, but their departure meant a welcome return to the museum's usual hushed reverence. How did teachers deal with it all day every day? No way did they get paid enough.

A flash of green caught her eye. Mrs. McPherson stood in the doorway, wrestling with an enormous umbrella a gust of wind had yanked inside out. Sloane started forward to help, but a suit-wearing man on the sidewalk beat her to it. Shifting the large cardboard box he carried to one hand, he held the door with the other.

"You got it?" he asked.

"I think so." Mrs. McPherson popped the umbrella back into place and gave the man a grateful smile. "Thank you."

"Welcome. Stay dry."

"I'll try." The teacher clambered aboard the bus behind her students, and the man strode into the lobby, the shoulders of his suit soaked, the lid of the box spattered with rain.

With his free hand he shoved drenched dark blond hair off his forehead. "It's a monsoon out there."

"Another gorgeous spring day in Kansas." Sloane flashed a wry grin and pushed her glasses further up onto her nose. "Can I help you?"

"Sure hope so." Ocean-blue eyes crinkled at the corners, and a crease next to the man's mouth deepened into a dimple. He was handsome enough, in a drippy, rain-soaked sort of way. "Are you the one in charge around here?"

Sloane gave a short bark of laughter. "Don't I wish."

"Maybe you can help me anyway." He set the box on the old wooden welcome desk and tapped its top. "My sister and I have been helping our grandma with a little decluttering."

Sloane stifled the urge to roll her eyes. She should've known his angle the second she saw that bedraggled box. The museum was constantly turning away people tasked with cleaning out the homes of elderly pack-rat relatives. People who thought the dusty, moldy junk they uncovered was worth a small fortune simply because it had a few decades under its belt. And that the museum, scraping by on barely there government funding and donations they had to beg for, somehow had piles of cash to fling about in exchange for these "treasures."

"I found this bag of some kind." He flipped open the box, flecking the desk with raindrops. "It looked old, so my sister suggested I donate it here."

"Sir, this isn't Goodwill. You can't just dump stuff here because it looks old."

The man blinked, as everyone did when faced with stark reality.

Sloane gentled her tone. "There's a whole process. You need to fill out a donation form, we have to assess the item, the acquisitions committee has to approve it, and—"

"Forms?" His face lit like she'd tripped some switch in his brain. "Of course. Whatever you need. I assume a separate form for each item?"

"Yes, but—"

"Good. Because there's more where this came from."

Of course there was. "Sir, I don't think—"

A phone trilled from deep inside the man's pocket. He pulled it out and glanced at the screen. "I'm sorry, I've got to take this."

"But I can't take this." She shoved the box toward him, but he was digging in a brown leather wallet.

"Look, here's my card." He placed a crisp, blue-lettered business card beside the box. *Garrett P. Anderson, Certified Financial Planner.*

"Mr. Anderson—"

"Please, just take a look. If you truly don't want it, call my cell, and I'll come get it." He backed into the door to push it open while pressing his hands together in a pleading gesture, his phone wedged between his shoulder and his ear. "Garrett Anderson. Hi. Thanks for returning my call . . ."

The door thudded shut behind him. With a sigh, Sloane eyed the box. Rain streaked its sides and added a fresh, damp note to the mustiness of the cardboard. Grabbing the box, she rounded the corner to the office she shared with the rest of the museum staff. Whatever was inside, whether it was worth anything or not—and her money was on *not*—it needed to get out of there.

Inside was a satchel. And she had to hand it to the guy, it was indeed old. Mid-nineteenth century from the looks of it. But its dust-dulled black leather was worn and cracked in several places, and rust reddened once-golden buckles. Amazing how people shoved things into dingy attics or damp basements, forgot about them for decades, and then got all miffed when museums weren't champing at the bit to display them.

And there would be no display for this satchel. Not when they had two just like it on exhibit, with another three in storage. Unless it belonged to someone historically significant, there was no reason to keep it.

But curiosity called nonetheless. Sloane smoothed her hand over the worn leather, her fingertips leaving tracks through the dust. Someone had owned this satchel once. Someone had gripped the handle when it was shiny and new. Worked well-oiled latches to secure priceless possessions.

Who was that someone?

Sloane cracked it open, the smell of stale leather puffing out. An inked inscription drew her in for a closer look.

*A. M. Collins.*

Collins…Collins…nope. The name didn't match any she'd uncovered during her years of researching Wichita's past and people. She'd double-check with her bosses, do a quick comb through the records, but chances were good she'd have to call Mr. Garrett Anderson back to retrieve what he'd all too eagerly dumped on her desk.

The thought gave her a perverse sense of satisfaction.

Setting the satchel carefully to the side, she sat down and rummaged through her desk for a tea bag.

A rainy, post-field-trip afternoon definitely called for some Earl Grey.

⸙

The windshield wipers of Garrett Anderson's Camry thumped a frantic rhythm against the incessant downpour. Raindrops pelted the car and wriggled like worms along the windows. Smooth pavement gave way to bone-jarring gravel as he turned off Jamesville Road onto the quarter-mile stretch of dirt leading to his grandparents' farmhouse. Instinct and experience, rather than visibility, guided him around ever-present potholes and that awful patch near the house that turned into a chasm of muck every time it rained.

But not even the rain could keep him from plowing through his to-do list, nor could it dampen his satisfaction at having crossed off a few items.

Cart unused kitchenware to the thrift store downtown? Check.

Take old towels to the animal shelter? Check.

Foist dilapidated satchel on unsuspecting museum curator? Check and double check.

Pulling to a stop as close to the house as he could, he dashed up the rickety porch steps and through the condensation-fogged storm door.

"So was I right? Did the museum take it?"

His sister's voice came from a greater height than usual. Garrett craned his neck to find Lauren perched on a stepladder, unloading a bookshelf.

He shrugged out of his rain-spattered jacket and hung it on the rack beside the door. "In a manner of speaking, yes."

"What's that supposed to mean?"

Rolling up his sleeves to his elbows, he walked toward the ladder. "It means I basically had to shove it into the curator's arms and promise to come back to get it if she doesn't want it."

"What makes you think she won't?" Lauren handed down a stack of books. Dust puffed up as he took them, and he sneezed.

"Call it a hunch." The disapproving look in the curator's dark eyes was all the evidence he needed, though an incurable head-in-the-clouds optimist like Lauren would doubtless need more convincing.

Next time he'd make his little sister run her own errands.

Dark blonde curls swished across Lauren's back as she reached for another handful of books and eyed the spines. "Think the library would want these?"

"*Reader's Digest* Condensed Books? Lauren, *no one* wants these."

"Maybe I can eBay them."

"If you can find people who'd rather have *Reader's Digest* Condensed Books than actual money, be my guest."

Defiance sparked in deep blue eyes. "I will, thank you. Now, be a dear and take these upstairs, would you? I've started a box of stuff to sell."

"Of course you have." Garrett took the books and trudged up the stairs.

This latest squabble was the umpteenth verse of a song they'd sung since

October, when their grandfather, fit as a fiddle last anyone checked, fell asleep watching television and never woke up. Orrin Spencer had been a rock for his wife as her memory failed and her mind betrayed her, but now Lauren and Garrett were at odds over their newly widowed grandmother's care. Living alone in the ancient farmhouse wasn't a viable option, but the sorry state of her savings account didn't allow for many alternatives.

The logical solution, of course, was to sell the house. Use the proceeds to finance a move to a long-term care facility. Both problems solved with a single perfect plan.

But Garrett's plan had run up against two formidable obstacles: his sentimental sister and his stubborn-as-all-get-out grandmother. Lauren had promptly given up her apartment, moved in with Grandma, and thrown herself into making the house livable for as long as possible. The arrangement was a stopgap at best, but Garrett couldn't talk them out of it. So he declared a temporary truce with Lauren, came down from Kansas City to help when he could, and did whatever necessary to facilitate the removal of decades' worth of accumulated possessions.

Like these useless books, which he had to set beside the eBay box, since the box itself was overflowing. Even so, plopping the stack down on the worn red carpet brought a small sense of accomplishment.

It'd all have to go eventually. This, at least, was a start.

When he returned to the living room, Lauren stood at ground level, surveying the freshly emptied shelf. "There. Dust it off, put a few of Grandma's knickknacks up there, and voilà."

"Good." Emboldened by progress, he glanced around the living room to see what else could make a quick impact. Ah. The knitting basket.

The knitting basket.

Garrett's heart sank. Half his childhood memories involved Grandma in her blue recliner by the fireplace, bathed in sunlight while silvery needles clicked away on her latest project. Piles of blankets, the pale pink sweater on the coatrack, intricate doilies draping every available surface, all testified to her favorite hobby.

But when was the last time she'd knitted? He picked up the basket and frowned at the tightly wound balls of yarn, at needles that had been eerily still for far too long.

Just one more thing the relentless thief known as Alzheimer's had stolen from his grandmother.

"What are you doing with that?" His sister's voice pitched low with suspicion.

"Lauren . . . she can't. Not anymore."

Lauren jutted her chin in the air, like the petulant toddler she'd once been. "You don't know that. Just because you haven't seen her knitting doesn't mean she can't."

Garrett looked once more at the dusty yarn. His latest sneeze was a far more eloquent argument than any verbal one.

Lauren folded her arms. "Fine. But how do you know she won't miss it? If something that's always been there, right by her favorite chair, up and disappears, don't you think that'll upset her?"

"Or having her favorite thing right here, knowing she's supposed to know what it is and what to do with it, but she doesn't? How will that *not* upset her?" Garrett shifted the basket to his other arm. "You know as well as I do she's gone downhill the last few weeks. I'm wearing a suit because she thinks I'm Grandpa."

"She'd think that even if she weren't sick. You look just like him."

"Fifty years ago, sure!"

Lauren rolled her eyes. "Stop yelling."

"I'm not yelling."

"Now, what's all this yelling?"

A frail, white-haired woman shuffled in from the dining room. Garrett felt, rather than saw, the I-told-you-so look Lauren tossed his way.

"Orrin. When did you get home?" Grandma's smile shone warm and genuine.

Swallowing a lump in his throat, Garrett met her in the center of the room. *Play along.* It was what all the Alzheimer's websites instructed.

"Hello, Rosie." He leaned down and feathered a kiss to her soft, wrinkled cheek.

"Where'd you find my knitting basket?" She reached into it, caressing a ball of buttery yellow yarn like a beloved pet. "I've been looking everywhere for this."

"Must've been put away somewhere by accident." Lauren rushed forward, took the basket, and returned it to its spot beside the chair. "There. Back where it belongs." She cut a pointed glance at Garrett.

"Wonderful." Grandma's pale blue eyes gleamed. "Tonight, after supper, I'll start on a new . . . a new . . . Oh, what am I trying to say? It's on the tip of my tongue."

"Sweater?" Lauren suggested. "Blanket?"

"No, it goes around your neck." Grandma swirled her hands in demonstration.

"Scarf," Garrett and Lauren replied in unison.

"Scarf. Right." Confusion flitted across Grandma's face. Her train of thought had derailed. Again.

Lauren stepped in with a gentle hug. "How about some TV, Grandma? I think the Royals are on."

Grandma's face lit. "Now that sounds like a plan."

Garrett helped her settle on the sofa while Lauren reached for the remote and clicked the TV to life. Within minutes, his grandmother was fixated on full counts and fly balls, waving the little felt pennant she kept in a 2015 World Series Champions mug on the end table.

This was the crux of Lauren's argument. Grandma was happy here, no denying it. And when the time came, it would break her heart to leave her home of more than sixty years. No denying that either.

But sooner or later, the bandage had to come off. Lauren and Grandma preferred to peel it away millimeter by millimeter. Mitigating the pain, sure, but prolonging it to a torturous degree.

He'd always preferred to rip it off.

Either way, it was painful. Garrett had known that from the moment of her diagnosis.

But he'd grossly underestimated how painful it would be.

>⸙<

"By the late flood, onion beds were paralyzed, beautiful lawns ruined, horrid stenches brewed, streets washed out and everybody inconvenienced."

Rustling from the next desk tore Sloane's attention from the *Wichita Daily Eagle*'s account of a 1904 flood to her office mate, Colleen.

"Taking off?" Sloane asked.

Tugging her silvery ponytail from beneath the collar of her trench coat, Colleen nodded toward the rain-streaked window. "You should too, unless you want to swim home."

Sloane glanced back at the black-and-white photos of floodwaters so deep people boated down Main Street. "I don't think it's quite that bad yet."

As her colleague departed, Sloane shifted in her chair and did a couple shoulder rolls. Lowering the lid of her laptop, she spied her mug of tea, still half full but no doubt stone-cold. That always happened when she was wrapped up in the past.

Her favorite place to be.

Well, second favorite. Her true favorite was her apartment, under her fuzzy orange blanket, a steaming order of Chinese carryout on the coffee table and an old movie on TV. *Romance on the High Seas* might be the winner tonight. Or maybe—

Her gaze fell on the worn-out satchel propped against her desk, and her bubble of daydreams popped. It wasn't just her tea she'd neglected this busy afternoon.

Okay, one more quick task, and then she'd take off. Call the guy—what was his name again?—and tell him, *You're right, it's old, but we've got half a dozen just like it, so I'm calling your bluff. Come take it back. Does Monday work for you? Great. And please, for the love of local limestone, don't bring us anything else from Grandma's basement.*

Now where was his card? Sloane pawed through piles of photos on her desk without success. It wasn't in any of the drawers either. Where in the world—

Oh. Right.

Sending up a silent prayer of thanks for a weekend that was apparently much needed, she reached for the satchel and peered inside. Bingo. *Garrett P. Anderson, Certified Financial Planner.*

Of course. Certified financial planners usually had names like Garrett P. Anderson. In fact, he—

Something deep inside the satchel caught her eye. Something she'd missed during her earlier examination.

It was small. Black. Leather. A Bible, maybe. Or some other book. Or—
Sloane's eyes widened as she slid the book out of the satchel and into the light.

It wasn't just a book.

It was a diary.

An old diary, from the looks of it. Slipping a pair of archival gloves from her desk drawer, she slid them on, cracked open the cover with care, and inhaled the earthy smell of ancient paper. Her pulse quickened at the childish scrawl on the opening page.

July 29, 1861

Deer Diary,

Hello. My name is Miss Annabelle Mary Collins.

I am nine years old.

## CHAPTER TWO

*July 29, 1861*

MERCY, IT WAS quiet here.

No teasing big brothers. No thundering footsteps.

And no Papa with his booming voice and hearty laugh.

Just a bird chirping outside the open window and leaves rustling in the slight breeze.

Annabelle dipped her pen in the inkwell and returned it to the crisp new page. At least the scratch of pen on paper would make a little noise.

> Uncle Stephen and Aunt Katherine gave me this diary. I have never seen so much blank paper before. I am not at all sure how to fill it.

She'd never had her own room before. And what a room it was. Blue and gold flowered wallpaper, the fanciest she'd seen. A lovely writing desk.

And the lace curtains at the windows took her breath away. She'd never seen anything so perfect, so delicate. Like the gown of a fairy princess. She was sure they were boughten, as they'd never had anything that fine, but Aunt Katherine *made* them.

This place was beautiful.

But it wasn't home.

> I am to live here with them until Papa returns. My room is nice. It has a blue flowered quilt on the bed and ~~boo beu~~ very pretty lace curtains at the windows.

But I would trade all the lace curtains in the world if I could have my Papa back.

A knock came to the door, and Aunt Katherine stepped into the room. She and Papa had the same slate-brown hair, though hers had more silver in it. Behind her spectacles shone eyes the same gray-blue as Papa's, like rain clouds before a downpour.

Those eyes peered back at Annabelle whenever she looked in a mirror.

Aunt Katherine beamed as she came up behind Annabelle. "I simply can't get over how much you look like Mary."

Annabelle frowned. People always said she was the spitting image of Mama. The same round cheeks, pointed chin, and thick honey-colored hair. But no matter how much time she spent in front of a mirror, no matter how hard she tried, she never saw Mama.

Maybe Papa did.

Maybe that was why he always seemed so sad.

"I am so happy you've come." Aunt Katherine wrapped her arms around Annabelle's shoulders. Annabelle started at the scent of her aunt's rosewater perfume.

The same kind Mama wore.

Perhaps if Annabelle shut her eyes tight and thought hard, she could pretend it was Mama hugging her. Not an aunt who was mostly a stranger.

It was no use. Not even she, with what Papa called her "fancy-full" imagination, could pretend that. The hug felt nice, but not quite right. It was a little too forced. Too fragrant. Too much.

Annabelle swallowed against the hurt in her chest and squeezed her eyes tighter to keep the stinging tears in. It wasn't Mama hugging her.

It wouldn't be Mama ever again, not until heaven.

Uneven footsteps creaked the floorboards as Aunt Katherine released her, and Uncle Stephen ducked into the doorway. So tall he nearly scraped the ceiling, yet his smile was warm, his brown eyes kind behind wire-rimmed spectacles.

"Now, isn't this nice?" he said. "All these years praying for a child, and here we are. Our own flesh and blood."

He meant well, but Annabelle squirmed. Papa had said on the way here that her aunt and uncle had always wanted a child of their own.

Hot anger had flared at that. "But I'm not their child. I'm yours. Yours and Mama's." She'd stamped her foot against the buggy's floor, but Papa silenced her with that look of his, that line in the sand she dared not cross.

"You know I've not got much choice in the matter, darlin'."

She'd stiffened. He'd been the first to sign his name to the list of volunteers at the rally. He'd been lauded as a hero, flags waving and bands playing. Everything about this had been his choice.

"Do you suppose Papa's made it to Indianapolis yet?" she asked.

Aunt Katherine opened the window a bit more, and the breeze ruffled those beautiful curtains. "I'm certain he has."

"Then is he fighting Johnny Reb?"

Uncle Stephen chuckled. "Not yet. He and your brothers likely have a lot of paperwork to fill out, and physical examinations to pass."

Mercy. That sounded almost as boring as being here.

Uncle Stephen's uneven gait filled the room. The result of a childhood riding accident, Papa had said. It didn't slow her uncle down any, but it must've been enough to keep him from joining up with Papa.

"I'd be there if I could." He sighed and slipped his arm around Aunt Katherine.

She patted his cheek. "Selfishly, I'm glad you can't."

Annabelle gave a silent harrumph. She would've joined up too, and she'd told Papa as much.

"Now, Annabelle," he'd said. "War is no place for a young lady."

For most young ladies that was doubtless true. But if Mr. President Lincoln could see her hold her own with her brothers, he'd surely make an exception.

"What if I cut my hair? Wore boys' clothes? Gave a different name? Could I come with you then?"

Papa had brushed his thumb over her cheek, the no in his eyes clear before it even left his lips. "You might be able to make them think you're a boy, but you'd never convince them you're old enough. Boy or girl, sweetheart, nine is nine."

Annabelle's heart had sunk, though she hadn't let her hopes get high enough to hurt when they fell.

"Do you like your new diary?" Aunt Katherine hovered like a hummingbird over the writing desk where Annabelle sat. "Your papa said you like to write and draw."

"You'll want a record of all your adventures," Uncle Stephen added.

Annabelle scoffed. "I haven't had any yet."

Uncle Stephen's eyes crinkled. "But you will. The good Lord is cooking one up for you as we speak. One that'll take everything you've got. He'll not let you go, though, not for an instant. He promised in his Word to always be with you."

Papa had promised that too. Yet not even twenty-four hours ago, she'd watched him ride away without a backward glance.

His country needed him. She knew that.

But no one stopped to think that maybe she needed him more.

><

Sloane's breath left in a whoosh as she laid the diary on her desk. Being abandoned by a parent, even for such a noble cause, would have left a deep wound.

A wound Sloane knew all too well. And one she'd rather not focus on right now.

So who was this Annabelle Collins? A census index might shed some light. And Sloane might be able to find Annabelle's father through Civil War records. If she'd lived in Indiana, her diary should go to historians there.

But if that were the case, how had her diary, her satchel, come to reside in a beat-up cardboard box in Sedgwick County, Kansas?

Sloane had no idea.

But she might know someone who did. She reached for Garrett Anderson's business card. He'd be pleased, no doubt, to learn he'd brought something of value after all. She could picture the smirk that would spring to his face when she told him.

But this wasn't about him, or the satchel, or his grandma's cluttered house. This was about Annabelle Collins and getting the words of her heart to their proper home. Besides, if he didn't know anything about Annabelle, which he probably didn't, then the call could be brief, and they could both go on with their lives.

Satisfied, she picked up her phone, sat back in her chair, and dialed.

>‹

"How's it going in here?" Garrett stepped into the kitchen, awash as usual with interesting aromas.

"Pretty good," came the absent reply from behind Lauren's clicking camera. "Just a few more shots and we'll be set."

Garrett eyed the artfully arranged plate in the crosshairs of the camera lens and suppressed a sigh. He was proud of his sister and her food blog, but given Lauren's obsessive need to get just the right shot, dinner might be stone-cold by the time it arrived on the table.

"Anything I can do to help?" He pulled a plastic pill reminder from a cupboard. "It's time for Grandma's meds, and she can't take them on an empty stomach."

"I'm just about"—the camera clicked a few times in quick succession— "done. Yay."

"Yay." Garrett's reply was much less enthusiastic as he grabbed a couple plates sensibly portioned with sliced chicken breast, some fancy whole grain he couldn't identify, and a heaping helping of something leafy and green. Lauren was always on the lookout for the latest health trends, and while this meal was gluten free, low-carb, and undoubtedly good for him, it would also lack the flavors he was used to from his simple bachelor fare. The few times he'd tried to cook dinner during his visits were met with well-meaning lectures from Lauren about the evils of every ingredient, so he'd ceded control of the kitchen when in Wichita and settled for the occasional late-night junk food run.

"Okay, Grandma, here's dinner." He set a plate in front of her, tipped the pills into his palm, and placed them next to her water cup. "And here are your meds."

Grandma blinked at the offerings, then looked up with a devilish smile. "Where's the beef?"

Lauren's lips curved. "You know red meat is bad for your blood pressure."

"I'm just teasing, sugarplum." Grandma reached out a withered hand and patted Lauren's. "It looks delicious as always. Now, who wants to say the, uh, the . . . ?"

"Blessing." Lauren finished her sentence as Garrett's phone buzzed in his pocket. He pulled it out and frowned at the number. The Wichita area code meant it probably wasn't a client, but it could be one of the care homes he'd begun researching on the sly.

He slid from his chair and silenced the phone. "I have to take this. You all go ahead without me." Ignoring Lauren's glare, he stepped out to the screened porch and raised the phone to his ear. "Hello?"

"Hi," a woman's voice replied. "Is this Garrett Anderson?"

"Speaking."

"This is Sloane Kelley from the Sedgwick County Museum of History. I'm calling in regard to the satchel you brought in this afternoon."

"Oh? Is it maybe something you can use after all?" His competitive urge surfaced, hoping for a victory over Miss You-Can't-Just-Bring-Stuff-In-Here. He tamped it down.

She paused. "Do you have any idea where the satchel came from?"

"I'd never seen it before. There's a ton of old stuff here. We've barely scratched the surface."

"Wonderful." She didn't sound impressed. "Does the name Annabelle Collins mean anything to you?"

He frowned at the puddles dotting the yard, the result of the day's downpour. Rain still fell but at a considerably gentler rate. "I'm afraid not."

"You said this was found in your grandparents' house? Did they ever live in Indiana?"

What was this woman getting at? "I don't think so. Grandma was born and raised here, and I'm pretty sure Grandpa was too."

"Did they ever travel to Indiana? Maybe pick up the satchel in an antique store on vacation, and the diary just happened to be in there?"

Garrett blinked. "Diary?"

"The one from 1861 I found inside the satchel."

"You're kidding. I could've sworn that thing was empty." Competitiveness tapped him on the shoulder once more. "So the diary at least has some use to you guys even if the satchel doesn't?"

"It's going to be useful to someone, yes, but I'm not sure it's in our jurisdiction, so to speak. That's why I'm giving you the third degree."

That drew a chuckle. "What do you know so far?"

"Annabelle was nine when she received the diary as a gift from her Uncle Stephen and Aunt Katherine. I don't suppose those names ring any bells?"

"Nope." Garrett ran a hand through his hair. It felt like this woman was giving him a quiz he never studied for and had no hope of passing. "I'm sorry, I don't know that much about my family history."

"Join the club." Sloane's voice lost its crisp, no-nonsense edge, and the resulting huskiness did strange things to his insides. Before he could analyze that, though, she hit him with another question. "What about your grandparents? Any chance I could speak with them?"

"I wish that was possible." He glanced out at the dilapidated red barn where Grandpa's beloved tractor stood silent, covered with cobwebs and dust. "My grandfather passed away last fall."

"Oh no. I'm so sorry to hear that." Genuine sympathy seeped through the line.

"Thank you. He didn't suffer, at least we can be thankful for that. And we know where he is now, so . . ." Garrett swallowed hard against a thickened throat. His grandfather's rock-solid faith in Christ left no doubt as to his eternal destination. It took the edge off the ache.

"That definitely helps."

The beautiful huskiness had returned to Sloane's voice, and with it that strange inward pull.

"What about your grandmother? I'd love to visit with her if I could."

Garrett switched his phone to the other ear. "I'm sure she'd welcome a visit, but you probably won't get much out of her."

"She'd at least know her parents' names, and whether she ever traveled to Indiana."

"I'm not so sure about that. My grandma has Alzheimer's. She's still functional and communicates well, but her memory's like Swiss cheese."

"Wow, I'm so sorry. That really sucks. For all of you."

Her offbeat forthrightness gave him pause. No one had ever said it in quite those words before, and their truth resonated in the very depths of him.

"This might sound weird, but I appreciate you saying that."

"You do?"

"Definitely." Everyone he shared the diagnosis with always said they were sorry. Then they asked if they could bring over a casserole. Or grilled him about her medications. Or questioned if he'd tried this doctor or that diet or these experimental treatments.

All of them meant well. They'd fix it if they could.

But some things couldn't be fixed.

And when that was the case . . . it sucked.

He hadn't realized how badly he'd needed to hear that from someone.

"Phew. I can be pretty blunt. It's sometimes a problem."

"Not for me." Garrett cleared his throat. "Anyway, it sounds like I'm not much help on this diary, but if I find anything else while I'm digging around, I'll—"

"Need any help?"

"Are you sure? There's a ton of dust and mold."

"Nothing I haven't seen before. Trust me." Her low, throaty laugh brought an unexpected ping of pleasure. "And if there's anything else of Annabelle's in the house, it might tell us more about where I should send this diary."

Her present eagerness couldn't be further from her earlier icy demeanor, but voicing that observation probably wouldn't win him any points. And if she was sincerely willing to come help with the house? He needed all the points he could get.

"Okay, I'll call your bluff. How about tomorrow?"

The thoughtful pause filled with soft tapping, like she was bouncing a pencil off a stack of papers. "I'm free any time during the day."

"Great. Ten thirty?"

"Perfect."

He gave the address. "Do you need directions?"

"The GPS should do fine. I'll call you if it does something squirrely."

After they hung up, Garrett slid his phone in his pocket with an amused shake of his head. Never in his life had he met someone who looked forward to digging through decades' worth of junk.

But if she did find something of historical value, it'd be one less thing he needed to make a decision about. One more item checked off the endless to-do list.

And one step closer to enacting his perfect plan.

＞＜

Friday's deluge had given way to a Saturday of brilliant sunshine and a sky of liquid blue. A beautiful day for a drive to Jamesville, a small town on Wichita's western outskirts. To Garrett's grandparents' house, and possible answers.

But as she rolled along the highway, Sloane stared, goggle-eyed, at the proliferation of new big-box stores and cookie-cutter McMansions, a far cry from the gently rolling farmland of not even five years ago. Subdivisions whizzed past, all with brick walls, lit signs, and names that sounded pretty but were utterly devoid of meaning. Harbor Pointe. Meadowlark Mountain. Pineridge.

Ugh. Suburbia had spilled across the countryside like red wine on a white tablecloth.

Just past the last cathedrals of conformity, the GPS chirped instructions to turn right. And when she did, onto a mud-and-gravel road marked by a shrubbery-obscured mailbox, Sloane's irritation with suburbia faded to nothingness.

Stately, thick-trunked trees stood at attention on both sides of the long driveway, kissed with the pale pinks, creamy whites, and tender greens of spring. Branches split the morning sunshine into shafts of magic that danced on the hood of her car.

She rounded a slight curve, and a white two-story house came into view. A delighted squeal bubbled up in her throat. This house, this beautiful, silent testimony to days gone by, stood in a cool oasis of evergreen and elm, flanked by the quintessential red barn and a scattering of smaller buildings. Sunlight dazzled like diamonds off the puddles in the bright green yard. The whole scene couldn't be more idyllic if it tried.

Envy welled inside her. Had Mr. Get-Rid-of-Everything spent any time here at all? He couldn't have, or he'd understand what a priceless pearl this place was.

As she drew closer, the home's age became evident. Paint peeled from both the house and the barn. One side of the screened porch listed to the left. Weeds sprang up with abandon. But despite these imperfections, its century-old charm was still there.

It was love at first sight.

She slowed to a near crawl, lost in daydreams and questions about the people who'd lived here, about their stories, their lives. It reeled her in up to her knees. Stuck fast with no hope of escape.

No.

Wait.

She wasn't just stuck in her daydreams.

She was stuck in a giant puddle of oozing mud.

# CHAPTER THREE

"WORK WITH ME, Edna." Gritting her teeth, Sloane revved the gas. "You can do it."

But the little Hyundai's only response was helplessly whirring and squealing its tires as it sank deeper into the muck.

Perfect.

With a great deal of trepidation, Sloane turned off the ignition and cracked the door to reveal a pool of shiny gray-brown goop. Goop that would be almost impossible to scrub out of the new pair of Toms she'd just treated herself to.

She kicked off her shoes, tossed them onto the passenger seat, and rolled her jeans to her calves, then set her jaw and climbed from the car.

Cold mud swallowed both feet up to her ankles, and she let out a yelp. When the shock passed, she leaned against Edna's smooth, dark blue side and carefully slogged to the rear of the car to assess the situation.

Ugh. The ground beneath the back tires was part rocky gravel, part tall grass, and part mud, but the front wheels were sunk halfway into the same slop that sucked at her feet. Somehow, in nearly fifteen years of driving experience, this had never come up.

With a silent prayer for guidance, she retraced her sloppy steps, leaned inside the driver's door, and groped around the passenger seat for her phone. Time to turn this problem over to Professor Google.

"Are you stuck?"

She straightened, and there was Garrett, leaning against the porch railing, his mouth quirked with amusement.

"Nope. Just a quick mud mask for my feet. Did you know they charge fifty bucks for this at the salon?"

His gaze slid from her face to the mud and back again. "So you don't need a hand or anything?"

"If all else fails, I'll call AAA." She lifted her phone. "Thanks, though."

"C'mon, I can have you out of there in two minutes." The porch steps creaked as he strode toward her. "Just put a few sticks under the tires for traction, and I'll get back there and give it a good shove."

"You think that'll work?"

He bent to examine the rear tires. "This isn't the first car to get stuck here, and it probably won't be the last."

Gone was his suit from yesterday, and in its place was a pair of faded jeans and a plaid flannel shirt over a Kansas Jayhawks T-shirt. He wasn't skin and bones, but he was no beefcake either.

"You don't really look like the sort of person who makes a habit of pushing cars out of the mud," she said.

That dimple in his right cheek deepened. "You don't really look like the sort of person who makes a habit of getting cars stuck in mud either. And yet here we are."

"All right." Swallowing her pride, she tucked her phone into her pocket. "If you can get me out of here, I'd be most appreciative."

"Happy to help. I'll grab some sticks."

She wasn't sure which was more irritating: the smirk on his lips as he turned away or how perfectly those jeans fit him. Heat blasting her face, she sank into the driver's seat, twisted awkwardly to retrieve an old hoodie from the back, and gave her filth-covered feet a cursory wipe.

When she looked up, Garrett stood beside her open window. "Okay, we've got enough traction, I think." He patted the roof and headed toward the back. "Go ahead and fire it up."

With a turn of the key, Edna vroomed to life.

"Now give it some gas," he called. "Don't floor it, though. Nice and gentle."

Mindful of the squalling fit Edna had just thrown, Sloane eased down the accelerator. The car whined a moderate protest, then lurched forward onto a patch of grassy gravel near the house. Relief washed through her as she climbed from the car, her bag over her shoulder, her shoes dangling from two fingers. The grass was cool and damp beneath her bare feet.

"See? Piece of cake." Garrett fell into step beside her, and her heart twinged with sympathy at the mud-spattered Jayhawk in the center of his T-shirt.

"Thank you. Truly."

He'd been right, of course. She couldn't have done it without him. And the satisfied smirk he wore told her he knew that, and he knew she knew that.

Being right was doubtless something he was used to.

"It was the least I could do, considering it's my fault you got stuck." He gestured toward the patch of mud. "This road's terrible, even without three inches of rain. I feel bad for not warning you."

"I was too busy gawking at the house to watch where I was going, so no harm, no foul." She feasted her eyes on the house once more. "This place is beautiful."

He gave a dry chuckle. "Even knee-deep in mud?"

"That patch of mud has probably been there for decades. There's beauty in that."

"There's beauty in pavement too." Garrett crouched beside a spigot next to the porch. "I should rinse off my shoes before I go in. You're welcome to use this, but this water's nowhere near as warm as what they'd give you at the salon."

"That won't bother me. I'll just be glad to get this mud off my feet."

"Can't say I didn't warn you."

The spigot squawked to life, and Sloane stepped beneath a flow of water so cold it drew a startled cry despite her efforts to suppress it. Ignoring Garrett's chuckles, she scraped off the worst of the mud with aching toes, then leaped to dry ground and glared daggers at him.

"Where'd this water come from, the iceberg that sank the *Titanic*?"

Blue eyes sparkling, he shed his plaid shirt and handed it to her. "Here. Rub some feeling back into them."

The rest of her froze as much as her feet. His T-shirt-covered shoulders were broader than they'd looked, his arms more muscled than she'd given him credit for.

Maybe he looked like the sort of person who made a habit of pushing cars out of the mud after all.

"Thank you." Bracing herself against the side of the house, she wrapped the soft, woodsy-smelling flannel around her grateful left foot. Garrett kicked off his mud-covered sneakers and held them beneath the spigot. The water ran brown, then beige, as the original bright blue of the shoes shone through.

The screen door banged open, and a young woman with long, dark blonde hair poked her head out. "Everything okay out—whoa, what happened?"

"Just a little mud," Garrett replied. "No big deal."

The woman switched her gaze to Sloane, and Sloane found herself staring at a female version of Garrett. Same eyes, same nose, same cleft in the chin, same dimpled smile.

What must it be like to look at another human being and see your own reflection?

"Hi." The woman stuck out her hand. Sloane glanced at her own to make sure it was clean enough to return the handshake.

"Sloane, this is my incredibly annoying sister, Lauren," Garrett said. "Lauren, this is Sloane Kelley from the historical museum."

Lauren held the door for Sloane. "Can I get you anything? Coffee cake? Blueberry buckle? Cinnamon rolls?"

That explained the fragrant mix of sweetness and spice hanging heavy in the air as Sloane stepped into the living room. At her apartment there was only one breakfast option—instant oatmeal—and she hadn't even bothered with that this morning.

"Lauren's a food blogger," Garrett explained.

"*Dollop of Delicious.* Maybe you've heard of it?" Lauren's smile was wide and hopeful.

"Sorry, no." Sloane handed the now-damp flannel shirt back to Garrett. "I'm not much of a cook."

"Let me get you something then." Lauren's blonde waves swished across the back of her plaid shirt as she headed to the kitchen. "You're probably starving."

Not until now, anyway. The drool-worthy aromas made Sloane's stomach gnaw its protest at the missed breakfast.

"Come on in." Garrett indicated a room to the right of the entryway, and Sloane drank in the sight. Though the floral wallpaper and deep green accents spoke of the 1990s, the bones of the house were from a century earlier. Wood-framed, thick-silled windows. Creaky hardwood floors. The gorgeous stone fireplace. This house was amazing.

"Land's sake, if it isn't Auntie Boop."

A slight, snowy-haired woman piped up from a blue recliner beside the fireplace, eyes twinkling behind large gilt-framed glasses.

"Sloane, this is my grandma, Rosie Spencer," Garrett said. "And Grandma, this is Sloane Kelley from the historical museum."

"Oh, hogwash. I know Auntie Boop when I see her." Rosie cut her broad smile from Garrett to Sloane. "You haven't changed a bit except your hair. Are you letting it grow out?"

Sloane put a self-conscious hand to her wavy chin-length bob. "Maybe?"

"You remember what we talked about last night, right?" Garrett's voice was low and close to Sloane's ear.

She nodded. "So who's Auntie Boop?"

"No idea. We just roll with it."

"Gotcha."

"Here we are," came Lauren's bright voice. "You didn't say what you wanted, so I brought you one of everything."

Sloane's mouth watered at the tray of goodies Lauren set on the coffee table.

"All gluten free, allergy friendly, non-GMO—"

"But they taste good anyway," Garrett interjected. Lauren rolled her eyes, and he planted a kiss on top of her head. "Save me a slice of that coffee cake. I'm going to go change."

"M'kay." Lauren pulled a TV tray from beside a large bookshelf, unfolded it, and placed it in front of Rosie.

"What a beautiful house." Sloane settled on the couch. "Do you all live here?"

"All except Garrett." Lauren poured coffee into a trio of mugs. "He's up in Kansas City. Comes down every couple weekends or so to help out."

Rosie blew a raspberry. "Garrett's a big worrywart."

Sloane chuckled. She liked Rosie.

She liked this cinnamon roll too. Warm and gooey, with the perfect blend of sweetness and spice. Who needed gluten anyway?

Lauren leaned back in the recliner, cradling a steaming green mug. "So Garrett says you're here about that satchel he brought in yesterday."

Sloane took a much-needed sip of coffee. "It's not so much about the satchel as what was inside it. A diary from 1861."

Lauren's eyes widened. "Wow. Do you know whose it is?"

"It belonged to a nine-year-old girl named Annabelle Collins." Sloane's heartbeat kicked up a notch as she watched Lauren for a reaction. "Does that mean anything to you?"

"No." She turned to Rosie and raised her voice slightly. "Grandma? Do you know an Annabelle Collins?"

"Annabelle . . ." Rosie's brow creased; gnarled hands curled into loose fists. "Blast it. If I ever did, I don't anymore."

"It's all right. I've never heard of her either." Lauren tore off a bite of cinnamon roll and turned back to Sloane. "Our mom died years ago, Dad moved to Florida, and with Grandpa gone, it's just Garrett, Grandma, and me. And we didn't know much about our family history to begin with."

"I'm sorry about your mom." Sloane lowered her mug to the table. "And you'd be surprised how little most people know about their heritage." *Try as they might to uncover it.*

"Wait a minute. You said Annabelle was nine?" Lauren rose and fluttered across the room. "I found a notebook last week that looked pretty old. The handwriting was a little unsteady and the spelling wasn't great. I thought maybe it was Grandma's from when she was a girl, but what if it's even older?"

"It's certainly worth a look." Excitement rose in Sloane's chest. She shouldn't get her hopes up.

But where history—and life—were concerned, sometimes hope was all she had.

><

Garrett spread an old towel on the hardwood floor of the guest bedroom. The bedroom he slept in when he visited, for as long as he could remember.

Stepping out of damp, mud-hemmed jeans, he glanced out the window to a view that remained unchanged: a vibrant green clearing leading up a slight rise to a grove of cottonwoods, on the other side of which ran Blackledge Creek.

Long weekends. Lazy summer days. Anytime he visited, sooner or later he'd find himself by that creek. Learning to fish with Grandpa. Wading in its cold, clear waters. Sitting on the banks and tossing in sticks, watching the current carry them away. City kid though he was, being here always brought him closer to some part of himself. To nature.

To God.

Those waters must've had that effect on people. His mother running barefoot through wildflowers and doing cannonballs into the creek's deeper sections remained among his most cherished memories. Even at the last, when cancer had devoured everything but her soul, when her cheekbones jutted sharp against the sheets and colorful head scarves did little to hide the ravages of chemotherapy, she still wanted to come home. Feel the fresh air against her skin one last time. The creek's rippling water on feet that would no longer support her.

Garrett yanked on a clean pair of jeans and whipped shut the lid of his suitcase. The past was long gone. Reminiscing would only heap pain upon pain.

The ancient stairs creaked beneath his footsteps as he descended to the living room, where Lauren, Grandma, and Sloane all huddled together, heads bent over something Sloane held.

"There he is." Sloane's smile was evident in her voice.

"Who?" He came around the edge of the sofa.

"Pretty sure we found Annabelle's dad." Sloane held up a tablet, eyes shining behind black-framed glasses.

The image of a stone monument filled the screen, a list of names and ranks engraved into its surface. Including a Lieutenant Collins, Company I, 19th Indiana Infantry.

"This is at Gettysburg," she said.

"Ah, the Iron Brigade."

Sloane's eyebrows arched, and he grinned, pleased to have impressed her.

"I'm surprised he made it out alive." He leaned down to study the picture. "That unit suffered some pretty heavy losses at Gettysburg, if memory serves."

"Look who knows something about history."

He shrugged. "I went through a bit of a Civil War phase as a kid."

"A bit?" Lauren scoffed. "Your cannon collection covered your entire dresser."

"Yes. Well." He wasn't about to let Lauren get started on embarrassing childhood stories. "Are we sure this is the right guy?"

"According to his service record, he's about the right age, and I found two more Collinses from the same town in Indiana. Nineteen-year-old Charles and seventeen-year-old Joseph. I have more sources I can check to confirm, but I'm ninety-nine percent sure this is him."

"Now, you let us know." Rosie raised a finger and peered at Sloane over the tops of her glasses. "Can't leave an old woman hanging in the middle of a good story."

Sloane took Rosie's hand in both of hers, and the gesture wrapped Garrett's heart in warmth. "I'll give you guys a call the instant I find out anything."

"You're looking a little tired, Grandma." Lauren rose from her chair. "Would you like to lie down?"

"I *am* feeling a bit tuckered."

"Can I help?" Garrett stood, but Lauren waved him off, a cryptic smile on her face.

"You stay. Give me the Cliff's Notes of whatever you find in that diary." Before Garrett could protest, his grandmother and sister rounded the corner to the bedroom, and he was left with Sloane.

"Diary?" he asked. "You guys found another one somewhere?"

"Lauren did." Sloane slipped on a pair of thin white gloves, her face alight. "Come on. Let's see what Annabelle's up to."

She looked so eager he couldn't resist, even if he wanted to. He sank into the spot vacated by his grandmother, and Sloane scooted closer, holding the diary between them. Some fruity scent wafted from her hair. Strawberries, maybe. It brought him back to childhood summers on the farm.

"So." He fixed his gaze on the faded pages. "What's going on with Miss Annabelle?"

"It's 1864 now. Annabelle's twelve, and her father's getting remarried." Sloane's finger traced the lines of childish handwriting. "'I've had a letter from Papa, and I am to have a new mama!'"

"What happened to her old mama?"

"Smallpox. The whole family caught it, and they lost both Annabelle's mother and baby sister."

"Wouldn't wish that on anyone." Garrett wasn't aware he'd spoken aloud until he caught a glimpse of wide, concerned brown eyes.

"Oh, I'm so sorry. Lauren said your mom . . ."

"Yeah. Breast cancer." The words were dull. Empty. "She's been gone six years."

Sloane's small gloved hand rested on his. "That must be difficult."

She sounded so sad he wanted to comfort her. "Her pain's over now. She's with Jesus. I wouldn't wish her back, not in a million years."

"Doesn't mean you don't miss her, though. And for that, I'm sorry."

"Thanks." He returned his attention to the page. "What happens next?"

Sloane scanned the next few pages, her long eyelashes flitting back and forth. "Here's something . . . Wow. Poor girl."

Garrett bent his head to read the text and caught another whiff of that fruity scent.

> My heart is broken. Papa and his new wife have bought a farm in Pennsylvania so they can be nearer to *her* family. And what's worse, she is going to have a baby! Papa says she has lost babies before and is "in a delicate condition," so she cannot travel and he cannot leave her. He assures me I will be happier with Uncle and Aunt than I ever would with him and Huldah.
>
> I thought I was to have a mother again. A family. But Papa has a new family now, and there's no place in it for me.

Garrett gave a bitter laugh. "Never thought I'd have so much in common with a tween girl from 1864."

Sloane arched a brow. "How so?"

"While Mom was sick, Dad found a kindred spirit in an online support forum. A woman whose husband died of pancreatic cancer a couple months before Mom. So when she passed, Dad flew down to Florida to meet Debbie. I thought they were just friends, but the next thing I know, he's calling from Jamaica telling me I've got a new stepmom." Garrett tented his fingers. "He sold his practice, the house . . . I've barely heard from him since. It's like he wants to close the book on that whole part of his life."

Sloane stared at him. "You've really lost everyone, haven't you?"

"Everyone except Lauren." He flashed a wry smile. "I keep hoping, but . . ."

Laughing, Sloane shoved his shoulder. "Come on. Lots of us would kill to have a sibling."

"And those of us with siblings would sometimes kill *not* to have them."

An odd expression flickered across Sloane's heart-shaped face, but before he could decipher it she was back to business, turning pages in the diary. "Annabelle's not writing as regularly anymore. Every few weeks instead of every few days. But at least she's still writing."

"Her handwriting's getting better too."

"She mentions school occasionally. Her aunt and uncle are doing right by her. In fact, she's—" Sloane gasped. Her gentle grip on his wrist sent a jolt of heat through his body.

"Oh, Garrett, this is big."

## CHAPTER FOUR

*September 23, 1869*

THE TICK OF the mantel clock echoed like gunshots. Annabelle gaped across the parlor, first at Uncle Stephen, then at Aunt Katherine. "He what?"

Uncle Stephen's eyes sparkled behind his spectacles. "Asked for your hand in marriage."

The room tilted. Annabelle gripped the arms of the velvet chair to steady herself. "I—I was unaware of William's intention."

William Barclay, the young man with impossibly blond hair and ruddy cheeks. Her uncle's apprentice and partner in medicine. She'd grown up with him, considered him a friend, but . . .

"He's been calling regularly." The creases around Uncle Stephen's eyes deepened.

Annabelle's brows shot up. "Calling?" Was that what all those Sunday afternoon visits had been? Visits during which William spoke more with her uncle than with her?

"And you'll be eighteen next spring," Aunt Katherine piped up over her teacup. "Not so young to wed."

"I suppose not . . ." Rebecca Mead, three months her junior, had married in May. "But he never . . . Perhaps he mentioned marriage a time or two, but as a concept, not with intent—at least none that he made clear." Her hand flew to her forehead. "Oh, am I truly this dull?"

Aunt Katherine beamed. "Annabelle, dear, you're in shock. Once you've had time to think it over, you'll see it's for the best."

*For the best.* Papa's voice bridged the gap of years. Yes, for him, and his shiny new bride, and their children—three of them now, according to his most recent letter—it undeniably was for the best not to have her hanging around, stirring up memories of a time when life wasn't so rosy.

She too had benefited from the arrangement. Her aunt and uncle were kind, and she'd been blessed with a thorough education, both academic and spiritual.

But there was no denying the hole her father's departure had gouged into her heart. The utter upheaval his decisions had brought to her life, upheaval in which she'd had no say. Upheaval that loomed larger with each word from Aunt Katherine's lips, at the look in her gray-blue eyes, eyes so like Papa's . . .

Annabelle drew herself up in her chair. "Uncle Stephen, you've always counseled me to approach important decisions carefully and with much prayer. Why must this move so quickly? William is a good friend, but I don't love him the way I want to love a husband. And he looks at me the same way he looks at his sister. Affectionate, perhaps, but not with love. Not the way Papa looked at Mama . . ." Annabelle studied her aunt and uncle. "What's really going on?"

The pair exchanged a telling glance, and Uncle Stephen cleared his throat.

"These last weeks I've felt a certain . . . disquiet in my spirit. I always planned to live out my days here, but I've recently received a call from the Lord to move to Kansas—"

"Kansas?" The word was a squeak.

"Please don't interrupt, darling," came Aunt Katherine's gentle reprimand.

But Uncle Stephen seemed not even to have heard. "The frontier communities are in desperate need of doctors. Preachers. Teachers. People of all walks of life. So I've filed for a claim in Sedgwick County."

Outside the open window a bird burst into song, its cheerful serenity out of tune with Annabelle's heart.

"But what about your patients?"

"They'll be in good hands. Dr. Barclay is more than qualified to take over my practice." Uncle Stephen's words tumbled out more rapidly than usual. "I arranged for him to do so when I retired. But it seems the good Lord has a different plan." He reached toward Aunt Katherine, who intertwined her fingers with his. They gazed at each other like a couple twenty years younger.

Annabelle scrabbled for traction. "How do you know this is the Lord's will?"

"The Great Commission calls us to go and make disciples of all nations, even to the ends of the earth. I've been drawn to that passage the last few nights, though I wasn't certain why. I've read it—prayed over it—countless times, asking the Lord to reveal to me what I am to do with his instruction." Uncle Stephen leaned forward, color in his cheeks. "Then one night I dreamed—vividly—of a young dark-haired man holding an infant, begging the Lord to send a doctor." His eyes shone. "That's when I knew."

"And you're in agreement?" Annabelle looked to Aunt Katherine, who nodded. "That's it then? You're moving to Kansas, and you want to marry me off so you won't have to worry about me? So I won't be in the way?" Panic turned the question shrill.

"Of course you wouldn't be in the way." Aunt Katherine's eyes were soft. Earnest. "We'd love to have you with us. But . . ."

"The frontier is a harsh, dangerous place." Uncle Stephen's voice lowered with warning. "And there are no shops. No railroads. Everyone is starting from nothing. The luxuries, the comforts to which you've grown accustomed simply don't exist there."

Annabelle stared. "You're bartering me off to William Barclay so I can keep my porcelain teapots and lace curtains?"

"It really is for the best." Aunt Katherine's gaze dropped to the floor.

"How is it for the best for me to sit on a shelf while everyone else does something worthwhile with their lives?" Annabelle braced for the inevitable reprimand, but none came. She pressed her advantage. "I'll not stay here and live in comfortable boredom, tethered to a man I don't love, merely reading about the Great Commission while the only family I have left is living it out."

"But—"

"Who will assist you with patients if William stays here? You know Aunt Katherine gets queasy at the sight of blood. Or you said they need teachers too. Why could I not do that?"

A line formed between Uncle Stephen's bushy brows. "You would forgo a comfortable, companionable marriage in favor of teaching in a ramshackle schoolhouse? Or setting broken bones and treating burns?"

Annabelle met her uncle's gaze. His was uncertain, but she'd never been more certain of anything in her life.

"I'll not be left behind again. I simply won't. Especially not without any say in the matter."

Her aunt and uncle exchanged another glance. The mantel clock ticked ever louder as Annabelle awaited their verdict.

Finally Uncle Stephen spoke. "I didn't realize you'd feel so strongly about it."

Aunt Katherine nodded. "We thought you'd rather stay here with William."

"Remember the day you gave me my first diary?" She looked from her aunt to her uncle. "And how you said the Lord was cooking up a grand adventure for me? One that would take everything I've got?"

Uncle Stephen smiled. "I do recall saying that, yes."

"I think Kansas may be my adventure." Conviction flooded her as her lips formed the syllables, and she lifted her chin. "I know it is. I feel it to the marrow of my bones."

><

Sloane paged through the diary as quickly as she dared. "I wonder if Uncle Stephen is Dr. Stephen Maxwell, one of the county's first physicians."

"And if it is?" Curiosity sparked in Garrett's cobalt eyes.

"Then these diaries are quite the find. We know a fair amount about Dr. Maxwell but not much about his family." She set the diary on the sofa beside her, then stripped off her gloves and reached for her tablet. With a few taps on the screen, she opened an early history of Sedgwick County, scrolled, and—

"Here. 'Dr. S. A. Maxwell, Jamesville, born in Ohio County, Kentucky, son of Arthur and Evangeline Maxwell. Married in 1849 to Miss Katherine Collins. No children, but brought his niece Annabelle with him to the county.'" Sloane beamed at Garrett, the joy of discovery bubbling within. "There she is."

"What's up, Annabelle?" Garrett waved at the screen, and Sloane dissolved into laughter. Maybe she was just that happy to find Annabelle.

Or maybe it was the thrill of sharing her passion with someone. Someone warm and strong, whose eyes were the same deep blue as the river on a clear day . . .

Before her thoughts could wander too far in that direction, Sloane skimmed the rest of the brief biography. "Let's see, came to Kansas from Brown County . . . settled near Jamesville in 1871 . . . founding member of the Methodist Episcopal Church . . ."

Garrett leaned closer, a hint of fresh soap and woodsy cologne in his wake. "Is Annabelle in there anywhere?"

"It's unlikely there'd be an entry about her, since most of the early histories focused on the men. But we could try the census index. Since they didn't take their land until 1871, it might be difficult to pin them down. There was another census in 1875, though, so let's check there." A few more taps to her tablet and the census popped up. "Martinson . . . Matthews . . . here we are. Maxwell. Stephen A., doctor, fifty-two, Katherine, forty-nine. That's got to be them."

"Where's Annabelle?" Garrett asked.

"Not living with the Maxwells in 1875. That's all we know for sure. Given her age, it's likely she married, but frontier life was no cakewalk. She may not have made it to 1875."

"Nah. She's made of tougher stock than that."

"You have a lot of faith in her."

Garrett's mouth quirked. "Just a stubborn sense of optimism."

Smiling, Sloane slipped the tablet into her bag. "Well, now that I know who Uncle Stephen is, I can do more research. Look at land records, find exactly where their claim was, see if I can track down Annabelle."

Garrett's brow furrowed. "That's a lot of trouble to go to for people who've been dead a hundred years."

"A few names get all the attention, but the ones who don't show up in the textbooks are just as important. We owe it to them to learn their stories. Sometimes it helps fill in our own blanks." Avoiding his probing gaze, she slid the diary into a protective sleeve. "I was abandoned as a baby. Adopted by strangers. So my family, my heritage . . . there are a whole lot of blanks."

Garrett was slow to answer. "I see."

She picked at the dry cuticle on her right thumb. "My parents—my adoptive parents—gave me everything I could've wanted. But . . ."

"You don't know who you really are."

The chasm within yawned, as it did whenever she allowed herself to consider the questions that had defined her existence. "Pretty much."

"Have you tried looking for your birth family?"

"Off and on. There's a website I search sometimes. Adoptees looking for birth parents and vice versa. But there's not much information available. I didn't even know I was adopted until I was nine."

Dark blond brows lifted. "Really?"

Sloane picked at her cuticle with more determination. "I wondered, y'know. Because my parents are both tall, fair, and blond. And then there's me. This short, chubby brunette." She sighed. "I remember watching my mom curl her hair one day, seeing how light it was compared to mine, how thin she was . . . half kidding, I asked if I was adopted."

Blue eyes turned serious. "And they told you?"

Sloane pressed her lips together and nodded. "They did, but it was just confirmation at that point. Because she paused. My mother *paused*." A mirthless chuckle slipped out. "What biological parent has to pause when their child asks if they're adopted?"

Garrett's hand rested lightly on her shoulder. "I'm sorry. That sounds painful."

"Thank you." She balled her hands into fists, then relaxed them. "So I asked a bunch of questions—"

"You?" Cautious amusement danced at the corners of his mouth as his hand slipped from her shoulder. "Surely not."

She threw him a half-hearted glare. "Do you ever have a thought you don't speak out loud?"

"Do you?"

"Touché." How glad she was for his wisecrack. It yanked her back from the painful path she was about to go down. The path she hardly ever let herself travel. "Anyway, I guess that's why I'm so passionate about history. If I can't know my own, at least I can help everyone else know theirs."

Garrett tilted his head to the side. "That makes perfect sense."

"I'm glad you think so." She shook out her hair. "I don't usually talk about my family issues with strangers."

Garrett's lips curved; his kind gaze swept over her face. "Surely we're not strangers at this point, are we?"

His smile drew out her own. "Well, you've seen me with mud up to my knees, and I'm digging through stuff you rooted out of your attic, so I guess not."

"Friends then?"

The word draped over her, warm and cozy. "Definitely. Friends."

>←

Garrett couldn't believe how much fun sorting through dusty old books could be with the right company. A whole afternoon had whizzed by, and they'd barely made a dent, but he was pleased to have several tubs of books boxed up to donate. Even more pleased to have discovered a couple more of Annabelle's diaries. Sloane had pounced on them, her eyes shining with an adorable eagerness that made him want nothing more than to scour every nook and cranny of his grandparents' house to see what other treasures he might uncover.

He walked her to the front door. "You'll let me know what you find?"

Hugging the stack of diaries to her chest, she rewarded him with a sassy smile. "Have I won a convert to the history-verse?"

"Learning about it in school was never anywhere near this interesting, I can tell you that much." Outdated textbooks, too-small desks, and dry-as-toast Mr. McConathy couldn't hope to make history come alive the way Sloane Kelley did.

Round cheeks flushed a delicate pink. "In that case, absolutely. You'll be my first call."

"Great." He pushed open the storm door, and her warm, sweet fragrance mingled with the fresh spring air as she passed. "Drive safe." Mischief tugged at his lips. "Don't make me push you out of the mud again."

Tossing a withering glare over her shoulder, she descended the porch steps, and his amusement turned to outright laughter.

As her mud-spattered car grumbled to life, Garrett surveyed the long driveway. The afternoon sun had shrunk the puddle considerably, and the scarred patch from their earlier struggle had lightened and dried. Sloane's chances of getting stuck now were practically zero, but he still watched the blue Elantra until the taillights disappeared.

"You like her, don't you?"

He whirled and found Lauren leaning against the doorway, arms folded, a teasing smile on her lips.

"How long have you been standing there?"

"Long enough to know you like her."

He pulled out his phone and checked for messages. "That's ridiculous. I barely know her."

"That's what you said in tenth grade about Jenny Hickok, and you ended up going out with her for, what, three years?"

Garrett stared at his smug, smirking sister. "Sloane is nothing like Jenny Hickok."

"I know." Lauren turned back toward the kitchen. "That's why *I* like her."

Shaking his head, Garrett started up the stairs. Sloane seemed nice enough, and this afternoon's conversation had definitely forged a bond between them. But with work and Grandma and all the plates he had to keep spinning, he had neither time nor inclination right now for anything more than friendship. And even if he did, it'd be with someone back home. Not here.

As usual, Lauren was reading too much into things.

His trips to Wichita were to tie up loose ends.

Not to create new ones.

# CHAPTER FIVE

GARRETT STOOD ON a moonlit sidewalk, staring at the rough brick building, the Wichita city flag mural beside the door, and the half-lit blue neon sign that had clearly seen better days. Marty's on Main—or *MA Y'S N M N*, if the sign was to be believed—didn't look like much.

Then again, the best places usually didn't.

He had to hand it to Lauren and her Google-fu. Sensing he needed to unwind, she'd suggested a long bike ride and an evening at a jazz club. He'd taken her up on the former, pedaling mile after mile through fresh air and green countryside, but scoffed at the latter. Whatever jazz scene Wichita boasted would pale in comparison to the one back home.

Lauren kept pressing him to give Marty's a chance, though, and after skimming several glowing reviews, he decided to call her bluff. At best, he'd hear some decent music. At worst, he'd be able to fling a well-deserved "I told you so" at his sister.

Tugging on the worn brass door handle, he stepped into a cozy yet swanky atmosphere. Over the laid-back thump of bass, the swish of brushes on cymbals, and the tinkle of piano, a sultry saxophone riff crooked a teasing finger at him and invited him to sit down and take a load off.

Hmm. Maybe Lauren would be flinging the "I told you so."

A perky maroon-haired hostess strolled up, menu in hand. "Booth or table?"

"Table."

"Right this way." She turned, and he followed.

And then a voice joined with the music. A smoked butterscotch of a contralto. Smooth and sweet, with enough of an edge to make it interesting.

No, not just interesting.

Irresistible.

The corner of a table thudded into his thigh.

"This okay?" the hostess asked.

With a distracted nod he groped for the chair and sat. Now he could focus on that voice.

Or rather, its source. He was seated near the stage but off to the side, resulting in a perfect profile view of a woman who looked as breathtaking as she sounded. Creamy shoulders peeked from a shimmery, dark blue dress, and shapely legs emerged from a shortish fluffy skirt.

His usual club soda with a lime thunked onto the table. Had he ordered already? He didn't remember doing so. He took a sip, still staring at that beautiful, crazy-talented singer in the blue dress. He was going to eat major crow with Lauren, but he didn't care. No one in Kansas City had ever transfixed him so completely. Not the way that gorgeous voice in this little hole-in-the-wall club had.

Full crimson lips issued the sound that dove deep into his soul. Bouncy dark curls shone a deep blue-purple in the stage lights. Sparkling earrings set off the gorgeous shape of her face. Wide cheekbones, long-lashed eyes, and—

Icy soda hurtled down his throat in a gulping attempt not to choke.

He *knew* those curls. Those eyes. That face.

That singer—how was this even possible?—was Sloane Kelley.

><

The applause from the small but enthusiastic audience rang in Sloane's ears as she reached for the water bottle on the wooden stool behind her. She took a few swigs while Eric chatted up the crowd. Stage patter was traditionally the singer's domain, but the standard "How y'all doin' tonight?" and "Thanks for coming out!" came far more easily to their ebullient guitarist than it did to her.

She could scat with the best of them. But small talk? Not so much.

"Got a live one tonight, mama." Jamal, the heavyset bass player, bent his head over the thick steel strings and adjusted a tuning peg.

"I'm sorry?" Sloane leaned closer.

"Cat over there at table two hasn't taken his eyes off you since he sat down."

Brow furrowed, Sloane glanced around the club. Table two . . . table two . . .

Was that . . . Garrett?

What was he doing here?

His gaze met hers, and he lifted a glass to her with an appreciative smile that still managed to be a smidge cocky. With the coolest nod she could muster, she turned back to Jamal.

"Oh, man. I cannot shake this guy."

Jamal peered at her over black-framed glasses. "He stalking you or something? Want me to put a stop to it?"

"No, he's not a creep. He's just popping up everywhere lately."

Jamal gave the tuning peg another crank. "Maybe there's a reason for it then."

"Maybe." She brushed the thought aside and pulled taut the strings of her stage presence. Only one number remained, an audience-favorite Sarah Vaughan cover. Normally by this part of the evening she could cruise.

But tonight her heart hammered. Her breathing was shallower than she liked. Her palms dampened, and her grip on the microphone slipped a fraction.

Why the sudden stage fright? This was her refuge. No one here knew she was a straitlaced academic who spent her days amid dusty artifacts. And no one from her day job knew what she did on her off time. The circles of her life were separate, and she liked it that way.

But Garrett had unknowingly hopped from one circle to the other. There he sat at table two. Chin propped on his right hand. Drink lightly grasped in his left. Watching her.

*Seeing* her.

The piano intro made her jump. Had she missed Eric's introduction? Was it time to sing already? Yanking her attention from Garrett, she called up an old trick from her voice teacher and sang not to the audience but to the exit sign at the back of the room.

By the end of the first verse, she'd calmed down enough to sneak a glance in Garrett's direction. To her relief, he wasn't watching her anymore. Eyes closed, he swayed slightly in time to the music.

Sloane fought a smile. In a million years, she'd never have pegged Garrett Anderson as someone who liked jazz.

When the song ended, the audience burst into applause. Garrett's eyes twinkled as he whistled his approval. She basked in the glow for a moment, warm and content.

The stage lights dimmed and the crowd began to disperse, and Sloane blinked as she made her way toward the staircase at stage left. The rickety stairs always made her nervous, especially in heels.

Sure enough, one of those blasted stilettos caught the edge of the second step and she wobbled—but a firm grasp on her elbow steadied her. She glanced up.

Garrett.

Of course.

"Thanks for bailing me out. Again."

"Are you kidding? It's the least I could do. That was incredible. Unbelievable. Sensational." The smile lines around his mouth deepened. "I'm running out of adjectives, so I hope you get the drift."

"Thank you." His effusive praise warmed her to the tips of her toes. Toes that suddenly protested being crammed into stilettos. She stepped out of the ridiculous contraptions, and her aching feet seemed to sigh with relief.

"Would you like to sit down?" He pulled out the chair across from his.

"That does sound nice." She sat, then kicked her shoes beneath the table while he made his way to his chair.

She smiled across at him. "So I didn't know you like jazz."

"Jazz, gospel, blues, I love it all. Grandma's always listened to gospel and jazz piano, and I guess it rubbed off." He cradled a half-empty glass of melting ice cubes and something clear and fizzy. "I think what I admire most is how you all improvise. The way you just let the spirit take you where it will. It's almost like prayer. Worshiping in church is great, but sometimes it's easier for me in a place like this. Does that make any sense at all?"

"Absolutely." For as long as she could remember, singing had been the best way for her to connect with God. And not always at church either. For whatever reason, the old jazz standards resonated more deeply within her soul. Not the words, necessarily, but the music. The spirit. The way her heart seemed to soar toward heaven when she improvised.

She'd never met anyone else who felt the same way.

It looked like Garrett hadn't either, from the slow smile spreading over his face. And was it her imagination or had his hand inched closer to hers on the scarred wooden tabletop?

"Could I buy you a drink?" he asked.

She held up her mostly empty water bottle. "Water's fine for me."

"Then how about dessert?" He reached for the menu. "Something good. Something with gluten."

A laugh burst from her lips. "If it's gluten you're after, their chocolate lava cake is worth your while. I usually treat myself to one after I sing."

"Perfect." He closed the menu as a server approached. "Two chocolate lava cakes, please."

"Great choice." The tall, sandy-haired server collected the menu from Garrett. "Can I get you another club soda?"

"I'll take a coffee. Dark roast, if you've got it. And could you bring her a glass of water, please? No ice?"

"We'll have those right out for you." The server bustled away.

Sloane studied Garrett. "No ice. How'd you know?"

"Lauren did some musicals in high school, and her voice teacher was a stickler about no cold drinks." Ice cubes clinked in his glass as he drained the last of his soda.

"Lauren's a singer?"

"Not so much anymore. It's a shame. She's got a great voice. So did our mom."

"Talent runs in the family then. What about you?"

"I play a little piano."

He certainly had the hands for it. Long, nimble-looking fingers. Neatly trimmed nails.

She arched a brow. "How little?"

A shy smile bloomed. "Okay, a lot. Started lessons when I was five and kept at it until college. My piano teacher thought I should major in performance, but ultimately I decided to go with something I could make a living at."

"Smart move."

"Yeah, my dad was pretty relieved he wouldn't be supporting a starving artist in his old age."

"Did you ever play any jazz?"

"I tried in high school. Turns out I can't improvise worth a lick. I need notes in front of me or it all falls apart. I guess that's why I admire you all so much."

She laughed. "Do you still play? I'd love to hear you sometime."

"Not a lot." He picked up his glass and turned it in his perfect piano hands. "Mom loved to listen to me when I practiced. She'd always hum along. But when she died, I guess the music did too."

Sloane's heart ached for him. She started to tell him she was sorry, but the look in his eyes changed from misty and faraway to focused and forward-thinking. He thunked the glass down. "What about you? How'd you get into jazz?"

"Well, my mother, in her constant effort to turn me into her mini-me, signed me up for choir as soon as I could walk. She was a beauty queen— first runner-up in the 1977 Miss Minnesota pageant and still bitter about it—and her talent was opera. She pushed me in that direction, but when I discovered jazz in high school, there was no turning back." Sloane quirked a grin. "One of a long list of reasons I'm a big disappointment. Mom was okay with it eventually, though. She said it was nice for me to have a talent even if I'd never be a beauty queen."

Garrett's brows lifted. "Charming."

"That's her." Sloane lifted the freshly arrived water glass in a silent, sarcastic toast.

"Did she push you to study music in college?"

"No, I arrived majoring in the ever-popular 'undecided.' But my gen-ed American history class roped me in. Not writing papers so much as the research. Learning how people used to live, how events shaped them. I was hooked."

"And the rest, as they say, is history." Dark blond lashes framed deep blue pools of mischief. "Bet you've never heard that one before."

She gave an affectionate roll of her eyes. "Never."

"So how'd you start singing with these guys?" Garrett gestured toward the stage. "Did you sing all through school?"

"No. Too many papers to write. But once I got settled with my job, I realized I missed singing. A couple weeks later, I saw a poster on the bulletin board at my favorite coffee shop. A band needed a new lead singer. I auditioned on a lark, and here I am. Second Saturday of every month."

"Life complete?"

A hunk of gooey, delicious-looking chocolate cake slid in front of her, and a matching one arrived seconds later in front of Garrett.

Mouth watering, she picked up her fork. "It is now."

⋇

It was past one in the morning when Garrett creaked open the farmhouse door and crept inside. Fatigue bled into his bones, reminding him of just how long it'd been since he saw that hour.

Worth it, though.

He and Sloane had stayed at Marty's long after most others had left, talking about music, faith, family, and anything else they could think of. Her singing had bolstered his spirits, but her presence afterward had slaked a soul-deep thirst. When was the last time he'd made it past small talk and truly connected with someone? When had a conversation about something other than dividends and portfolios flowed so easily?

Probably about the last time he'd stayed out until one in the morning.

Something rustled in the living room, and a curly blonde head peeked over the back of Grandma's blue recliner. For a second he was seventeen again, sneaking in after curfew and hoping this was the one time his mom had gone to bed early.

But that was Lauren in the chair, not Mom.

"So." Lauren rose, her smile devilish. "Wichita's jazz scene. Nothing to write home about, huh?"

"Yeah, yeah. Rub it in." Rolling his eyes, Garrett swept past his sister to the kitchen. Something smelled delicious, and his stomach growled. How could he be hungry? That chocolate lava cake wasn't small. And it had real sugar. Gluten, even.

But he couldn't remember eating it. All he remembered was Sloane.

A plate piled high with cookies proved the source of the aroma, and he popped one into his mouth. Odd that she'd described herself as chubby earlier. Chubby certainly wasn't the word he'd use. Curvaceous, maybe. Voluptuous. In that dress, she'd looked—

"You're in a good mood." Lauren stood in the doorway, one arm propped on the burnished wooden frame.

He reached for another cookie. "Heard a good band."

"Must have. It's one in the morning."

"You sound like Mom." He rummaged through the fridge for something to wash down the cookies. Soy milk . . . almond milk . . . hemp milk? Was there no room in the world anymore for normal milk produced by cows, the way God intended?

"So I was right then? About Marty's?"

"One-hundred-percent." Almond milk looked the least offensive of the choices. He reached for the carton, closed the fridge, and found Lauren behind him with a glass in her outstretched hand.

"You met someone." It wasn't a question.

He took the glass and set it on the counter. "What makes you say that?"

"Because you just admitted I'm right. You never do that. So you either met someone, or you had something stronger than club soda with a lime." She leaned in and sniffed the shoulder of his shirt. "No, you smell more like chocolate than anything else. Maybe a little perfume."

Garrett stepped back. "Did you literally just smell me?"

"Who is she?"

"You mean you didn't know?" She'd been awfully insistent he go to Marty's, and trying to fix him up was not beyond her.

But Lauren's expression was blank. "Know what?"

"Sloane's the lead singer."

Lauren's eyes almost popped out of her head. "Sloane is the singer? Oh ho. No wonder you stayed out so late."

"Okay, whatever you're conjuring up right now, don't. Sloane and I are just friends. I live three hours away, remember?"

Lauren tilted her head. "Uh-huh. Is she why you smell like chocolate?"

"We had dessert, yes. Delicious dessert, with sugar and carbs and everything." He sloshed a little almond milk into the glass, took an experimental sniff, then tossed the cold beverage down his throat.

Hmm. Not bad. Not anything he'd ever mistake for actual milk, but . . . not bad.

"Can't have been that delicious, the way you're chowing down on my cookies." Lauren jerked her head toward the pile on the plate, which had shrunk considerably. "Who bought this carb-a-palooza?"

"That's not the point."

"So you did."

"A man can buy a woman dessert without ulterior motives."

"And keep her out until one in the morning? Also without ulterior motives?"

He slid his empty glass into the dishwasher. "Lauren. Sloane sang beautifully, and then we sat and had cake and a conversation. We're friends. That's it." The statement didn't ring quite as true as he'd like.

But that had to be it. He had Grandma to think about. His Series 7 exam to prepare for. Clients to focus on. He couldn't let himself get distracted, no matter how enticing those distractions might be.

Jenny Hickok had been one such distraction. And look what a disaster that turned out to be.

"Okay." Lauren still looked like she didn't believe him.

His brow creased. "You really didn't know Sloane sang at Marty's?"

"Don't you think I'd be gloating like nobody's business if I did?"

"Good point." He grabbed another cookie, then pulled Lauren close for a quick hug. "G'night, Lo."

"Night night, lover boy."

Her singsong voice chased him all the way upstairs.

# CHAPTER SIX

SUNDAY AFTERNOONS DIDN'T normally find Sloane in the depths of the museum's archives, but her burning curiosity about Dr. Stephen Maxwell meant a post-church date with dusty documents, regardless of the day and time. The good doctor's tireless dedication to caring for the earliest settlers was well-known, as was his rise to prominence as a physician and surgeon. But she was fuzzy on some of the details, like how one of the first churches in the area had met in his home. How he'd donated a portion of land in 1884 for the construction of a permanent church building.

How one of the first schools in the township had met nearby. Taught for two terms by his niece, Miss Annabelle Collins.

Eager to share her findings, Sloane pulled out her phone to call Garrett, but it buzzed in her hand before she got the chance. The flash of his number on-screen drew a smile.

"I was just about to call you," she said by way of greeting.

"You were, huh?" Was she imagining it, or was there a flirtatious note in his voice? The sound brought a wash of memories from last night and a rush of pleasant goose bumps to her arms.

"Not like . . . I mean, I found some stuff about Uncle Stephen. Not my Uncle Stephen. I don't have an Uncle Stephen. Annabelle's Uncle Stephen. Dr. Stephen Maxwell."

He chuckled. "You're cute when you're flustered."

"You're annoying when you're perceptive."

"So what'd you learn?"

Sloane cleared her throat. "I confirmed that Stephen Maxwell filed for a quarter section in Sedgwick County in 1870, and another source mentioned his niece Annabelle teaching at a school nearby. I was about to look through the school district's records to see if I could learn more."

"I suppose you could find out that way. Or you could hear about it from the girl herself."

Sloane's eyebrows shot up. "You found another diary?"

"Knew that'd get your attention." His I'm-so-proud-of-myself smirk was audible, but her anticipation was too great to care. "Lauren found it in the spare bedroom."

"Have you read it? What does she say?"

"Come on. What fun would it be if we didn't look through it together?"

Together. The word brought an exhilarating zing.

"That does sound fun." She reached for her day planner. "When can we meet?"

"Are you near a window? Say, facing Main Street?"

She crossed the room. "I am now."

"Look down."

She did, down three stories of limestone to the sidewalk, and there was Garrett, phone to his ear and that smirk on his face. In his other hand was a small book, with which he gave a jaunty yet careful wave.

"I swung by on the off chance you might be digging up some dirt on Annabelle. Patience doesn't seem like your strong suit."

Right again. As always.

"I'll be right down."

She stepped from the dim lobby into bright spring sunshine and found him sitting on a bench beneath a tree, surrounded by a sea of colorful blossoms. Their sweet fragrance wafted on the breeze as she settled beside him.

"Hello again." His eyes crinkled at the corners, the same way they had last night at Marty's. But now up close, in broad daylight, through a pair of tortoiseshell sunglasses ...

"Hi." Pulling her archival gloves from her bag, she turned her attention to the diary. "What do we have?"

"First page says May 29, 1871. Annabelle's, what, eighteen? Nineteen now?"

"Nineteen. Hey, I thought you said we'd read it together."

"I peeked." One corner of his mouth quirked in an adorably mischievous way. "Surely that doesn't count as reading."

"I suppose I'll let you off the hook." She threw him a glance of mock severity. "This time."

"Good." Garrett leaned closer as she opened the diary.

He must not have shaved since last night, because a hint of reddish blond stubble glinted in the sunlight. Sunlight that threw his cheekbone into shadow and highlighted the crease beside his mouth, and—

Why was she staring at stubble and sunglasses when Annabelle Collins's voice called to her from the pages of the diary in her hands?

"Shall we?" Her voice was a little too bright. Her cheeks felt hot. Had Garrett noticed? She didn't dare look at him, not now, but she caught a hint of a charmer grin out of the corner of her eye anyway.

Drat. He'd noticed.

The charmer grin deepened. "I thought you'd never ask."

>‹

*May 29, 1871*

Pushing back her bonnet, Annabelle breathed deep of fresh spring air and tilted her face to the sun's warming rays. There was a time long ago, so long she could scarce remember, when she'd have been reluctant to let sunlight kiss her skin lest she freckle. Back in Indiana. In the land of before.

That covered-wagon trip to Kansas was the curtain separating the girl she'd been from the woman she'd become.

Parts of that girl came with her. Like the diary on the corner of the worn quilt beneath her, pinning the tattered edge of fabric in place. She'd expected to need something heavier—a stone perhaps, or a sturdy branch—but the normally ceaseless wind was still today. As though even it were willing to take a Sabbath rest.

The creek wasn't, though. A week of rain had muddied its banks and stirred its lazy waters to life. Wild indigo bloomed brilliant in the fields. Sunbeams danced through shimmering cottonwoods, whose fluffy tufts drifted before her face like snowflakes. God's presence brooded thick here on these Sunday afternoons by the creek. Thicker than it ever had in Indiana.

A lock of sun-streaked hair blew across her eyes. As she brushed it back, movement in the creek caught her attention. Splashing. An otter perhaps?

Annabelle's breath caught. It was no otter. It was a child. A little boy.

She sprang to her feet and raced for the water's edge. Stumbled through the brush, half tripping, almost falling, but unwilling to tear her gaze from the struggling form. The boy's head disappeared and her heart stopped, but then a thatch of dark hair surfaced. His mouth gaped. His eyes wide with terror.

A fallen cottonwood branch caught her eye, and she grabbed it. If she acted now—got his attention, gave him something to hold on to—perhaps she could save him. Frantic, wordless prayers burned in her chest.

"Hey!" The swollen stream drowned her words. She tried again. Louder. "Hey!"

Spinning in the current, weighed down by his clothes, the boy looked up. His eyes locked on hers.

"Take hold." She held the branch out over the water. The boy's small hand reached for it but missed by several inches. His head bobbed beneath the surface again.

Too far away. She needed to get closer.

Sinking in cold, muddy water to the tops of her shoes, Annabelle grabbed the trunk of a nearby cottonwood for support. Stretched the branch as far out as it would go. If she didn't grab him now, she'd never catch him. And that was a possibility too painful to consider.

"Take hold! Now!"

The boy's hand stretched from the water. Tantalizingly close. Just an inch or two. *Father God, just give me one more inch.* She leaned over the water as far as she dared. Her palm stung with the pressure of the tree's rough bark. *One more inch . . .*

There. Small fingers gripped the branch. One hand, then the other. She stumbled under the weight of the boy and his waterlogged clothes but remained upright, and the lad held on.

*Thank you, Father.*

"Now hold tight. I'm going to pull you up. Whatever you do, don't let go."

The boy nodded his agreement, and Annabelle pulled with all her might. She dragged and yanked until his booted feet touched the muddy bank and he fell to his knees, coughing and spluttering. Wobbly with relief, Annabelle tossed the branch aside and knelt before him. Chilly mud seeped through her skirts.

"Are you all right?" Placing her hands on the soaked shoulders of his cotton shirt, she peered into deep blue eyes that looked much too old for a face so young. He couldn't be more than four or five.

The trembling boy burst into tears.

"You poor dear." Annabelle scooped up the drenched child and carried him the short distance to where she'd been sitting. "How frightened you must have been. But you were very brave. And you're safe now."

Pulling the quilt from beneath her belongings, she wrapped it around the boy and comforted him as best she could. When his sobs subsided, she released him from her embrace and tightened the quilt around his shoulders. "There you are. You'll be warm and dry before you know it."

The boy wiped his nose on the worn edge of the fabric.

Who was he? Too young for her schoolroom, but perhaps a student's sibling? She scanned the small face for familial resemblance but found none.

"My name is Annabelle." She sat back on her heels, hands folded in her lap. "What's yours?"

"Oliver." He gave a small sniffle.

"It's a pleasure to meet you, Oliver, though I wish it were under better circumstances." Smiling, she glanced around. "Where's your mother?"

The boy shook his head. "I don't have one, ma'am. Not anymore."

Her heart gave a painful squeeze. "Your father, then?"

"Don't have one of those either."

Cooing with sympathy, Annabelle drew the lad closer. "Haven't you anyone in this world?"

"Oliver!"

The deep, desperate shout carried on a cotton-tufted breeze. A dark-haired man sprinted along the banks of the creek behind her, his attention fixed on the fast-moving waters.

"I've got him, sir," Annabelle called. "He's all right."

The man stopped and stared, wild-eyed. "Oliver?"

Joy dawned on the boy's face. "Uncle Jack!"

Breaking into a run, the man easily covered the remaining distance, then dropped to his knees and wrapped Oliver in a fierce embrace.

"Thank the Lord." He pulled back to look at the boy, concern etched in fine lines around his eyes. "Are you all right, lad?" A hint of an accent colored his speech, one Annabelle couldn't place.

Oliver managed a shaky nod. "I—I think so."

"I thought I'd lost you." His voice ragged, the man pulled the little boy close once more.

Annabelle rose and shook out her soaked, mud-covered skirts, eyes stinging at his unabashed display of emotion. Most men weren't as forthcoming with their feelings. Despite the cold, wet patch where she'd cradled Oliver's head against her bodice, there bloomed a curious heat in her chest.

The man kissed the top of Oliver's head, then stood, his hand resting on the boy's shoulder. "We were fishing by the creek, you see, and young Oliver tripped over a tree root and lost his balance. He knows how to swim, but the current was fast with all the rain—I'd no idea how fast—and . . ." He trailed off, still winded from his sprint, and looked at his nephew with love in his eyes. "The good Lord was watching out for you today."

"The good Lord and this lady." Oliver rewarded Annabelle with a shy smile.

"You saved him?" The man's deep gray eyes, fierce and cloudy as a prairie thunderhead, fixed on her, and she flushed under their intensity.

"I was here, where I spend Sunday afternoons, and I saw his struggle. A branch was nearby." She gestured to the lifesaving limb. "I held it out to Oliver, and he grabbed on. He was so very brave, and strong, and—"

Whatever else she might have said was cut off by the man's lips on her forehead. Warm, firm hands cupped the back of her neck. His beard and mustache tickled her sensitive skin.

It was over in a heartbeat. As though scorched, he released her and backed away, blinking. He looked as stunned as she felt.

This kiss wasn't her first. That little imp Thomas Warner, who'd dipped her braids in his inkwell more times than she could count, had stolen a kiss in the schoolyard one warm autumn day when she was eleven.

But that was a child's kiss. This kiss had come from a man. A man who was all muscles and glittering eyes and dark beard and strange accent. A man whose forehead shone with perspiration, whose tanned cheeks flushed a deep scarlet.

"I'm terribly sorry, Miss . . . ?"

"Collins, sir." Her face flamed. "Annabelle Collins."

"*Miss* Collins?"

"Yes."

"Well, at least you haven't a husband to come after me." With a sheepish smile, he brushed a thick lock of hair off his forehead. "Forgive me, Miss Collins. I don't know what came over me."

"You were worried for your nephew." She glanced toward young Oliver, still huddled in her quilt, dark eyes wide and curious. "No harm done, Mr. . . . ?" *Oh, dear.*

"Brennan. John's my Christian name, but please . . . call me Jack."

She managed a smile. "I suppose we have moved through the usual niceties rather quickly, haven't we?"

Mr. Brennan—Jack—burst into deep, rich laughter that chased away the lingering awkwardness. That laugh was as unabashed as his relief had been earlier, one that begged her own to bubble forth. When it did, she met his eyes, creased at the corners and sparkling with mirth. The warmth in her chest grew all the warmer at their shared amusement.

"Uncle Jack?" Oliver tugged on his uncle's trouser leg, and Jack turned his attention to the boy.

"What is it, lad?"

Oliver rubbed his left shoulder, the motion causing the quilt to slip to his waist. "My arm hurts."

The lightness of laughter disappeared from Jack's face, replaced by lines of concern.

"Now that the shock's worn off, the pain may be setting in." Annabelle stepped closer. "May I have a look? I know a bit about it."

Blue eyes large and wary, Oliver nodded.

"I'm going to move your arm a little. I'll be gentle, and it shouldn't pain you, but if it does, I promise I'll stop at once."

Oliver braced himself. Praying she wouldn't cause the lad any more discomfort than he'd already suffered, she bent down and carefully guided the tiny arm in all directions, as she'd seen Uncle Stephen do time and again. Though the boy moaned slightly on the last rotation, the blood-curdling shriek for which she'd braced herself never materialized. With a sigh and a smile, she let go of his arm and tucked the quilt back around the small shoulders.

"It doesn't appear serious," she said to Jack as she rose. "No dislocation, and likely no fracture either."

"God be praised," murmured Jack, who then eyed her with skepticism. "Where did you learn all that?"

"From my uncle." She lifted her chin. "Dr. Stephen Maxwell. I'm certain he would be happy to take a look at Oliver, to be safe. He has the formal training, of course, but I've learned much from assisting him."

A shadow flitted across Jack's face. "I've not yet met the man, but he is the answer to many prayers."

"That he is," she said.

Was it sinful to be proud of her uncle? She hoped not. A wonderful doctor, and an even more wonderful man, he'd been a tremendous help to these struggling settlers. God truly had called them here, of that she was certain.

A frown creased Jack's brow. "Would he see the boy even on the Lord's Day?"

She stooped to retrieve her diary. "He always says if Jesus healed on the Sabbath, he reckons he can as well."

Grinning, Jack offered her his arm. "Then will you do us the honor of escorting us?"

Annabelle returned his smile and rested her fingertips in the crook of his elbow, as though their destination was a grand ball. "It would be my pleasure."

✢

Garrett's chuckle was low next to Sloane's ear, mingling with the swish of a passing car. "Sounds like Miss Annabelle is one smitten kitten."

"Sounds like it." Sloane closed the diary and pulled off a glove. "But even more than that, do you realize what she's given us?"

"What?"

"Another name. John Brennan." She reached into her bag and grabbed her tablet. Angling it to avoid the sun's glare, she pulled up the township map she'd been studying earlier, then leaned closer to Garrett and indicated one of the cursive-labeled squares with a fingertip.

"S. A. Maxwell." Garrett glanced up at her. "That's Uncle Stephen?"

"Mm-hmm." Excitement coursing through her, she dragged her finger over the screen to move the map. "Jack and Oliver couldn't have been too far away." She scrolled across the nearby properties. "Abrams . . . Stevens . . . Oh, right here."

"J. F. Brennan." Garrett slipped off his sunglasses and peered at the map. "Is that Jack?"

Sloane zoomed the map out to double-check. "No other Brennans anywhere nearby, so, yeah, that's gotta be him."

"Wow. So, wait. What happened to Oliver's parents? Why is he with Jack? Is Jack married? I'm assuming not, since he just planted one on Annabelle, but does he have family other than Oliver?"

"Look who's full of questions now."

"Well." His voice deepened, and he fixed her with the full intensity of that ocean-blue gaze. "You've got me invested."

Her heartbeat kicked up a notch, and she tore her attention back to the map . . . Aha, a landmark.

All the pieces clicked into place.

"I'm glad." She pointed at a little square with a cross on it. "Because see this church right here? St. Matthew?"

A crease formed between Garrett's brows. "That old Catholic church out west?"

"One and the same." She scrolled the map over a few sections. "So we start there and go three miles straight east to where the claim backs up to Blackledge Creek—"

"Wait, that's Blackledge Creek?" Garrett leaned closer. "That S curve in it sure looks familiar." He looked up, wide-eyed. "Is that . . . ?"

"It is indeed." She beamed. "Jack Brennan's claim is your grandparents' farm."

# Chapter Seven

Jack Brennan. The name bounced around Garrett's head, much like the gravel clanking against his car as he drove back to the farmhouse. Knowing this land once belonged to that long-ago settler was interesting, but what did it mean? What bearing, if any, did it have on the present?

Sloane would find out, of course. She was relentless in her pursuit of information, and she'd promised to keep him in the loop. It was a little alarming how much he hoped her name would flash across the screen every time his phone chirped. Whether the information she uncovered had any significance, it was fascinating.

She was fascinating. Her enthusiasm for digging around in old boxes charmed him. Her frankness refreshed him. Her dry sense of humor lightened his heart. And her vulnerability stirred protective instincts he didn't know he had. She'd shared the tragic circumstances of her birth with him as matter-of-factly as he discussed investment portfolios with clients, but the hurt in those golden-brown eyes revealed her abandonment's true cost. The depth of her sorrow, the brave cover for barely healed wounds, made him want to gather her in his arms and whisk her away someplace where her past couldn't hurt her, and her present couldn't confuse her, and—

And these were not the sort of thoughts one had about someone who was just a friend.

But just a friend she had to remain. Because anything more was not part of his plan, couldn't be part of his life. Her life was here and his was hours away.

Pulling up outside the house, he parked the car, boxed up all thoughts of Sloane, and strode through the back door into a kitchen perfumed with strange spices. Lauren stood at the stove while Grandma sat at the table watching finches flit around the feeder outside.

"Hello, all." He crossed the kitchen and retrieved a glass from the cupboard. A large pot simmering on the stove seemed to be the source of the aroma. As usual, he had not a prayer of identifying it.

"Hey." Lauren tapped her spoon on the edge of the pot. "You find Sloane? Was the diary a hit?"

"It was." He stuck his glass under the faucet. "Especially the kissing part."

"You guys *kissed*?"

"Who's kissing?" Grandma piped up from the table.

Heat stung Garrett's cheeks at how grossly he'd underestimated Lauren's imagination. More so at the image that popped, unbidden, into his head. Sloane's perfectly shaped mouth, her full red lips . . .

"No, I'm not . . . It's Annabelle. The girl from the diary. She's nineteen now, getting kissed by a neighbor guy named Jack." He took a hasty gulp of water. *Friends.*

"Ooh. Jack. Sounds sexy," Lauren said.

"I knew a Jack once," Grandma added. "He wasn't sexy, though."

Spluttering, Garrett choked down the water and yanked the conversation back to the past. To a simpler time, when thoughts of Sloane didn't intrude and his grandmother and sister didn't fling the word *sexy* around like a Frisbee.

The past Annabelle had so richly described in her diary.

When he finished recounting Annabelle's rescue of Oliver and Jack Brennan's impulsive display of gratitude, Grandma's face lit with a satisfied smirk. "Attagirl, Annabelle."

"No joke." Lauren stirred the simmering concoction. "If there's one thing this neighborhood needs more of, it's hunky farmers with cute accents."

Grandma's chair scraped against the floor as she pushed herself back from the table. "If you'll all excuse me, I need to go see if the Royals' bats woke up yet."

Garrett moved toward her, but she waved away his offer of help.

"Thanks just the same, Garrett." She stood, stretched to kiss his cheek, then shuffled from the room.

*Garrett.* Today she remembered his name.

Lauren gave a few raspy turns to a pepper grinder over the steaming pot. "She's having a good day."

"She is." No arguments.

But for every good day, another bad one always lurked around the corner.

"So, do we know any more about this Jack guy?" Lauren spooned up a sample from the pot, gave it a taste, and reached for one of the spice jars littering the counter beside the stove.

"He was one of the area's original settlers. Sloane found a map—and get this. Jack's claim was right here."

Lauren turned, spice jar in hand. "So this could've been his house?"

"It's possible, although land changed hands fairly often. Even if this was his claim, he may not have stayed long enough to prove it. Sloane's on the case, though." Draining his glass, he slid it into the dishwasher. "Better get upstairs and get packed."

"Not sticking around for dinner?"

"Got a client bright and early, so the sooner I get back home, the better."

"In that case, how about some for the road? I've got Very Veggie Tikka Masala with cauliflower rice."

So that's what it was. Rice was the only part that sounded remotely appetizing, and with the word *cauliflower* preceding it, even that lost its luster.

He gave a polite smile. "That's sweet, but I'll just pick something up on the road."

"Nonsense. Do you have any idea how much sodium and fat is in that stuff?"

"That's why it's delicious."

"But this is healthy." Rhythmic chopping underpinned Lauren's words as she disassembled a handful of parsley. "And it's free."

She had him there.

"You know my kryptonite."

Lauren scraped the parsley into the pot of vegan goo. "Back in two weeks then?"

"Actually I'm coming back Friday."

"Why? Hot date?" Lauren bent to retrieve a glass container from the cabinet.

"I'd be more inclined to call it 'plans.'" His cheeks warmed again. "But yes. There's a combo playing at Fitzy's next week. Sloane says they're fantastic."

Lauren stood, container in hand, eyes glittering with amusement. "I was totally kidding, but wow, look how red you're getting. You're so adorable when you've got a crush on someone." She patted his flaming cheek.

"It's not a crush."

"All right, what would a stuffy, brainiac big brother call it? Let's see . . ." She deepened her voice. "A mutual attraction based on common interests."

"Sure. Call it whatever you want."

"You have to at least admit you're attracted to her or I'll make you take some of this Perfectly Paleo naan along with you." She gestured with the container toward a plate of odd-smelling flatbread.

"Okay, yes. Objectively, Sloane is an attractive woman." His pulse skittered at the memory of her in that blue dress. "But that doesn't mean I'm attracted to her. All it means is—"

"Oh, please." Lauren rolled her eyes. "This is Jenny Hickok all over again."

"That may be. But now I don't have to take any of this naan . . . nonfood you're trying to foist on me."

"Just for that, I'm giving you extra." Lauren ladled a steaming spoonful into the container, and Garrett laughed all the way up to the second floor.

＞＜

*May 29, 1871*

The tick of the clock on the mantel marked the passage of seemingly endless seconds as Annabelle sat beside Jack in Uncle Stephen's parlor—or what passed for one in a hastily constructed cabin. Two muffled voices bled in from behind the door: Oliver's high-pitched chatter and Uncle Stephen's smooth, reassuring baritone.

Jack hadn't said a word since they arrived. Eyes locked on the floor, he worried a worn Stetson in his hands. His right leg bounced, the soft thump of his heel at odd counterpoint with the ticking clock.

"He'll be fine." Annabelle placed a reassuring hand on his forearm. "At worst, it's a small fracture. And Oliver's young. Strong. He'll be back to his old self in no time."

Coal-black lashes fluttered as Jack raised his eyes to hers. "I know. At least in my head I know."

"But?"

The darkness in his gaze, the heaviness in his countenance, spoke of something deeper than concern for his nephew. He sighed and turned back to his hat. "I believe in the Almighty, Annabelle. At least, I did once. But if he is real, then I feel he's set his hand against me. Ever since we left Wisconsin."

"Is that where you're from?" It was the wrong thing to fixate on now, but perhaps she'd finally placed his delightful manner of speech.

A smile touched his lips. "If you're wondering about my accent, no. That comes straight from the Emerald Isle. Aghadrumsee, if you've heard of it." The slight twinkle in his gray eyes suggested he'd guessed the truth: she hadn't. "It's on the northern side of Ireland. 'Field of the fairy ridge,' the name means."

"It sounds beautiful."

"It is. At least, what I remember. I was even younger than Oliver when we came to America. First to Wisconsin, then Illinois." He cleared his throat. "Last year, my wife, Sarah, and I left, along with her sister and husband and Oliver, their son, to take a claim in Kansas."

His wife. He had a wife.

Or he'd *had* a wife. The slump of his broad shoulders confirmed it.

"Elisabeth—Sarah's sister—was the first to go. Cholera. Her husband, Charles, followed two days later. By some miracle it passed the rest of us, so Sarah and I took in Oliver to raise as our own." He rocked forward to rest his elbows on his knees, and that lock of hair fell across his forehead. "But then we learned Sarah was with child."

Sympathy quickened Annabelle's pulse.

"If I'd known when we started, I'd have never made the trip. But Sarah didn't tell me, precisely because she knew I'd have never made the trip, until we'd gone too far to turn back. I prayed—every day, every hour—for her. For the baby. And she was strong. Right up until the delivery." Pain shimmered in his eyes. "But the birthing was difficult. There was no doctor, and the neighbor who served as the midwife, she . . ." He pressed his lips together. "There was nothing anyone could do."

"Oh, Jack." She grasped his hand and gripped it tight. "I'm so sorry."

"Our son—Josiah—he lived four days." He shook his head. "And since then, I can't help but think . . . what if coming here was a mistake? What if God's punishing us? What if there *is* no—"

"Mr. Brennan?"

Uncle Stephen's eyes shone; his voice held a happy lilt. He had good news. Relief coursed through Annabelle before he spoke another word.

Jack leaped to his feet to meet Oliver as he stepped through the doorway into the parlor. A smile cracking the sadness, Jack crouched down and clasped the boy's round face between work-worn hands. A quick kiss to the small freckled cheek, then he rose and turned to Uncle Stephen. "How is he?"

"No breaks or dislocations. Only a small cut on his leg. I bandaged it, and you'll need to rub this salve on it each night before bed." Uncle Stephen held out a small tin, which Jack stuffed into his pocket. "Come back if the wound reddens or swells, but I don't expect it will. Keep it clean and it should heal nicely."

"My deepest thanks, doctor." The depth of Jack's voice made Annabelle's heart thump.

"It's my pleasure."

Jack reached into his pocket. "How much do I owe you?"

Uncle Stephen waved a hand. "No charge, Mr. Brennan."

"Are you certain? It's no trouble, I can pay."

"No, no. It's the Lord's Day. Any healing I do on this day is purely out of service to God."

"Then I'm much obliged, Dr. Maxwell. And to you, Miss Collins." Replacing the Stetson on his head, Jack took Oliver's hand.

"I'll be praying for you, Mr. Brennan." She stepped toward him. "That God will reassure you of his love, and give some sign that you're where he's purposed you to be."

Jack's intense gray gaze pinned her in place. "Perhaps he's done exactly that."

Her face flamed. Only after the wooden door creaked open and shut did she turn to her uncle, her pulse still racing, her breath caught in apprehension of the questions he was certain to ask.

But he stared at the door, a thoughtful expression softening craggy features. "Funny thing. Even before I met that man, I knew him."

Annabelle frowned. "How?"

"That dream I had back in Indiana, the one with the man holding the infant—"

Her eyes flew open. "That was him?"

"It was." Uncle Stephen placed a hand on Annabelle's shoulder. "The Lord works in mysterious ways, doesn't he?"

Her gaze traveled to the gingham-curtained window and the retreating figures of Jack and his young nephew, her skin warm from the memory of those fierce lips.

"He certainly does, Uncle. He certainly does."

><

"Must be good, whatever you're reading."

Colleen's voice over Sloane's shoulder made her jump. Lowering the diary, she turned toward her coworker, who was settling in at her desk, her enormous WuShock coffee mug wafting steam into the office air.

"Didn't realize you'd come in."

"I gathered that. Said hi to you three times."

Sloane slipped a bookmark into the diary and set it aside. "Sorry."

"So what's got you so absorbed?"

Quickly, Sloane caught her colleague up on the diary's author and contents.

Colleen, a mischievous smirk on her face, stuck a pencil into her graying ponytail and turned to her computer. "Now I gotta know if Annabelle got her man."

"No." Sloane nearly lunged across the space between them in her vehemence. "No spoilers."

Colleen stopped, mid search query. "But we can probably dig up all the dirt on her in two minutes."

Sloane sighed. Her thirst for knowledge was raging, the temptation intense. "I know. But I'd like to learn it from Annabelle. In her words. As she experienced it."

"Suit yourself. At my age, I don't have the patience."

"Dig up whatever you want. Just don't spoil it for me."

Colleen reached for the diary and carefully leafed through the worn pages. "Where'd you even find this thing?"

Sloane recapped her day of discovery at Garrett's grandparents' farm.

Colleen's gray brows arched. "The Spencer place? Up near Jamesville?"

"That's the one."

"They getting ready to sell?"

"Not that I know of. Why?"

Colleen handed the diary back to Sloane. "Warren Williams has had it in his sights for a long time."

"As in Williams and Son Development?" Sloane's gut tightened. The Williams empire, responsible for many of Wichita's upscale subdivisions, had been gobbling up farmland, Pac-Man style, for over three decades.

Colleen sipped her coffee. "My ex-husband had some dealings with his former partner. If memory serves, the Spencers sold some of their land to a neighbor about fifteen years ago."

Sloane pursed her lips. That timing lined up with Garrett's mother's cancer diagnosis. Maybe the Spencers had needed money to help with her treatments.

"The neighbor agreed to farm the land, but a couple years later he sold it to Williams for a pretty penny." Colleen chuckled. "The Spencers were none too pleased and made that crystal clear when ole Warren came to try to buy the rest."

*Way to go, Rosie.* Garrett's grandma definitely had some fire in her. Doubtless her husband had too.

"For the sake of preserving an old property, I sure hope stubbornness runs in that family." Colleen turned back to her computer. "All the same, I wouldn't get too attached."

"Right." Reeling, Sloane set the diary on her desk. Warren Williams turning that beautiful land into a sea of suburbia? The idea made her sick.

It wouldn't happen, though. Rosie and Lauren were happy there, and the decluttering binge seemed geared toward making the house more habitable for Rosie, not more attractive for a potential buyer. Besides, if he were planning to sell, Garrett would've mentioned it, but he hadn't said a word.

Her shoulders relaxed. The Spencer place, Jack Brennan's claim, wasn't in immediate danger. At least, she hoped it wasn't.

Because despite Colleen's warning, it was too late.

Sloane was already attached.

# CHAPTER EIGHT

SHAFTS OF SUNLIGHT sneaked between the blinds of Garrett's office and took up residence in their customary spot on the far side of the gray carpet. Normally he felt extra virtuous when he arrived before the sunbeams did, but this morning, as he slid his second cup of coffee from beneath the Keurig's spigot, he barely noticed. Wednesday already, and despite two days of early mornings and late nights, he was still playing catch-up.

Such was life when he took time off for a trip to Wichita.

It never used to be like this. Not long ago, he'd come in early to sip coffee at leisure, not gulp it out of desperation. The relative quiet was a perfect opportunity to skim the latest industry news, maybe draft a blog post, and reach Inbox Zero before the chaos hit.

These days, he'd settle for Inbox Double Digits. Especially since yesterday's dip in the Dow meant he'd doubtless spend the morning reassuring his more panicky clients.

Sure enough, as soon as his clock clicked to eight, the phone rang. Garrett reached for the receiver with wry amusement. He'd speak with several clients this morning, but only one was this predictably punctual.

"Morning, Mrs. Krantz."

"Good morning, Garrett." The elderly widow's sheepish smile was audible. "I suppose you can guess why I'm bothering you this early."

Garrett leaned back in his chair and twirled a pen between his fingers. "Wouldn't have anything to do with the Dow, would it?"

"You know me well."

He chuckled. "I try. And it'd be great if all my clients were this vigilant. But a seventy-point swing is nothing to get excited about."

His client's soft sigh whooshed into his ear. "I know. I just needed to hear it from you."

"That's what I'm here for." Affection for his anxious client curved his lips. He'd reassure a thousand Geraldine Krantzes if it meant sparing them the financial struggles his grandmother was mired in.

Garrett returned the phone to its cradle just as a knock came at the door. His boss, Joseph Sterling, stood in the doorway, a blue Sporting KC coffee mug clutched in one deep brown hand.

Sterling smiled. "Geraldine Krantz, I presume?"

"The one and only."

"Sweet old ladies, man, that's your wheelhouse." Sterling's broad smile faded slightly. "Speaking of, how's your grandma?"

"About the same. Which is good, considering."

Sterling nodded, then raked a sharp gaze over Garrett's face, the office lights glinting off his glasses. "You've been putting in a lot of late nights. Early mornings."

The chair squeaked as Garrett shifted his weight. "I do what needs to be done. You know that."

"I do." His boss paused. "Y'know, I usually have to give the work-life balance speech to people whose work takes over their lives. But it's not healthy to let your life take over your work either."

The gentle reprimand brought heat to Garrett's cheeks and an anxious knot to his chest. "I know, sir."

"I've got nothing but respect for what you're doing. It can't be easy, especially with the travel. But you're one of my best guys. I need you at the top of your game. Your clients do too."

With a tap on the doorframe, Sterling retreated, and Garrett turned back to his computer, reeling from the unexpected encounter.

He'd only ever received accolades at work, not chastisement. Sterling's visits to his office had always been limited to small talk and strategy sessions, with a good deal of positive feedback and appreciation for his hard work.

These weekend trips to Wichita must be taking more of a toll than he'd thought. But he'd already wracked his brain for a different solution and come up empty. Lauren's day job as a wedding photographer meant she frequently worked weekends, and securing quality, consistent home care for Saturday and Sunday had proven difficult.

The situation wasn't sustainable, and the wrenching decision he'd been putting off now stared him straight in the face.

The decision shouldn't even be his to make, but no one else was willing or able to make it. Mom and Grandpa were gone. Lauren's emotions sometimes clouded her judgment. And Dad? Ha. Happy in Florida with his new wife and new life, Paul Anderson offered only vague, breezy, don't-bother-me-with-this encouragement. "You're way closer to the situation than I am, Garrett. You're smart. You'll figure it out. You always do."

And so the weight settled on his shoulders. A weight he accepted, even viewed as an honor sometimes. But he'd be lying if he said he didn't resent it sometimes too.

Humiliation and anxiety churning in his gut, he clicked out of Mrs. Krantz's files and into the bookmarked folders of websites and research. While the basic plan—find a care facility for Grandma—seemed simple, it contained a complicated number of moving parts. Which place would provide the best care? At what cost? What would insurance cover, and what would they need to come up with on their own?

And what about the house? What could they get if they sold it? What work would need to be done to make a sale possible?

Perhaps it still wasn't time for Grandma to leave her home.

But it was time—past time—to get some answers. Solidify questions and uncertainties into actual facts and workable plans.

Reaching for his coffee, he clicked to his online calendar. He was already heading down on Friday for the concert with Sloane, but if he left a couple hours early, he could meet with a real estate agent. Lauren wouldn't like it, but Lauren wouldn't be there. According to their shared calendar, she'd be taking Grandma for a checkup.

It was the perfect opportunity. One he'd be an idiot to forgo.

Surging with caffeine and motivation, he glanced through the list of Wichita real estate firms he'd researched, selected one more or less at random, and picked up the phone.

Even this small step would give him a modicum of control over a squirming, unpredictable situation.

Perhaps that control was an illusion. Perhaps not.
Either way, he'd take it.

→←

*June 4, 1871*

The strains of "O for a Thousand Tongues to Sing" filled Uncle Stephen's parlor as Annabelle stood with the group of neighbors who formed their little congregation. Though she longed for the day when they could build a real church building, with a bell and a steeple and an organ like her church back in Indiana, these weekly gatherings, all packed together in her uncle's parlor, were lovely in their own way. The common struggle of eking out a living had removed petty arguments and denominational squabbles. Now that their Savior was all they had, it was starkly clear he was all they needed. And the thought of it made Annabelle's heart overflow during the hymn's final stanza.

No sooner had the notes died away than the door creaked open, bringing in a gust of rain-soaked air. Annabelle turned at the intrusion, and her breath caught.

Jack. With Oliver by his side.

"Miss Collins!" His face alight, Oliver bolted across the crowded space and flung his arms around a startled Annabelle.

"Well, hello, Oliver." Her cheeks warmed at the whispers and titters of the congregation.

"Oliver." Jack's face loomed large as he scooped up the boy, then turned to Uncle Stephen. "I'm deeply sorry, Dr. Maxwell. I'm afraid it's been a long while since the lad's been to a proper meeting."

"No harm done, Mr. Brennan." Uncle Stephen, the Word open in his hand, regarded Jack and his nephew with a kind smile. "Jesus himself said to let the little children come unto him. Stands to reason that those who strive to be like him would follow in his footsteps."

As the whispers died down, Jack nodded his thanks and squeezed through the sea of skirts and boots to the only empty chair, a few feet to Annabelle's left. Close enough to catch a whiff of rain-soaked leather as he passed, to glimpse a fleck of shaving soap clinging to his neck.

Amusement glimmered in his eyes as he ushered Oliver past, settled into the chair, and pulled his nephew onto his lap. "So much for an unobtrusive entrance," he muttered.

Uncle Stephen began the week's lesson, and Annabelle turned her attention to him. She tried her best to focus, but the whole left side of her body tingled with the awareness that Jack was near. A force more powerful than discipline tugged her gaze in his direction.

Mercy, he was handsome. And not in a pretty, refined way like the boys she'd known growing up. No, Jack Brennan was this country personified. Wild. Fierce. Untamable. The hollows beneath his cheekbones and the fine lines around his eyes spoke of hardship, but the tightness of his mouth, the breadth of his shoulders, spoke of determination to overcome.

His dark gaze darted to hers, and she hastily looked away. The quick movement caused her Bible to nearly slip off her lap, but she caught it with a soft slap of palm on paper that drew a sharp, disapproving look from Aunt Katherine. Properly chastised, Annabelle fastened her gaze on Uncle Stephen's thin, bespectacled face. She wouldn't allow her eyes to wander again.

And wander they didn't. But she couldn't say the same for her focus. Rather than listening to Uncle Stephen's message, she found herself praying for Jack. That her uncle's words would sneak past his defenses and fan that spark of hope she'd glimpsed the last time they sat in this parlor.

That Jack was here, that he'd risked the humiliation of a late arrival, that he'd stayed even after Oliver's impulsive interruption . . . Oh, the Lord had to be calling him back into the fold. *Please, almighty God. Finish the good work you have begun in Jack.*

*And if you see fit to use me in that good work . . . then here am I, Lord. Send me.*

When the time of teaching ended and they rose for the closing hymn, Annabelle hazarded one more glance at Jack, who stood with a hand on Oliver's shoulder, sharing a hymnbook with the gentleman next to him.

*Oh.* It was impolite to stare, but she couldn't not stare. Because gone was the darkness of Jack's earlier expression, the tight, drawn pallor of his skin. Now his face radiated richness, and his gray eyes held an inner light they hadn't before.

Those eyes locked with hers and he smiled. Not one of those quirked, humorless half smiles, but a full-bodied one that transformed his whole countenance. Joy rushed into her soul with the ferocity of a prairie wind. Whatever faith Jack had lost in his struggle, it seemed God had given at least a portion of it back.

No force in all the world could have kept her from returning that smile.

The fiddler struck up the closing hymn, and though Jack's lips moved along with the rest, his gaze remained fixed on her. Looking at her. Looking *into* her, as though he could see her very soul.

The quiet clearing of Aunt Katherine's throat broke the spell. Annabelle glanced at her aunt's reproachful face, then ordered her gaze to white page and black notes.

But nothing could steal the joy of answered prayer.

❄

The insistent buzz of Sloane's phone against the desk dragged her out of the nineteenth century and into the twenty-first. Setting the diary aside, she answered the unfamiliar number, her voice as foggy as though she'd just woken up from a nap.

Thank goodness it was Friday.

"Hey, Sloane, it's Lauren Anderson. Garrett's sister." She sounded on the verge of squealing with excitement. "I found something I think you'll want to see."

Sloane straightened. "Ooh, another diary?"

"Better. I may have found a photo of Annabelle."

"Really?" Sloane was wide awake and fully in the present now.

"I'm not positive it's her, but it says 'Granny Annie' on the back, and the clothes look like they might be the right vintage. I can text you a picture."

Sloane already had her keys in hand. "Cell phones never do those pictures justice. I'd love to see it in person if that's okay."

"You're coming all the way out here just to look at a picture?"

"History nerd, remember? There's something deeply wrong about looking at a century-old photograph on the screen of an iPhone. I can swing by in about twenty minutes, if that works?"

"Sure," Lauren replied. "I have to take Grandma to the doctor at three thirty, but if you're heading out now, that should give us a little time."

Sloane was halfway to the elevator before they even ended the call.

><

When Sloane arrived, Lauren stood in the living room holding up two zippered cardigans for Rosie's examination.

"Okay, Grandma. Do you want the red sweater or the pink?"

"Pink," Rosie answered with confidence, and Lauren draped the knit garment over her stooped shoulders, then swept past and hung the red sweater on a rack near the door.

"That's one of the things I've learned about dementia," she explained, her voice low. "If you give someone two options, most of the time they'll pick the last thing they hear. And as cold as Grandma gets at the doctor, pink was the best choice."

With a broad smile, Rosie turned to Sloane. "Why, hello there, Auntie Boop. Was I expecting you today?"

"No, Grandma." Lauren zipped up Rosie's cardigan. "Auntie Boop just stopped by to pick something up. She knows we're off to the doctor."

"Oh. All right." Rosie blinked at Sloane, her blue eyes faraway and unfocused.

"While I get Auntie Boop what she came for, why don't you see how the Royals are doing?" Lauren clicked on the TV, and Rosie's attention instantly locked on the screen.

"That should buy us a few minutes. The pictures are in here." Lauren started for the kitchen. "And sorry about the Auntie Boop thing."

Sloane fell into step. "I'm happy to be mistaken for her. She sounds fun."

"I've got no idea who she is. Just like these pictures." Lauren switched on the kitchen light, revealing a table covered not with health food but with dozens upon dozens of photographs. Color, black-and-white, framed, free-floating . . . The sight was a feast for Sloane's eyes.

"They've been on the wall in the stairwell forever," Lauren continued, "but today Grandma got upset because she couldn't remember who the people were. I feel terrible. I never thought to protect her from pictures, or to ask her about them before it was too late."

"Pictures are never the first thing on anyone's mind, and we've got lots of ways to find out who these people are. It might take a little sleuthing, but..." Sloane spread her hands. "Nancy Drew, at your service. What have we got?"

"Here's the one I called you about." Lauren handed a black-and-white photo to Sloane.

Her heartbeat quickened. A fiftysomething woman peered back from the photo, clad in a shirtwaist and skirt typical of the early twentieth century. She stood alone next to a water pump, her hair pulled back in a bun, the corners of her eyes creased in a gentle smile.

Sloane flipped the picture over, but the back bore no identifying details other than "Granny Annie" scrawled in blue ink.

"Is this your grandma's handwriting?"

"I thought of that, but I pulled out some of her recipes to compare, and it's not the same."

Sloane eyed the photo again. "Well, whoever Granny Annie is, I'd say she was probably born in the 1850s sometime. Maybe early 1860s."

Lauren's eyes widened. "So this really could be Annabelle?"

Sloane's excitement surged. "It's definitely possible. She's the right age. And Annie could be a nickname."

The deep lines in the woman's face, the silver hue of her hair, spoke of a life filled with hardship. But her expression held a peace, a soft serenity, with just a hint of fire.

Had this woman penned the pages Sloane kept turning long into the night? Was it she who'd reached through time and so quickly captured Sloane's heart?

Lauren chuckled, holding another black-and-white photo.

"These are my grandparents, right after they got married." She handed the photo to Sloane.

She stared through the gilt-framed glass in disbelief. Because there, his arm around a young, golden-haired Rosie, was a man in a 1950s-era suit and fedora, a cleft in his chin and a rakish smile on his lips.

He looked exactly like Garrett.

A bubble of infatuation formed fast. "Wow. They're practically identical."

"Grandma's called Garrett by the wrong name since we were in high school. That's part of why it took everyone so long to figure out she was sick." Lauren tugged her long hair into a messy bun and grabbed an olive-green backpack from a chair. "Okay, I gotta get Grandma to her appointment. The door locks by itself, so feel free to stay as long as you like. Thanks for coming out. It's great to see you."

"Absolutely. Anytime."

Lauren's rapid footsteps retreated through the living room, and the front door thudded shut a moment later.

Much as she'd have loved to linger, Sloane couldn't spare the time. On impulse, though, she pulled out her phone and snapped a couple pictures of Granny Annie as well as one of Orrin and Rosie Spencer.

As Sloane slipped out the front door, a large white Lexus SUV pulled into the gravel driveway, and a glamorous-looking, fortysomething woman stepped out. The wind harassed carefully styled auburn hair; she corralled it with a manicured hand and took a look around.

"Can I help you?" Sloane asked, keys in hand.

"Hi. Kimberly Walsh with Carter and Macy Realty. Are you"—squinting, she consulted her notes—"Erin?"

Sloane frowned. "No . . ."

"I'm sorry, it's just I'm supposed to meet someone named Erin here at four."

It was odd to see such a put-together woman fumbling to this extent. "Are you sure you're in the right place?"

"This is the address." Another gust of wind caught Kimberly's hair, and she fought it back. "So if you're not Erin, then who are you? And who am I supposed to meet?"

Tires on gravel underlined her last words, and a beige Toyota Camry with a bike rack on the back rolled up beside the Lexus.

Wait a minute.

Sloane had seen that Camry here before. Just last weekend.

The car stopped, and Garrett stepped out. An eager smile beamed toward her, but it wobbled slightly when he looked at the real estate agent.

He cleared his throat. "Hey, everybody."

# CHAPTER NINE

GARRETT HAD MADE an appointment with Rick Macy. So who was the redhead with the flustered expression and the fluttering clipboard? Was Rick still on his way?

More importantly, what was Sloane doing here? She wasn't supposed to be here. And she definitely wasn't supposed to be making chitchat with someone from the real estate office. Not before he even had a chance to ask questions or assemble anything resembling a plan. And why did it matter so much what this tweed-skirt-wearing historian with wind-tossed hair thought?

Her quirked brow brought an uncomfortable awareness that he was staring, and probably not in a hey-there's-my-friend kind of way. He shut the car door and pulled in a quick breath, praying she'd ignore the implications of him meeting a real estate agent at Grandma's house.

"Hi," he said.

Sloane pushed her glasses up on her nose, a half smile on her lips and the expected questions in her eyes. "Hey."

High heels crunched on gravel as the redhead stepped forward and extended a hand. "I'm Kimberly Walsh with Carter and Macy Realty. Are you the Aaron who had an appointment with Rick?"

Garrett returned the handshake. "I am Rick's four o'clock, but my name's not Aaron. It's Garrett Anderson."

"Aha." A triumphant smile crossed Kimberly's face. "So I am in the right place. Rick had a family emergency last night and had to fly out to California. I took over most of his appointments today. And Rick's a little hard of hearing, so that explains the name mix-up." She glanced from

Garrett to Sloane and back again. "But anyway, hi. You two were interested in having me look at the property?"

Garrett drew back. "Oh, we're not—I mean, she's—"

"Leaving." Sloane bailed him out with a jangle of her keys. "I'm with the historical museum, and Lauren wanted to show me some old pictures."

Lauren and Sloane? Together? That could be dangerous. "Maybe you can fill me in tonight?"

"Sure." Her smile was a twitch of the lips rather than the full-on one he'd hoped for. "Six thirty, right?"

"Six thirty. Looking forward to it."

"See you then." With a wave, she climbed into her car and took off, and the tension across Garrett's shoulders loosened slightly. Her demeanor left him feeling like having Kimberly out to the house was a mistake somehow. But the house and Grandma weren't Sloane's responsibility. They were his and Lauren's. Not that he was keeping Lauren in the loop either.

Later. He'd sort things out with Sloane later. For now, it was time to talk business.

He turned to Kimberly to find her staring after Sloane's retreating Elantra, a frown creasing her features. But when the car's taillights disappeared around the bend, she erased the confusion from her face, slapped on a bright smile, and gestured toward the house with her clipboard. "Shall we?"

Garrett led her across the driveway to the listing porch. "My grandfather was fixing this up last fall when he passed unexpectedly."

Kimberly gave the predictable sympathetic murmur. "I'm sorry to hear that."

"I've been looking into contractors to finish the job." The wooden steps seemed more warped and faded than he remembered. One corner of the screen, sagging loose last time he visited, had fallen down completely, the newly freed corner scraping against its frame with each gust of wind.

Had the porch always looked this bad? Or was he simply seeing it with more critical eyes?

"I've got a couple carpenters I can recommend." Unfazed, Kimberly stepped into the living room. Garrett held his breath as her keen gaze swept over every nook and cranny.

"Wow. This place has been here a while, hasn't it?" Lines around her eyes deepened with her smile. "It's a good size. Cozy, but not cramped. Loads of charm and character. The wallpaper's got to go, of course." She pointed to a chunk of peeling floral paper in the corner.

Garrett switched on the reading lamp beside Grandma's recliner. "That's already on my sister's master plan. Our grandma has Alzheimer's, but Lauren's trying to keep her here as long as possible."

Kimberly arched a brow. "I take it you feel differently?"

"You're here, aren't you?"

She conceded his point with a nod.

He stuffed a stack of magazines into the end table drawer and winced at the dust left behind. "Our research on Alzheimer's care suggested bright paint instead of patterned wallpaper."

Kimberly's heels clicked against the hardwood floor. "If you plan to list the place soon, I'd recommend neutral rather than bright. Gray is super-hot right now."

Gray? He frowned. Couldn't picture it. "I'll talk that over with Lauren."

But Kimberly had already stepped through the wooden-framed doorway into the kitchen. "What's all this?"

Oh no. Lauren hadn't been kidding about the pictures. The table was so covered with them he couldn't see its surface. "Sorry about the mess."

"What mess? I love old photos." A smile softened Kimberly's features as she picked up one of the black-and-white pictures. "Relatives of yours?"

Garrett craned his neck for a better look. "My grandparents."

"You really favor your grandpa." Kimberly replaced the photo, then picked up another, slipping on a pair of reading glasses. She blinked a few times, and her mouth fell open a fraction. "Bet these gals have some stories to tell. Do you know who they are?"

The black-and-white photo captured a pair of young women in what looked like 1920s-era garb. The blonde bore a vague resemblance to Grandma, though if the photo really was that old then it couldn't be her. Her mother perhaps? The other woman had dark hair and wore a sequined headband. The photographer had caught her mid laugh, her face turned to the side. Garrett could almost imagine her dancing the Charleston to one of the jazz standards Sloane had sung at the club. She and Sloane would get along famously, no doubt.

Where had Lauren even found this picture? Maybe it had been stuffed behind another photo in the frame, as had been Grandma's custom for as long as he could remember. He shook his head. "I'm afraid not."

Kimberly flipped the photo over, but the back was blank. "No worries. I'm just being nosy." She replaced the photo and clipped her glasses to the front of her shirt. "Shall we take a peek at the kitchen?"

After a quick survey of the rest of the house and a good portion of the land, Garrett and Kimberly returned to the living room and settled on the sofa.

"Okay, here's where I think we stand." Kimberly consulted her notes. "The house has good bones, but it needs a lot of cosmetic work. Fresh paint indoors and out, fix the porch, replace the roof, things like that. The kitchen could use some updating if you've got the budget. New counter-tops, new appliances, replace the cabinets. Outdoors, the landscaping's pretty neglected, but nothing professionals can't fix." She peered up at him, the lines across her forehead deepening. "But if I may be frank?"

"Please."

"With this property, you're looking for a very specific buyer. I'm seeing a young family who want their kids to grow up with the best of both urban and rural living. People who want to grow their own vegetables. People whose HOA won't let them have chickens."

"Chickens?"

"Oh yes. Our hipster homesteaders will definitely want chickens. And you've got the barn, the creek, the acreage, plus you're not far from shopping and restaurants, and you're in a good school district. That all works in your favor. But most buyers who've got the cash for a place like this want a cul-de-sac lot in a gated subdivision with a playground and a pool. You need to find people who don't care about those things."

Garrett nodded. "And if we do find these people, what might they be willing to pay?"

"Provided you take my suggestions, have it updated, fixed up . . ." She named a figure that didn't lift the weight from Garrett's shoulders but did make it lighter. That figure could see Grandma comfortable for several years, especially if he invested wisely on her behalf. Given her condition and her age, it would likely be enough.

"But that's only if everything breaks in our favor," Kimberly said. "This place might get snapped right up, but it could also linger on the market for a while." She crossed her legs at the ankles and leaned forward. "Now, we do have other options. Given the location and the acreage, developers would definitely be interested. And selling it for the land would save you the time and expense of fixing the place up."

Garrett's lips tightened. Watching a developer bulldoze the old farmhouse wouldn't fly with Grandma and Lauren. Truth be told, he wasn't wild about the idea either.

"And our last option is to put it up for auction."

Garrett straightened. "Like for foreclosures?"

"Foreclosures or anyone who wants a guaranteed minimum and a quick sale with no need for renovations."

*Guaranteed.* The word feathered into his soul. Guaranteed money for Grandma's care. A guaranteed sell-by date. No renovations. No contractors. And it could move quickly, so if his grandmother's health deteriorated faster than expected, there'd be no need to wait for those perfect buyers and their flock of fictional chickens.

In an ocean of chaos, an auction presented him with an island of calm.

But he'd have his work cut out for him. Lauren would be apoplectic if she knew he was even talking to Kimberly, let alone entertaining the possibilities of gray paint and new countertops.

Or an auction.

Or a developer.

Sloane wouldn't be thrilled with any of the options either. Especially that last one. He could practically hear her passionate defense of the history that would be forever destroyed.

Not that she was part of this. Friend though she might be, he couldn't afford to factor her opinion into the equation.

"Anyway." Kimberly's crisp voice broke into his thoughts. "It looks like you have a few things to think about."

A few? Ha.

Understatement of the decade.

>‹

*June 4, 1871*

A bank of heavy clouds to the east was all that remained of the morning's downpour, and rays of sunlight cast dappled shadows on the puddle-strewn ground in front of Uncle Stephen's porch, where Annabelle stood with her aunt and two other women from the congregation. She'd been a lively participant in the conversation, but now their words flitted only on the surface of her awareness.

Jack was striding around from behind the house toward a group of youngsters tumbling in the grass. He called to Oliver, then crouched, heedless of mud and mess, to speak with his nephew. He was far enough away that his words were inaudible, but there was softness in those rugged hands, cradling the boy's cheeks. Love in those gray eyes, crinkled at the corners and glinting with amusement as Oliver chattered on and on.

Warmth spread through her. Why, Jack looked at Oliver like he was the most important thing in the world. Many men didn't even look at their own children that way, much less someone else's. The memory of her papa brought a twinge. He'd once looked at her that way . . . until the call of adventure grew too loud to ignore.

"He's a good man, that Jack Brennan." Uncle Stephen's deep voice jolted Annabelle from her reverie. The group of women with whom she'd been half conversing had dispersed, but when? Had Jack really commanded the sum total of her attention?

Annabelle's gaze fell to the black tips of her shoes, peeking from beneath her flowered go-to-meeting dress. "Yes, he is." She glanced up with a smile. "He reminds me a little of you, Uncle."

Uncle Stephen's brown eyes softened behind his spectacles. "How so?"

"The way he loves Oliver. Took him in as his own." As surreptitiously as possible, she glanced toward Jack, who'd taken Oliver's hand and shortened his normally long stride to match the boy's. "Like you did for me."

"You've been a blessing, Annabelle, and I'm grateful you insisted on making this journey with us. The Lord's plans were indeed far better than mine."

Annabelle frowned at her uncle. There was something of goodbye in his tone. In his words. His tender expression.

His lips curved in response to her silent curiosity. "I had quite the conversation with Mr. Brennan just now."

"You did?" She smoothed her skirts and tried to look nonchalant, but the lift of Uncle Stephen's silvered brow told her he didn't believe her ruse.

"You know he lost his wife last year. Their son. It's been . . . difficult for him." Uncle Stephen weighed his words, as though debating what was prudent to share. "But today was a big step. Though he was raised in the faith, recent tragedy caused him to doubt God's goodness. His very existence. But the Lord used today's sermon to remind our Mr. Brennan of the true depth of his love and faithfulness."

Tears stung Annabelle's eyes, and emotions tumbled within her breast. She blinked furiously and swallowed hard against the lump forming in her throat. When at last she felt in control, she smiled up at her uncle. "God be praised."

With a nod, Uncle Stephen started to go, then stopped and turned back, eyes twinkling. "That wasn't all we spoke about."

Annabelle's stomach knotted. Her hands went numb. Uncle Stephen was wise. Perceptive. Could he see the evidence of Jack's impulsive kiss? The signs that its memory had kept her awake more than one night, that she'd been astir since the moment it happened, wondering how it would've felt on her cheek. Or—*have mercy*—on her lips . . .

But her uncle's expression was one of kindness, not reproach. "He asked my permission to court you."

Annabelle's breath stopped, suspended between inhale and exhale. "And . . . what did you tell him?"

Uncle Stephen's face relaxed into a wide, easy smile. "I told him it was fine by me, but your answer is the one that really matters."

Her body was incapable of motion, but her heart leaped for joy.

"He also said he planned to take Oliver out fishing again this afternoon, though at a much less active part of the creek. A bit farther downstream." Uncle Stephen eyed her over his spectacles. "I assume you catch his meaning."

Annabelle's mouth opened. Closed. Opened again. Speech, why had it deserted her? All she managed was a piteous-sounding squeak.

It didn't matter. Uncle Stephen was already gone.

Jack was on his way too, having climbed astride a waiting horse, Oliver seated safely in front. But the delicious grin he tossed her as he flicked the reins did nothing for her ecstatic, terrified, stunned state.

This afternoon. By the creek. Downstream.

Perhaps by then her words would have returned.

# CHAPTER TEN

*June 4, 1871*

IT WAS SUNDAY. An ordinary Sunday by the creek.

That's what Annabelle told herself time and again, though her hands and heart fluttered like cottonwood leaves in the relentless wind.

She'd no guarantee of seeing Jack. No promise save that knee-weakening wink. But she'd remained clad in her best dress anyway. Brought along a pitcher of lemonade and a plate of homemade cookies just in case. And she'd taken great care to spread out her quilt in a spot that, while secluded enough for comfort, remained in full view of her uncle's cabin.

No sooner had she put trembling pen to diary page than a cheerful greeting lifted her eyes and her spirits. Jack. Accompanied by Oliver and an energetic spaniel, ears flopping in the breeze as he bounded after his masters. With a smile that turned her heart to liquid, Jack sat down next to her.

She'd never been courted this way, out in the open, bathed in warmth beneath a summer sky unable to decide between sunshine and clouds. Yet, for him, it seemed right. She almost laughed at the image of a formally dressed Jack perched uncomfortably in their stuffy makeshift parlor while Aunt Katherine fluttered in and out, pouring weak tea into tiny cups far too fragile and fussy for a man of the frontier. Here, with the wind tugging his clothes and his features dappled by shadows, his smile easy and his posture relaxed, Jack Brennan was in his element.

He and this prairie land were one.

After thanking Annabelle for the two glasses of lemonade and handful of cookies he'd downed, Oliver turned hopeful eyes on his uncle. "May I go play fetch with Buster?"

Beaming his pride, Jack brushed crumbs from the boy's lips. "Yes, you may."

"C'mon, Buster." Oliver scampered off, the dog at his heels. "Let's go find a stick."

Oliver's quest took him too close to the creek for Jack's liking, judging from the way he tensed when the boy's toes touched the water's edge. Annabelle, too, kept her eyes fastened on him, her muscles ready to spring into action. But the creek was far calmer than the week before, and Oliver's only interest in it was pulling out a small stick poking up from the muddy banks. The perfect size for throwing to his canine companion.

Relief loosening her shoulders, Annabelle refilled Jack's glass of lemonade. "It's good he doesn't fear the water."

"It's also good he's no closer to it than he is." Something simmered beneath the surface of Jack's words, and his face was shadowed by more than the brim of his Stetson. Oliver may have forgotten all about last Sunday's misadventure, but his uncle still bore the scars.

"It's not your fault, Jack. These things can happen in half an instant."

"'Tis why the good Lord meant children to have two parents." His gaze followed the boy, knee-deep in prairie grass, flinging the stick to the eager spaniel, his injured shoulder showing no ill effects. "I try—God knows I do—but there's no escaping it. Oliver needs a mother."

A cloud passed overhead, and Annabelle's heart poised at the precipice of free fall. So this was why Jack had so quickly sought permission to court her. Her fanciful imagination had led her to believe he'd asked because of tender affections toward her. Because he perhaps saw in her the same qualities he'd seen in his first wife. Because his impulsive kiss to her forehead had upended his world as surely as it had her own.

A knot formed in her chest. What a foolish girl she was. Jack Brennan was a practical man, and the prairie was a practical place. Raising a five-year-old alone while trying to prove a claim? Well-nigh impossible. And in such a sparsely populated area, the number of eligible ladies was low. In fact, it likely stood at one.

"Of course." Her words came out remarkably calm, given the dust and noise of girlish dreams crashing down around her. The frontier was no place for those dreams. Jack was a good man. He'd work hard to provide for her. Take excellent care of her. She could do far worse, of that there was no doubt.

But if she wanted to marry a man who sought her hand for practicality rather than love, she'd have done so already. Without leaving the comforts and conveniences of Indiana.

"Something wrong?" Jack peered at her, a stalk of tall, fluffy-topped grass in one hand, his expression impossible to read.

"So this is why you've asked to court me. To give Oliver a mother."

One broad shoulder lifted. "'Twould be a lie to say that wasn't a reason."

Irritation burned white-hot. *Your answer is the one that matters,* Uncle Stephen had said. Balderdash. Though his offer appeared magnanimous, he was still trying to put her in a neat little box, as he'd done before they moved here. As Papa did when he left her behind all those years ago.

Her uncle had probably planned this from the moment he met Jack. As obvious as her infatuation must have been, Uncle Stephen had predicted— if not expected—that she'd jump at the offer. That she'd see the necessity, the practicality, of the situation, and slide into this man's home to cook his meals and raise his child. *It's for the best, Annabelle,* she could hear him saying. *Surely you see that.*

Or was it her father's voice she heard?

Annabelle yanked a late-blooming black-eyed Susan from the grass and plucked off a brilliant yellow petal. "I'll not consent to being a mere pawn, Mr. Brennan."

"It's Jack."

Ignoring his mild correction, she pulled off another petal. And another. And another. "All my life, people have charted my course. Stuffed me into whatever trunk best suited their fancy. Coming to Kansas was the first decision I ever made for myself, and I had to fight tooth and nail for it." Two more petals fluttered to the quilt at her feet. "If Uncle Stephen and Aunt Katherine had their way, I'd be back in Indiana, married to William Barclay."

"And you found that arrangement unacceptable?"

How could the man be so daft? "Of course I did." She reached for another petal, but she'd already torn them all off. Annoyed, she tossed the barren stem to the side. "I didn't love William, nor did he love me. Not the way I wanted to be loved."

"Ah." Jack twirled the stalk of grass between work-roughened, infuriatingly casual fingertips. "So you'll marry only for love then?"

With a sigh, she hugged her knees and focused on the blue-and-white floral pattern of her skirt, on the neat black shoes peeping from beneath the fabric. It was embarrassing, letting this handsome still-a-stranger see so deep inside her.

Sharing dreams she'd no idea she held so dear.

Until she needed to let them go.

"I've seen it, Jack. I was only eight when Mama passed, but I remember how she and Papa loved each other. No matter how long her day or how tired she felt, Mama lit up when Papa came into the room. And Papa . . ." The memory clutched at her heart. "Papa had a special smile just for her. Even when they disagreed, they did so knowing that however large the problem, their love was enough to overcome it."

She unclasped her hands. "When Mama died, a part of Papa died too. And while I wouldn't wish that pain on myself, or anyone else, I couldn't help but wonder, even as a child, how would it feel to be so loved that—if he lost me—a man would also lose part of himself?"

Jack's eyes darkened, and Annabelle bit her tongue. Had she really shared her ridiculous fantasy with a man who knew that pain all too well? His own Sarah, scarcely a year gone. He'd married for love, and look where it had gotten him. No wonder his reasons were more practical this time around.

And no wonder he couldn't feel for her what she sorely wished he would. His late wife had already laid claim to his heart.

"I'm certain you now think me selfish and foolish and childish. And you'd be right." A gust of wind tugged a lock of her hair loose. She shoved it back and looked him square in the eye. "But my mind is made up. I'll spend my life a spinster schoolteacher before I marry someone who sees me only as a solution to a problem or a fulfillment of a need. Foolish and selfish and childish as I am, Jack Brennan, I'll marry for love, or I won't marry at all."

"I appreciate your honesty." Jack's words were slow. Measured. Directed more to the grass in his hand than to her. He was doubtless disappointed, and she hated being the cause.

A shout and a bark rose from the meadow and wrenched her heart. Oliver, retrieving the stick from Buster's jaws, his cheeks pink with joy and exertion. Bless him, he truly did need a mother. She prayed God would provide one. That he would lead Jack to a bride far less muleheaded than herself. One selfless enough to properly care for a young child. Surely she'd just now demonstrated how ill-suited she was for the task.

That wrenched her heart too. Because, despite everything . . . she could love Jack Brennan. And Oliver. So easily, she could love them both.

In fact, she was certain she already did.

Jack shifted his weight, his sleeve brushing her wrist, and she braced for his inevitable departure. He'd flash a stilted version of his heart-stopping smile, spin out some polite yet patently false words thanking her for a wonderful afternoon, gather up Oliver and the dog, and retreat to his claim. Lick his wounded ego and start his search anew.

But he didn't leave. He sat there, twirling that infernal blade of grass and not looking at her. Why was he still here? Had her words not affected him in the slightest?

Something had. The muscle at the corner of his jaw twitched in rapid rhythm beneath the neatly trimmed thatch of coal-black beard. Tension emanated from him, like the electricity of a gathering storm.

"'Tis a good thing my mam taught me to be a gentleman, Miss Collins." The formal title weighted his half-growled brogue. "Because were I not so well taught, I would demonstrate—most emphatically—how wrong you are about my reasons for courting you."

Beneath the Stetson, his eyes glittered with a fire that left no mistaking the truth in his words. She opened her mouth to argue, to apologize, to— to do what exactly?

Whatever words she might've uttered died in her throat, cut off by the intensity of Jack's gaze. An intensity lightened by a satisfied glint, as though her response—or lack thereof—was exactly what he'd intended.

"Reverend Little's been through four times since Sarah passed, and if all I wanted was a mam for Oliver, I'd have already stood before him." A corner of Jack's mouth turned up. "Daniel Swanson over in Park Township has three unwed daughters. He'd be happy to see me take any one of them off his hands."

Oh, that the earth would swallow her whole. She'd misread the situation badly, and she deserved every bit of the chastisement to come. Marrying for pure practicality would've been bad enough, but this? Torching her chances with a man whose motivations she'd sorely misjudged? That loomed far worse.

"But I've not pursued anyone, Annabelle. Not until you. Because I didn't feel . . ."

Her head snapped up. Her pulse pounded. "Feel what?"

"The way I feel when I look at you." He tossed the stalk of grass aside. "I feel as tongue-tied as a schoolboy, but somehow like I've known you all my life. Looking into your eyes—I'm lost. But at the same time, I'm found. Being with you feels like I'm on the cusp of a grand adventure, yet it feels like I'm coming home too. Like you see me for who I was always meant to be. I feel . . . so much for you, so strongly, in so short a time, that it terrifies me." Jack stopped, his breathing fast.

She couldn't breathe at all.

"Now, if you still think all I want is a mam for Oliver, then clearly I'm not a very persuasive speaker, and I'll have to prove my point another way." The weight of his gaze pressed her to the spot. "But remember, lass. I was raised a gentleman. And the way I've in mind to prove it isn't the most gentlemanly thing to do."

Annabelle trembled under torrents of chaos and anticipation, fear and exhilaration, love and need, and want like she'd never felt before.

Jack didn't need to prove those words. Not with the way he was looking at her.

But oh how she wanted him to.

*Mercy.* She was playing with fire, and she knew it. Here they were in broad daylight, unwed, steps away from a five-year-old and a dog and meddling Aunt Katherine, who would burst out the back door any second with a well-deserved reprimand. But none of that mattered. All that mattered was Jack. His gorgeous words tumbling around inside her.

His lips and how desperately she wanted to feel them on her own.

She lifted her chin, heart hammering, throat desert dry.

"Prove it, Jack."

A quiet challenge, but his mouth claimed hers even before she finished. His every movement was proof. The sudden tangle of one hand in her hair. The tight grip of the other on the back of her neck. And his lips—they seared her with proof. Branded her with it, even more than those words had, and—

Jack broke away, but the rapid rise and fall of his chest and the tension in his hands as he released her spoke of how difficult it was for him to do so. Somehow his hat had fallen off, and he leaned in, pressing his damp forehead to hers, caressing her jaw with callused fingertips.

"Annabelle." Never had her name sounded so luscious as it did in Jack's husky whisper. "The next time Reverend Little comes through, so help me, it's my full intention to be standing before him, your hands in mine. For nothing short of love."

His smile was so delicious she couldn't help but lean in for another kiss. A short one. Given how disheveled they both were already, and that they weren't wed—not yet anyway—it was all she could allow. When she pulled away, a quiet groan slipped from him, one that resonated in her own heart.

She caught his gaze and beamed. "Then I'll pray he comes through soon."

⇥⇤

*Prove it, Jack.*

Goose bumps broke out on Sloane's bare arms despite the warmth of the westward-leaning sun as she walked toward the colorful little downtown park where she'd agreed to meet Garrett. The normally fascinating mix of aged brick buildings and sleek modern art installations faded into the background this night. Because prove it Jack had. Most decisively.

He and Annabelle seemed a perfect match, and they'd known it lightning fast. Granted, frontier courtships could move quickly. But many of those marriages were for more practical reasons. Reasons that weren't quite enough for Annabelle Collins. It was admirable tenacity—or sheer stubbornness—to hold out for a love match in an era when such insistence was impractical at best and risky at worst.

The walk signal lit, and Sloane crossed the street, skirt swishing around her legs, high heels clicking on the sidewalk, and a jealous twinge in her heart. She'd never experienced anything close to what Annabelle described. Her tendency to hold people at arm's length no doubt had something to do with it, but even when she noticed a good-looking guy, there'd never been fireworks or wobbly knees or missed heartbeats. Like Garrett, who sat at a bright orange table, head bowed over his phone. Empirically, he was an attractive man, but—

He looked up, and a slow smile spread over his face.

Whoa.

Were his eyes always that bright? That blue?

He stood, stashed his phone, and started toward her. "Hi."

"Hi." Her heart gave a curious *ker-thump*, and her knees seemed a bit less sturdy.

"You look . . ." The lines bracketing Garrett's mouth deepened, and his eyes shone with the same intensity they had the other night at Marty's. "That dress is . . . you look . . . nice."

"Thanks." Never had the word *nice* rippled with the implication of words he could've chosen instead. And never had it instantly brought a spark to her heart and a smile to her lips.

Hmm. Perhaps she should spend less time buried in the musings of lovestruck nineteen-year-olds.

Garrett turned his attention to a color-splashed taco truck, and the two made their way toward the cluster of people waiting in line. He didn't look half bad himself in that sun-dappled navy jacket and crisp plaid shirt. A pocket square poked out from the left side of the jacket, and he'd left the top buttons of the blue-and-white shirt undone just enough to make her mind go places it probably shouldn't.

*Knock it off.* This was Garrett. Her friend. Her fellow jazz aficionado. And the man who, if that real estate appointment this afternoon was any indication, could very well sell that beautiful house and not think twice about it.

But he was also the first man to make her feel anything close to the attraction Annabelle had for Jack.

Minutes later, they sat at a metal table beneath a bright blue umbrella, two steaming baskets of mouthwatering street tacos before them.

"Would you mind if I said a blessing?" Garrett asked as Sloane spread a napkin on her lap.

She smiled across at him. "Not at all."

It surprised her when he reached for her hand, but she wasn't about to object. His fingers wrapped hers in a gentle embrace, yet they had strength to them too. Regardless of how long it had been since they danced across a piano, they'd doubtless remember how.

When he finished praying, he released her hand but held her gaze. "Before we get too far, I want to apologize."

She paused in her reach for a taco. "What for?"

"For the real estate agent this afternoon. I'm sorry if it was awkward. That . . . wasn't the way I wanted you to find out."

His words started a slow leak in the balloon of her mood. "So you're selling the house?"

"It's not definite. But my grandma's not getting any better." His gaze shimmered in the sunlight. "She's happy at home, and for now she's safe. But Alzheimer's is so wildly unpredictable, we don't know how long that'll be the case, so it seemed wise to start formulating some plans."

The shadows beneath his eyes and the tightness around his lips underscored his burden, and her heart went out to him. He bore up bravely, but the weight of the decisions he faced, of his grandmother's future, had to be staggering.

"The meeting with Kimberly was mostly a fact-finding mission. I wanted to know how much work the house needs, what we could reasonably expect from a sale. And she gave me a lot of options to think about."

*Was selling to Warren Williams one of those options?* Sloane bit back the question. Much as she loved the house, she had no claim on it. The decision was Garrett's to make, and he had to do right by his grandmother. As his friend, Sloane needed to support him, not add to his already-obvious strain.

But could she support his selling to Warren Williams or another of his ilk? Could she stand by while that beautiful piece of paradise was plowed under to make room for another interchangeable subdivision?

She grabbed her taco and took a far larger bite than decorum dictated. Maybe it wouldn't come to that.

But the possibility loomed, and the bite went down with effort. Perhaps sheerly because of its size.

Or the heaping helping of emotions that struggled down with it.

## CHAPTER ELEVEN

NIGHT HAD FALLEN by the time Garrett strolled along the brick street outside Fitzy's, Sloane by his side. She seemed to have a destination in mind, so he fell into contented step with her, awash in a pleasant buzz of great music, a gorgeous evening, and the nearness of someone he truly connected with.

Connection—putting people at ease, letting them know he cared—was the soul of his job. But those connections were ultimately a means to an end. A vehicle to gain his clients' trust. There was always an agenda.

Connecting with Sloane, though, was simply the natural fusing of similar minds and hearts. There was no agenda driving it. No guessing games either. Not like most of the women he'd dated, where everything was stiff and stilted, all plastic smiles and best foot forward and *no, please, I insist, let me get the check.*

Not that this was a date, of course. Not really.

It wouldn't be anywhere near this comfortable if it were.

When they rounded the corner, a tall, stylized statue of a Native American warrior provided Garrett his bearings. The Keeper of the Plains, one of Wichita's most recognizable symbols. Recent years had seen a large interactive plaza added to the exhibit, and the bare-bones bronze sculpture he remembered from his youth now stood atop an enormous pedestal, surrounded by a stone path and a ring of firepots. Piped-in Native flute music wafted on the breeze, giving the whole exhibit an earthy feel. Clusters of teens took selfies. A *paleta* vendor called out in Spanish from his cart on the bridge. And Sloane made a beeline for a circle of historical plaques.

Garrett caught up to her, a smile tugging his lips. "Surprised you don't have these memorized."

"Oh, I do. Most of them. But I like reading them anyway." She gestured to the area around the statue, where the Little Arkansas River met and mingled with the Arkansas. "It's easy to think this city's always been here, but in history terms, it's just a baby. Nomadic tribes roamed this area for centuries, following the bison. The first white people didn't show up until the 1860s."

The downtown skyline's golden lights shimmered in ink-dark waters. "And all this came from that."

"It's amazing to think about." Sloane's slow, meandering steps led them onto a bridge overlooking the river. "Settlers like Jack and Annabelle weren't perfect. They did a lot of things wrong. But they survived against incredible odds, they endured so much hardship, all because of a dream. This beautiful city is the fruit of that dream, and . . . I'm talking too much, aren't I?"

What on earth had given her that impression? "Not at all. This is fascinating stuff."

"Yeah, well." Her gaze darted away, like a shy bird. "If I really get going, I'll talk forever, so just elbow me and tell me to shut up if I bore you."

His lips curved. "I'm a financial planner, Sloane. It takes a lot to bore me."

Sloane gave a chuckle that zinged all the way to his toes, then she leaned against the bridge railing. Dark wavy hair and fluffy red skirt ruffled in the evening breeze; creamy skin glowed in the moonlight.

"Sometimes when I come here, I can almost see how it used to be. Tallgrass prairie from here to the horizon, thundering with the hoofbeats of bison and the hunting cries of the Osage. Then trading posts and settlers' cabins pop up, then a string of buildings. Just enough to qualify as a town. Then a small city . . . a bigger city . . . then this." She indicated the skyline. "All because people fought against incredible odds for a dream they believed in."

"You see all that?" His heart swelled. What a wonder this woman was.

"Sometimes." She looked his way. "What about you? What do you see?"

Leaning on the cool metal railing, he looked out over the rippling river. "This place has a lot of memories. Some happy, like fishing with my grandpa. Some painful, like when my mom was dying and we brought her down here one last time. But"—his gaze slid toward Sloane—"I see a lot of beauty here too. I see passion and elegance and strength. Resilience. Vulnerability, yes, but a tough vulnerability—"

Wait, what? Was he still talking about Wichita, or had he shifted to talking about Sloane?

So what if he had? What he'd said was true. And friends built each other up. Encouraged one another.

But the tempo of his heartbeat was well beyond what he normally associated with friendship. And Sloane, with the breeze softly blowing her hair and the city lights reflecting in her eyes, her lips full and ripe and cherry-delicious—

Something slammed into his back, knocking him off-balance and lurching him forward. Sloane caught him, small hands braced around his biceps.

Behind him traipsed a bubbly brigade of twentysomething blondes, the shortest wearing a tight skirt, tiara, and white sash. BRIDE TO BE, it proclaimed in silver sequins.

"Oops! Sorry," she slurred, with the loopy giggle of the hopelessly intoxicated.

"It'sh her *bash-lorette*," proclaimed the girl next to her, who dissolved into doubled-over laughter, accompanied by identical chortles from her friends.

"It's all right," Garrett replied, but the girls were tittering too loudly to reply.

"Good luck," Sloane called to the departing gaggle, then grinned at Garrett. "To her husband-to-be, that is. He's sure gonna need it."

Garrett laughed and jerked his head toward the *paleta* vendor. "How about some dessert?"

"Sounds great." She fell into step alongside him.

The laughter, the movement away from the bridge, the unwelcome but well-timed interruption all combined to breathe calm into Garrett's inner turbulence. Had he really almost kissed Sloane?

It had to be a fleeting, momentary impulse. A natural reaction to a beautiful woman in a romantic setting. A flutter of foolishness that floated away on the breeze. Because he was here on a mission. He had plans to make for his grandmother's care. Finding a friend in the midst of it was certainly welcome.

But anything more?

That wasn't part of his plan.

⇥⇤

*Birth Mother seeks Adoptee born 10/25/99*

Nope. Too young.

*Birth Mother seeks Adoptee born 6/6/86*

Not that one either. Too old.

Snuggled beneath her favorite orange blanket, Sloane sipped lukewarm chamomile tea and scrolled further through the list. The clock on her screen displayed an hour she hadn't seen for some time, yet sleep eluded her.

Part of her railed against that drunk-as-a-skunk bachelorette for bumping into Garrett and ruining their moment. But the rest of her was relieved beyond measure. Because if that kiss had actually happened? Then this thing with Garrett would be a Thing. With rules. Expectations. Standards she couldn't possibly meet.

"Deep-seated abandonment issues," her therapist called it. At first, Sloane had rolled her eyes. *Someone who was left on a city bus as a six-day-old has abandonment issues? Ya think?*

But while the diagnosis may have been obvious, its impact had been less so. Marjorie had shed light on how Sloane's intense fear of rejection led her to lock herself away in a bubble of isolation, never letting anyone get too close. Sloane couldn't argue. She had colleagues, but no confidantes. Bandmates, but no best friends. A handful of relationships over the years, one or two men she'd grown to really like, but no one she'd ever given herself fully to.

How could she when she herself wasn't whole?

And so another late-night trip through Adoption Bridge's list of Seattle-area birth mothers searching for their cast-off children.

*Birth Mother seeks Adoptee born 1/15/98*

*Birth Mother seeks Adoptee born 4/12/96*

And that was the end of the list. No leads. Not that she should expect anything different. Five years she'd been combing this site off and on. Five years she'd come up empty.

Clicking over to her profile page, she stared at the terse, bare-bones description for the millionth time. Everything she knew about her beginnings, her identity, was right there in black and white.

*I am: Adoptee*

There it was. Her scarlet letter. The reason she carried different DNA than the people she called Mom and Dad. The reason why, in the sea of slender Scandinavians that comprised her family, her dark hair and curvy build made her stand out. Like a spotlight shone on her. Every day. All the time. It never went dark.

Most people could see something familiar when looking at family photos.

She couldn't.

And it shouldn't matter.

But it did.

*Adoptee name at birth: Unknown*

Had the woman whose womb she'd grown in even given her a name? Six days she'd been with her. Had the woman held her? Fed her? Kissed her goodbye?

Patricia Kelley certainly hadn't thought so and made it clear the day Sloane dared ask. The harsh words were as daggerlike now as they'd been two decades ago.

*That woman left you on a bus, Sloane. She didn't want you. I did. I'm the one who raised you. Who took care of you. Who gave you everything. That woman was nothing for you but an incubator. She gave you life, but I gave you your life. I am your mother. Not her.*

Stunned at the outburst, Sloane had backed away and retreated to her bedroom. A bedroom worthy of a princess, with its four-poster bed and frothy pink curtains.

She never asked questions of the Kelleys again.

But she didn't stop wondering.

Her adoption meant she'd been chosen. Wanted. That people who had no biological obligation to raise her had taken her in. Taught her right from wrong. Loved her and cared for her and brought her up in the church.

But it also meant the woman who'd grown her, who'd given birth to her, had looked her in the eyes. Cared for her, at least to some extent, for nearly a week.

And then she'd left her on a bus.

*County/province of birth: King*

*Hospital: Unknown*

She'd spent her first five years in Seattle. Home of the Space Needle, grunge music, complicated coffee drinks, and rain that never quite quit. She didn't really remember it. Her father's transfer to Wichita the summer before she started kindergarten meant a greater familiarity with wheat fields than mountains, with unending wind rather than ceaseless rain.

She'd visited Seattle after college. Wandered its streets for days, searching for something—anything—familiar.

But there was nothing. No connection. No sense of belonging.

The hole in her heart wouldn't be filled here.

*Birth Mother maiden name: Unknown*

*Birth Mother name at Adoptee's birth: Unknown*

*Birth Father: Unknown*

Three years ago, she did one of those swab-your-cheek-and-send-it-in DNA tests. Six weeks later, she received the colorful results: Italian and Irish. English and French and Welsh. And a large chunk Ukrainian.

One Sunday, on a whim, she'd forgone services at her smallish community church for those at the large Orthodox cathedral on the east side of town. Maybe she'd connect with the ancient liturgy. The incense. The centuries-old hymns. Maybe they would resonate with whatever flowed through her veins.

They didn't.

*Adoption agency: Child Protective Services*

*City/state of adoption: Renton, WA*

Her heart had rejoiced a few years back when the state of Washington unsealed its closed adoption records, allowing adoptees access to their original birth certificates.

Unless, of course, the birth mother had denied permission. A nasty loophole which Sloane learned about after she made the request.

Yet another rejection from the person who was supposed to love her most.

Not that Sloane should feel anything but grateful for her upbringing. The Kelleys had made that perfectly clear. And she couldn't deny the opportunities she'd been given. Ballet classes. Voice lessons. All the choirs she could have ever hoped to sing in.

But it seemed the Kelleys were trying to mold her into the perfect, pristine princess they'd always dreamed of. A thin, gorgeous blonde who never mouthed off, who sang opera and danced en pointe and won beauty pageants. A girl who, though not visible and never spoken of, still hovered like a specter over Sloane, silently mocking her for all she'd never be.

In her early years, Sloane strove to measure up to that girl. As a teen, she quietly rebelled. Quit concert choir and only sang jazz. Stayed in Kansas after high school when her parents retired in Idaho. Throughout her life, she sensed a total befuddlement from them, a desperate helplessness as to how to raise this girl who wasn't theirs and who didn't turn out the way they expected.

Her birth parents didn't want her.

Her adoptive parents, though they wanted, chose, and loved her, didn't know what to do with her.

In both cases, she was something unexpected. Something people had to deal with. Plan B.

She was nobody's plan A.

That was the one hurdle she'd never overcome. The thorn in her flesh that, pray as she might, God simply wouldn't remove. So she'd made an uneasy truce with this unwanted dinner guest, set a place at the table, and accepted it as best she could. Like it or not, it was part of her.

But sometimes it loomed large. Unbearable. Intolerable. She wanted it gone.

And tonight was one of those times.

Garrett was wonderful. She liked him. She could maybe even *really* like him, if she let herself. And if she found a way to fix that part of herself, to truly let him in, then maybe they'd stand a chance. If not Garrett, then someone like him. Someone who loved jazz and liked to hear her sing. Someone who laughed at her jokes and let her prattle on about local history.

Someone who looked at her the way Garrett did. Like he couldn't fathom looking at anyone else.

It all came back to that one moment in time. That one choice. And if she could find the woman who made that choice, grab hold of the answer to the question that haunted her, then maybe she could get off this website and get on with her life. Filled in. Complete.

Despite the late hour, Sloane returned to the top of the list and scrolled through it one more time.

*Birth Mother seeks Adoptee born 10/25/97*

# CHAPTER TWELVE

"Hey, Anderson. We're making a burrito run. Want in?"

Garrett glanced up from his computer to find two of his coworkers, Nicky and Rajesh, framed in the office doorway.

He offered a smile. "Thanks, but no thanks, gentlemen. I'm working through."

"Told you." Rajesh elbowed the heavyset Nicky, who gave the door-frame a hefty pat.

"Catch you later then." They disappeared, their animated conversation growing fainter with their progress down the hall.

Garrett leaned back in his chair and unzipped the insulated lunch sack that had become a permanent fixture these last weeks. When was the last time he'd gone out to lunch? Taken a midday break to leave the office, order off a menu, and enjoy a lighthearted meal with his colleagues?

His phone buzzed on the desk. Lauren. Seeing her number in the middle of the day was rarely a good sign. And a stark reminder of why he couldn't afford lunch hours away from his desk. Stomach knotting, he reached for the phone.

"What's up, Lo? Is Grandma okay?"

"Yeah, she's fine. I'm not calling about her."

"Good." The knot eased enough for a bland bite of turkey and Swiss.

"I found another stash of books in the spare bedroom. I think there are a couple of Annabelle's diaries in there. Same handwriting anyway."

Sloane would be thrilled. "What'd they say?"

"I took a peek but didn't read much." Her voice took on a note of mischief. "I figured you and Sloane could take care of that this weekend."

The third consecutive weekend trip to Wichita, in fact. Going longer than that without Sloane would be more than he could take.

Yet another reason he was eating lunch at his desk.

"So what are you guys doing for her birthday?" Lauren asked.

His second bite of sandwich slid down awkwardly. "Her what?"

"Her birthday. Friday."

"This Friday?"

Lauren gave an exasperated huff. "Honestly, don't you ever check Facebook?"

"Have you met me?" His little sister the blogger loved all forms of social media, and though she'd talked him into getting an account, he rarely used it. Scrolling for hours through political memes and pictures of high school classmates' dinners? He'd never understood the appeal.

"Oh, for the love—okay, listen closely. Sloane. Has a birthday. This Friday. The twenty-third." He could picture Lauren rolling her eyes. "What would you ever do without me?"

"Eat gluten on weekends, for starters."

"I'll ignore that because we've got bigger issues. You have to celebrate somehow."

He popped open a single-serving bag of potato chips. "We're already planning to have dinner Friday, and she did mention wanting to try that new pizza place in Old Town."

"Mirabelli's? Good luck with that. I drove by last week, and the line was halfway around the block. On a Wednesday."

"That's what reservations are for." His mouth full of salty, crunchy deliciousness, he found Mirabelli's website, clicked the reservations tab, and—

"Crud. Reservations only for parties of six or more."

Lauren gasped. "Wait a minute. I just got a brilliant idea."

"Uh-oh."

"What if we throw a party for her?" Excitement raised Lauren's voice to near-squeal territory.

He paused. "A party?"

"We can have it at Mirabelli's, and that'll get us our reservation. No mile-long line."

He did like the sound of that.

"I'll bring some balloons, make a cake . . ."

"A cake?" He didn't like the sound of that.

She huffed again. "Just for you, I'll make one from a box. Sugar, gluten, the works. You two can give yourselves diabetes together. It'll be super romantic."

"Just keep it small, okay?"

"No problem." A pen clicked in the background. "Who's she close to?"

Hmm. Sloane had mentioned a couple of colleagues, but her relationship with them seemed strictly professional. "There's her band, but I don't know much about them."

"That's not a problem. They have a Facebook page too."

Of course they did.

"Anyone else? Any family?"

An obvious sore point. "Nope. She's an only child, and her parents live out of state."

"Poor thing. No wonder she seems lonely."

Lonely? He thought of her as someone who—like himself—preferred a smaller social circle. But she hadn't mentioned any birthday plans last night on the phone, even as they worked out dinner for Friday. So maybe Lauren was right. Maybe Sloane was a little lonely.

"Ooh, you know what would make it even more fun?" Lauren sounded on the verge of squealing again. "Let's make it a surprise. Obviously she knows you're going out to dinner. But don't tell her any more of the plan. It'll be just like Mom used to do. Remember?"

Nostalgia hugged his heart. Of course he remembered. Sometimes it was a bedroom filled with balloons. Sometimes a packed bag waited at the foot of the bed with a note instructing him to grab it and hop in the car for a day of fun. Sometimes it was a full-on surprise party, complete with a darkened room and people leaping out from behind furniture. There was no way to predict what or when the birthday surprise would be, but it was a constant of birthdays in the Anderson house. Mom had made sure of that.

"Just . . . no jumping out from behind the furniture, okay?"

"Don't worry," Lauren replied. "I figure unexpected cake and a bunch of friends is probably enough for someone who's not familiar with the Anderson Family Surprise Dynamic."

Bittersweet warmth bloomed at the idea of sharing something so personal with Sloane. Though he couldn't introduce her to his mom—much as he might want to—this was a small part of her, a piece of her legacy, he could let Sloane see.

One small part of himself too.

><

*August 13, 1871*

A scant few hours had passed since the simple ceremony, yet Annabelle had no recollection of Reverend Little's words. Only the vaguest remembrance of the vows she'd taken, of the feasting and merriment afterward.

Seared in her memory instead was the look in Jack's bottomless gray eyes. Her heart had swelled at the adoration shining there, at the thin film of moisture pooling along pink lower rims. At the thickness of his voice as he pledged himself to her. Though close to the edge of his composure, he'd never quite lost it.

Neither had she. Far from it.

She was soaring.

Summer's wind caressed her skin as her husband's strong, skillful hands guided the horses toward his claim. Her claim now too.

Her home.

Her cheeks hurt from smiling, but she couldn't stop. Not when the man who owned her heart was so near. When he'd vowed that very morning to love, honor, and cherish her. When a beautiful garnet ring wrapped her finger in its snug embrace.

She studied that ring, dazzled by the dance of sunlight through deep red stone, the brilliant shine of gorgeous gold filigree, then slipped her hand beneath the warm, solid curve of Jack's arm. The bunch and ripple of his muscles beneath her fingertips started a tingling that spiraled through her whole body and made her ache in a delicious, tender way.

It made her . . . want.

But that was allowed now. They were man and wife. She was Mrs. John Francis Brennan, and she could want him all she liked.

They crested a slight hill, dappled gold in the late afternoon sun, and Jack's cabin came into view, small but homey. Rough cottonwood logs still yellow in their newness. A door and a single window. A barn behind. The chicken coop. Maisie, the black-and-white cow, and Millie, her half-grown calf.

She'd seen all this before, on many a Sunday drive.

But now it was home.

Jack extended a hand to help her down from the buggy. "And now, Mrs. Brennan, we've come to the part where I offer my deepest apologies."

Giddiness bubbled at the new title as her dainty black shoes thumped onto thirsty grass. "For what?"

"For the house." Doffing his hat, he knocked off the dust and pushed open the wooden door. "Bachelor quarters, to be certain."

Annabelle stepped inside and blinked to adjust to the dimness. Jack had been nothing but honest. Though freshly scrubbed from top to bottom, these were indeed bachelor quarters. No curtains fluttered at the window. A rudimentary stove squatted in the corner near a small, rough table. Two beds lined the far wall, separated by a scrap of dingy canvas.

Jack cleared his throat. "I thought perhaps we'd want a bit of privacy..."

Heat flooded her cheeks. Privacy wasn't a concern for the next few days, however, since her aunt and uncle had offered to care for Oliver.

The marriage would begin here. Alone. Together.

The implications heated her cheeks even more.

"Sarah had a few things. Pretty. Feminine." Jack's voice was low and husky. "But I couldn't bear to use them. Not after..."

Annabelle placed a finger against his lips. "It's all right, Jack."

Something flickered in the depths of his eyes. Something that made the tingling ache inside her grow.

Slowly, not even daring to breathe, she traced the smooth fullness of Jack's lower lip.

His eyes closed, his coal-black lashes carving half moons against skin dusky from sun. A soft groan slipped out, vaulting her heart into her chest with anticipation. This was the power she had over him, and he over her.

It was dizzying. Dangerous.

His hand closed around hers. Lowered it as his eyes eased open and love shone from their depths.

"After I lost Sarah . . . our son . . . I lost myself too. My optimism. My dreams. But the Lord gave it all back to me again." Rough fingertips feathered over her cheek, and she shivered. "Now I have all kinds of dreams."

She broke into a wide smile. "Tell me."

He stepped back and turned to the window. "That drive we came up just now? I dream of lining it with trees. Flowers for spring, sweet fruit for summer. Cherries maybe. And apples so we'd have some in the fall."

Joy percolated at the gleam in his eyes.

"And at the end of that drive, I'll build a house. Not a cabin like this. A real one." He strolled around the cabin, strong hands gesturing as he gave his imagination free rein. "Big. White. With an upstairs for the bedrooms and a proper parlor . . . right here." He stopped and nodded. "I'll put in a window looking out on the creek. And I'll build a writing desk too, so you can fill up those diaries of yours."

Her eyes stung. What had she done to deserve the blessing of this man?

"And over here"—he made his way to the other side of the cabin—"a dining room. One with a big table, so our six children will have plenty of room."

An astonished laugh burst from her lips. "Six?"

"Seven, including Oliver. I see them as clear as if they stood before us, love. Three dark like me, two fair like you, and one fiery redhead like my own dear mam." His eyes twinkled. "That one might be a troublemaker, I'll warn you."

Annabelle chuckled. "You're quite the dreamer, Mr. Brennan."

"The kitchen'll go here. With a large sink and a proper stove and plenty of space. And over there, a room with a big stone fireplace. Paper on the walls. Maybe even a piano."

Her brows lifted. "A piano. How fancy."

"You deserve nothing less, love." His expression suddenly sobered. "In fact, you deserve much more. So much more than a rough Irishman and his nephew and a tiny cabin in the middle of the prairie."

As he had that morning, in front of God and their witnesses, Jack clasped her hands in his. "But that Irishman has dreams. And, God willing, he's going to make them come true for you."

"Oh, Jack." His excitement was catching. "It sounds wonderful. But I don't need a stone fireplace or a writing desk to feel at home." She wound her arms around his neck. "All I need to feel like I'm home—all I will ever need—is you."

His eyes darkened, his lips neared, and then they were on hers. Seeking. Savoring. Probing. Promising. She threaded her fingers through the hair at his nape; his strong arm pulled her against him.

When he drew back to look at her, his breathing was rough and fast, as though he'd run a great distance. So was hers.

It was all a touch overwhelming. She stepped back on weakened legs and pressed numb lips together. Lips that tasted like him.

"You . . . and maybe one more thing," she said.

"What's that?"

She crossed the room to her hope chest, which Jack had carted in the day before, and removed the wedding gift from Aunt Katherine: a new set of handmade lace curtains. Quickly, she tacked them up over the window and turned toward her husband with a sense of triumph. "There. Now it's a home."

His smile was so warm and tender her heart nearly broke. Closing the distance between them, he took her in his arms and pressed his lips to her temple. "I adore you, Annabelle Brennan."

"And I you."

Oh, the love in his eyes. Love . . . and a question. *Are you ready?*

Was she ready to truly become his wife? To leap hand in hand into all the future held for them? The joys? The sorrows? The dreams?

How could she not be when he looked on her with such love?

She nodded. He caressed her cheek with his fingertips, then claimed her lips in a kiss filled with passionate promise.

✧

"Getting juicy?"

With a quiet gasp, Sloane yanked her gaze from Annabelle's diary to Colleen's smiling face. "Oh, hey, Colleen. Didn't see you come in."

"I gathered that." Colleen bustled to her desk, insulated lunch sack in hand.

The blink of the cursor on Sloane's laptop, the bright green flash on her phone, the scratchy peeling apart of Velcro as Colleen dove into her lunch all pulled her back to the present. Had she even eaten yet?

She'd started at least. A metal fork stuck out of the bowl of pasta on her desk, and the taste of tomato sauce lingered on her tongue. She lifted another bite to her lips, but it was stone-cold.

"So." Colleen spun in her chair, plastic container of salad in hand and a gleam in her eyes. "What's going on with Miss Annabelle?"

"Well, she's Mrs. Annabelle now."

Colleen's eyebrows arched over her glasses. "Ole Jack put a ring on it, did he?"

"Just read about their wedding day."

"And their wedding night?" Colleen's brown eyes took on a mischievous shine.

"It's not like that. She's very discreet."

"Can't be that discreet," Colleen retorted around a mouthful of salad. "Your cheeks are about the same color as your spaghetti sauce."

"Ha ha." Sloane picked up her pasta and headed for the microwave.

"Mind if I take a peek?" Colleen's container thumped softly on her desk, and her chair creaked.

"Knock yourself out," Sloane called over her shoulder. "But I promise, there are no details."

"We'll see about that," was Colleen's parting shot.

Sloane shook her head as she reached the little kitchen and popped open the door of a microwave that was itself nearly old enough to be in their collection. It wasn't the content of Annabelle's diary that had her cheeks aflame. Not really.

It was that every time Annabelle described kissing Jack . . . Sloane saw Garrett. Garrett's eyes, deep navy in the moonlight. Garrett's cheekbones, thrust into light and shadow by the Keeper's ring of firepots. Garrett's lips, quirked in a quick, shy little smile, moving closer . . .

The microwave beeped, and she jerked the door open. She had to snap out of this. He'd be here again in two days. Would he be able to read her thoughts? To know how many times he and that near miss of a kiss had been their sole focus? To know how much brainpower had gone to wondering if it had been a fluke, or if there was actual intent?

How many times she'd relived that moment—and mentally finished it—minus the gaggle of drunken bachelorettes?

When she returned to her desk, Colleen held the diary in gloved hands, her gaze scooting back and forth over the page with impressive speed.

"See?" Sloane set her lunch down. "PG-13 at worst."

"Disappointingly, yes." Colleen turned back a couple pages. "I know you told me, but when was Grandma's house built?"

"1890. Why?"

Colleen held the diary out to Sloane. "Take another look at the part where Jack talks about his dream house. I'm surprised you missed this."

Frowning, Sloane peered at the faded cursive. Honed in on the details of Jack's dream.

The sitting room window, looking down on the creek. The same view Rosie had in her den.

The large stone fireplace. Just like the one in Rosie's living room.

The tree-lined drive leading to the big white house.

Heart somersaulting, she grabbed her phone. Garrett. Garrett would know. She had to call Garrett.

He answered on the second ring. "Now there's a sound for sore ears."

"Hey. Got a minute?"

"Sure." He hesitated. "Are you all right? You sound out of breath."

"Fine. I just—I need to know—what kind of trees line the drive up to your grandma's house?"

"Are you sure you're all right?" His furrowed brow came through in his voice.

"Promise. Just tell me about the trees."

"They're apple trees. At least some of them are. The rest are cherry, I think. Yeah. Grandma used to make pies in the summer. Why?"

The truth settled in Sloane's midsection and spread over her face in a smile. "Because Jack planted those trees. He's the one who built that house. Your grandma's house . . . Jack Brennan built it. For Annabelle."

# Chapter Thirteen

At four minutes past five thirty that Friday, Garrett pulled up outside the castle-like historical museum. Traffic jams and road construction along the turnpike had delayed him, and he'd started late anyway thanks to a client who wouldn't take a hint. He'd hoped Sloane wouldn't have to wait on him even these extra four minutes.

He didn't want to have to wait the extra four minutes either.

But his heart lifted the moment he glimpsed her, sitting on a sun-dappled bench, looking at her phone, the wind tousling her hair. She glanced up, smiled, and got to her feet. He threw the car into park and hopped out to open her door.

Her eyebrows arched over a pair of funky vintage-looking sunglasses. "Why, thank you."

She seemed surprised. Was chivalry really that rare? "You're welcome," he replied as she passed. A whiff of sweet perfume cut through the diesel exhaust of a passing bus.

He walked around to his side and climbed behind the wheel. "Sorry I'm late."

"It's only"—she peered at the clock—"five thirty-five."

"I know. But I wanted to be here when you got off work."

"Well, it's a gorgeous day, so you're forgiven." She was even more beautiful than he remembered. Being another year older was definitely treating her well.

Grinning like a fool, he reached into the back seat. "Got something for you."

"Oh?"

He presented her with a bouquet of springy yellow flowers. "Happy birthday."

Plastic crinkled as she accepted his gift, but her smile froze halfway to her eyes. "You didn't have to do that."

"I wanted to." He swallowed against a jolt of apprehension. Birthday flowers were within the boundaries of friendship, weren't they? "Besides, it's Friday. Field trip day. Figured after those swarms of kids, you might need a day brightener."

Jackpot. The smile reached her eyes with a nearly audible ding.

"You're sweet." She sniffed the flowers appreciatively, then lowered them to her lap. "Thank you."

"So how were the little rascals?" Glancing over his shoulder, Garrett pulled away from the curb.

"Third graders are their own kind of special. Especially five classes' worth."

He winced. "Ouch."

"Meh. My day's looking up."

"Good." He stopped at a red light and turned to her. "How's Mirabelli's sound for dinner?"

She chuckled quietly. "Sounds great if you feel like waiting in line for two hours."

"What if I told you I had a reservation?"

Sloane blinked. "You do?"

"Yep."

"Well. Color me impressed, Mr. Anderson." She settled back in her seat, eyes closed, looking as relaxed as if she were lying on a beach. "Guess there are perks to hanging out with people who like to plan."

"Guess so." Never mind that this whole thing was Lauren's idea.

If it was going to make Sloane this happy, he'd gladly hog the credit.

⭢⭠

The tangy scent of marinara sauce and the comforting, yeasty aroma of dough grabbed Sloane by the elbow and guided her, gently but irresistibly, through the heavy wooden doors of the crowded, speakeasy-like Mirabelli's. While Garrett spoke with the hostess, Sloane breathed deep of the tantalizing smells and feasted her eyes on the century-old converted warehouse. The walls, though covered in neon lights and witty signage, were rough red brick, and the ceiling boasted patterned tin tiles.

She'd yet to take a bite and this place was perfection.

"Fancy meeting you here, sugar."

She turned at the familiar baritone. Sure enough, there was Jamal, her band's bass player. Drink in hand, his trademark tweed cap atop his head.

"You playing here tonight?" In addition to their band, he and a couple others formed a jazz trio that routinely gigged around town.

"Nope. Just stuffin' my face with some pepperoni and extra cheese." He lifted his glass. "Good to see you."

"You too," she called as he disappeared into the crowd, moving more quickly than usual.

The hostess stepped between Sloane and the retreating Jamal, menus in hand. "Right this way."

She escorted Sloane and Garrett toward a cozy-looking booth for two in the back. The perfect place to duck away and wait for this day to be over.

It was April twenty-third. Just another square on the calendar. Twenty-four more hours of life under her belt.

And as long as she kept telling herself that, she'd be okay.

So locked was her vision on that cozy corner booth that she almost ran smack into the hostess, who had inexplicably stopped at a large rectangular table in the center of the restaurant.

A table where Jamal was hastily pulling out a chair.

A table that contained Eric. Patrice. The rest of the band. And a beaming Lauren Anderson.

A table festooned with shiny Happy Birthday balloons.

Oh. Oh *no*.

"Surprise!"

"Happy birthday." Garrett's voice was so close to her ear that she jumped, even as he threw an arm around her shoulders and pulled her close.

Sloane swallowed hard, braced herself, and pulled out the smile she pasted on when people did things like this to her.

No. Not *to* her. *For* her. They liked her. They were being nice. They had no idea how hard this day was. How could they? She'd always shrugged off her birthday as no big deal.

Nothing could be further from the truth. It was a very big deal.

But if she told them that . . . she'd have to tell them why.

So she willed her smile wider and started toward the table on legs that felt like Jell-O.

>←

Maybe Sloane didn't like surprises.

Maybe she was tired after a long day with the field trip kids.

Maybe she'd hoped for a quiet dinner for two at that cozy booth in the corner.

Garrett's brain worked overtime, trying to uncover what was wrong. Because something was. She'd plastered a smile onto those lovely lips, but it was as shiny and artificial as the plastic on the menu she held. She was a lively participant in the small talk, witty and laughing as always, but the stiff set of her shoulders sparked a squirmy sense of worry in his chest.

Had they gone too far? Was this whole thing a colossal screwup? He reached for his water glass, praying he was wrong. That this surprise birthday party wasn't a mistake.

Or if it was, that it could be fixed.

"This is a milestone, y'all." Across from Sloane, the band's blond, bearded guitar player lifted his glass in tribute. "All these years, and you finally let us celebrate your birthday with you."

She waved him off. "I've never made a big deal about it, Eric. It's just another day."

To Eric's left, a brown-skinned woman with magenta-streaked corkscrew curls—the drummer, Patrice, if memory served—peered at Sloane with a sly smile. "Guess she's turning over a new leaf, what with the new boyfriend and all."

Alarmed, Garrett glanced at Sloane, who studied her menu as though it contained ancient secrets. "We're just friends," she said.

"Right," he echoed, atop an irritating sense of disappointment. Because suddenly he wanted so much more. Plans be hanged.

"Mm-hmm." Patrice flipped her menu over. "Can't recall any of your other friends putting together a shindig like this for you."

"Pshaw." Lauren waved a hand. "It was nothing, really. Just a thank-you for all Sloane's help with the house and digging around in our dusty boxes. Plus our mom was super big on birthday surprises."

Patrice's eyes lit. "Your mom sounds fun."

"She was," Lauren replied. "My seventh birthday, she came to school and got me sprung for lunch, anywhere I wanted. So we had ice cream. And when I turned nine, she filled my room with—"

A rustling beside Garrett drew his attention. Sloane's hand rested gently on his shoulder. She still wore that strange, painted-on smile. "Will you excuse me for a minute?"

She stood and walked quickly toward the front of the restaurant, where a neon arrow pointed to the restrooms. But she bypassed that little alcove. Threaded her way through the crowd waiting by the door.

He craned his neck, alarm pinching his gut. What was she doing?

When that door opened and Sloane strode straight through it, he had his answer.

⇥⇤

Safely around the corner from Mirabelli's, Sloane dropped onto a bus stop bench and focused on the patch of pavement between her shoes. Her pulse pounded. Her hands shook with fury.

*Breathe. Just breathe. They didn't know.*

But she wasn't angry with them. Not really.

She was angry with herself.

Because normal people didn't flip out when someone did something sweet for them. Normal people didn't spend their thirtieth birthday alone on a cold metal bench after sabotaging their own surprise party.

But normal people weren't left on a bus a week after birth either.

So maybe it wasn't really herself she was angry with.

Cautious footsteps cut through the swish of traffic and stopped a few feet behind her. "Sloane?"

Garrett. Relief and apprehension mingled in her midsection.

"I'm sorry." Her hands fisted and loosed, fisted and loosed. "I'll go back in there. I just . . . need a minute, is all."

"I'm the one who should apologize. I didn't mean to upset you." A couple more slow footsteps. "I should've realized Lauren talking about Mom would remind—"

"It's not that." She stared at her skirt, burning the navy-and-white polka dot pattern into her retinas. "It's just this day. My birthday."

Moving more certainly, he sat down beside her. A hint of woodsy cologne wafted on the evening breeze.

"I'm sorry." The words vaulted from her mouth, desperate to undo the damage. "I know you guys put a lot of work into this, and I'm not supposed to be sad on my birthday. Everyone loves birthdays. Cake and presents and balloons. You're supposed to be happy."

"You're crying."

Was she? She put a hand to her cheek. It came away wet.

She buried the evidence in a tightly closed fist. "I'm fine. I'll be fine."

"Hey." He put his arm around her and pulled her into his warmth. "You don't have to be fine."

Something shifted at his quiet words. He'd given her permission to be who she was. Messy. Complex. Sure of simple things, like her love for jazz and history and vintage clothing, but clueless about the deeper things. Her origins. Her birth. She'd tried so hard, for so long, to be fine with it.

And here was someone telling her she didn't have to be. Someone who knew she wasn't okay, and was perfectly okay with that.

What sweet freedom.

Leaning against Garrett, she wiped away the last of her tears. Tension seeped from her shoulders. Her neck. Wherever Garrett's arm rested, warmth flowed.

"My parents always went all out for my birthday," she said. "Magic shows, costumed princesses, even a live pony one year. And I want to celebrate and be grateful when people do things like that for me, because it means they love me and want me to be happy. And I am."

"Are you?" Garrett's concerned gaze flitted over her face. He still hadn't released her from his embrace.

She hoped he never would.

"Mostly. But my birthday is also this huge, glaring reminder of the decision my birth mother made. I've tried to imagine what kind of person would leave a baby on a bus, what had to be going on in her life to drive her to that decision, and I . . . can't. I mean, does she even remember what day it is today? Does she care at all about what happened?"

Garrett's embrace tightened. "For what it's worth . . . I care. About what happened, sure. But mostly I care—a whole lot—about you."

His words were sunshine on her soul. Closing her eyes, she leaned her head on his shoulder. "I feel like such an idiot. You guys had no clue about my birthday issues. All you wanted was to throw me a nice party, like your mom did for you." She sighed. "I should go back in there."

"There's no rush." Garrett stretched long legs in front of him and crossed one on top of the other. "We'll stay right here until you're ready. And if it's never, then that's okay too. I'll tell Lauren you have a migraine. Food poisoning. You're in witness protection. How far do you want me to go with this?"

It felt so good to laugh. "Somewhere between salmonella and WITSEC should cover it."

"You got it." He gave her a gentle squeeze.

"I'm kidding. I'll go back in a minute. Gotta admit I'm morbidly curious what a gluten-free, paleo, whatever-else-it-is birthday cake tastes like."

Garrett's lips curved against her forehead. "I have it on good authority Lauren put gluten in there."

"Sugar too?" She pulled back to look at him.

"That's what I hear."

"Hmm. I may have to go check that out."

"Before you do, I have something for you." Loosening his hold on her, he reached down and retrieved a plain purple gift bag from beneath the bench. "I hope a gift is okay. If not, I'll take it back."

He looked so sweet and earnest and endearing that even if she'd wanted to refuse, she wouldn't have been able to.

"Don't you dare. I like presents."

He held out the bag, then pulled up short. "It's nothing big, but I was pretty sure you'd like it. And I didn't know what else you'd want, or if you needed anything, or—"

"Garrett?"

"Yes?"

"Shut up and let me open my present."

He handed over the gift. "Yes, ma'am."

She dove into the bag, rooted through the tissue paper, and let out a quiet gasp at the sight of a small brown leather notebook.

She peeked at the first page. March 21, 1872. Could it be?

> The rain has finally ceased, praise the Lord. Jack has been near to climbing the walls . . .

"I would've given it to you anyway." Garrett's voice brought her back to the present. "But since it was your birthday, I figured I'd wrap it up and—"

"It's perfect." She cupped his cheek in her hand. "Thank you."

His eyes widened at the sudden contact.

She felt the same jolt.

She should take her hand away. She should.

But how could she when his cool, smooth skin felt like home?

Then Garrett moved closer. His lips parted. His heavy-lidded gaze fell to her mouth.

It was inevitable what they were about to do. She wanted to race toward it, but she also wanted to freeze this moment of delicious anticipation.

The last moment before their first kiss.

His mouth met hers then, and she melted. His hand slid behind her neck. The kiss was tender and slow, unwinding and unraveling as though they had all the time in the world. As though he wanted to savor each second, commit each moment to memory.

More power to him if he could think.

All she could do was feel.

When they pulled apart, she cleared her throat. "That was . . ."

"Unexpected."

"But good." Right? He seemed just as addled as she felt, so there was at least a chance.

"Yes. Good. *Very* good." He swept a curl behind her ear, then lowered his hand, letting his fingertips trail along her cheek. "Happy birthday."

"It really is."

"Good." Garrett flashed a mischievous smirk. "I was afraid I might have to kiss you again."

Laughing, she got up and retrieved the gift bag. "C'mon. Let's go back." She extended her hand to him, and he took it with questions in his eyes.

"You sure?"

She laced her fingers with his. "I've got a birthday cake to eat."

＞＜

Diary and steaming mug of chamomile tea in hand, Sloane padded from the kitchen to her bedroom. Tired but not yet sleepy, she looked forward to some quality time with Annabelle and Jack. A peek at the worn pages while Garrett drove her home had revealed that the pioneer couple's first baby was on the way. Her heart had quickened. A baby meant a new name. A new detail. A new nugget of information that gleamed with promise.

Her birthday really had been wonderful, all things considered. The pizza had been delicious, the birthday cake stellar, and Garrett's warm, reassuring presence helped her to relax and enjoy the mixing of social circles.

And Garrett. Though he'd played it cool around the band—and his sister—the evening had been peppered with shy glances. The wonderment in those deep blue eyes echoed her own. They'd *kissed*. Which meant their assertions of being just friends were probably no longer true.

Especially since he'd kissed her again outside the restaurant when they returned to his car.

And again when he walked her to her door.

Not quite suppressing the smile pushing at her cheeks or the fluttery feeling in her chest, Sloane set the mug on her night table, pulled back her cozy blue comforter, and climbed into bed.

She'd just opened the diary when her phone buzzed. Irritated at the interruption, she picked it up and glanced at the screen. Whatever it was could doubtless wait until morning—

*Marinera72 has sent you a message on AdoptionBridge.com!*

Frowning, she clicked the link, then froze.

*I never forgot.*

*Happy birthday.*

## CHAPTER FOURTEEN

GARRETT NUDGED THE kitchen faucet off with his wrist and plunged the sauce-encrusted skillet into a sink full of soapy water. Much had changed in the last couple decades, but the Spencer family tradition of men washing the dishes remained a constant. Ever since he was tall enough to see over the counter, Garrett had been summoned after meals to scrape plates and fetch soiled silverware. "World-class cook shouldn't have to do her own dishes," Grandpa would insist as he rose from the table, plates in hand.

Garrett never minded. There was something satisfying about sorting through the chaos of dirty plates and bowls and sliding them into neat rows in the dishwasher. Taking a haphazard pile of pots and pans and making them shine once more.

If only the chaos in his life were so easily managed.

Granted, the most recent chaos was self-inflicted. Because while friends went to concerts together and threw birthday parties—even ones including flowers and gifts—friends did not kiss.

But he'd kissed Sloane. More than once.

And Lord help him, he never wanted to stop.

Those impulsive kisses had been a brick through the glass of friendship, and what in the world could he do about it? How could he fit these new developments into his already packed-full life? How would it work once he wasn't coming to Wichita all the time anymore? With Sterling breathing down his neck, could he afford to wedge a romantic relationship into his plans? And with the scars of Jenny Hickok still on his heart, was it even wise to try?

But if he turned his back on this, would he be missing out on something wonderful? Something life altering? Something—

His phone buzzed, and he swiped his hands on a nearby towel, grateful for the interruption.

"Garrett. Hi. Kimberly Walsh. Just checking to see if you'd had a chance to talk with your family about the property."

From one confusing mess to another. "Not yet." Wedging the phone between his ear and shoulder, he channeled his anxiety into scraping stuck-on crud from the skillet.

"Then this might help. I ran into Warren Williams's assistant at the gym this morning. She says he's definitely interested in your grandparents' land." Kimberly's words tumbled out over themselves. "He actually approached them about it a while back, but they refused to sell. Maybe now things would be different."

Garrett's eyebrows shot toward his hairline. Warren Williams had tried to buy the land before? This was the first he'd heard about it. No doubt his grandparents had turned down a handsome sum too. One that could've saved them so much heartache.

He renewed his attack on the skillet. "Maybe."

"When Williams wants land, he does whatever it takes to get it. He's not above paying top dollar for a property he's passionate about. If you want my advice, that's the route I suggest. But it is, of course, up to you and your family."

And there lay the rub.

Garrett ended the call and finished the dishes, his mind a stew of prognostications and projections, numbers and possibilities. So much that he nearly jumped out of his skin when the doorbell rang.

"Oh, Garrett," Lauren called from the living room, her voice singsong. "Sloane's here."

Quickly, he dried his hands and headed for the living room, where just a glimpse of her quieted his mind and brought a smile to his lips.

"Hi."

Sloane quirked a brow. "Little overdressed to go dig around in dusty boxes, don't you think?"

Garrett glanced down at his black dress pants and shiny shoes. "Grandma's stuck in the past again today."

Lauren patted Garrett's shoulder. "Or he's trying to impress you."

He glared at Lauren, who fired back a smirk. Mercifully, Sloane gazed out the window toward the creek, seemingly a million miles from this little sibling exchange.

With a toss of her head, Lauren spun on her heel. "And now I'll leave the room for no reason whatsoever."

Garrett rolled his eyes and started up the stairs. Since Grandma was napping, there was a chance he could get away with more casual attire. "Make yourself at home. I'll be right down."

After changing into a Jayhawks T-shirt and shorts, he returned to find Sloane elbows-deep in one of the cardboard boxes he'd brought down from the attic. Dust motes flitted around her head in a shaft of sunlight, giving her an otherworldly appearance. A cream-colored sweater sagged off one shoulder, and one denim-covered leg was tucked beneath the other. Her teeth grazed her lower lip, and memories of their velvety firmness came flooding back. Would her cheek be that soft? What about her neck? Her shoulder?

Jaw tight, he grabbed a box and plopped down on the other end of the sofa. Given where his thoughts were headed, distance was doubtless a good idea.

They worked in silence for a few minutes, which was odd. Usually she'd be making pithy statements or tossing some snark his way. But today she was quiet. In fact, other than that first glance when she arrived, she'd barely even looked at him.

Perhaps he wasn't the only one grappling with the shattered boundary of friendship.

"Finding anything good?" he ventured.

She tossed a paperback Western into an empty crate destined for Goodwill. "Nope."

"At least you've got that new diary to keep you occupied. Dig into it yet?"

"Yeah." A Robert Ludlum book thwacked into the crate.

"How's Annabelle?"

"Pregnant." *Thwack.*

All right. Lauren always ragged on him for being dense and missing obvious hints, but if Annabelle Brennan was pregnant and Sloane didn't want to talk about it? Something was definitely wrong. And it wouldn't take a genius to figure out what.

Gut knotted, he piled a few more weathered paperbacks into the box. "Look . . . I'm sorry if I overstepped."

She stopped, book in hand and brow furrowed. "What?"

"Last night. When we . . . when we kissed. I thought you were okay with it, but if you weren't, then I apologize, especially since friends don't—I mean, it's been a while, if I'm honest, and I may be a little rusty on the finer poi—"

Leaning over the boxes, Sloane wrapped her free hand around the back of his neck and pressed a kiss to his lips. Firm enough to shock him into silence, and just short enough to leave him aching for more.

"It's not you, all right?" She eyed him. "I'm sorry if I made you think it was."

Okay. Boundary officially obliterated. He'd sort out its impact on his plans later.

"I'm glad for that. But if it's not me, then . . . what is it?"

Sloane studied the worn cover of an Agatha Christie novel. Finally, she sighed and pushed her glasses up on her nose. "My birth mother emailed me last night on that adoption website I look at sometimes."

"What?" He couldn't have been more shocked if she'd reported an email from the Queen of England. "That's huge."

"Yeah." Sloane gave the book a cursory glance, then tossed it into the crate.

"What'd she say?"

"She wished me a happy birthday, if you can believe that. Said she never forgot." A pair of faded romance novels sailed into the box atop the mysteries. "But if that's true, then why'd she wait thirty years to drop me a note? Did it never occur to her to do so before?"

"Maybe she had a good reason not to."

Sloane's eyes shot sparks. "The woman left me on a bus, and now you're defending her?"

"No. I just . . ." He floundered for something that wouldn't hurt her further. "This is what you wanted, isn't it? To find her? To make contact?"

"Yes. No. I don't know." Sloane ripped some old tape off the box and folded it into tiny squares. "I thought it was. But now that she's surfaced, now that there's an email from her on my computer, it's this weird emotional tossed salad I don't want to deal with. Or talk about. Or even think about."

"Well then." He gingerly withdrew a small brown notebook from the box, a notebook he'd just discovered beneath a pile of old *National Geographic* magazines. "Maybe this'll take your mind off it for a bit."

"Ooh. Gimme." Sloane dove for her gloves, slipped them on, and took the diary. But when she opened it, instead of the wide smile he hoped for, she covered her mouth with her hand, and . . . were those tears in her eyes?

"Oh no."

His heart lurched as she held the diary out to him.

⤜⤛

*October 27, 1872*

Annabelle knelt under the cottonwood on the small rise overlooking the creek. The sky was overcast, and a cold, stiff wind blew from the north. As long as she'd been out here, that wind should've made her cheeks raw.

Maybe it had. She had no way of knowing.

The little mound of sandy dirt beneath her skirts crowded out everything else.

Seventeen days.

Seventeen days since pain engulfed her world.

It was subtle at first. Twinges in her lower back while preparing dinner. But those twinges turned into aches she couldn't ignore. And the aches became outright pains, pains that dimmed her awareness and blurred her vision and sent an ashen-faced Jack galloping off for Uncle Stephen.

She hadn't had a chance, their Emmaline. Not this soon. Not this small. She should have. She was so perfect. So complete.

But the womb that was supposed to protect and nurture her until February had failed, and now their little girl slept in a womb of cold, soulless earth.

Annabelle's body had betrayed her. And it had betrayed Jack, whose beloved Sarah lay nearby, her grave marked by a simple stone carved with her initials and grown over with grass.

Another infant lay there too, but at least little Josiah wasn't alone.

As her neighbors coaxed Emmaline's resting place from unforgiving soil, the scrapes of the shovels gouging holes from her heart, it had taken everything in her not to leap into the grave and let them cover her too. So she could hold her daughter in her arms and fall asleep and wait for the resurrection together.

Only Jack, holding her up as her knees gave way, kept her from doing exactly that.

Jack. When had they last spoken more than a handful of words to one another? From within grief's suffocating shroud, she couldn't even look at him. Couldn't bear to see the pain in those gray eyes. The streaks of tears he tried so valiantly to hide. The tightness of his jaw, his pale skin, all because of her failure to do the one thing she'd dreamt of doing since the day she fell in love with him.

She had failed him. Failed Emmaline.

Agony upon agony. Which was worse, she couldn't begin to know.

Footsteps crunched on the fallen leaves behind her. A hint of a brogue broke through the silence.

"I should've known I'd find you here."

Why was Jack here? Where was Oliver? What time was it? The leaden clouds gave no hint of the hour, and pain had removed all awareness of time.

Jack cleared his throat. "Oliver came out to the barn when he got home from school and couldn't find you."

She turned to look at her husband but only got as high as his mud-stained boots. "Is he . . . ?"

"He's fine. I fixed him some milk and cookies. He's playing with Chester." The black-and-white barn cat with whom she'd consented to share her home, provided he kept the mice away.

"I'm sorry, Jack." A tear slipped out, stinging her cheek.

"It's all right, love. Oliver's big enough to be alone now and then. And I came here often myself when . . ." Sorrow roughened the words, and she doubled over with the pain of it. Jack shouldn't have to be here again, standing by another too-small grave. He shouldn't, he shouldn't, he *shouldn't*.

In an instant, he knelt beside her, wrapping her in an embrace she didn't deserve.

"It's not Oliver," she gasped between sobs. "It's . . . Emmaline." It was only the second time she'd spoken their daughter's name aloud since that terrible day.

"You—you think it's your fault?"

The iron grip of grief choked any words out of her, so she merely gulped and nodded.

Jack's sigh resonated through his muscular frame as he drew her closer. "Oh, my love."

While she waited for the latest storm of tears to subside, Jack held her. Whispered reassurance into her ear. He didn't blame her. Of course he didn't. And whether she deserved his comfort or not, she clung to it, hard and fierce. The warmth of his embrace, the passion beneath the kisses he lavished on her hair, her cheeks . . . how lonely he must have been.

How lonely she'd been too.

"Oh, Jack. I can't move. I can't breathe. I can't do anything except hurt." She heaved a shuddering breath. "How did you survive this?"

"I didn't. Not for a while." He pressed his lips together. "I wanted to die. I was so mad with grief that I lay abed for days, weeping. Begging God to please, please take me too."

A tear dove down her face at the crack in his voice. For God to take her. To be with Emmaline. That was what she wanted. More than anything.

"Eventually I stopped asking. In fact, I stopped talking with God altogether. Either he didn't exist, or his purpose was to gut me like a fish. Whichever it was, I was through."

Annabelle raised her head from his tear-soaked shirt. Looked him in the face. Fully. Finally. The man she adored. The man for whom she'd walk through fire. "I didn't understand those feelings before. Now I do."

Beloved gray eyes shone bright. "I may have given up on the Lord, love, but he never gave up on me. Even when I stopped clinging to him, he never for one moment stopped holding on to me. He sent friends, neighbors. People whose own survival was at stake took the time to come help me when I couldn't manage. To keep things going until I got back on my feet." Tears wobbled on red-rimmed lids. "And when I feared I'd lost Oliver too, that every last soul I loved had been torn from my arms . . . God rescued him. Rescued me. And led me straight to you."

Another tear slipped out. Sweet mercy, how did she have any left? But though pain still consumed her with each breath, hope flickered. For the first time in seventeen days.

"I miss her, our little Emmaline Rose. Till the end of my days, I'll miss her." A tear trickled down the side of his nose, and he reached up to brush it away. "But as true as that is, and as deeply as I grieve, I also rejoice. Because if you were in that grave too . . ."

His voice broke, and she gripped his hand. What would it have done to him if he'd been forced to mourn another love lost, another grave dug in this desolate place? How selfish her earlier wish had been, and how gracious was God not to have granted it.

"I'm not, Jack. I'm here."

He took her hand and kissed her fingertips. "And all my moments now are both piercing pain, because of Emmaline, and indescribable joy, because you lived. With every breath I thank God that I can still hold you. Kiss you. Love you. Weep with you. And dream with you." His shimmering gaze sought hers. "Do you remember?"

She swallowed hard and nodded.

"The big white house. The table full of food." His words were slow. Measured. Spoken with great effort, as though he needed to cling to them as much as she did. "The seven little ones. Four dark like me, two fair like their mam, and one wee redhead . . ."

One hand wandered to her hollowed-out womb. "It seems so far away. So impossible."

"I know, my love. I know."

They clung to each other and wept. And for the first time in seventeen days, grief was no longer a burden she bore alone.

⇥⇤

A solemn heaviness draped over Sloane's shoulders as she followed Garrett up a slight rise to a copse of trees behind the house.

"This is about the only place that counts as a hill around here." His words bounced on a gust of wind. "But I'm not sure, since the diary made it sound like that cottonwood was off by itself."

"It probably was back then." Sloane's foot caught on a gnarled tree root.

"Cottonwoods are one of the few species native to Kansas. All these others must have been planted on purpose."

"If I remember right, there's a cottonwood in the middle of all this." Garrett's pace quickened as he crunched through twigs and leaves and years' worth of growth. Sure enough, amid twisted dead branches and sprigs of pale green newness stood a stately cottonwood, infant leaves shimmering in the incessant wind.

Sloane walked around the thick trunk of the old tree, and her pulse quickened. "I'm no arborist, but this thing's been here a hundred years, easy. And Annabelle said it was on a hill near the creek. This has to be it."

The ground was strewn with autumn's leftover leaves and choked with dead brush.

Wait. There. Buried in a thatch of tangled undergrowth. A corner of stone peeking out.

Could it be . . . ?

"I think I see something." Sloane grabbed the branches and tugged. The dead ones snapped easily in her hands. "Help me."

Garrett crouched next to her, and together they cleared away enough brush to see the stone clearly.

Satisfaction and sorrow mingled in her core. There it was. A small, rough stone, its letters filled with lichen and worn with the passage of time. Still legible, but only just.

*S. B. & J. B.*
*1870*

And next to it, another stone.

*E. B.*
*1872*

Right here. Right where she stood, the heartrending scene had played out. Sloane had never felt closer to Jack and Annabelle.

Garrett's arm slid around her shoulders. "I can't imagine. Losing a child."

"It was sadly common back then. But that doesn't mean it didn't still hurt."

"Yeah." His voice sounded thick. His lips were tight, and a muscle at the corner of his jaw worked. Her heart wrenched at the losses he'd faced. His mother. His father by extension. His grandfather. And now his grandmother by infinitesimal, torturous degrees.

He turned to her then, something alight in his eyes. "What if your birth mother missed you? Sorta like Annabelle missed Emmaline? I know it's not the same, but what if she did?"

Ah, the Pollyanna pipe dream she'd forced herself to suppress. The idea that somewhere out there was a perfect princess of a mother who loved and missed her, who'd spent her life regretting a terrible choice. Who'd whisk her away to the land of rainbows and roses and happily-ever-after.

Sloane scuffed the ground with the toe of her sneaker. "Then why'd it take her thirty years to say hello?"

"I don't know." Something about Garrett's voice drew her gaze back. "But she finally did. She reached out. So maybe she wants to know a little bit about you. Just like you want to know a little bit about her."

Hope struggled from the piles of cynicism and bitterness she'd buried it beneath. The effort made her chest ache. "Even if that's true . . . what do I say? All she said was happy birthday. For the first time. What am I supposed to say to that?"

"Well, there's always 'thank you.'"

"Thank you." She rolled the words around in her mouth, like a familiar food covered in an unfamiliar sauce. "I could do that."

"You could."

She smiled at him. "Thank you."

"See? Piece of cake."

And late that night, long past when she should've been asleep, after multiple false starts and several laps around her living room, Sloane typed, with trembling fingers, those two little words in the reply box to Marinera72 and hit send before she could lose her nerve.

*Thank you.*

# CHAPTER FIFTEEN

*To: HistorICT*
*From: Marinera72*

*In closing, you asked about my screen name. I'm not ready to reveal many personal details yet, but I can tell you I love the Mariners even though I no longer live in Seattle. I'm also part Italian and was born in 1972, so put all those together with some creative spelling, and there you have it.*
*Hope to hear from you again soon.*

A half-eaten microwave burrito in hand, its flavor ignored in favor of far more pressing matters, Sloane stared at the words on her laptop. Just as she had with each message from Marinera72 over the past nine days.

All Sloane's life, her birth mother had achieved almost mythical status, but now she had proof. Marinera72, her mother, was a real flesh-and-blood woman. A woman who, only an hour ago, sat at a computer and typed words onto a screen and sent them straight to the eyes and heart of the daughter she'd never known. Myth melted away with each detail that sprang from the screen.

She liked baseball.

Had a playful knack for screen names.

And she'd been only nineteen when she gave birth. Nineteen. Sloane shook her head. Even as studious and responsible as she'd been at nineteen, enough goldfish had died on her watch that she'd half expected a cease-and-desist order from PETA. No way would she have been able to handle a baby.

But even at nineteen she'd have taken her newborn daughter with her when she hopped off the bus.

*So why didn't you?*

As much as the question burned, she wasn't ready to ask it. Not yet. She needed to work up to it.

*To: Marinera72*
*From: HistorICT*

*The Italian I knew about. I took one of those DNA tests a while ago. It said I'm a mix of Italian, Ukrainian, Irish, and some smaller bits of British Isles and Western Europe. Do you happen to know the story behind any of that? You don't need to share anything you're uncomfortable with, but I have always wondered where I came from.*

She clicked send before she could talk herself out of it, then forced another bite down her throat and waded through her work emails, trying to find something else—anything else—to think about. Thirty years without a word and she'd been fine. But now minutes seemed like months. Seconds like centuries. The only thing more nerve-racking than waiting for a reply was—

*Ding.*

Getting one.

Stomach flip-flopping, heart pounding, she clicked to the Adoption Bridge inbox. Marinera72—her mother—was on the computer right now. Sitting out there somewhere, looking at a screen, just like Sloane.

With a trembling hand, she opened the message.

*To: HistorICT*
*From: Marinera72*

*Yes, the Italian is for sure from us. My great-grandmother—we called her Nonna—was born there and came to the US with her family as a little girl. There's an old letter somewhere from her where she talks about her life. Give me a day or two to look for it. Not sure about the Irish. My dad's side maybe?*

*The Ukrainian must be from your father's side. I am not in contact with him.*

Her father.

Of course she had a father. One who, from the minimal information Marinera provided, must still be a sore point.

As with all research, each nugget of new information led to several other mysteries. Questions piled on questions. Who was this man? What had their relationship been like?

Did he even know he had a daughter?

As reluctantly as Marinera revealed information about herself, she'd doubtless be doubly so when it came to the other half of Sloane's DNA.

But there was a letter from Nonna. So maybe, just maybe . . .

*To: Marinera72*
*From: HistorICT*

*I would love to learn more about Nonna, your family, or anything else you're comfortable sharing. If you can find that letter, that would be amazing . . .*

>←

Garrett held a hastily assembled sandwich in one hand and clicked at his computer with the other. With the Patersons due in at one o'clock, he once again didn't have time for a normal lunch.

Nor did he have time for the call he'd ignored from a mysterious Wichita number. Or yet another call coming in now. His teeth on edge from the incessant buzzing, he reached for the phone and glanced at the screen.

Lauren.

"Are you out of your mind?" That was her greeting, so shrill he jumped up and shut his office door. If her pitch and decibel level were any indication, things were about to get ugly.

"I'm afraid you'll have to be more specific, Lo." He crossed his office and sat back down.

"Were you ever going to clue me in on your big elaborate plans? Or Grandma? Or were you going to sell the house out from under us and let us find out when the bulldozers showed up?"

His mind whirred, trying to keep up. "What are you talking about?"

"Don't play dumb with me." She sounded like Mom. "I just got home from a shoot, and there's a message from Warren Williams on Grandma's machine."

"Warr . . ." The rest of the name tumbled down his throat, unuttered. "What?"

"You're telling me you don't know who Warren Williams is? Now I know you're playing dumb. That developer who's gobbling up every square mile between here and the highway to build cul-de-sacs and crappy McMansions?"

Now she sounded like Sloane.

Garrett rubbed his right temple. Williams must've been the Wichita number he'd ignored. "I know who he is. I just never expected him to call. All I told Kimberly was I'd think about it."

"And who is Kimberly?"

"She's a real estate agent. Now I know it's—"

"Garrett Paul Anderson, you are unbelievable. You went behind my back? Talked to a real estate agent? A developer?"

He dragged a hand through his hair. This whole thing was spiraling out of control, an unmitigated disaster. He'd wanted time to organize his options and present them to Lauren at a quiet moment when they had time for reasonable conversation.

But all that had been torn away with one unexpected phone call.

"Typical." Fury shook his sister's voice. "You don't even have an excuse. You've just decided the house is inconvenient, so you'll dispose of it as quickly as you can. Y'know, you're exactly like Dad."

He gritted his teeth. "Are you finished?"

"Yes." The word knifed through the phone.

"Would you like to hear my side?"

She gave a bitter laugh. "Oh yes, I'd love nothing more than to hear you explain your way out of this one."

He pulled in a breath through his nose. "My explanation is this: unlike you, I'm willing to face reality. Grandma's going downhill. Every time I visit, she's lost the ability to do something she could the time before. Every single time, without fail, she loses something."

"Don't you think I know that?"

"You're not acting like you do. You're acting like she's got a cold or something, and she'll snap out of it any minute."

"Sure. That's why I moved in with her. Because I think she has a cold."

"But because you moved in, you don't see it." Garrett's chair creaked as he vaulted out of it and began to pace the small office. "You don't see that she won't be able to live at home much longer. The stairs, the land, there's no way the two of you can keep up with it. I have to come down there every weekend as it is."

"You don't have to do anything, Garrett." His name sounded like an insult the way she flung it at him. "You want to wash your hands of this whole thing and take off like Dad did, fine. Be my guest. I didn't ask for your help, and if it's so inconvenient for you, then I don't want it."

"Would you stop being emotional for half a second and listen to me?"

The frigid silence over the line was permission enough.

"I'm a planner, okay? I focus on the future, because that's what I'm good at. It's what my clients depend on me to do. What my family depends on me to do, because nobody else bothered to think of the future. Ever. That's why we're in this mess. Grandma's life savings are practically down to nothing."

"What about Medicare?"

"Medicare won't kick in while she's got the house. It's worth too much. And if she's got any of her wits about her at all, she'll flat out refuse anyway. You know how she and Grandpa always were about accepting any kind of charity."

"So now you're willing to admit she's somewhat qualified to make her own decisions?" Lauren's voice dripped with derision. "If that's the case, why are you going behind our backs talking to Warren Williams?"

"I wasn't going behind your back. I was formulating a plan!" Through his office window, the administrative assistant shot Garrett a concerned glance. He plastered on a reassuring smile and turned toward the opposite wall.

"Without consulting me. Or Grandma," Lauren hissed.

"Because whenever I try, you shut me down and tell me I'm being ridiculous."

"Maybe you are."

"Fine. Maybe I am. But at least I'm trying to do what's in Grandma's best interest."

Oops. Too far. He ached to reel in the words, but they were already out there.

"And you think I'm not?"

"I'm sorry. That came out wrong."

"You think?" Her voice was so shrill he half expected to hear dogs barking in the background.

"Look. All I'm doing is gathering information. Learning what our options are, what we could potentially get for the house, the land—"

"I should've known. Money. That's the only thing that matters to you, isn't it? You don't give a flip that Warren Williams wants to turn Grandma and Grandpa's farm into Prairie Palace or Meadowlark Moonscape or whatever. You won't even consider selling it to some family who'll love it and take care of it. You just want to do the quickest thing, the easiest thing. Get it over with. Tell me again how that's not exactly like Dad?"

"Oh, for—are we really having this fight again?" His throat tightened. "Dad was by Mom's side every day for eight years. He went with her to doctor's appointments. Chemo sessions. Watched her lose every meal she tried to eat and her hair fall out strand by strand. As far as I'm concerned, Dad was a saint, and whatever he wants to do now, he's more than earned it."

"So it's fine with you that he abandoned his entire family and ran off to Florida with some floozy we've never even met?"

"You've never met her. Debbie is a wonderful person, if you'd give her a chance to—"

"We are not. Talking. About this." Each word was an icicle.

"Couldn't agree more." He sighed and switched tactics. Anger was getting him nowhere. "Lauren. You're doing a great job with Grandma. Everyone in her situation should be blessed with the kind of love and care you give her. I need you to hear that."

"Flattery won't get you anywhere, jerk face." His sister still sounded angry, but her strident tone had softened. That and the use of her favorite childhood insult told him he could proceed, albeit with extreme caution.

"I only spoke with Kimberly to get an idea of what kind of work the house needs and what it might go for. Because there's going to come a time when it's not safe for Grandma to stay there anymore, and unless we get started on some of these repairs now, we won't have a snowball's chance of selling."

He paused to give Lauren a chance to argue. Mercifully, she didn't.

"But Kimberly was honest and said that even if the place were in mint condition—which you and I both know it's not—it could still sit for a long time, waiting for that perfect family. Meanwhile, months tick by and Grandma's not getting any better." He started another lap of his office. "Kimberly suggested an as-is auction, which would guarantee a set price and sale date without the need to fix it up. She also told me Warren Williams is interested in the land and would give us a fair price. Generous, even. I've committed to nothing, Lauren. I haven't even spoken with the man."

"But you're willing to consider selling to him."

"Yes, I am."

"Even if it means tearing down this house." Her voice wavered. "Watching these hundred-year-old walls get turned to splinters and seeing all the beautiful old trees ripped out and knowing that a bunch of soccer moms are driving their SUVs on the very land where Grandpa gave us tractor rides and let us chase the chickens?"

The vivid memories brought a sting to his eyes. "This isn't easy for me either. I have as many memories in that house as you do."

"And yet you're willing to toss them aside."

"Because I have to be." The words burst from the depths of him. "Grandma can't make informed decisions about her care anymore, and you know Grandpa would want her to be taken care of. Which is why you've bent over backward for months. Turning your life upside down, moving out of your apartment, all while maintaining your blog and running your photo studio . . . God love you, Lo, aren't you tired?"

Silence. A sniffle. Then a sob that reached down and yanked his heart inside out. "Yes, Garrett. I'm exhausted."

He swallowed against the lump in his throat. "I love you, all right? And what you've done for Grandma is amazing. It makes me so proud to be your brother. To be able to tell the world, hey, that generous, caring, kind-hearted woman who put her whole life on hold—who reminds me so much of Mom—that woman is my sister."

"Thank you." She sounded so small and pitiful, he wished he could reach through the phone and give her a hug.

"I mean it. Every word." With a weary sigh, he sank into his chair. "And I'm sorry. This isn't how I wanted you to find out."

"Yeah, well." She blew her nose. "I'm sorry too."

"We're all we've got. We have to stick together."

"I know. But that doesn't mean I don't hate you a little bit right now."

A small smile dared to surface. "I didn't expect it would. But please . . . For you, for Grandma, will you at least think about this?"

"I don't know, Garrett. Right now the idea, it's just . . . I can't."

"Then could we talk more this weekend?"

"Maybe."

A moment later, he ended the call, set his phone on the desk, and cradled his face in his hands. He'd give all he owned to have his bike with him right now. To hop on and ride, mile after mile, far away from here. To let the wind in his face and the fire in his lungs obliterate everything else.

But of course he couldn't.

As always, he had to be the responsible one.

⤞⤝

Sloane reached out from her cocoon of blankets to plug her almost-dead phone into the wall charger. It was nearly midnight, as usual with Garrett, and they'd hung up only out of respect for the morning that would come all too soon. That had become usual too.

What wasn't usual was Garrett himself. He seemed distracted. Upset about something maybe. He seemed reluctant to discuss the matter, so she didn't press.

But she did wonder.

A couple taps on her music app and Billie Holiday's sultry voice wafted out of the speakers as Sloane reached for her archival gloves and

Annabelle's diary. Despite the late hour, she wanted to check in with the girl before going to sleep.

No sooner had she opened the diary's worn pages, though, than her phone pinged. Her heart leaped as she grabbed it. Garrett again?

No.

Not Garrett.

*To: HistorICT*
*From: Marinera72*

*Hi Sloane,*

*Here's that letter I told you about. I'm not sure why we have it, and the first page is missing, so I don't know who it's to or when it was written, but it should answer some questions about where we came from. I think you'll be able to read it, but if you can't, let me know and I'll try again.*

Sloane sat up in bed. Her fingertips pounced on the screen, but it proved too small for letter reading, so she tossed it aside and reached for her tablet. Tapped the email app and waited and waited and why, why, *why* was it taking so long?

There.

Slanted cursive on faded paper.

Her great-great-grandmother's handwriting.

Nonna's handwriting.

The same DNA that flowed through the writer of those words flowed through the one who drank them in.

So many words, as Nonna seemed to be telling her life story to the letter's recipient. Sloane read in great, greedy gulps, trying to slake a lifetime's thirst in a few short seconds. Some of the details would inevitably slosh over the side, unabsorbed, but she'd come back for them later.

They'd come to America from Sicily when Nonna was only a toddler, settling in Cleveland, Ohio. Nonna had grown up there, marrying her husband, John, after a whirlwind courtship and simple church ceremony that had taken place shortly before the letter was written. She, the Italian immigrant, and he, the red-haired son of an Irish American farmer. *What a country this is,* Nonna marveled.

The final paragraph was mostly personal salutations and well-wishes. Sloane started to scroll back up for another read, a deeper drink of the details she'd sought for so long.

But then she saw the closing. The name. And all her muscles locked in place.

*I remain faithfully yours,*
*Domenica Brennan*

# Chapter Sixteen

Tension knotted Garrett's shoulders as he crunched across the gravel to his grandmother's kitchen door early that Saturday afternoon. In the aftermath of Wednesday's argument, he and Lauren had been civil enough, so long as they stuck to bland, nondescript conversations about work, the weather, and the Royals' four-game winning streak.

But thanks to his morning tour of Plaza de Paz, the second of three retirement communities he'd see this weekend, that fragile truce could remain in place no longer. They had to discuss Grandma's future. And he wasn't looking forward to it in the least.

He squeaked open the screen door to a warm, delicious-smelling kitchen. Cherry pie? Turnovers maybe? What would Lauren's versions of those things taste like anyway?

Didn't matter. The aroma alone made his mouth water.

"So how awful was it?" Lauren's back was to him, though whether that was intentional or because she was reaching into the cupboard, he couldn't tell.

"Actually, not awful at all." He placed Plaza de Paz's informational brochure on the counter beside her and beat a hasty retreat to the table.

Lauren set down a stack of small plates and glanced at the brochure with the same wrinkled-nose expression as if he'd put an insect there instead. "Looks like flipping *Mister Rogers' Neighborhood.*"

"That's the new memory care unit." Pulling out a chair, Garrett prayed for the right words. "Lots of bright colors and pictograms to help residents find their way around, plus all kinds of special therapies and activities to help them maintain quality of life for as long as possible. It's very state of the art."

"Sounds expensive."

"Looks like I'm rubbing off on you."

If she looked disgusted before, it paled in comparison to the face she made now. "Ew, you're right."

At the teasing glint in her eyes, some of the tightness across his shoulders gave way.

Despite this mountain of a disagreement they faced, they'd be all right. Like always.

He cleared his throat. "As far as cost, it's pretty brilliant. Residents are required to have a certain amount in the bank when they move in. It's not a small amount, but if that ever runs out, Plaza de Paz guarantees care for the rest of their life, rent free. No charity, no government aid. They consider the care bought and paid for."

"Huh." Lauren picked up the brochure and flipped through it. "Grandma might get on board with that."

A timer dinged, and Lauren opened the oven to retrieve a pan of—yup, cherry turnovers. "But I'm guessing she doesn't have that required amount."

"She does not."

Lauren slammed the oven shut. "And we're back to the elephant in the room."

"You said we'd talk about it this weekend."

"I said maybe we'd talk."

"You knew I was taking some tours."

"All right, fine." Lauren tossed her oven mitts onto the counter, right on top of the brochure. "Let's talk. Where else did you go?"

He blinked at her sudden shift. "Sunset Manor. It's a little older, not quite as nice, but it could be adequate."

"Adequate." Coffeepot poised over a ceramic mug, she spat out the word as though it tasted bad.

"Those aren't our only options. Sycamore Grove looks promising."

"Doesn't that one have a two-year wait list, though?"

"Yes. And depending on how long she's there, it could cost even more than Plaza de Paz." He tented his fingers. "Any way you slice it, Grandma's going to need a lot more cash than she's got, and there's only one way to fix that."

"And now I'm done talking." Lauren set a tray of coffee and turnovers on the table in front of Garrett. "Go take Grandma her snack."

Garrett glanced up at her. "You're avoiding reality, Lo."

"And you're not?"

Lauren's pointed question was a knife thrust straight into his mounting irritation. "Excuse me? Who's the one spending the weekend touring care facilities and going over finances and making tough decisions?"

"And in the meantime you're not spending any time with Grandma. You come down every weekend, but you're always running around taking donations to Goodwill or hanging out with Sloane or any of a hundred other things that mean you're never here. So that begs the question, are you distracting yourself with busyness? And before you answer"—Lauren held up a hand—"I know what that looks like, because I've done it. When Mom was sick, I flitted around chasing boys and being in musicals and going halfway across the country to art school. I couldn't handle seeing her sick. But you stayed."

The truth landed with a thud. "And now you feel guilty."

Lauren dropped into the chair across from him. "I missed so much, Garrett."

"No, you didn't." Leaning forward, he clasped her hands. "Mom would want you to remember her as she really was. Vivacious and bubbly and loving life. Not the sick shell she was at the end." His throat tightened. "I'd give anything not to remember her that way."

"But you were there. And she knew you were." Lauren's blue eyes grew bright with tears. "Grandma forgot me yesterday. I know, she calls me Barb a lot, but she did that even before she got sick. Yesterday, though, she looked at me like she'd never seen me before. It's better today, but . . ."

Her words were a kick to the gut. Things were worse than he'd thought.

"She's slipping away." Lauren swiped at a tear. "And you're missing it. And one day you'll regret it, like I do with Mom. So go. Take her a snack. Stop doing things for her, and be with her. Just for a little while."

As usual, Lauren had him nailed to the wall. He was always running around. Doing. And it wasn't wrong, because things needed to be done. But there was a selfish reason for it too.

If he stopped, the pain would catch up with him.

Garrett picked up the tray, dread coiling in his gut like when he was a little kid about to get a shot at the pediatrician. "It's gonna hurt, Lo."

"I know." Lauren offered a sad smile. "But do it anyway. You'll be glad you did."

The tray seemed to triple in weight as he took it into the living room, where Grandma sat in her favorite chair. She looked his way, and the crepey skin of her face fanned into a thousand crinkles, each with its own story to tell.

Stories that were disappearing from her memory, one by precious one.

"Orrin. What a nice surprise."

"Hey, Gr—Rosie." He set the tray on the coffee table and settled into the matching armchair. Grandpa's chair.

"When did you come home?" She took the coffee from his outstretched hand. "I didn't think you got off work until five."

"It's Saturday, sweetheart. Remember?" He bit into a turnover, hot and juicy. Maybe it was healthy, but it was so delicious he didn't care.

"Oh. Right." She looked vaguely disoriented, then smiled again. "In that case, you'd best get to practicing."

He frowned. "Practicing?"

"For church tomorrow." She nodded toward the dusty piano in the corner with an expression of mild reproach. "I haven't heard you play in so long."

Garrett's mind raced. Grandpa never played piano. The man was completely tone-deaf.

But Garrett wasn't. And during his weekends on the farm, he'd routinely been called on to play a hymn or two for his grandparents' church. They had a regular organist and pianist, of course, but the aged congregation always loved offertory specials from Orrin and Rosie's grandson.

And that she remembered.

"You're right. You haven't." The last time he played for anyone was at that same little church. Mom's funeral.

He'd scarcely touched a keyboard since.

"What are you waiting for then? Go tickle those ivories."

Garrett looked down at his hands as though they belonged to someone else. "I'm a little rusty."

"Nonsense. You could play those old hymns in your sleep." She smiled fondly. "It's been ages since I've heard a good hymn."

His heart sank. Lauren faithfully took Grandma to church each Sunday. Their old one had closed, but another nearby still held a traditional service, featuring the hymns Grandma loved. He'd gone with them just last week.

But that she didn't remember.

"I'll take a look." A mess of conflicting emotions, Garrett crossed the room, peeked into the piano bench, and there it was. The old green hymnal. Sticky notes marked the hymns his mother had selected for her service. He could still see her clearly, lying on the couch, a scarf covering her hairless head, the summer sunshine giving her emaciated face an ethereal glow. A smile curving her lips as he played.

The lump in his throat reaching softball size, he sat on the creaky bench and set the hymnal on the music rack. It fell open to "Great Is Thy Faithfulness," a longtime family favorite and the first hymn Mom had requested.

It was almost like she was there.

Blowing out a shaky breath and blinking tears from his eyes, he set his fingers on the smooth, firm keys.

His playing was clunky at first, with more sour notes than he'd ever have liked to admit. But by the second verse, the cobwebs had dissipated. His fingers fell back into the dance he'd spent years training them to do.

And then a thin, warbly soprano joined in:

> Join with all nature in manifold witness
> To thy great faithfulness, mercy, and love.

Garrett glanced over his shoulder. His grandmother's eyes were closed, her lashes shiny with tears. She wasn't reading the music or looking at a song sheet. These words, this music, were locked deep in her mind.

No. Not her mind.

Her heart.

That was why they hadn't disappeared.

A surge of gratitude overwhelming his usual self-consciousness, he lifted his voice to join with hers:

All I have needed thy hand hath provided—
Great is thy faithfulness, Lord, unto me!

⇥⇤

*January 30, 1881*

A strong puff of steam and an even stronger fragrance slapped Annabelle's face as she uncovered the pot and gave the stew a final stir. Glancing up, she peered through the snowstorm outside to catch a glimpse of Jack and Oliver, choring in the frozen barn. She was determined to have a hot, delicious meal ready when they returned.

But her other three children had not made that an easy task. Six-year-old Thomas sprawled near the fireplace, nose still red and chafed from a recent illness, stockinged feet hitting the rug with slow, rhythmic thumps. Gray eyes, a gift from his father, scanned the book before him, but the angry slap of each page turn indicated he was still displeased with her decision to keep him inside and away from his usual place beside Oliver and his pa.

His attitude needed correction, but this latest battle of wills with her headstrong son left her too exhausted to do anything but allow for a silent, if uneasy, truce.

"Ma-ma?" A chubby, dimpled hand tugged at Annabelle's skirt.

"Mary, not so close to the stove." Annabelle stepped around her sixteen-month-old on the way to the shelf for a stack of bowls.

"Mama?" Another childish request, this in the more fluent speech of four-year-old Caroline. "Where's Abigail?"

"Ma-ma?" Tiny fists grabbed Annabelle's skirt again.

"In a moment, little one." Annabelle ladled the pungent stew into a bowl. "Caroline, I haven't seen your doll. Where did you play with her last?"

"Ma-ma up." With a mighty yank, Mary pulled herself to standing, knocking Annabelle off-balance and nearly causing her to slop steaming stew onto the toddler's golden curls.

"Mary, please."

Mary's wail rent the air of the cabin, and Annabelle almost tripped over a child once more. Caroline, this time, chestnut braids dangling as she searched for her beloved doll.

Biting back her frustration, Annabelle set the dishes on the table and bent to pick up her youngest, wincing at the pressure against heavy, aching breasts. "Thomas, would you please help Caroline find Abigail?"

The petulant boy looked up, eyes sparking protest.

"*Now*, Thomas." The sharp retort flashed fear across the boy's face, while Mary wailed all the more. Her final nerve dangerously frayed, Annabelle plopped the child into her chair and handed her a slice of fresh bread, then glanced at Thomas, who—thank the Lord—was trotting off toward the bedroom he shared with his siblings, Caroline at his heels.

With a weary sigh that puffed up escaped tendrils of hair, Annabelle turned back to the stove. When had this house gotten so small?

She corrected herself at once. It was a true blessing to have a house of any kind, let alone one that had been built onto time and again by a hardworking husband. It was warm and dry, filled with laughter and love. Yet on days like today, when Thomas was in a mood and Caroline and Mary begged for attention and the weather was such that she couldn't send them all outside, having her offspring confined in such a small space was enough to drive her mad.

Well. It wasn't the small space or the weather driving her mad. Not entirely.

It was the same thing that made her breasts ache. Her stomach roil at the scent of the coffee she poured into Jack's mug. Her eyes pool with tears at the slightest provocation.

It was a good reason, the best possible reason.

Despite her exhaustion, her frustration, she felt a wave of love for the little life growing inside her. Her dresses were already tight around the waist, though she doubted anyone else noticed. Jack certainly hadn't, but he'd been so busy lately, that didn't come as a surprise.

This would, though. And she could hardly wait to tell him.

The door burst open, ushering in a gust of wind and puff of swirling snow along with Jack and Oliver. Mary looked up from her bread and squealed in delight, while a beaming Thomas and Caroline barreled in from the bedroom, Caroline clutching her long-lost doll.

A broad smile melting away lines of fatigue, Jack hung his snow-covered Stetson on the peg beside the door, scooped up Thomas and Caroline, and dropped a kiss atop Mary's curly head.

Adoration squeezed Annabelle's heart. What a wonderful papa he was. To have taken in Oliver—who at thirteen was nearly as tall as she—and raised him as his own, to have showered the same love on his sister-in-law's child as he did his own flesh and blood . . . she would never be able to express how much that meant to her.

And what of her own dear Papa? It had been years since she had a letter. Was he still living?

Mercy. What a thing to wonder about one's father.

Yet that was all it was. Wondering. The anger that once accompanied questions about Papa had lost its edge. Though it surfaced on occasion, it did so faded and fatigued. A faint shadow of its former self.

Children crowded around the table then, and while Jack blessed the food, Annabelle peeked at those five much-loved faces. Another would arrive this summer, while dear Emmaline awaited them at heaven's banquet table.

And none of them would exist if she hadn't come to Kansas. If Papa hadn't left her with Uncle Stephen and Aunt Katherine.

The family joined in a recitation of the Lord's Prayer, and Annabelle's mouth moved as her mind whirled. Though painful, Papa's abandonment had led her here.

To Jack.

To this hard, messy, wonderful adventure of a life. The Lord had indeed wrought beauty from her life's most bitter moments.

"Forgive us our sins; for we also forgive every one that is indebted to us." And when her lips formed the words, realization struck. Somewhere during the last years, in the safety of Jack's love and care, she'd finally forgiven her father.

Peace settled over her soul as Jack ended the prayer and Oliver dove into his dinner. Laughter and chatter quieted to the scrape of spoons against bowls and the crispy crunch of bread crusts, the music of sated appetites and filling bellies.

"Lot of mouths to feed," Jack commented, raising his coffee to his lips.

Annabelle leaned over to cut a chunk of meat for Caroline. "And there'll be another by summer's end." Heart pounding, she awaited his reaction.

Jack paused, mug in midair. His wide-eyed, open-mouthed stare slid down to where the table concealed her midsection. She could almost see the wheels in his head turning, moments from past days that hadn't made sense now settling into certainty.

"For sure now?" Emotion thickened his brogue.

"Sometime in August, I think."

Jack's face split into a broad smile. He rose from his seat. Accompanied by small, questioning gazes and the bang of Mary's spoon on the table, he slipped his hands behind Annabelle's neck and claimed her lips.

Her fingers threaded through the dark hair at his nape, damp from the miserable weather.

"What's happening?" This from the always-inquisitive Thomas.

"Mother and Uncle Jack are kissing," Oliver replied around a mouthful of stew.

"I know that," Thomas shot back. "But why?"

"Because they're in love."

"Wuv," Mary repeated. "Wuv, wuv, wuv."

Jack leaned his forehead against hers, but the coffee on his breath sickened her stomach. Wincing, she turned away.

His callused thumb caressed her cheek. "Are you all right, love?"

She nodded. "The smell of coffee . . ."

"Sorry." Eyes twinkling, Jack covered his mouth with his hand. "'Twas like that with Thomas, if I recall."

"But not with the girls."

"Another boy then?"

She smiled. "Thomas will be thrilled if I'm right. The boys would out-number the girls again."

Jack rewarded her with a lopsided grin, that fallen lock of hair giving him an almost rakish appearance. "The lad's got a competitive streak a mile wide."

"And I wonder where he got it," she teased.

"Haven't any idea." He kissed her cheek, then slid his arm around her shoulders and glanced around the small kitchen. "Well, now. Looks like we might need more room in here."

Her breath caught. Could it finally be time? "Really?"

"You don't think it's a bit cramped?"

Tears stung once more. "Oh, Jack, it is, and I'm so sorry, and I don't want to complain—"

"Annabelle." His gaze held hers. "It's not a complaint. The house has suited our needs, and I'm most grateful, but God's blessed us much in recent years. Our cup's overflowing. So what say after dinner we do some dreaming?"

She laid her head on his shoulder, her heart so full of gratitude and love she almost couldn't speak. "Sometimes I think dreaming is what we do best."

><

With shaking fingers, Sloane keyed the name Domenica Brennan into the genealogy website's search window.

It couldn't be.

Ohio was the wrong state, after all. And Brennan was a fairly common surname.

So it couldn't be.

After a few seconds, a marriage record popped up. One from Cuyahoga County, Ohio. Cleveland.

*Name: Domenica R. Giordano*
*Form Type: Marriage*
*Marriage Date: 6 September 1904*
*Age: 18*
*Gender: Female*
*Birth: Abt 1886*
*Birth Place: Italy*
*Father: Antonio Giordano*
*Mother: Benedetta*
*Spouse Name: John Patrick Brennen*

*Spouse Age: 23*
*Gender: Male*
*Birth Year: 1881*
*Birth Place: Kansas*
*Spouse Father: John Brennen*
*Spouse Mother: Anna Collins*

John Brennen? Anna Collins?

No. It couldn't be.

But Jack Brennan's given name was John. And Annabelle could easily have sounded like "Anna," particularly if the room was crowded or the registrar was in a hurry. And the last name could be a simple misspelling, an all too common discrepancy.

It *couldn't* be.

But it had to be. How many Brennans were born in 1881 in Kansas? To parents with similar names? And a mother whose maiden name was Collins?

Hope searing her heart, Sloane reached for the diary. Annabelle was pregnant at the end of January 1881. She suspected a boy.

Confirmation could lie within these yellowed, time-softened pages.

An entry toward the end stole her breath. One dated August 9, 1881, in a bold, slanted scrawl that didn't belong to Annabelle.

> *My beloved wife gave birth last night to a healthy, good-sized boy, just past nine o'clock. It was a difficult birth—for a few terrible hours I feared the worst. But the Lord saw fit to spare me loss— God be praised!—and sweet Annabelle is still with us. Though she is weak, the sparkle has returned to her eyes, and Stephen assures us she will recover fully. May the Lord answer our continued prayers.*
>
> *We named the boy John Patrick—John after both his father and mine, and Patrick after hers. He has a full head of fiery red hair and a temper to match.*
>
> *Consider yourself warned, love. I told you we'd have a redhead.*

Sloane read the short entry over and over until tears blurred the faded ink and her hands shook so badly she nearly dropped the precious book. No wonder these people had reached through time and grabbed her soul.

Though she'd yet to connect Annabelle with Garrett's family, she'd found treasure far greater. Proven in Jack Brennan's own hand.

John Patrick Brennan, husband to Domenica—to Nonna—was her great-great-grandfather.

Which meant Sloane's family—her blood, her DNA—came directly from Annabelle Collins Brennan.

# CHAPTER SEVENTEEN

SLOANE GAVE A few firm raps to the weathered farmhouse door, then stepped back and waited. The afternoon air was warm. Heavy with humidity. Gusty winds tugged her clothes and tossed her hair into disarray. Her phone buzzed in her pocket, and she pulled it out to glance at the screen.

*The National Weather Service has issued a tornado watch for portions of central and south-central Kansas . . .*

Sloane chuckled. The weather-heads had yammered about today's setup for over a week. Something about cold fronts and dry lines in springtime always got the TV meteorologists so riled up their hair almost moved. And the more they hyped a potentially dramatic weather event, the less dramatic it usually turned out to be.

Today looked like one of those anticlimactic days. Despite the reminder that conditions were ripe for tornadoes, the sky showed nothing but a towering pile of cotton-ball clouds against a pale blue backdrop. With a slight roll of her eyes, Sloane slipped her phone in her pocket and rapped on the door again.

No one answered, but Garrett's car was out front, and faint whispers of music through the door told her someone was home. Gentle pressure against the creaky front door proved it unlocked, and the music swelled. Tinkly chords on an out-of-tune piano underpinned a warbly soprano and a tenor that, though pitchy in spots, was rich and warm.

She rounded the corner and—that was Garrett playing. And singing along with Rosie. Strong hands drew the strains of "Amazing Grace" from the depths of that dusty old upright; his cello-like voice floated on top.

Sloane wrapped her arms around herself, warmed by the homey scene. *I play a little piano*, he'd said. Ha. To play that fluidly would take years of lessons or a boatload of natural talent. Probably both. Eyes closed, he swayed slightly with the rhythm, and the words to the old hymn slipped dreamily from his lips, as if the music he pulled from those rickety keys had carried him along with it.

She'd known for a while that Mr. All Business had a heart in there. Now here it was, on full display, and it filled her own to the point of precious pain. This side of Garrett she'd never seen was bringing up feelings she hadn't known in quite some time. If ever.

Could she be . . . ?

No. Not this soon. She couldn't be.

Could she?

As the hymn approached its end, the truth settled into her heart with the gentle fluttering and folding of wings.

She could very easily be falling in love with Garrett Anderson.

→←

"That was beautiful."

Garrett startled at the words. It sounded like a low, husky version of Sloane's voice, behind him to his left. But she wasn't here. Was she?

Still enveloped in a musical fog, he turned, and there she was. Real as anything.

"Oh, Sloane. Hi."

Her dimples deepened. "Hi."

"When did you get here?"

"Couple minutes ago."

"Couple minutes ago." He'd become a parrot.

"Relax." Her hand landed on his shoulder, warm through his shirt. "You sounded wonderful."

"Are you kidding, Auntie Boop?" Grandma piped up. "He sounded sensational." She tossed him a wink he'd expect from a much younger, more flirtatious person.

He squirmed on the piano bench. "Thank you."

Sloane sat beside him, her concerned gaze flitting over his face. "Are you okay?"

"Yeah." He cleared his throat. "It's just . . ."

"Your mom?"

The weight of grief settled in his chest, and he fixed his attention on the keyboard. The ordered pattern of ebony and ivory.

Sloane gripped his hand. "I'm sorry." Her voice was low and soothing. "I can't imagine how painful that was, or how hard it must be to play now. I'm honored to have heard you."

He stole a quick glance toward Grandma. As confused as she'd been today, he didn't want to take any chances, but she seemed content watching finches flit around outside, so he gave in to his heart and pulled Sloane close.

When she slid her arm around his waist and rested her head on his shoulder, he blinked in surprise at how right it felt. The warmth of her body snuggled against his. The sweet fragrance of her shampoo. The whisper of her thumb over the back of his hand.

And yet. He didn't live in Wichita. She did.

And he didn't have room in his life for the kind of relationship he wanted with her. Not now. Not until Grandma was settled and his career more established. Sloane couldn't be more right, but the timing couldn't be more wrong.

She stirred in his arms, and he pulled her closer. He didn't want to lose her. He couldn't lose her.

He'd sort out the details later. *You're smart, Garrett. You'll figure it out. You always do.*

He feathered a kiss to the top of Sloane's head. "Thank you."

The door banged open, a stark contrast to the silent way Sloane had slipped inside. Lauren appeared with an armload of bags from the drugstore, and Sloane lifted her head from his shoulder.

"Hey, all." Depositing the bags on the sofa, Lauren scooped up a handful of windblown blonde hair and attempted to corral it into a ponytail.

"You get caught in a hurricane?" Garrett asked.

"Starting to get a little stormy out there." She quirked a brow. "Of course, it looks like you've been too busy to notice."

Garrett tossed his sister a withering glare, but she wasn't wrong about the weather. Though it had been sunny when he arrived after lunch, the western skies were now thick with dark, rain-swollen clouds.

"You probably aren't aware we're under a tornado watch either." Lauren gave her ponytail a final tug.

Garrett reached for his phone, neglected on the coffee table. Sure enough, he'd received a couple weather alerts during his private concert with Grandma.

Sloane waved a hand. "They always go overboard with the gloom and doom. The first 'severe weather alert day' of any spring is always so melodramatic."

"Especially since it's so late this year." Lauren glanced at the clock. "You give Grandma her meds yet?"

Garrett frowned. "It's three already?"

"I don't believe it. Mark this down. Mr. Punctuality lost track of time."

"Grow up." Grinning, he stood. "I'll get her meds."

"I got it." Lauren was already helping Grandma up from her chair. "She's supposed to take them with food, and you look like you were busy. Or were about to be." She gave a suggestive wiggle of her eyebrows on her way to the kitchen.

Resisting a juvenile urge to stick his tongue out at his sister, he turned to Sloane. "So what was it you wanted to tell me about? Your text said you had some developments."

She retrieved a colorful tote bag from a doily-covered end table, then pulled from its depths a piece of paper not unlike a March Madness bracket. "Ta-da."

He glanced at the names and dates covering the paper. "Is that a family tree?"

"Yep. For Jack and Annabelle and their kids. I finally got enough info to put one together."

A web of lines radiated from Jack's and Annabelle's names at the top. "Wow. That's a lot of kids."

"They ended up with six plus Oliver. Just like Jack predicted. And this guy is of particular importance." Her fingertip tapped a name amid the sea of lines. "John Patrick, Jack and Annabelle's fourth child. He was born in

1881 and went to optometry school in Cleveland, where he married this woman." Her finger slid to the name joined to John Patrick's.

"Domenica Giordano. Sounds Italian."

"Domenica's family came from Sicily when she was a toddler. She and John Patrick had four kids of their own."

Garrett squinted at the names below John Patrick and Domenica, all in Sloane's slightly messy cursive. "Four girls?"

"Four girls." Sloane's voice trembled. "And one of them—not sure which one—"

"Is related to me somehow?"

"No." Frank, gold-flecked brown eyes held his. "She's related to me."

Garrett's jaw unhinged. "Wait a minute. Jack and Annabelle are *your* ancestors?"

"Uh-huh. Isn't that crazy?"

"That *is* crazy. And it's huge for you. You found your family. Your blood family." He folded her into his arms for a quick embrace, then peeled his attention from her to the paper. "How'd you figure all this out?"

"My birth mother sent me an old letter from her great-grandmother. Here." Sloane pulled out her phone and held it for him to see, the slanted, old-fashioned handwriting an odd contrast to the sleek modernity of her phone. "Look at the signature."

"Domenica Brennan. Wow."

"I found a marriage certificate and some census records to prove it. This is the same person." The tremor returned to Sloane's voice. "Jack and Annabelle are my great-great-great-grandparents."

Garrett squeezed her shoulder. "Can this information help you identify your birth mother?"

She shook her head, giving off a new wave of fruity fragrance. "I traced the daughters as far forward as I could, but since I don't know my mother's name, I can't figure out which of them is her grandmother. And they all stayed in Cleveland, so that's no help."

"Still, though. Jack and Annabelle, they're your family."

"They're my family." Her wistful gaze caressed the family tree, then rose to his face. Fragility was in every inch of her tremulous smile, but her eyes were nothing but strength. That combination must be his kryptonite, because he suddenly wanted nothing more than to kiss that delicate smile, to capture those gorgeous lips with his own—

"Wait." He stopped just short of her mouth. "Are *we* related? Please tell me we're not."

"Nope. Not by blood anyway."

Cool relief washed through him as she stretched up and pecked him on the cheek, then flipped the paper over to reveal more lines and brackets. "I got all this off a couple genealogy websites. Here's your grandma. And if you follow the generations back . . ."

He scanned the list. None of these names meant a thing in the world to him, but all these people were instrumental in his existence.

Wait. That one he knew. "Oliver?"

"Yup. Jack's nephew. His sister-in-law's son."

Garrett frowned. "So if Oliver is my ancestor and John Patrick is yours, what's that make you and me?"

"Absolutely nothing." The truth pulled that delicious mouth into a broad smile that sent warmth buzzing to the tips of his toes.

"Good. Because I'd like for us to be . . . something else, I think."

The look in Sloane's eyes answered his unasked question, so he bent forward and claimed her beautiful lips.

She wrapped her arms around his neck, and her contented murmur shot straight to his heart. He pulled her closer. They really did fit well together, didn't they? Like two pieces of a puzzle. Two halves of a whole. Two—

"Hey, guys, did anyb—oh. Sorry."

Lauren's voice shattered both mood and moment. Garrett jerked away, scrubbing the back of his hand over his mouth in case Sloane had left him a lipstick souvenir.

"No, you're fine." He glanced Lauren's way, but instead of the mischievous smile he expected, her brow was creased with concern. "Is everything all right?"

"I'm not sure." Lauren stepped to the window and brushed back the curtain. "I thought I heard tornado sirens."

Over the hammer of his pulse and the thrum of his need to be back in Sloane's arms . . . yes. There it was. The unmistakable, chilling wail.

Confirming what he heard, his phone buzzed. Other buzzes echoed around the room as he reached for it and scrolled through the weather-speak on his screen.

*Tornado warning . . . northwestern Sedgwick County . . . rotation . . . radar indicated . . .*

Lauren turned on the TV, and Garrett swiveled toward it, his arm draped over Sloane's shoulders. On-screen, a dark-haired meteorologist chattered anxiously, pointing at an angry-looking red blob on the radar.

But something about that meteorologist caught his eye too.

"Lauren? Isn't that . . . ?"

"Carter Douglas. Yeah." Her voice was flat, her face similarly devoid of expression.

Sloane leaned in. "Who's Carter Douglas?"

"Lauren's old boyfriend," Garrett said softly.

"You okay?" Sloane moved to Lauren's side and laid a supportive hand on her shoulder.

Lauren stared, unblinking, at the screen. "I don't wanna talk about it."

"Good. Because look at the storm track." Sloane pointed at the tele-vised list of locations and times. "This thing'll be on top of us in about eight minutes."

Heart pounding, Garrett sprang into action. "I'll get Grandma."

But Lauren was already halfway to the kitchen. "I've got her."

"Do you guys have a basement or anything?" Sloane asked.

"There's a cellar. Nothing to write home about, but it'll do." What else did he need to do? Tornado warnings weren't as common up in Kansas City. In fact, the only time he'd ever taken cover from an imminent threat was here, the summer after second grade. They'd all huddled under blankets in the dank cellar, Grandpa spinning tall tales and acting like nothing in the world was wrong, even as the storm raged outside—

"Blankets. We need blankets." He yanked a red-and-blue crocheted afghan off the back of the couch and handed it to Sloane, then grabbed the cushions for good measure.

"What are you doing?" she asked.

"We'll want to protect our heads just to be safe." Permission asked and obtained with a glance, he dumped the pile of cushions into her arms and headed for the stairs. "I think there's a flashlight in the hall closet."

Lauren tore into the living room, her face pale. "I can't find Grandma."

"What?" He paused, one foot on the second step. "What do you mean?"

"Exactly what I said. I can't find her."

Anxiety pricking his chest, Garrett followed his sister to the kitchen. The soft thumps of pillows and blankets on the sofa and rapid footsteps at his back told him Sloane was close behind.

"She was right there. Finishing her snack." Lauren indicated the empty space at the table.

A half-eaten turnover sat on a plate beside a mostly full cup of coffee and three pills of various sizes and colors. But Grandma's chair was pushed back, and she was nowhere to be seen.

"Is she in the cellar?" The siren's wail was even louder here in the kitchen. If Grandma had heard that, she might've had the presence of mind to take shelter.

"I already checked."

"Grandma?" Garrett peeked around the corner into the half bath, but it was empty.

"Rosie?" Sloane called from the laundry room.

He flipped on the light in his grandmother's bedroom. "Grandma?"

But the only voice he heard was Lauren's, shrill and panicked. "I don't know what happened. I was only gone for a second."

Sloane gestured toward the kitchen stairs. "Think she could've gone up there?"

"She'd have had to climb over the safety gate," Garrett replied. "Or she could've unlocked it."

"I'll check." Sloane's footsteps thudded up the stairs.

"Okay, Lo, start from the beginning." He looked between the bed and the wall—no Grandma—and forced calm into his voice. "You brought her into the kitchen and gave her another turnover and some coffee."

"And her pills," came the shaky reply. "But I forgot the new blood pressure one, so I went back for it."

Grandma probably wasn't in the bedroom closet, but he checked anyway. "What happened next?"

"I brought her the pill and put it with the others. Then we heard the thunder. I looked out the window and told her it seemed a little stormy outside."

"Grandma?" He peeked into the laundry room. Sloane already looked there, but he needed to see for himself.

"And then I thought I heard sirens, so I came in to ask you about it, and by the time I came back, she—" Lauren broke off with a terrified gasp. "Oh no."

He whirled to face her. "What?"

"The last thing she heard me say was . . ."

His stomach dropped. "Outside."

Lauren nodded.

Garrett glanced at the dark clouds churning overhead. Then he tore out the back door and into the gale.

# CHAPTER EIGHTEEN

SLOANE BURST FROM the kitchen into a midafternoon dark enough to pass for evening. The dissonant moan of sirens blended with howling wind and frantic cries of Rosie's name. A putrid greenish-gray sky roiled overhead, the kind of sky common sense said they had no business being beneath.

But common sense had no place right now. Rosie was out here, somewhere under this sinister sky. She must be confused. Terrified. Sloane's gaze darted around the yard, her heart pounding frantic prayers.

"Where do you think she went?" Garrett peered between the shrubs along the south side of the house.

"How should I know?" Lauren tossed back on a vicious blast of wind. "She's in her eighties. She can't have gone far."

"Well, do you see her nearby?"

"No, do you?"

"Garrett. Lauren." Sloane stepped between the warring siblings. "We'll have a better chance if we split up."

"You're right." Lauren sprinted toward the driveway. "I'll check the front."

"I'll get the back." Garrett barreled toward the copse of trees by the creek.

Sloane stayed near the house, peeking around the east corner as fat raindrops smacked her forearms. An old clothesline poked through overgrown trees, and a rusty wheelbarrow lay on its side, half hidden in a patch of brush speckled with pale green leaves.

No sign of Rosie. But Lauren was probably right. At her age, she couldn't have gone too far.

Rain rendering her glasses useless, Sloane slipped them off, jogged to the blurry red barn, and pushed the door open.

"Rosie?" Her eyes took a moment to adjust to the near-pitch blackness inside. Polishing her glasses on her shirttail, she put them on, and the blurs crystallized into an ancient, dust-covered tractor and various other tools she couldn't identify. The barn smelled of hay and horses, though she doubted either had inhabited the structure in years.

No Rosie here either.

Adrenaline sluicing through her veins, she shut the barn door, slipped off her glasses, and darted through intensifying rain toward a small toolshed. A thick, gnarled tree root caught her by the toe and yanked her off-balance. She braced herself against the rough bark, regained her bearings, and—

There. A flash of pink through the cracked doorway of the toolshed.

Pink. Like Rosie's sweater.

Sloane jogged the rest of the way and shoved the shed door open. Lightning zigzagged through the sky and lit up the dank interior. And there, cowering in the corner, was Garrett's grandmother.

"Rosie. Oh, you poor thing." Nearly sobbing with relief, Sloane pulled Rosie close and whispered words of comfort into snowy, hair spray–scented curls.

"Auntie Boop." Rosie clutched Sloane's shoulder and buried her head in the folds of fabric. "Thank the Lord you're here."

The door banged open, startling her and making Rosie jump.

"Grandma. Thank God." Garrett turned to shout over his shoulder. "Lauren! In the shed!"

Rather than look relieved to see her grandson, though, Rosie trembled all the more.

"Rosie?" Sloane sought her gaze. "It's just Garrett. Lauren's coming."

Pale blue eyes and a blank expression peered back at her.

"Orrin's here too," she hastened to add.

"Who?" Rosie looked at Garrett, but no recognition flickered across her face. Sloane's stomach churned.

Another thunderclap announced Lauren's arrival.

"Grandma. There you are. Listen, we've got to get you inside. There's a storm coming."

Rosie glanced toward Lauren, then back at Sloane. "A storm?"

"Not a bad one." Sloane hated to lie, but she didn't want to worsen Rosie's panic. "I think we'd all be safer in the cellar, though."

A wall of wind slammed the side of the shed, and rain drummed the metal roof. Rosie glanced around, eyes wide with fright.

"It's okay, Toots." Sloane gave a wink and a jaunty fluff of her hair, as she imagined someone who answered to the name of Auntie Boop might do. "We'll help you get down there, quick as a whistle."

As if to emphasize her point, the wind grew louder, and with it the telltale pop of hailstones.

"O—okay," Rosie agreed.

Garrett didn't waste a moment. Closing the gap between them, he scooped his grandmother into his arms. "Come on."

"I'm right behind you, Toots," Sloane reassured Rosie. "You'll be just fine."

Lauren tugged open the shed door, and Garrett darted into the deluge. Sloane ran close behind, shielding her head awkwardly with one hand. Cold rain drenched her clothes; small hailstones stung her skin and bounced at her feet.

Within seconds, they reached the stone steps of the cellar. Lauren yanked the door open, and Sloane held it until everyone was safely through. Inside, she pulled her glasses from her pocket and slid them on, but all that did was make the darkness less fuzzy.

"I never got that flashlight," came Garrett's voice behind her. "But I think Grandpa left a lantern down here somewhere."

"Here." Sloane fumbled in her pocket for her cell phone. Good. Still dry. She switched on the flashlight, and a narrow beam of bright light split the blackness. It rested on wooden shelves, doubtless stacked in decades past with the farm's bounty. Ready to see the family—the Brennan family, *her* family—through another prairie winter.

"Here it is." Lauren stretched on tiptoe and retrieved an ancient-looking green camping lantern from a shelf. "Let's pray this thing still works."

It did. Breathing silent thanks, Sloane switched off the flashlight and tucked her phone into her pocket.

"Grandpa had us take cover over here." Garrett guided his grandma to a corner and helped her to a sitting position. Lauren knelt beside Rosie and wrapped an arm around her, while Sloane crouched on the other side of Garrett.

His skin seemed to glow in the lantern light. His clothes were soaked with rain, and a chunk of wet hair draped over his forehead. When he quirked a smile and pulled her close, her chest filled so full of love for him she was certain her body couldn't contain it all. The cellar might not even have room for it.

"The wind stopped," Lauren announced from Garrett's opposite side. "Guys, the storm's passed."

But Sloane's ears filled, then popped, and she knew. It hadn't passed at all.

As if on cue, the wind picked up, but it sounded different this time. A waterfall, a steady whoosh at a constant crescendo, peppered with the thump of her heartbeat. The whooshing waterfall grew louder and louder until it was right on top of them.

"This is it," came Lauren's quiet, tremulous voice.

Garrett pulled Sloane closer. "I thought it was supposed to sound like a freight train."

The whoosh became an angry hiss, and Sloane's ears popped again. "Me too." *God, please keep us safe. Please keep us safe. Please keep us safe.* It was all she could think to pray.

Crashes and bangs punctuated the shrieking wind, a stark contrast to the heavy, humid calm inside the musty cellar. Nothing within these earthen walls moved, but above it sounded like a giant, demonic snake had been let loose to wreak havoc across the farm. Something cracked, then thudded, and Sloane's mind spun nearly as fast as the storm. Was it the barn being torn apart? The shed where they'd found Rosie? The house?

*Dear God, please. Not the house.*

To her relief, the storm began a slow yet certain retreat. The hissing lessened. The thumps and bangs came less often, then stopped altogether. The wind died down.

And then it was over. Calm. As though nothing had happened.

Seconds. Mere seconds.

But it felt like a year.

"Is it over? It's over. Isn't it?" Lauren's shaky voice echoed the trembling in Sloane's legs as she cautiously stood.

"I think so." Garrett got to his feet, and together they helped Rosie stand.

"Goodness, that was a doozy," the older woman exclaimed.

Sloane managed a smile. "A doozy" was the only way to put it. And yet they were all in one piece. God had kept them safe. Tension melted into gratitude that warmed her fear-chilled hands.

Lauren pushed the door open, and Sloane's eyes ached as bright light spilled into the cellar. As dark as the sky had been moments ago, now there were shadows. A weak one hovered on the stone steps. One that looked like . . . a tree?

Whew. That meant at least one still stood.

She climbed from the cellar on Jell-O legs to a landscape littered with branches, along with a few hailstones and a handful of shingles. The largest of the downed limbs lay directly between the house and the shed where they'd found Rosie, its dark, leafy tips standing out against the pale, exposed wood on the jagged end. That must've been the loud crack. Sloane shuddered, thinking how near they'd come to meeting that tree limb up close.

But the house still stood, stately and white. A regal serenity radiated from the whole structure, foundation to rooftop. A quiet triumph at having withstood yet another prairie assault. The only damage looked to be a shutter from one of the second-floor bedrooms, which now dangled from a single hinge.

The image blurred with a flood of grateful tears.

Her family's house still stood.

"Looks like we escaped the worst of it." Garrett stopped beside Sloane and slid his arm around her waist. As Lauren guided Rosie to the kitchen door, he sighed and kissed the top of her head. "Are you all right?"

She blinked away her tears. Yes. And no. Not really.

Because in the cellar, right before the storm hit, when she looked into his eyes . . .

She loved him.

Despite all her baggage and her damage and her fear of loving him—of loving anyone—she loved him.

"I think so." Her fingers skimmed his cheekbone. "Are you?"

His response was a fierce kiss. One that stole breath, stole sense and reason and thoughts of anything except him. The tension of his hand on her skin. The heat of his chest against hers. The desperate movement of his mouth as he clung to her and drank deeply, as though slaking some bone-deep thirst.

It was too much, this kiss.

And yet it would never be enough.

Breathless, he pulled back, his eyes a deep sapphire. "I am now that I know you're all right."

Shaky, her legs rubbery, she slipped her hands along his shoulders. "Good."

And then she returned to the well from which she'd just drunk so deeply.

><

"Good night, Orrin."

Grandma's sleepy voice drifted from her nest of pillows and blankets, and her eyes slid closed.

From where he sat on the edge of the bed, Garrett leaned forward to kiss her forehead. "Good night, Rosie."

After Sloane left for the evening, it had taken a while to get Grandma settled, what with the trauma of the tornado. She'd wanted to talk about it but couldn't summon the right words, which sent her into a tailspin of panic and tears. It took much pacing, patient negotiation, and a bowl of vanilla ice cream to get her calmed down and into bed.

When Grandma's breathing evened and slowed, Garrett carefully stood, pulled the blankets to her chin, and crept from the room. A soft hallway lamp illuminated the creaky wooden staircase.

Time had worn the banister to a smooth patina. Striped wallpaper bore nail scars and faded spots where the gallery of family photos had been displayed. This staircase had carried his ancestors up and down, likely for generations. Pioneers. Flappers. Veterans of two world wars. His grandparents.

Mom.

It all could've been obliterated this afternoon. More than a century of history wiped out in seconds. Instead, the twister had passed to the north, its short-lived path damaging only a few outbuildings at a neighboring farm. No one had been injured. And the house still stood.

But would it survive his plan? A plan their frantic afternoon had proven more necessary than ever?

He switched on the kitchen light, but Lauren's startled yelp made him switch it right back off again.

"Sorry, didn't know you were in here."

"'S okay."

She sat at the table, bathed in a pool of moonlight. A cabinet door, slightly ajar, cast an eerie shadow over the domed plastic lid of . . . was that a cake?

Chocolate, looked like. With frosting and everything. The kind of cake you bought at the grocery store, that was patently not paleo, keto, gluten free, or anything else his nutrition-obsessed sister would ordinarily eat.

Yet there she was, shoveling it into her mouth at a frenzied pace.

Alarm churned in his chest. "Lauren?" She hadn't done this for over a decade.

"Don't judge," she snapped.

"I won't. Long as you're willing to share." He retrieved a fork from the silverware drawer and sat across from Lauren, who wordlessly slid the cake toward him.

He sank his fork into it and fished out a bite. "Grandma's finally asleep."

"Good."

"Took a while."

"I'll bet." Just like it had been while watching her ex-boyfriend give the weather forecast, Lauren's voice was flat. Emotionless. She shoveled bite after bite of cake into her mouth but gave no indication of even the slightest enjoyment. And after all these years of dedication—and deprivation—she *should* enjoy it.

He placed his hand over hers. "Lauren, I—"

"I know." She slammed her fork down. "You don't have to lecture me or rub it in or be all high-and-mighty big brother, because I know, okay? I was irresponsible. I left her alone, and she wandered off. But she's never done that before, not even once, and I—"

"Hey, *hey*." He squeezed her hand. Rant stilled, she looked up at him, caution and challenge sparking in shadowed eyes.

"I'm not blaming you. Not in the slightest. Promise. Because it's not you. It's her disease."

Lauren took another bite of cake, though at a more reasonable speed. She actually seemed to taste it this time.

"I've been thinking," she said. "A lot. About how Grandma was. Y'know . . . before."

"Yeah." Garrett stuffed more cake into his mouth. He'd been trying not to remember. It was too painful.

"Didn't matter what time of day or night, she'd be waiting for us at the front door." Lauren's voice held a smile. "And the second we got there, she'd hurry off to the kitchen to pull a chocolate cake out of the oven."

Ah. That explained Lauren's choice of comfort food.

It was good cake.

But nowhere near as good as Grandma's.

"The local news would always be on in the background, remember?"

Warm memories tugged at the corners of Garrett's mouth. "And Grandpa always pulled out his grouch act and pretended to be annoyed that we were interrupting his program."

"But then he'd pick us up and spin us around in circles."

Garrett chuckled. "I think he regretted that decision the time you had stomach flu and nobody had any idea."

"I'm sure he did." Lauren laughed, but her laughter quickly dissolved into a sob. She looked across the table with tear-filled eyes. "It's time, isn't it? For us to move her, I mean."

Garrett's heart broke, even as relief flooded in. "Yes. It's time."

Her tears spilled over, and he got up and wrapped her in a hug.

"I miss Mom," she sobbed against his chest. "And Daddy. And Grandpa. And Grandma. I miss them all."

The litany of their losses brought a lump to his throat. "I miss them too. So much."

"And this house is all we have left of them." She sniffed. "Grandma didn't even remember you today. Not as you, not as Grandpa, not as anyone."

And that blank look had scared Garrett to his core.

"So . . . it's time." Lauren's voice was quiet but resolute.

"It's time."

Lauren's heartbreak stung his eyes. But gratitude mingled with the grief. Finally, she saw the truth that moving their grandmother to a skilled nursing facility was the only choice. Finally, she understood.

He could only hope and pray that Grandma would understand too.

# CHAPTER NINETEEN

*September 30, 1882*

ANNABELLE SNIPPED ANOTHER strip of muslin and added it to the growing pile on the worktable in Uncle Stephen's spare bedroom. Just this summer, Jack and Oliver had helped build this room, a space for patients requiring overnight observation and care.

She never imagined Jack would be its first occupant.

He was still asleep in the bed behind her, though his increased tossing and occasional moans indicated he'd awaken soon. Dread knotted her stomach, and she snipped more quickly. When he awoke, they'd need to redress his burns.

A sudden pop split the air, jolting her with terror and sending her scissors clattering to the wooden floor.

*It's only the fireplace, you silly goose.* The logs shifted and settled, as if to chide her foolishness.

Trembling, she bent to retrieve the scissors, the coppery taste of fear washing through her mouth. How long would something so safe, so necessary, make her want to curl up in a ball and hide like a terrified child?

Of course, there was a world of difference between a friendly home fire and the frenzied fury of a prairie wildfire. She'd learned that all too well Wednesday afternoon. Jack and the neighbor men had fought to beyond exhaustion, beating at the flames with wet sacks and blankets, but their valiant efforts proved useless against the ferocious wind. Annabelle and the children had made trip after trip to the creek, soaking the parched ground around their little cabin in hopes of persuading the ravenous flames to feed elsewhere.

In the end, only the cabin was left.

They'd lost the barn.

Two-thirds of the stock and most of the chickens.

The seed for next spring.

The half-finished house on which Jack had spent every spare minute.

Years of toil incinerated in moments.

Though she longed to weep at the enormity of the loss, Annabelle refused to allow the luxury of self-pity. Their family was intact. Their children unharmed. Their home spared. And though Jack's hands and arms bore blistered burns and his lungs struggled to clear the smoke he'd inhaled, he was alive. Uncle Stephen reassured them that, in time, his damaged limbs should regain full function.

A quiet knock came at the door, and her uncle stepped inside. "Is he awake?"

"Not yet." She added another strip of muslin to the pile.

Uncle Stephen glanced at the ticking clock on the mantel. "I'm afraid we can't wait any longer. Perhaps he'll sleep through it."

"Perhaps." A fanciful thought, and they both knew it. But her uncle was right. To prevent infection, it had to be done.

Swallowing hard, Annabelle picked up the bandages and the little dish of pungent salve they'd apply and stepped to the bed, where Uncle Stephen took up residence on the opposite side.

He eyed her over his wire-rimmed spectacles as he spooned a little brandy into Jack's barely open mouth. "You needn't stay. I can manage."

She shook her head. "Jack needs me."

"All right." Uncle Stephen squared his shoulders and slipped into his professional façade, but it took a beat or two longer than usual, as it always did when the patient was family.

The work began, and with it the heart-wrenching moans from Jack. Gentle as could be, Uncle Stephen removed the bandages, snipped away dead skin, and applied the salve, but even slight contact with the burns was excruciating.

This was why they were staying here rather than at home.

So the children wouldn't witness their father's agony.

Finally, mercifully, Uncle Stephen finished and slipped from the room. Her legs wobbly, Annabelle sank onto the bed beside Jack and looked into eyes almost ebony with pain.

"It's over." She stroked his sweat-soaked hair with a shaky hand, speaking as much to herself as to him. "It's all over. You were very brave."

She winced at the words, something she might say to the children. Jack must've thought so too, because he grunted and closed his eyes.

Annabelle dipped a cloth in the cool water of the washbasin and smoothed it over her husband's pale, stubbled face. The fire had singed off his beard, at first glance making him look younger. But the fan of lines beside his eyes, the defeat etched around his mouth, aged him at least a decade.

"Uncle Stephen says you're healing nicely. No sign of infection."

"Good." His voice was still thick and heavy from smoke.

"You'll make a full recovery in time."

Jack glanced at his hands and forearms, swathed in fresh muslin. "Then as soon as these useless things will let me, I'm writing to my brother."

"Robert?" The two hadn't spoken in ages. Some falling-out upon which Jack refused to elaborate. "Why?"

"The folks say he's doing well for himself. Perhaps he'll rent us some of his land."

Her fingers tightened on the wet cloth as she trailed it down to the hollow of his cheekbone. Robert was in Wisconsin. What was Jack saying?

"Or perhaps we can live in town. I could find a job."

Her mouth fell open. "A job doing what?"

Anger sparked in his eyes. "So you think there's nothing I can do then? That the fire left me a cripple? Is that what you're saying?"

"That's not what I'm saying at all."

"You implied it." He turned his face to the wall.

Mercy. Her nearly thirty-seven-year-old husband was acting like fourteen-year-old Oliver, all sullen and surly.

Setting the cloth aside, she swallowed her irritation and breathed calm into her words. "All I meant was I can't picture you doing the same thing day after day, working your fingers to the bone for someone else's dreams."

Jack made a noise, half laugh, half cough, and all bitterness. "And what good is working for my own?"

She scanned his face. Though he occasionally lapsed into dark moods, she'd never seen him quite like this.

"This country took Sarah." His voice was rough yet quiet. "Our son. It tried to take Oliver. It took Emmaline. It nigh took you when you birthed John Patrick."

The pain in his eyes tore at her heart.

"And now it's taken our barn. Our stock. Our house. Our dream. Every time I raise my head, this country kicks me in the teeth. Perhaps a stronger man could tough it out. A better man could overcome the odds. But I'm not that man. I can't do this anymore, love. I'm not strong enough."

"Oh, Jack." Aching for him, she bent forward and laid her cheek against his. She wanted to believe this was the influence of the brandy, but Jack had never spoken like this before, and Uncle Stephen had given the usual dose. "You're merely exhausted. You're merely in pain."

"I'm not merely anything." His brogue rumbled against her chest. "I'm a man who's smart enough to know when he's licked."

All the breath left her lungs. Jack licked? Never. *He can't really believe that, Lord. Can he?*

"So that's it then?" She pulled back. "You're giving up?"

His mouth twisted in a parody of a smile. "There's a certain nobility in no longer bashing one's head against a brick wall, don't you think?"

"Is this truly what you want?"

"Does it matter?" His inky eyes wouldn't meet hers but instead stared up at the ceiling, blinking fast, the muscle in his jaw twitching in steady rhythm. "What I want is for us to survive. To thrive. To see you and the children have the life you deserve. Not . . . this." He spread his bandaged hands.

"I've never needed material things to be—"

"There's a difference between tea cozies and fripperies and the security of knowing where your next meal's to come from." His voice contained a steely edge she'd never heard before. "Have you forgotten the grasshopper plague in '74? The blizzards? The winter we all nearly froze?"

"But we survived all that."

"This country's not fit for man or beast. Certainly not for our children. They deserve better. You deserve better."

She rested her hand lightly atop his bandaged ones. "Do you sense God leading us away from here? Have you prayed about it?"

Tears swam in his eyes. "I've prayed and begged and cried out until I'm hoarse, and he says nothing. Silence. I'd like to say I know he hasn't turned his face from me, that he's still present with me . . . but I can't." His voice broke. "And I think it'll be the death of me."

He crumbled then, and with a whisper of his name, she cradled her tireless, indomitable rock of a husband against her chest and let him weep for layer upon layer of loss. His Sarah. His son. Their daughter.

His dreams.

Leaving was the last thing she wanted. They'd been hard-hit to be sure, but they weren't starting from nothing. They had friends here. Family. The church. The mere idea of severing all those ties, of leaving home . . . she couldn't imagine it.

But that wasn't the cry of her heart, the aching groan of a prayer she heaved toward the heavens.

It was for God to make her broken husband whole again.

⊁⊰

"Look at her."

Garrett followed Lauren's gaze across the ornate sitting room in the memory care unit at Plaza de Paz, and there sat Grandma in a plush blue chair near the fireplace, chatting with a couple other snowy-haired ladies. One of them leaned over, a conspiratorial gleam in her eyes, and Grandma's Texas-sized smile turned to a laugh. The hooting, whooping laugh lodged in his childhood memories.

The one he hadn't heard since Grandpa died.

He looped his arm around Lauren's shoulders and squeezed tight. Grandma was . . . happy.

From the moment Garrett arranged her tour, he'd prepared for all the possible reactions. Confusion, absolutely. Disgust, a definite possibility. Utter heartbreak, the one he'd dreaded most.

But he hadn't expected happiness.

Lauren slid her arm around his waist. "It never occurred to me how lonely she must've been since Grandpa passed. But it should have. Remember how they were always running off to some card game or bowling tournament? Mom told me they even used to vacation with other families. Why didn't we think of this sooner?"

He had. But there was no advantage in belaboring the point. Instead, he dropped a kiss onto Lauren's head. "What matters is we're doing it now."

Perky high heels clicked on the tile floor, and Julia, the admissions coordinator, strode toward them.

"So what do we think?" she asked, her smile enormous.

"I think she likes it." Lauren beamed and made a gesture oddly reminiscent of jazz hands. "Yay!"

"Yay!" Julia's bracelets clanked as she echoed the gesture.

Garrett wasn't about to join in their cheerleader enthusiasm, but he couldn't deny the truth. "She seems happy. That's nice to see."

"And it looks like someone's happy to see her." Julia's penciled eyebrows gave a suggestive wiggle in the direction of a dapper gentleman seated in a brown leather recliner on the other side of the room. Tweed cap on his head, cane clutched in a gnarled hand, his attention was locked and loaded on Grandma.

Garrett shuddered. He wasn't quite ready for that.

Moments later, Grandma joined them in a row of chairs opposite a photo-littered desk in Julia's office.

"I like it here," Grandma declared.

Julia clicked at her keyboard. "That's what we like to hear."

Lauren leaned in with a searching look. "Are you sure this is what you want to do?"

Grandma's cottony curls bounced as she nodded. "This is probably one of the last de . . . di . . . oh, what's the word?"

"Decisions," Garrett offered.

"Thank you." Her wry smile curved wrinkled lips. "This is probably one of the last *decisions*"—she said it slowly, as though she'd never heard it before—"I'll ever make for myself. And I think it's a good one."

"It is," Garrett agreed.

On Grandma's other side, Lauren nodded. "I think so too."

"You've both taken wonderful care of me." Grandma slipped her cold fingers into Garrett's grasp and did the same with Lauren. "But you two are far too young to worry about an old biddy like me all the time. I'll be just fine here."

Lauren squeezed Grandma's hand, tears pooled along her lower lids. "Okay."

"Okay." Relief slid through Garrett's body. Grandma's good day—her best day in weeks—couldn't have come at a better time. She was on board with the move. More than that, she wanted it.

"Okay!" Julia scrolled on the computer screen. "As I mentioned before, we do have one suite available. To hold it, we'll need your deposit, first month's rent, and proof of finances. You said you have a house you're selling?"

"Yes." Garrett dug in his jacket pocket for Grandma's checkbook.

"Wonderful." More clicking. "Any other assets? Savings accounts? Retirement funds?"

"No."

Julia's long nails hovered over the keyboard. "But you believe the sale of the house and land will meet the requirement?"

"That won't be a problem." *Please, God, let it not be a problem.*

"All right. No rush, as long as she's able to stay current with rent."

Garrett paused, the checkbook in his hand, and did some quick number crunching. His grandmother's liquid assets would cover two months' rent and part of a third, but that didn't include the deposit. All before they even listed the house.

Kimberly's warning about how long it might take to find a buyer loomed large.

So did her suggestion of an auction. No waiting. No repairs. No redecorating. Just a quick sale to the highest bidder.

And if that happened to be Warren Williams, bulldozer at the ready?

Then so be it. Whatever the outcome, he couldn't afford to feel anything about it, good, bad, or otherwise.

Decision made, he replaced his grandmother's checkbook and pulled out his own instead. Paying the deposit himself would dent his savings, but it'd also buy some time just in case.

"We've got it covered." He scribbled his signature and handed the check over before his inner cheapskate could protest.

"Thank you so much." Julia tucked the check into a drawer and withdrew a large manila envelope. "Just a few more forms to sign, and we'll be all set."

Garrett slipped his checkbook into his pocket, stomach queasy. Finally, *finally*, it was done. Plans were made. Set in motion. Plaza de Paz was undeniably the best place for Grandma, and the cherry on top? She was happy about it.

They'd done the right thing.

So where was the relief? The vindication?

Why did doing the right thing feel so horribly wrong?

⇥⇤

*October 4, 1882*

Annabelle sat at the kitchen table, pen scratching over the pages of her diary. With the four oldest at school and John Patrick down for a nap, she'd received a slice of silence. One of which she intended to take full advantage.

She'd filled half a page when the bedroom door creaked and Jack walked out. Fully dressed, though how he'd managed it with his bandaged hands was a mystery. His hair was combed as neat as could be after a week in bed.

She started to question him, but his eyes glittered, dark and determined, his shoulders set. Gone was the pallor of days past, and in its place was a slight flush. Not crimson as with fever, thank the Lord, but the pink of health.

Whatever he'd decided—and he'd for certain decided something—it was going to be nigh impossible to talk him out of it.

She hoped she wouldn't need to try.

"Have you any spare paper?" He settled into the chair across from her. Her stomach knotted. "Yes."

"Can't write quite yet, so I'd be obliged if you'd do it for me." His voice was granite, and her heart sank. The letter to Robert.

"You've made up your mind then?"

"Aye."

Tears stung her eyes, tears she quickly fought back. *Your will, Lord. Your will, not mine.*

With a deep breath, she pulled a sheet from the back of her diary. "What would you have me write?"

"I want you to write a list of everything you want in your house."

She paused, pen hovering over the inkwell.

His eyes locked on hers. "The Lord broke his silence. If there ever was a silence. Maybe it's that I finally stopped shouting at him and started listening."

A smile tugged the corners of her mouth, and she leaned her pen against the inkwell and waited.

"Because when I was quiet . . . I heard our children. Their joy. Their laughter. I heard them running and playing outside my window. It doesn't bother them that we lost so much. It didn't dampen their joy that they won't be moving to a larger house soon. They're happy. They're content. Because they trust me. They know I'll fight for them until my last breath, that I love them more than my own life."

Adoration swelled. "I've never seen a father who loves his children more."

"And the way they trust me should be the way I trust my heavenly Father. So I quieted my spirit and surrendered to him anew. When I did that . . . oh, Annabelle, the peace I felt. It was like the sun shining on my soul."

Her throat thickened, and her heart filled with gratitude.

"I read some Scripture—Scripture I've sorely neglected the last few weeks—and everywhere I looked was guidance to persevere. The verses leapt off the page, as though meant for me. I'd never known what the phrase 'living word' meant until this morning. So I believe God wills us to stay. To persevere."

"Oh, Jack." Relief washed through her. They were staying.

"It won't be easy, love. It'll take years to rebuild."

"I know."

"But rebuild we will. He'll care for us. He'll not leave us. I know that now, to my bones. Even when I don't feel him, he's there." Joy shimmering in his eyes, Jack tapped the paper with his fingertip. "So don't hold back. Let your imagination run wild."

Annabelle opened her mouth to protest, but he beat her to it. "And I know you're about to tell me that you don't need a big house, that all you need is this little cabin. And that may well be true." He swallowed hard. "But I'm not asking this for you. I ask it for me. Because I need to dream again, and you're the one person who's always given me the courage to try."

Warmth filled her as she studied the man who'd so swiftly won her all those years ago. He needed her. Needed her like she needed him.

"All right," she said, and he captured her hands with his cottony bandaged ones and kissed her fingertips.

Her lips curved. "You'll have to free my hands if you wish me to write, Mr. Brennan."

The humorous glint in his eyes reassured her that he was back. That though physical recovery was still to come, his heart and soul were whole again.

"You make a valid point."

"As always."

He pressed kisses to the back of each hand. Each knuckle. Each fingertip. Then, his gaze tender, he released them.

Overflowing with joy, Annabelle picked up her pen.

# CHAPTER TWENTY

SLOANE PUSHED OPEN the farmhouse door with her shoulder. "Anybody home?" One hand cradled the most recent diary, while the other carried savory-smelling bags of takeout barbecue.

"In here," Garrett called from down the hall, accompanied by the scratchy squawk of packing tape.

Sloane set both food and diary on the coffee table and rounded the corner into Rosie's bedroom, where Garrett crouched amid a sea of boxes. Closet doors gaped, piles of clothes obscured the quilt on the bed, and dust motes danced in a shaft of late afternoon sunlight.

Sloane blinked. "What's all this?"

"You know how you wait and wait and wait for something, but when it finally happens, it happens fast, and no matter how prepared you were, you still feel behind?" He thumped a box to secure the tape he'd rolled across it. "We found a place for Grandma. Plaza de Paz. They had an immediate opening, so we jumped on it this afternoon. She moves in next weekend."

"Wow, that is fast."

"Yeah, well." Garrett rose with a quiet grunt and added the box to a stack in the corner. "The tornado sped things up a bit."

Sloane crossed the room and slid an arm around Garrett's waist, his skin warm and damp through his T-shirt. "I'm glad you found a safe place for her."

"Me too." Relief lightened his eyes. His face, flushed and shining with effort, was devoid of its drawn, tight appearance from recent weeks. That sight alone made her glad for him. For Rosie. For all of them.

But uncertain sorrow snaked around her joy. If Rosie's move had been stepped up, then surely the plans for the house had as well.

So what would happen to it?

And how could she ask without seeming enormously selfish?

Garrett's stomach growled, and he pressed a quick kiss to her temple. "Guess that means it's time for a dinner break, huh?"

"Absolutely." She stepped from his embrace. "I'm starving."

Lacing her fingers through his, she led him into the living room, where the delicious aroma from the takeout made her mouth water.

He reached for one of the bags, and a corner of his mouth tipped. "Can't believe this Kansas City kid likes Wichita barbecue better than anything back home. That's gotta be at least two different levels of blasphemy."

"Blasphemy or not, good is good." Sloane ducked into the kitchen for a couple of plates. When she returned, Garrett had his nose in the diary.

"What's Annabelle up to these days?" he asked.

"We can look at it after dinner if you want."

"Or you could read me an entry while I get stuff ready."

"Twist my arm." Sloane set the plates on the coffee table and took the diary from his outstretched hand.

＞＜

*August 23, 1890*

Annabelle's skirts jostled as the children thundered through the wooden door Jack held open and burst headlong into the house.

The new house.

*Their* house.

Gleaming wooden walls echoed with the whoops and shrieks of children unable to contain their excitement. Five-year-old Maggie Ann, their youngest, spun circles in the foyer until she toppled over in a heap, honey-brown ringlets forming a gilt halo in the sunshine. Her nearest brothers, Stephen and John Patrick, tore into the spacious living room, while the older boys thudded upstairs, Mary close behind. Even quiet, dreamy Caroline strolled around the dining room, wide-eyed and chattering.

They were loud, those children. But not Annabelle.

She was speechless.

It wasn't as if she hadn't seen the house before. She'd watched the neighbor men hoist the roof and hammer the walls. She'd seen her Jack out there, sawing and painting in wilting heat and bone-cracking cold. She'd witnessed the blood, sweat, and tears that went into its construction.

But that was before it was finished.

Now . . .

The fresh smell of new varnished wood. The stone fireplace. The large window framing a gorgeous view of the creek, complete with lace curtains.

Her breath caught. "Oh, Jack." Aunt Katherine's advancing age meant she could no longer do delicate needlework. So where had these curtains come from?

He pulled her close, his smile weathered and knowing. "I worried they wouldn't be here in time, but they arrived on Tuesday's train."

She tore her focus from the room to the man who'd coaxed it, inch by inch, from dream into magnificent reality. "It's breathtaking."

"Yes. It is." The intensity in his deep gray eyes made it clear he wasn't talking about the house. Love surged as their lips met.

"Jack," she murmured against his questing mouth. "The children."

"They're not paying us any mind."

It was true, they weren't, and her paltry resistance died at his kiss, at the heat of the hand resting at the small of her back—

The door banged open, and they broke apart, Annabelle smoothing her skirts.

"Uncle Jack." Oliver's deep voice and confident stride sliced through their mood.

Jack cleared his throat. "Yes?"

Oliver held up a shingle in his reed-thin hand, and Jack frowned.

"Where'd that come from?"

"Our roof."

Jack took the piece of slate. "I dropped a few of them over the edge when I was putting them on the other week. Thought I'd gotten them all, but I suppose not."

"This wasn't there yesterday," Oliver pointed out. "They must've come off in the wind."

Yesterday had indeed been blustery, even by Kansas standards.

Jack drew back. "They?"

"Maybe a dozen. I'll nail them back on if you like."

"No need. I'll take care of it."

"Does this mean the move is delayed?" Annabelle asked. Excited thumps and shrieks still echoed upstairs. She'd hate to disappoint them.

Jack gave a reassuring smile. "Not at all, love. Only I'll need to get up there and fix it before it rains next."

"So we've all the time in the world then," Oliver said dryly.

Jack laughed, but beneath it lay real concern. The bone-dry summer meant constant scans of the horizon for that ominous red glow. Despite the warm day, Annabelle shivered, remembering the fire that nearly wiped them out. Nearly cost her husband's life. Scars from that day peeked from Jack's shirtsleeves, mementos of his darkest hour.

*Please, Lord. Protect the house from fire.*

Pressing a kiss to her temple, Jack drew her to his side, and she relaxed into the warmth of his embrace. He didn't say a word, but he knew her worry. That alone brought comfort.

*Oh, Lord. Thank you for Jack. What would I ever do without him?*

He searched her face; she reassured him with a smile. Satisfied, he nodded, then turned to the stairs and called each of the children by name in that agile-tongued way of his that never ceased to summon them from the far-flung reaches of their exploration. Within moments, their seven young ones had gathered in the empty sitting room.

"Before we all get too excited, I think we need a prayer of blessing, yes?" Jack looked around the circle of offspring. "To dedicate this house to the Lord, the source of all it took to build it and the sustainer of all who'll live within it."

Seven shining faces surrounded Annabelle, seven precious souls who'd grow within these walls. Perhaps even some of their children, and their children's children . . . and this home would still stand, a testament to the Lord's faithful provision.

It was a house. A pile of wood and stone.

And yet it was so much more.

Oliver stood at her left. The boy she'd rescued from the flooded creek, who now towered head and shoulders over her. The child who didn't share her blood but may as well have been her firstborn. The young man who'd put nearly as much work into the place as Jack himself.

And Jack to her right. The man in whose chest her own heart beat. The man with whom she'd truly become one flesh. Who could guess her thoughts, who knew her better than she knew herself.

She joined hands with them both.

"God bless the corners of this house, and be the lintel blessed." Jack's light brogue thickened with emotion, and the children added their voices to the chorus.

"And bless the hearth, and bless the board, and bless each place of rest."

Overwhelmed with love for God, for Jack, for her family, Annabelle squeezed his hand and stepped closer to his warmth, her lips moving in unison with his.

"And bless the rooftree overhead, and every sturdy wall . . ."

✦

"The peace of man, the peace of God, the peace of love to all." Garrett's voice joined with Sloane's, a faraway look in his eyes. "We moved from Shawnee Mission to Olathe when I was nine, and my mom prayed that over our new house. I never knew where it came from."

"It's a traditional Irish home blessing. Goes back a long time." Sliding a bookmark into the diary, Sloane laid it on an end table, far from barbecue sauce and potato salad. The plain wooden walls Annabelle described were covered now with floral wallpaper, but they'd been hoisted by Jack Brennan. His sons. Their neighbors. Annabelle's beloved lace curtains no longer graced the large picture window, but the view of the creek was timeless. The Brennans never would've imagined the flat-screen TV mounted over the fireplace, but they'd recognize that fireplace, having built it stone by stone.

The entry Sloane had just read had taken place in this very room. She could almost sense them in the house with her. Watching.

Did they know their labor of love still stood?

Did they know it might soon disappear?

"Sloane?" Garrett held out a plate piled high with food, questions dancing in his eyes. "Are you all right?"

"Yeah. Fine." She took the plate and laid it on her lap.

"You're thinking about the house, aren't you?"

How could she not be? "It's nice to see how it began. To picture them standing here, blessing it."

He plopped a spoonful of potato salad on his plate. "I know. Gives me goose bumps."

After he blessed the food, she picked up her sandwich and tried to keep her voice light. "So what happens to the house now? Are you listing it with Kimberly?"

Garrett shook his head and hastily swallowed a mouthful of brisket. "Given our time constraints, we've decided on the auction route."

Sloane paused, barbecue sauce dripping from her sandwich. "Really?"

"I called McCue's earlier. They had an open date at the end of the month, so I snapped it up."

"Wow." Her heart sank to her shoes. An auction. Sold to the highest bidder.

Warren Williams, no doubt. Or another of his ilk.

"It wasn't my initial plan." Garrett reached for his iced tea. "But it makes the most sense. Grandma's got to have a certain amount in the bank to stay at Plaza de Paz, and if we sell the house and land for what Kimberly says it's worth, we'll get there."

Sloane forked up a bite of potato salad. "Mind if I ask how much that is?"

He quoted a number. A high one. Many times more than the cash she had on hand.

But maybe she could take out a loan. Her credit was good. Her salary stable. She had some savings, and her parents had a nest egg for her as well. Maybe that would tip the scales in her favor. Give her a better bargaining chip at the auction.

And if not, maybe Garrett would be willing to haggle.

"What about parceling it? Selling off the farmland and keeping the house?" Buying the house without the land would definitely be more feasible for her.

"Who'd take care of it? Even if we rented it out, the price would be too high to be practical, and we'd still be responsible for all the maintenance. Lauren doesn't want to live here alone, and my life's back in Kansas City."

The living room lurched. His life *was* back in Kansas City. He was here so often, his permanent residence three hours away was easy to overlook. But once the house was sold and Rosie's future secured . . . what then?

"Right." Sloane gave a thin smile. She didn't want to be that girl. "Guess we'll give the long distance thing a whirl then, huh?"

He blinked. Paused for far too long. "I guess so."

"FaceTime, weekends . . ." Although how many road trips could she really afford? Especially if she found herself with a mortgage.

"To be honest, there's been so much going on, I haven't figured that part out yet."

"Of course." It made sense. No way would he have had time to make decisions about their relationship with his grandmother's future weighing him down.

But he was Garrett P. Anderson, advance planner extraordinaire. From his wardrobe to his menu, he left nothing to chance, always staying two steps ahead of every decision he had to make.

But he'd yet to make a plan with her. And that spoke painful volumes.

Forcing down another tasteless bite, she stared at her shoes on the worn wooden floor. It had been here for decades, but along with the rest of the house, it was rapidly running out of time.

From the sound of it, she and Garrett might be heading the same way.

# Chapter Twenty-One

Sloane ducked into a little coffee shop in a strip mall a couple miles south of the farmhouse. The scent of coffee and spices wrapped her in a comforting embrace, and the collection of baked goods in the glass case was a powerful temptation. But rather than her usual mocha and scone, she ordered a simple black tea.

Four bucks saved. Only a few hundred thousand more to go.

She retrieved the warm to-go cup and was halfway to the door when a woman called her name. There, by the window, sat Kimberly Walsh. Her silver laptop lay open on the wooden table, and white earbud wires draped over her shoulders.

"Kimberly. Hi."

Crimson lips curved. "I wondered if that was you when they called your name."

"Never had to worry about there being more than one Sloane in my class, that's for sure."

"It is unusual. But beautiful." Over the rims of her reading glasses, Kimberly scanned Sloane's face. "It suits you."

"I'm glad I ran into you." Sloane rested her cup on the corner of the table. "I have a couple questions about the old farmhouse up on Jamesville Road. Do you have a minute?"

"Absolutely. Have a seat."

Sloane pulled out a chair while Kimberly closed her laptop, then fixed Sloane with an eager gaze. "What's up?"

"Garrett probably told you they've decided to auction the property."

At Kimberly's nod, she continued. "What would a prospective buyer need to do?"

"Is the museum interested?"

"No, but I am."

Kimberly grinned. "Want to raise some chickens, do you?"

"Not necessarily. I'm just pretty attached to the place. It belonged to my great-great-great-grandparents."

It felt strange saying that out loud.

Strange, but wonderful.

Penciled brows arched. "You're kidding."

"Nope." Sloane popped the lid off her cup and pulled out the piping-hot teabag. "Jack and Annabelle Brennan. Some of the first settlers in Sedgwick County. I just found out they're my family. I was adopted and grew up knowing basically nothing about my roots, so this is kind of a big deal."

"I can imagine." An odd expression flitted across Kimberly's face. "How did you make that connection?"

"I found my birth mother online recently, and she sent me an old letter with a name matching one of Jack and Annabelle's children. I've been reading Annabelle's diaries, and those plus some marriage records and census data confirmed the match."

Kimberly shook her head slowly. "That's amazing."

"And probably TMI." Sloane waved a hand. "But that's why I want the house."

"Makes sense." Kimberly sipped from an enormous coffee mug. "Well, given what that place is worth, even as is, unless you've got a ton of cash lying around . . ."

Sloane gave a derisive snort, and Kimberly laughed.

"Then you'll need to look into getting a loan. I've got a lender I work with regularly who's great with first-time buyers. Assuming you are one."

Sloane nodded.

"No contingencies then, so that'll work in your favor. But these guys'll walk you through everything. There's a bunch of paperwork . . ."

Kimberly continued talking while Sloane scribbled in a notebook she pulled from her bag.

It was a long shot, going up against Warren Williams.

But no way did he want that house more than she did.

⇥⇤

The heavy plastic crate thudded in the trunk of Garrett's car that Sunday afternoon, and the Camry sank slightly under its weight. Not unlike his heart, knowing this was the last load of things Grandma wanted with her at Plaza de Paz. So much was still left inside, destined for the estate sale. Little things, random things, that flooded him with memories.

They couldn't keep them all, though.

He loaded another crate. This one was mostly pictures, ready for a sort-a-thon when he got home. The ones he recognized he'd scan and store online. As for the rest? Sloane might want them, as obsessed as she'd become with the house and its history.

Not that he blamed her. It was her family's house too, after all. But the stories she'd uncovered, her deepening devotion, all made the upcoming auction even more difficult than it already was.

And the question she'd raised last night, the question he'd wrestled with until the wee hours . . . talk about difficult. He hadn't yet faced reality, but now it stared him in the face.

Her life was here. His wasn't. Neither of them had any plans to change that.

Should he try to convince her to move to Kansas City? Were there job openings in any of the historical museums up there? Would she want one if there were?

And if Sloane didn't want to move, should he chuck his burgeoning career and start over down here? Was it even wise to consider such a step given how new their relationship was? He and Jenny Hickok had been together far longer, and it still blew up in his face. What made him think this wouldn't end the same way?

The crunch of tires on gravel behind him signaled the arrival of an enormous maroon Mercedes SUV, from which a balding, heavyset man emerged, his plaid flannel shirt, jeans, and giant belt buckle totally incongruous with the luxurious vehicle.

"I'm sorry," the man drawled. "Didn't know anyone would be here."

"I was just leaving. Can I help you with something?"

The stranger stuck out a meaty hand. "Warren Williams, Williams and Son Development."

Aha. That explained the car.

And his presence.

"Garrett Anderson." He returned the handshake, and the churning in his stomach kicked up a notch.

"You're Orrin Spencer's grandson, aren't you?"

"Yes, sir, I am."

"Figures. You look just like him." Williams ran a hand over the top of his head. "I was real sorry to hear when he passed last fall. Stubborn old coot, that Orrin."

"That's Grandpa," Garrett replied with a chuckle.

"I remember when I first approached him about this land. He wouldn't hear a word of it. Not for sale at any price, your grandpa said. It had been in the family for generations, and they weren't about to be the ones to let it go."

Garrett winced. Because now he was the one.

"Figured they'd change their tune eventually, though. Most folks do. Bodies get older, maintenance gets to be too much, and sometimes the thing they fought so hard against becomes the ideal solution."

Garrett's jaw tightened. It was official: he did not like Warren Williams. But that didn't mean the man was wrong.

"Look, I'll be frank." Williams hooked a thumb in his pocket. "I've loved this land from the moment I laid eyes on it. Great location, fantastic views . . . the perfect little slice of the American dream."

Williams's lips drew back in a manufactured smile, and Garrett stiffened. He knew a sales pitch when it was coming, and this one was cocked and ready to fly.

"That's what those pioneer ancestors of yours thought, am I right? Building this place was their American dream come true. And now, a hundred and fifty years later, what better way to honor that legacy than to make the American dream a reality not just for one family but for dozens?"

Despite Garrett's preparation, the pitch caught him off guard. Using his family's dream as a plug for plowing it under? He hadn't expected Williams to go there. The guy was good, he had to admit.

"Now I've got an architect in mind, a real up-and-comer. Young guy, but talented. Eager. He's got some great ideas for homes. Green construction, arts and crafts design. That kind of thing's makin' a comeback. Like the past, only better." He swept his arm over the horizon. "Can't you just see it?"

Garrett could.

And it made him ill.

"There are graves here," he blurted. "Some of the original settlers. A young wife. Couple kids. Babies, really."

Williams's lips turned down in an odd expression that still seemed to be something of a smile. "Real shame, that. Not the first we've seen. No cemetery yet, so what else could you do? They marked?"

"Yes, sir. They're under a big cottonwood, between the barn and the house."

"Well then. Should we be so fortunate as to purchase this land, we'll put up a fence for protection. We'll even get a real nice headstone for 'em. Make it look brand-new for the next hundred years."

A cemetery in the middle of a subdivision? Would that truly honor Jack's wife and children? Or would the incongruity of a chain-link fence and freshly carved stone make a mockery of the whole thing?

Williams leaned in with a conspiratorial wink. "What would it take for you to call off the auction, son?"

Garrett drew back. "I'm sorry?"

"We can go through the dog and pony show if you'd like, but I want you to know I'm dead serious." Williams withdrew a checkbook from his shirt pocket. "You and I both know what this land's worth, and I'm prepared to give you a deposit here and now. We'll meet with the lawyers in a few days and get it finalized."

Garrett's name formed on the check in Williams's angular scrawl.

"I . . . That's very generous, but I need to think about it."

Williams's pen tapped against his checkbook, right on the line where the all-important amount would go. "I'll even give you ten percent over market value. How's that sound?"

Ten percent over. Could it fetch that much at auction? The offer would have to come from someone with deep pockets, and Warren Williams was the only one fitting that description who'd shown serious interest.

The developer must have interpreted his silence as a no, because his bushy gray brows arched. "All right. Fifteen percent over."

"Sir, I—"

"Mind you, this ain't how I normally do business. Wouldn't be where I am today if I overpaid for every plot of land I bought. But that's how special this place is to me."

Numbers bounced around Garrett's skull. Fifteen percent over would cover Grandma's expenses and then some. Leave her a nice little nest egg in case of something unforeseen. After so many years of watching his grandparents scrape the bottom of their meager savings, of worrying about how they'd care for themselves, the idea of that problem wafting away on the warm spring breeze was almost intoxicating.

The scratch of Williams's pen mingled with the song of a nearby bird. "Here's my offer. Fifteen percent over, and half now. Consider it earnest money, if you like."

A number appeared on the line. Garrett had seen numbers that large before, of course, but never on a check made out to him.

"You want to wait for the auction and see if someone wants this land more than I do, be my guest. But we can settle this in a couple weeks and both walk away happy." Williams tore out the check and extended it to Garrett. "What do you say?"

There it was. That number. A number representing security. Stability. A lifting of the thousand-pound weight he'd carried for months.

Could this be an answer to prayer?

It had to be. It made perfect sense.

So why was his stomach churning? Why did his neck feel hot?

"Do we have a deal, son?"

That number. Regardless of how he felt about it, this was the logical course of action.

It had to be the answer.

"Yes, sir. We have a deal."

Williams thrust the check into Garrett's left hand and pumped his right, beaming. "You're gonna be proud of what we put in here. Real proud. I promise you won't regret this. Not for an instant."

But as Garrett looked over the developer's shoulder at the stately white house, the house that held half his memories, the house he'd just doomed to a date with the wrecking ball . . .

He already regretted it.

✦

*November 16, 1890*

Steam bathed Annabelle's face as she bent to retrieve the bread from the oven. Reveling in the yeasty aroma, she tapped the outside. Nice and hollow. Perfectly done. Crispy crust, melt-in-your-mouth interior. Jack would love it.

She set the loaf on the counter and leaned back, fanning herself with the pot holder. She shouldn't be working this hard on the Lord's Day. But after the stomach illness that swept through the house this past week, she was hard-pressed to remember what day it was, let alone observe it. She and Jack had been spared, mercifully, but all the little ones had taken their turn, and her days had become a blur of washing and caregiving, drying and doctoring.

John Patrick had been the last to fall ill, and though he still looked pale today, the worst was over. He even felt well enough to traipse to the creek earlier this afternoon with his father and brother. Out the gorgeous kitchen window, still shiny and new, Jack's dark hair peeked through the trees, a sharp contrast to Stephen's light blond and John Patrick's fiery red.

Annabelle breathed a silent prayer of thanks that God had once again restored the health they usually enjoyed. This bread, and the fish from the creek, would disappear from the dinner table in a heartbeat, and she couldn't be happier about it.

A rumble reached her ears, and she paused. Was that . . . thunder? It'd been so long since she'd heard it, she wasn't sure she'd know the sound. While the drought wasn't nearly as severe as the one in '74, the ground bore deep cracks, and their fall crops had suffered. Harvest was adequate, though, and she was grateful.

But thunder? Today?

Another rumble came, louder than the first, and Annabelle tossed the pot holder on the table and stepped out the back door. Sure enough, a thunderhead was forming right over top of them. The air was thick with humidity. Lively with the scent of . . .

Rain? Could it be?

No sooner had the question formed than its answer arrived. On her forearm. Her cheek. The cracked earth at her feet. Splotch after splotch. Delicious, delirious proof of much-needed moisture falling from the sky.

Footsteps thudded behind her. Jack and the boys jogging up from the creek, fishing poles in hand, lines of fish bouncing with each step.

"Stow these for me, would you?" Jack thrust his fishing pole and tackle box into the outstretched hand of young John Patrick. "And Stephen, will you take care of these?" He handed the fish to the boy and took off toward the barn. A moment later, he reemerged, tools in hand and a smile on his face. "The roof was on the list for tomorrow. Thought I had plenty of time for a Sabbath rest."

"Apparently not." Annabelle echoed his smile, then whirled with a start. Mercy—the laundry! Three beds' worth of sheets hung on the line, and if she didn't hurry, she'd have to wash and dry them all over again.

She poked her head in the door and yelled to the girls to take over supper preparations, then hoisted her skirts and sprinted around back to the clotheslines. But no sooner had she loosed the first clothespin than the sprinkles turned to a downpour.

"Oh no," she wailed, moving ever faster. But the rain was relentless, and a gust of wind smacked one of the hanging sheets into her face, cold and wet. Grumbling under her breath, she twisted and fought, pushing back the sodden sheet and trying to untangle it from around her waist.

Amid the hiss of rain and another rumble of thunder came laughter.

*Laughter?*

She looked up, and there was Jack atop the roof, hammer in hand, dimples deep and mouth open in a belly laugh.

Irritation burned. "You're laughing. At me."

"No, love," he shouted. "I'm not. I promise."

"Liar." Another sheet wrapped around her.

"I'm laughing because we've prayed and prayed for rain, and at the least convenient and most unexpected moment, here it is. It's raining, Annabelle." Beaming, he turned his face to the turbulent sky, his skin shining with rain, his hair soaked and clinging to his forehead, and bellowed his joy. "It's raining!"

Irritation faded to guilt, then gratitude. It bubbled in her chest and pushed outward in laughter to rival Jack's. Tilting her head back, she stared straight into the deluge and let it fall. It soaked her bodice, her skin, muddied the hem of her dress, drenched the laundry that she'd have to do all over again, but it was too wonderful to care.

Jack was right.

It was raining.

Her laughter growing louder, she held her arms out to her sides and spun in crazed circles. Most undignified behavior for a woman nearing forty, but her joy was too great to contain. Everything had come together. They'd weathered hunger and hardship, limits and loss, but they'd persevered. They'd remained faithful.

And now here they were, the Lord's blessings showering down on them.

It was raining.

Oh, that it would never stop.

A blinding flash and deafening crack stopped her dance in its tracks, and she leapt back with a startled shriek. Her hand fluttered to her chest, from which her pounding heart felt certain to leap. Mercy, that was close. Lightning hadn't struck their farm, but the acrid smell lingering in the air meant it hadn't hit far. Perhaps the Jansens'?

"That was unbelievable," she shouted. "I hope the Jansens are all right."

Jack didn't answer.

"Jack?" Whirling around, she looked up at the roof.

But he wasn't there.

"Jack?" Her voice took on a panicked edge, her terrified gaze swept over the property.

And there, half hidden by the house, a sprawl of tangled limbs . . .

"Jack!" She sprinted toward him.

The sodden sheet she'd been holding fluttered to a puddle of mud, forgotten.

# CHAPTER TWENTY-TWO

THE STRAINS OF Ella Fitzgerald's "Cry Me a River" spilling from an aqua turntable mingled with the scrape of chopsticks on Styrofoam, the soundtrack to a quick takeout dinner at Sloane's cozy apartment. Garrett reached across the yellow Formica kitchen table for the container of pad thai, still fascinated by the eclectic mix of vintage finds that comprised her place. The framed movie posters. The antique typewriter on a corner shelf. Her home itself was a museum. One he never grew tired of visiting.

Sloane grabbed another skewer of chicken satay, humming along with Ella. He froze, the noodles in his mouth half chewed, heart somersaulting at the sound. He'd always liked the song, but to hear its sultry melody coming from Sloane's throat . . .

He must've been staring, because she stopped, her cheeks flushed a delicate pink. "Sorry."

*Don't apologize.* But he swallowed the words, along with his bite of pad thai.

"This one's in our set at Marty's in July." She glanced up. "Maybe you could come down for that."

He'd never been wonderful at picking up hints from women, but that one was so obvious even he couldn't miss it.

She wasn't just asking about her gig. About when he planned to visit next.

She was asking about them.

They had danced around the subject all evening, a palpable awkwardness hovering over the scattered takeout containers. She hadn't come right out and asked him where they were headed, nor had she shared any thoughts on the subject. In fact, since he'd decided to auction the house, there'd grown a distance between them that had nothing to do with geography.

A distance that reminded him of Jenny Hickok.

He'd fallen fast, and fallen hard, when he met her running cross-country his sophomore year. Bubbly, energetic, and driven to succeed, Jenny checked all the boxes on a list he'd never thought to make. It wasn't long before they were planning their future. They'd go to KU together—he for business school, she for the soccer team and a communications degree—and when he was firmly established in his career they'd get married.

But then Jenny received a soccer scholarship at a small college in Missouri. An offer KU didn't match, and one she couldn't afford to turn down. So he altered his plans, revised his vision of the future, and enrolled in a school of twenty-eight hundred instead of twenty-eight thousand.

He hated it. It was too small. Too cliquish. The business school had none of the reputation or connections that KU's did. And the woman he'd torn apart his life for suddenly had no room for him in hers. First it was bonding with the team, then studying, and by Christmas she'd met someone else. Even worse, Mom's cancer was back, and his parents struggled to pay both tuition and treatments. He was able to correct course the next year, transferring to the school he'd wanted to attend all along, but he did so with a broken heart and a depleted bank account. Both took years to recover.

And none of that would've happened if he'd just stuck to the plan.

Sticking to the plan now meant sustaining things with Sloane via video chats and weekend visits. Maybe they could make that work somehow.

But maybe the distance would be too much. Maybe he'd lose Sloane too. Inch by agonizing inch.

Maybe he'd survive that.

But maybe he wouldn't.

He swallowed hard and looked across the table, that innocent question about the July set at Marty's suddenly so much more.

"Yeah. Maybe."

✎

*Maybe.*

Normally that word was ripe with promise. With hope. With possibility.

But with that close-lipped smile of Garrett's, the one that touched his mouth but not his eyes, *maybe* promised nothing but heartache.

She'd wanted to raise the subject—not in an obnoxious, am-I-the-one sort of way—since she had a right to know where she stood. How serious he was about her.

But now she didn't need to ask. Because he'd just answered her question. He wasn't.

He wasn't making long-range plans about them. Not that she'd been looking at wedding dresses or dreaming of babies or mentally signing her name Sloane Kelley-Anderson.

But she'd hoped.

And now those hopes had taken a serious ding, all because of a two-syllable word.

*Maybe.*

With tomorrow suddenly murky and today too painful to deal with, she retreated into the cocoon of yesterday and the plastic crate of photos and other old things Garrett had brought along with the Thai food.

"Mind waiting on that coconut ice cream?" she asked with a too-bright smile. "That box of stuff is calling my name."

"Not at all." He stood, their plates in hand. "Tell you what, I'll take care of these, and you dig in."

She was already halfway across the room. "Won't say no to that."

While Garrett boxed up leftovers and chucked them into the fridge, Sloane sat on the floor in front of the sofa and tore into the crate. Anything related to Jack and Annabelle she wanted to look through now. So tempting though the 1955 Roosevelt High School yearbook was, it could wait. As could a 1927 issue of the *Wichita Beacon*.

But something was wrapped in one of those newspapers. She unfolded the ancient, yellowed newsprint and gasped at the sight of a gilt-framed, sepia-toned photograph.

A couple in their forties peered up at her. The man, his hair and mustache ink-black, sat in a velvet chair, while a woman stood beside him, her arm draped artfully onto his shoulder. Her Victorian-era dress bore ruffles and a high collar, and her pulled-back hair was several shades lighter than his. Neither smiled, but the man's dark eyes shone with a charismatic glint, while the woman's expression held the same quiet confidence as the older woman in the photo Lauren had found all those weeks ago.

Could it be? It was definitely the right vintage.

Hands shaking, Sloane popped off the ancient frame and slipped the photo from behind the glass.

*Granny Annie and Grandpa Jack, 1889.*

Confirmation in faded cursive.

"Garrett! It's them. It's Jack and Annabelle. I found a picture."

The roar of her excited heartbeat drowned out any response. There she was. The woman whose story had grabbed her by the heart from the beginning. The woman who'd shaped her, molded her, changed her in ways she could never have imagined.

Sloane grabbed her phone and pulled up the picture Lauren had found. No doubt it was the same woman. The same eyes, though webbed with wrinkles in the older photo. The same poised set of the shoulders, the same tilt of the chin—

Wait. That narrow jaw. That pointed chin. All tapering from a pair of wide-set cheekbones.

Her stinging eyes blurred the image. She knew that jaw. That chin. Those cheekbones.

She saw them every time she looked in a mirror.

It wasn't much. Frankly, she hadn't expected anything, given how many generations lay between Annabelle and herself. But here, finally, was something familiar. Something that meant she belonged to someone.

To her family.

She couldn't wait to show the photo to Marinera.

"Garrett?" She turned toward the kitchen, but he'd already joined her in the living room. He peered at her, head to one side, a small book in his hand. How long had he been standing there?

"I found this picture of Jack and Annabelle." She thrust it at him like an overexcited five-year-old. "Look. She has my chin. My jaw. I mean, I know it's not much, but . . . what?"

The somber expression in his eyes cooled her excitement. Wordlessly, he handed her another diary. Tucked inside the front cover was a clipping from the *Wichita Eagle*, yellow and softened with age.

"I'm so sorry."

*J. F. Brennan Dies in Accident at Home*

*Jamesville, Kan., Nov. 18 — A bereaved wife, seven children, and an entire community are left to mourn the loss of one of its pillars, John Francis "Jack" Brennan, who passed from this life on Sunday after a fall from the roof at the family homestead . . .*

➤⬩

*November 19, 1890*

At last, they were alone.

Three days. Three full days of friends and neighbors. The parson. The undertaker. The children. Their presence provided comfort Annabelle would doubtless need in the days to come. The weeks, the months—

No. She couldn't face those.

All she could face was right now.

Right here.

Alone with Jack.

The ceaseless activity had quieted. The children were in bed. What time was it even? She glanced toward the mantel—the mantel he'd carved from a cottonwood that blew over in a windstorm, a reminder that God could create beauty from anything—but the clock was stopped, its endless ticking stilled, its hands frozen at five thirty-seven.

A thoughtful tradition, stopping clocks at the time of death, though she'd never paid it much attention before. It provided a pause, a respite from the relentless march of minutes to allow the bereaved to absorb that moment where hearts shattered and life ceased to make sense. The single instant that tore existence into *before* and *after*.

Indeed, it hadn't taken much more than that. Uncle Stephen assured her that the Lord had spared Jack any suffering. By the time she reached him, fell to her knees in the mud beside him, shook him, said his name, said it louder, screamed it . . . he was already gone.

Oliver, riding in from a drive with young Kate Emerson, had known at once. He didn't say a word, but his horror-stricken eyes, the way he peeled her off Jack and ushered her inside, spoke volumes.

"Thomas will fetch the doc," he'd said, voice clipped. "Come inside before you catch your death."

Her death. That the Lord would be so merciful.

Through the window, as her uncle bent over her husband in the pouring rain, she'd seen what shock had hidden from view. The unnatural angle of Jack's neck. The sickening twist of limbs. He was—

No. He couldn't be. He was right here in the parlor. With her. Alone. She could talk to him. Laugh. Spin in circles, like before. He was asleep, that was all. Fixing the roof had plumb worn him out. He'd wake up soon.

But her Jack would've never crammed himself into such a small space. He needed to spread out. He'd built their bed bigger than most for precisely that reason.

He would've hated this box.

He would've hated the suit too. Who'd decided on that? He only wore one when he had to. Though he'd celebrated when the church building was finally complete, he'd quietly grumbled about stuffing himself into his suit once a week.

This one was new. Store-bought for the wedding that was doubtless in young Oliver's future. Sooner than Annabelle might like, based on the way he and Kate looked at one another. And Jack was to be sitting in the front pew beside her, wearing that new suit. She would grip his hand and smile at him through eyes filled with tears and a heart overflowing with joy and sorrow and bittersweet pride for the man Oliver had become. And Jack, more handsome than ever with his silver-streaked hair, would look down at her, squeeze her hand, and give her that lopsided grin, the one that said more than a thousand words ever could that it'd all be okay. That they'd get through this, as they had everything else.

That was what the suit was for.

Not this.

And the flowers. Endless flowers pressing around her, trapping her in a nightmarish garden. Beautiful but sinister, with no way to escape. Their cloying scent made her head ache. Or maybe it was the embalming chemicals.

She didn't want to smell those things. She wanted to smell Jack.

Black skirts swished as she rose from the chair—the velvet one he'd ordered at shocking cost from the furniture store in town, but . . . oh, he knew her. He knew what she liked, and no mountain would remain unscaled, no stone unturned, to give it to her.

He lay in front of the fireplace. He looked quiet. At peace.

But he didn't look like Jack. His hair was combed too neatly. That stubborn lock that forever fell into his eyes, the one he always threatened to lop off once and for all, was slicked back with pomade.

On sudden impulse, she flicked it down onto his forehead. Almost laughed at the effect. It would annoy him so. He'd sit up and glare at her with mock severity, but those depthless gray eyes wouldn't quite be able to conceal their mischievous glint. A smile lurking beneath his mustache, he'd tug down a lock of her hair.

"Two can play this game, love," he'd say. And she'd muss his hair even more, and he'd pull down another strand, and they'd dissolve into the carefree laughter of the young.

And then his amusement would meld into adoration, his laughter into love, and he'd claim her lips and draw her down onto him and gently grasp her face in work-roughened hands and whisper in that barely there brogue of his . . .

Except he wouldn't.

Because Jack, her husband, her love, her life . . .

He was gone.

This man stuffed into the casket, into the suit . . . this wasn't Jack. The playful, passionate soul who'd captured her heart had flown heavenward, like a newborn butterfly. And this, left behind, was his cocoon.

And all the days they'd dreamed together, all the tomorrows and next weeks and next months and next years . . . she'd have to walk them alone.

Without Jack.

His name ripped from her a sob, and she doubled over, the simple wood of the casket digging into white-knuckled hands.

Tears dropped onto his shirtsleeve. Tears like the rain at five thirty-seven on Sunday.

The rain before.

The rain after.

She'd give anything for that moment not to exist. To go back to the bliss of before, to order him down off the roof. To tell him the shingles didn't matter. The house didn't matter.

It was only a house.

And here in the world of after, without Jack, could it ever be a home?

>‹

Sloane raised her head from the shoulder of Garrett's tear-dampened plaid shirt and blew her nose. Jack Brennan. Gone. So young. And poor Annabelle. The first entry in the new diary splotched with her grief.

At the quiet sniffle beside her, Sloane glanced up into red-rimmed blue eyes.

His dimple deepened. "Aren't we a couple of saps?"

Despite everything, she chuckled and wadded up the damp Kleenex. "Would you mind grabbing that box of tissues over there?" She nodded toward the old trunk she used as a coffee table.

"Sure thing." As Garrett got up off the floor, a slip of folded paper worked its way out of his pocket and landed amid the newspapers and yearbooks.

She reached for it. "You dropped—"

The rest of her words died on her tongue as she stared down at the piece of paper.

It was a check.

A sizable check.

From Warren Williams.

# Chapter Twenty-Three

"Garrett?"

Sloane's voice—half wounded, half accusing—rang dissonant against the velvety tones of Ella Fitzgerald from the phonograph. Tissue box in hand, he turned to find that same blend shimmering in her deep brown eyes.

And a small paper rectangle held between two fingers, fluttering like a cottonwood leaf.

The check from Williams. It must've fallen from his pocket.

His stomach went into free fall; his blood turned to ice.

"Please tell me this isn't what I think it is."

He couldn't bear the betrayal in her eyes. Jamming his hand into his pocket, he stared at the crimson-and-blue swirls of her Oriental rug.

"Garrett." Her plaintive plea tore at his heart.

"It just happened today. I was waiting for the right time." With a cautious step toward her, he set the box of tissues back on the coffee table. "I was going to tell you over dessert, but you wanted to sort through the box, and then Jack died . . ." He gestured helplessly at the strewn-about newspapers and photographs, at the diary and the yellowed clipping that had shattered their evening and altered his plans. "I didn't want to upset you."

She flung the check onto the coffee table, then stood and folded her arms across her chest. "Well, your plan failed. I'm upset. Let's talk anyway."

"Fine." He straightened and swallowed against the churning in his gut. "Warren Williams came out to the house today while I was packing."

"And?"

"And he made me a generous offer if I agreed to call off the auction."

Her eyes narrowed. "How generous?"

"Generous enough that I couldn't say no."

"Humor me." She shifted her weight to one hip. "He gave you your asking price?"

He squared his shoulders. "Fifteen percent over, actually. Not that it's any of your business."

"That's all it took?" She gave a derisive chuckle. "You're easier than I thought."

Frustration bubbled and burst. "Do you have any idea how much money that is?"

"Enough to make you do a one-eighty on those precious plans of yours. Unless you never intended to go through with the auction at all. Maybe it was just a ruse to get as much money out of Warren Williams as possible."

"What?" Her accusation knifed him. He pulled in a breath through his nose, desperate for even a whisper of calm. "From the beginning, this has been about providing for my grandmother. About paying her back for all the money she and Grandpa poured into Mom's cancer treatments." He flung out his arms. "They didn't have a plan, Sloane. My whole family, they're all ready, fire, aim. When life happens, they're caught shorthanded. I'm the only one who plans for the future."

"This isn't about your grandma. I'm glad she's getting the care she needs."

"Then why is this such a problem for you?"

She stared at him as though he were certifiable. Maybe he was.

"Because I met with Kimberly. I've been approved for a loan." Fire burned in her eyes. "I was going to come to the auction. I was going to bid on the house."

>&<

Over all the weeks she'd known Garrett Anderson, Sloane would never have described him as dumb. But right now, that's exactly how he looked. Like a goldfish staring out of its bowl. Just standing there. Blinking at her.

"You?" he finally asked.

"Why wouldn't I? I love that house. Every square inch. Everything it represents. For you. For me. For us. I was prepared to sink my last penny into it. I want to make it what it used to be. What Jack and Annabelle always dreamed it could be." She swallowed against the lump in her throat. "Doesn't that mean anything to you?"

His expression softened. "Of course it does. If circumstances were different, believe me, I'd love nothing more than to sell that place to you."

A wild idea seared her. "So call off the deal and sell it to me."

"Can you afford what we need to get out of it?"

"No. Can you cut me a deal?"

"No!" His hands sunk deep into his hair. "I can't. I have to have what I'm asking. Otherwise Grandma can't stay at Plaza de Paz. There's simply no other way. Believe me, if there were, I'd be going that route."

"But what if I could get you that much? What if I could match Warren Williams's offer?"

"Sloane." Blue eyes held infinite sadness. He didn't believe she could come up with the money.

And he wasn't wrong. He was a financial planner. He could guesstimate what kind of loan she'd qualify for, and he knew it would fall woefully short of what a wealthy real estate developer could conjure up.

He was all about logic. Things that made sense in his head.

His folded arms said it all. He had utterly ruled out the power of the heart.

The lines around his mouth deepened. "Okay. How?"

"I'll sell my car." It was the first thing that came to mind. "It's fairly new. Low miles. Aside from a tendency to get stuck in mud puddles, she's fit as a fiddle."

"All right. Car's gone, how are you going to get to work from out in the hinterlands? Is there a bus stop nearby? Will you bike?"

"I'll quit the museum. Find something closer."

"Then there goes your income. Do it before you buy, you won't get a loan of any kind. Do it after and you'll fall behind on your house payments."

Why, why, *why* did he have to be so right all the time?

"I'll ask my parents." She was grasping at straws. "They've got an account set aside for me—that's what I'll use as a down payment—but I'll ask for more. Get an advance on my inheritance. Maybe I'll convince them to go in with me, and then we can all live there together in Jack and Annabelle's house. One big happy family!" Never mind that she only saw her parents at Christmas, that nearly every conversation was strained. Never mind that they were happily ensconced in the mountains of Idaho and had no desire to live anywhere else.

"Sloane." Garrett grasped her shoulders. "Stop. Please. You're embarrassing yourself."

And she was hurting him. She could see it in the indigo sheen of his eyes.

"What's done is done." He let go and stepped back. "I don't like the idea of Warren Williams buying the place any more than you do. But saying no to this . . . that would be irresponsible. Impractical. Completely illogical."

Practicality. Logic. Planning.

Those called the shots with him.

His reasons for making a deal with the developer were noble, but his methods were not. The second a check was offered, he took it, even knowing he'd effectively signed the home's death warrant. He claimed the decision was difficult. But if that were true, a check from Warren Williams wouldn't be sitting on the coffee table.

Garrett didn't care what happened to the house. Not really.

He just wanted to be rid of it. To pocket the money, let the chips fall where they may, and be done with this chapter of his life.

And everything that had been a part of it.

He bent to retrieve the check. "It's over, Sloane."

Crystal clarity cut through as he stuffed the check into his wallet. Whether he intended to be or not, he was right again.

It *was* over.

"I guess it is." She pushed up her glasses, trying to calm her swirling emotions. "I'm glad you and Lauren won't have this on your shoulders anymore. And I'm glad your grandma's someplace she likes, where she'll be taken care of. I'll always remember her fondly."

Garrett's brow creased. "She's not dying. Lord willing, she's got a lot of years left." He paused, absorbing the true meaning of her words. "Wait. Is this—are you ending this?"

"It's for the best, don't you think? We had fun . . . and you brought me to my family. My blood." The portrait of Jack and Annabelle blurred through her tears. "I can't even begin to tell you what that means to me."

"Sloane . . ." His voice was low. Husky. Pain speared her heart at the thought of no longer hearing it over the phone. No longer drowning in those lake-blue eyes. A future without the caress of his fingertips, the comfort of his arms, the crush of his lips against hers.

He stepped closer and cupped her cheek in his hand. The featherlight touch of his thumb across her skin threatened her already shaky resolve.

"I'm crazy about you," he whispered.

His words tugged an echo from the deepest part of her. "I'm crazy about you too. So much it scares me."

Pain swam in his gaze. "Then why are you throwing this away over an old, run-down house?"

"Because you still think this is about an old, run-down house."

He removed his hand from her cheek and dragged it through his hair. "Then you've gotta help me, because I don't get it. What is this about?" He sounded desperate. Undone.

"It's about you. And your carefully scheduled grid of a life. There's no room for surprises. No flexibility. No space to see what might happen if you deviated from your precious plan for a minute or two."

His expression darkened. She must've hit a nerve. "I have to have a plan or it all falls apart."

"But you don't have a plan for me." The truth hung there, agonizing, between them.

"No," he said quietly. "I don't."

The three simple syllables shattered her heart.

"I didn't expect you. I came down here to get the house cleaned out and sold and to find a place for Grandma. Meeting someone—meeting you— wasn't part of my plan. I veered off course for someone before, and it fell apart, and . . . I don't know if I can risk that again. I just—I don't know what to do about you."

Of course he didn't. No one did.

She was just a diversion they were forced to deal with. The unexpected wrinkle in their carefully ironed plans.

"And that's why this is for the best." She trailed her fingertips along his stubbled jawline. "Because you're a plan A person. That's who you are. And me? I'm the person nobody plans for. Someone nobody expects."

She dropped her hand and shook her head. "I'm plan B, Garrett. I've always been plan B."

><

Half an hour later, Sloane still leaned against the couch, wrapped in her favorite orange blanket despite the warm evening. Two Styrofoam containers lay at her feet, both empty save for a melted puddle of what had once been coconut ice cream. A spoon rested inside the one closest to her.

One spoon. Not two like she'd planned.

After her "I'm plan B" declaration, Garrett had kissed her forehead and slipped out without a word. He'd left the leftovers in the fridge. The ice cream in the freezer. The crate and all its contents strewn about her living room.

He'd doubtless meant to leave them. Most of the things belonged to her family anyway, and what didn't, he knew she'd find good homes for.

A nice gesture. At least, he'd probably thought it was. But it was also one more reminder of how his mission all along had been to leave Wichita behind.

Well. What he'd discarded, she'd treasure. The diary. The newspaper clipping.

The photo.

She reached for the gilt frame. Ran her fingertips along the carved edges. How confident Jack and Annabelle looked. How optimistic. How utterly unaware of the tragedy lurking on their doorstep. The sparkle in Jack's eyes, the slight smile on Annabelle's lips, spoke of plans for the future.

Plans shattered in a single second on a stormy Sunday afternoon.

Sloane knew all about shattered plans. Broken dreams. Their rubble surrounded her right here on the living room floor. Just as rubble would litter the old homestead as soon as Warren Williams could get his wrecking ball out there.

She'd tried and she'd failed.

She'd battled and she'd lost.

With Garrett. With the house. With everything.

"I tried, Annabelle. I'm so sorry." A tear splashed down onto the portrait of her great-great-great-grandparents.

The family she'd found.

The family she'd failed.

# Chapter Twenty-Four

*September 30, 1893*

THE TABLE JACK had painstakingly constructed was full once more. Full of family and delicious food, prepared in large part by Mary and Caroline. Even eight-year-old Maggie Ann, whose light brown braids swung over her shoulders as she carefully laid a platter of biscuits on the table, was becoming quite the cook. The turkey they served was the result of John Patrick and Stephen's successful hunting trip yesterday, and Oliver's wife, Kate, had contributed her famous apple pie. Of the children, only Thomas, in his second year of medical school, was absent.

But even at this crowded table, one chair remained empty.

Jack's chair.

Annabelle's heart ached at the vacancy whenever she sat down to a meal. But removing it would tear the wound open anew. So it stayed.

"More gravy?" Kate held out the gravy boat, and Annabelle took it from her small, thin hands. Oliver's rosy-cheeked, delicate-featured bride looked like she'd be more at home in an English tearoom than on the Kansas prairie. But Kate had proven tougher than she looked, and she and the headstrong Oliver clearly adored one another. It was a good match.

"You all still thinking about moving?" John Patrick asked from the other side of the table. Annabelle passed the gravy to Stephen and stifled the knot in her stomach. Oliver had discussed striking out on his own since shortly after Jack died. At first, she thought it was restlessness. Eagerness to marry Kate and start his own family. And after the wedding, he'd stayed put. Built a cabin on a corner of their land and farmed.

But talk of leaving hadn't stopped. He'd spoken of Harper County. Sumner County. Even the newly opened territory of Oklahoma.

Oliver's dark eyes met Kate's pale blue ones in a glance that spoke volumes. "We were going to wait until after dinner to tell you, but . . . we've a firm destination in mind."

Annabelle froze, fork halfway to her lips.

"Where?" Caroline asked.

Another glance between husband and wife. "San Francisco."

The words coldcocked Annabelle. "California?"

"Why so far?" Mary looked as wounded as her mother felt.

"Kate has a cousin there, working for the railroad." Oliver laid tanned, work-roughened fingers over his wife's porcelain hand. "He says there are jobs. And the land's fertile. The climate mild. Not like *here*." He spat the word.

Annabelle's heart tore with the same pain she'd felt at nine, watching Papa ride away. The same as when she'd rushed to Jack's side and found him already gone.

"So that's it?" She strove to keep her voice from rising. "You're up and leaving then?"

"It's still under consideration, Mother." Oliver's tone carried a hint of chastisement. "Nothing's finalized yet."

Kate turned to Annabelle. "Perhaps you could come with us?"

"What?" Annabelle couldn't have been more taken aback if her soft-spoken daughter-in-law had shouted her suggestion.

"Come with us," Oliver echoed. "To California."

"I couldn't simply . . ."

"Yes, you could." Oliver's eyes held a wild glint. "Thomas is grown, Caroline and Joseph will be wed and living in Colwich by year's end, and the rest could come along."

Maggie Ann gasped, and her gray eyes lit. "Are we moving?" The child carried Annabelle's own adventuring spirit.

At least, the spirit she had once.

Annabelle laid a hand on her daughter's head. "I don't know. I . . ." Leave the house? The land? Three of her children a thousand miles away? "I moved cross-country in a covered wagon once. I'm not sure I've got it in me to do again."

Oliver waved a hand. "We'd take the train all the way. No oxen required."

"But what would I do about the house? The farm?"

"You'd sell it, of course."

Annabelle shut her eyes against the panic roaring through her. "No. I can't sell this land."

"Why not?" Oliver pressed. "It's only a house. Only land."

Her eyes snapped open. "It's not only any of those things. This land—this house—was Jack's dream. His labor of love. His legacy. I'll not dishonor his memory by pawning it off to the highest bidder."

"So you'll farm the land yourself?"

"If I must, yes."

Oliver's fork slammed to the table. "Don't be ridiculous, Mother."

"I'm not the one who's being ridiculous."

Between them, Kate's face paled, and she stared at her lap, looking as though she wished for the earth to swallow her whole.

Annabelle took a shaky breath and lowered her voice. "You've both worked so hard, and you're finally seeing the fruit of your labors. You've had good crops the last two years, despite drought. Why would you leave when everything's starting to go well?"

"*Because* everything's starting to go well." Oliver's mouth tightened and twitched under a great struggle. "That's what this place does to you. It lulls you into complacency. Makes you think you're through the worst of it and you can finally get ahead. But a fire comes. Or a blizzard. Or a run-of-the-mill afternoon thunderstorm that knocks you off-balance and throws you to your death."

Annabelle's lips parted at the pain in her son's voice. He'd been the fastest to bounce back from Jack's passing. The first to put hand to plow and do what needed to be done.

And in so doing, he must have stifled a world of grief.

"This place killed my parents. The aunt who took me in, and the uncle who raised me. If not for you, it'd have killed me too." Flashing eyes fixed on her face. "And you yourself lost a baby and a husband to this godforsaken land. Why would you ever want to stay?"

Oh. It made so much sense it hurt. How could she have been so blind to the agony Oliver carried?

"But the Lord himself promised there'd be trouble. Life is hard. Things like this can happen anywhere."

His jaw tightened. "That may be. But I never knew loss until I came here. And one by one, the people I love get picked off by illness or natural disaster or plain old bad luck. And I've no intention of sticking around to watch the rest of you die too."

Wood scraped against wood as Oliver shoved his chair back, nearly toppling it in his race to escape the room. With a worried glance, Kate set her napkin aside and hurried after him. Maggie Ann's face crumpled, while the rest of the children exchanged murmurs of shock and concern.

Annabelle cradled her youngest to her chest and grappled with the enormity of it all. Oliver's pain. His decision.

The decision that now required one from her.

It would kill her to be abandoned again. To watch Oliver and Kate pack up and leave for California, perhaps never seeing them again.

But to pawn off Jack's dream? The one thing she had left of him?

That might kill her too.

><

Sloane set the diary aside with a frustrated sigh and pushed back from her office desk. Looked like her brilliant plan to forget Garrett and lose herself in Annabelle's life qualified as an epic fail. Given the content of the most recent entry anyway.

Emptiness. Loss.

The gaping hole a loved one left with his departure.

She stalked to the fridge and fished among the lunch sacks and takeout containers for the leftover enchilada she'd packed. Maybe she should set the diaries aside for a while. Find some less emotionally involved way to learn the rest of the story. Census films and cemetery records would tell her in an instant if Oliver and Kate had gone to California. If Annabelle went with them. That would be the logical way.

Garrett, no doubt, would heartily approve.

Colleen entered the little kitchen area, brow creased. "Are you all right? I just heard."

Sloane stuffed the enchilada into the ancient microwave. "Heard what?"

"Warren Williams bought the Spencer place."

"Yes. He did." She jammed the start button, and the microwave whirred to life.

"Are you all right with that?" Colleen's gentle brown eyes sought Sloane's. "I know how attached you are."

"Yep. Fine."

"Really?"

Sloane removed the enchilada from the microwave early and gave it an experimental taste. Blech. Still cold. "The money's for his grandmother. He did what he had to do." She returned her lunch to the microwave and slammed the door.

"I'll believe that when you do."

Sloane harrumphed quietly as Colleen bustled around the corner to her desk.

"So, not that this is any of my business." Colleen's chair creaked under her weight. "Are you pretending you're fine for the sake of the relationship?"

"There is no relationship. Not anymore." The microwave dinged off the surface of her sorrow, and Sloane popped the door open. Fragrant steam puffed up from the enchilada. A good sign. "Garrett's a planner. I didn't fit in with his plans. He's moved on. So should I. It's for the best."

"Simple as that."

Was Colleen being sarcastic? It was hard to tell. But there was no point in dwelling on it. Sloane forked up another bite of enchilada. Still cold in the middle. Back into the blasted microwave.

"Shame," Colleen said over the microwave's hum. "I thought you two were good together."

The simple phrase pushed at the lid she'd slapped onto her emotions. They *were* good together. Garrett's sharp wit and keen intellect matched her own. His dry sense of humor and innate knowledge of when to use it helped her not take herself so seriously. His deep blue eyes never failed to draw her in. Those creases in his cheeks when he smiled always made her want to smile right back. He shared her faith. He loved his family. He liked jazz.

"You're right, we were." It was the truth. Feelings aside, they were, indeed, good together.

And yet there was no room for feelings. Garrett had made that perfectly clear. Despite the shimmer in his eyes, the huskiness in his voice, the tremble in his thumb when he brushed it across her cheek and told her he was crazy about her . . . she still wasn't part of his grand master plan. The plan logic dictated he follow.

The microwave dinged once more, and she retrieved her lunch for a third time. She plunged her fork straight into the middle, took a bite, and—

*Ouch.* Their diva of a microwave had finally come through. And now she'd have a burned tongue to contend with the rest of the day.

Perfect.

At least it distracted her, if only momentarily, from all she felt about Garrett. Good thing too, because it didn't matter how she felt. That his departure left her feeling as dull and colorless as the plastic container in her hands. That she woke with his name on her lips, aching for him and angry with him and awash with all sorts of things she shouldn't feel, didn't want to feel.

Garrett clearly wasn't feeling any of those things. He'd made his plans, checked off his list, and stuffed her neatly into a box marked Pleasant Diversions. Nice for a time but never meant to last.

He'd made his choice. He'd moved on.

So should she.

*Help me do that,* she pled as she sank into her chair and set her lunch on her desk. *Help me think about something else, help me—*

Her computer chirped and she pounced. Then froze.

*To: HistorICT*
*From: Marinera72*

*Hi, Sloane! This is a bit out of nowhere, but I'm going to be in Wichita on business next week. I don't know if you're ready for this, and I don't know if I'm ready either, but—deep breath—I'd really like to meet you.*

Sloane blinked. Gaped at the message on her screen.

It was quite possibly the swiftest answer to prayer she'd ever received.

❊

Half-hearted rain spattered the windshield as Garrett drove down the turnpike to Wichita. Gray clouds hung heavy overhead, a dismal, disheartening start to what would no doubt prove to be a dismal, disheartening morning.

He reached for his cup of gas station coffee and took a bitter, lukewarm sip. It was early. Too early. Not that it mattered. He'd tossed and turned most of the night. And the night before that. And the night before that.

Every night, in fact, for the last two weeks. Since he shook Warren Williams's hand and took the man's enormous check, the knot in his gut had grown ever tighter. So much so that he couldn't even deposit the check. It still sat there, snug in his wallet.

His grip tightened on the wheel. In a couple hours, this would all be over. His meeting to finalize the sale was at nine, and then he'd be free. Free from all the angst and strain and stress and hassle. It would be done. Finito.

Maybe then the knot in his stomach would ease and he could bring himself to deposit Williams's check.

Maybe then he could work on his broken heart.

He missed Sloane. Every minute of every day. They hadn't been together that long, and frankly he hadn't expected it to hurt this much. But hurt it did. And sear, and ache, and every other verb for pain he could possibly think of. His missed those dimples in her cheeks when she smiled. The sparkle in her eyes when she made some new historical discovery. The mischievous quirk of her mouth when she was about to let loose another snarky comment.

Desperate for distraction, he turned up the radio. Traffic reports and stock market updates would keep his mind off things.

But the frequency that was all talk, all the time in Kansas City simmered with a sultry Diana Krall number here in Wichita. One that instantly called up a vivid image of Sloane onstage in that don't-you-dare-blink blue dress.

He'd give anything to hear her sing just one more time. To listen to her mesmerizing voice massage the ebbs and flows of the melody. To see her heart-melting smile as she basked in much-deserved applause. To guide her down the stairs offstage, cup her face in his hands, and kiss her senseless—

This wasn't helping. Not at all.

He gritted his teeth and switched the radio off.

At last, he exited the highway onto Jamesville Road. In a cruel irony, the offices of Williams and Son Development were on the same street as his grandparents' farm. Just a couple miles to the south.

He slowed as he approached the familiar gravel road to the left. After today, the property wouldn't be theirs anymore. A few months from now, it'd be unrecognizable. So maybe he should take a minute to pay his respects. See the place one last time.

He was already miserable. What could it hurt?

Memories assaulted him as he bumped along the rutted driveway. The first time he ever drove was here, at the tender age of fourteen, behind the wheel of Grandpa's ancient Chevy pickup. His mother, grandmother, and the chickens had all squawked their disapproval, but Grandpa was steadfast. His patience infinite.

Much of what Garrett learned about driving—about life—came from him.

From here.

And over there. Grandma's garden. A lump formed in his throat at the memory of the tomatoes she used to grow. Summer wasn't complete until he bit into one, flavor exploding in his mouth and juice running down his chin. They'd ruined him for all other tomatoes. And the county fair ribbons Grandma brought home every year proved he wasn't alone in that assessment.

Nothing but weeds grew there now. Grandma hadn't gardened for years.

And there. The patch of mud where Sloane got stuck the first time she came out here. He pulled up beside it, the brown puddle rippling in the rain. Sloane, shoes in hand, mud halfway up her calves. The adorably embarrassed way she'd admitted her need for help. The grateful shine in her eyes when he bailed her out. Heaven help him, he'd push cars out of the mud until he dropped if it meant she'd look at him like that.

What he wouldn't give for things to be different. For her to be sitting in the passenger seat right now, giving him that *don't be an idiot, Garrett* look he'd grown so fond of. To tell her, *Y'know what? Let's keep the house. Let's live here. You and me. Let's get married and make adorable, snarky babies. Let's eat bad-for-you desserts in the kitchen and kiss on the front porch and make love in the clearing by the creek. Let's make this house what it was always meant to be.*

*Let's make it a home.*

He wanted that. Craved it. He'd never known an ache so strong, a longing so deep. It volcanoed up from his very core, up and up until it erupted in a cry of anguish. His fist pounded the steering wheel once. Twice. He gripped the wheel so hard it hurt, and his head fell forward onto white-knuckled hands.

He gasped under the weight of pain. Of clarity.

He loved Sloane.

And if it were up to him, she'd be in all his plans. Every last one of them, from now until the end of time.

But it wasn't up to him, was it?

He had to do right by Grandma. Had to stick with the plan.

Even if that plan would utterly shatter his heart.

With a shuddering breath, he raised his head from the steering wheel. Took one last look at the house and scrubbed his hands over stinging eyes. Then he swallowed his anguish, stuffed all the emotions down deep where they belonged, and put the car into gear.

He'd given his feelings free rein for long enough. It was time to put logic and reason back in the driver's seat.

Time to enact his plan. Time to sign on the dotted line.

Time to get this over with.

# CHAPTER TWENTY-FIVE

GIVEN THE OMNIPRESENCE of Williams and Son Development signs between the highway and the company's offices, Garrett expected a towering skyscraper. Instead, the command center of one of the city's largest developers was an unassuming beige brick building sandwiched between a Presbyterian church and a Dairy Queen.

Inside, a receptionist escorted him to a conference room, where a trio of suit-clad men milled around a large wooden table. All of them balding, all of them middle-aged, all of them talking about golf.

He hated golf.

A box of doughnuts from the expensive place around the corner festooned the center of the table, flanked by a pair of French presses and an array of matching mugs. Real coffee. Not the convenience-store swill that had kept him going all morning. He started to reach for some, but a sudden queasiness made him step back.

"Mr. Anderson, I presume?" One of the suits approached with an extended hand and introduced himself as a member of Warren Williams's legal team. And then another. And another. All of them had names like Bob. In fact, maybe their names *were* all Bob. He wasn't paying enough attention to be sure.

"Is Warren not here yet?" one of the Bobs asked.

Another Bob jerked a thumb toward the opposite wall. "He's in his office. Said he'd be a second."

"Justice isn't here yet, either," put in Bob the Third.

Bob the Second rolled his eyes. "Fashionably late, as always."

Wait, Justice was a person? Surely he couldn't have heard that right.

Then Warren Williams's bulky presence filled the doorway. He'd exchanged the plaid shirt and blue jeans for a polo shirt and khakis. The enormous belt buckle, though, was still the same.

The developer's car-salesman smile beamed toward Garrett. "There he is. The man of the hour." His meaty hand encased Garrett's in a painfully tight handshake. Not physically painful, Williams's handshake was carefully calibrated to ideal professional firmness.

But emotionally it felt like handcuffs.

"Did you get coffee? A doughnut?" Williams gestured toward the spread. "Today's a celebration a long time in the making."

A celebration? Ugh.

"No, thank you." Garrett waved a hand. "I'm good."

Williams leaned in with a conspiratorial gleam in his eye. "I had Kinzie pick up some gluten-free ones if that's what you're worryin' about. You kids today are always avoidin' this and that. Good thing we're too old to worry about all that nonsense, right, Bob?" Patting his ample stomach, he elbowed the nearest Bob, who responded with a burst of workplace-appropriate laughter.

"It's . . . not the gluten," Garrett said quietly.

"Suit yourself." Williams shrugged and reached for a doughnut so covered in pink frosting and sprinkles that Garrett's teeth hurt just looking at it. "Mavis'll have a conniption, but I figure if ever there's a day to hop off the health food wagon, it's the day when somethin' you've been dreamin' about for over two decades comes to fruition, am I right?"

The Bobs all nodded and murmured their agreement.

Williams fixed his gaze on Garrett, dollar signs dancing in his eyes. "Good things come to those who wait, though. And this is definitely a good thing."

Garrett forced a smile and fought off a wave of nausea.

A tall, hipster-looking guy in all black entered, and Williams beamed. "But if I'd had that land when I first went after it, this genius would've still been in grade school. And I wouldn't have dreamed up half of what he does. This here's my son, Justice." Cupping his mouth with his hand, Williams lowered his voice to an exaggerated stage whisper. "His mama picked his name."

At six one, Garrett wasn't used to people towering over him, but Justice

Williams did. What he had in height, though, he lacked in width. Unlike his rotund father, Justice was reed thin. All arms and legs and loping gait, he resembled a giraffe with black plastic glasses and a soul patch.

"Justice, this is Garrett Anderson," Williams said. "The man who's about to make our dreams come true."

Justice sized up Garrett in a way that made him uncomfortable. Or maybe it was just today's general discomfort, and the sharp-eyed appraisal did nothing to alleviate it.

*Focus. Get it over with. A few more minutes, and you'll be free.*

Justice stuck out a pale hand, which Garrett shook. "Mmm," was all the taller man said.

"Have a seat, son." Williams rolled out the leather chair next to him. "Kinzie brought doughnuts."

Settling into the seat, Justice held up a hand. "I'm carb cycling."

Garrett sat across from them, between two of the Bobs. He wouldn't mind cycling right now. Pedaling mile after mile until he collapsed from exhaustion somewhere far, far away from here.

"Whatever keeps those creative juices flowing." Williams elbowed his son, then turned to Garrett. "Justice is the brains behind my best work. Meadowlark Mountain, Honeycomb Terrace . . ."

"Can't say I'm familiar."

The Bob to Garrett's left looked aghast. "Those are some of the most innovative residential developments in the whole Midwest." He seemed to take Garrett's lack of knowledge about the ins and outs of suburbia as a personal affront.

"I'm sure they are." His cheeks hurt from all the fake smiling.

"What else has he done?" Williams tented his fingers. "Let's see. Pine-ridge, of course. Conch Shell Cove—"

"Conch Shell Cove." Justice shuddered. "It's so pedestrian."

"Conch Shell Cove is a vision," the Bob on the right protested.

Justice shook his head. "It was my first attempt. I can scarcely bear to look at it now."

"C'mon, now, we're all our own worst critics." Williams reached for another frosting-drenched doughnut. "Conch Shell Cove is great. Half-million-dollar homes, three playgrounds, two swimming pools, a golf course. But that's nothin' compared to what we're gonna do for Beachy Meadows."

Beachy Meadows? Even the name made Garrett nauseous.

Williams nudged Justice's shoulder, sending a shower of sprinkles over his son's dark clothing. "Tell 'im what you've got cooked up." While Justice brushed off his shirt with a look of disdain, Williams smirked at Garrett. "You're gonna love this, I just know it. You'll tell your grandkids about it one day."

Garrett choked back bitter laughter. Yeah, right. *C'mon, kids, gather round and hear the tale of how Grandpa Garrett sold the family land to a sleazy developer. Right over there by the fifth hole? That's where the barn stood. And there by the swimming pool? A house used to be there. One Jack Brennan built with his bare hands.*

Nope. Not happening.

He'd take this day to his grave.

The lights dimmed, and a presentation appeared on the screen before him. "Beachy Meadows," the logo proclaimed, complete with the incongruous image of a field of sunflowers along an oceanic shoreline. Justice launched into a low monotone riddled with unfamiliar words like *gestalt* and *liminal*.

"Start with the creek lots, son," Williams instructed. "And you don't mind if I do the talkin', do ya?"

Perfect. Now Garrett would have some clue what was going on.

Although maybe he didn't really want to know.

Justice clicked a slide to reveal a simulated drone flyover of a suburban street. Garrett recognized the twists and turns of Blackledge Creek at once, though now it was lined with piles of brick and stone instead of stately cottonwoods. The simulation showed artfully placed, fully leafed trees in every front and back yard, of course. But those would take decades to reach the level of cool, soothing shade pictured there.

"And now, the pièce de résistance." Williams's butchered French made Garrett cringe. "What'll set Beachy Meadows apart."

The next slide presented a serene lake view, ringed with private docks.

"This isn't your standard, run-of-the-mill neighborhood retention pond. No sirree. This is a state-of-the-art ski lake. Jet Skis, canoeing, fishing, any kind of water activity people want right outside their back door, off their own private beach."

A map of Beachy Meadows came next, and Williams looked ready to pop with glee. Large home lots fringed the edges, but the center of the land, the heart and soul of it, was the ski lake.

"There she is. Fifty-five sweet acres of lake, and thirty-plus lots of beach-front property. And the ones that aren't on the beach will have in their back yard a beautiful meadow leading right down to the creek."

Garrett's stomach turned. Beachy Meadows wasn't just a smarmy name. It actually meant something.

Williams kept prattling, but the words seemed a million miles away as Garrett stared at the map, all the air whooshing from his lungs at the spider-shaped ski lake that comprised the majority of his grandparents' land.

They weren't simply going to plow the house under and build bigger, newer ones in its place. No, they planned to obliterate it. Dig up that beau-tiful land and drown it beneath a lake.

The tomato patch.

The puddle where Sloane got stuck.

The graves beneath the old cottonwood.

All so yuppies with seven-figure houses could ride Jet Skis in their own back yard.

"Would ya look at that?" Williams elbowed his son. "The boy's gone speechless!"

Garrett blinked. Williams, Justice, and the Bobs all studied him. Was he supposed to say something? React somehow?

"What about the graves?" he blurted.

Right Hand Bob straightened in his chair and eyed Williams over the rims of his glasses. "Human graves? You never said anything about that."

Williams pasted on that salesman smile. "Justice has a plan for that too. Show 'em."

Justice clicked to another slide featuring a fenced-off area with a gran-ite stone in its center, the names represented by a scribble. To its left was a shaded picnic spot, to the right a playground, all against a beachfront backdrop.

People picnicking by the Brennans' stone. Kids running around shrieking and tackling each other next to a memorial to three people who gave their lives on this very soil. Two of whom never lived long enough to run or play.

All while their actual resting place lay at the bottom of a man-made lake.

This was supposed to honor them?

"This was not our agreement." The words burst from Garrett, clipped and short.

Williams glanced up. "What are you talking about? You told me about the graves, and I said I'd put up a stone. Fence it off."

"But you never said where, did you?" *And I never asked.*

The realization was a punch to the gut.

"What about putting the lake somewhere else?" The mere idea of the lake galled him, regardless of location. But at least maybe then he could live with himself.

Both Williamses shook their heads, and the elder pointed at the map. "The most important part of a ski lake is its shape."

"But I specifically asked for the graves not to be disturbed."

Williams stifled a sigh. "I'm prepared to exhume the remains at my own cost. Rebury them at a cemetery of your choice. Just tell me where."

"Where I want them buried is at the base of that old cottonwood. *Not* under a ski lake."

Williams's eyes narrowed, and he leveled a meaty finger at Garrett. "Think carefully about what you're sayin', son. You need me far more than I need you."

Garrett gulped. He *did* need the money. His grandmother's future hung in the balance.

But . . . beachfront property? A ski lake?

The land Jack Brennan had slaved and sweated over, the land that had been in Garrett's family for over a century, buried beneath thirty feet of water?

The very thought gutted him.

And Sloane. She'd know exactly what lay beneath that lake. What had been sacrificed at the altar of urban progress. And it would destroy her.

All too clearly, he could picture her heartbreak—heartbreak he'd cause at the stroke of a pen—and his eyes stung. He bit his lips lest he break down all over again.

*Dear God. What have I done?*

He'd followed his own plans. Leaned on his own understanding. In his obsession with trying to do the right thing, he hadn't consulted God at all. Not the God of the Bible anyway. Just the god of logic. His own financial expertise. His own intellect. He'd left the only one who truly knew the right plan completely out of the equation, and now he was moments from doing something that would utterly devastate his grandmother. His sister.

And the woman he loved.

His heart filled to groaning with a wordless cry for forgiveness. For guidance. Right there, in front of the Bobs and the Williamses, he silently begged God to intervene. To fix this somehow. *Forgive me, Lord. It's yours now. Your plans are higher. Your ways are greater.*

*Please. Show me what to do.*

Something shifted and gave way within him. The fist clenched around his heart loosened and blissful release flooded into its place.

He didn't know what he was going to do. Not yet.

But he couldn't do this.

He *wouldn't* do this.

Not to his family.

And not to the woman he loved.

Garrett cleared his throat and met Warren Williams's eyes across the table. "I'm not certain I'm comfortable with these plans."

"I'm not certain that matters."

"I am. Because this land belongs to some of the first settlers in the county. Without them, we wouldn't be here. Wichita wouldn't be here. And I think they deserve better than to have their land turned into a ski lake."

"Now just you wait a minute." Williams's voice took on a menacing tone. "We had a deal."

"We had a verbal agreement. That's not a deal."

"Where I come from, a man's word is a deal."

"Then why are all these Bobs here?" Garrett gestured around the table. "I've signed nothing. Legally, I'm under no obligation to sell the land to you."

"But I wrote you a check."

"Which I never cashed." Garrett fished the check from his wallet. "Never even endorsed it." Holding the check by its edges, he turned it around. "Would you like it back? Or should I tear it up?"

No response.

"I'll just leave it here then." He set it in the center of the table, next to the doughnuts, and a three-ton weight lifted from his shoulders. He gripped the side of the chair so he wouldn't float away.

Williams turned to the Bobs, red-faced. "Can't you do something?"

"He's right, Warren," one of them said. "A verbal agreement means nothing until it's signed."

"Which it won't be. Not now. Not ever." With his first genuine smile of the morning, Garrett rose and snagged a doughnut from the box. "Good day, gentlemen."

Sinking his teeth into the sweet, pillowy pastry, he strode to the exit on legs rubbery with relief. With freedom. The full-bodied release he thought he'd feel when he signed on the dotted line. Here it was, at last, and it tasted far sweeter than he could've ever imagined.

He wasn't trying to convince himself he'd done the right thing. Not anymore.

He knew.

He still wasn't sure where the money would come from. Not at all certain how to secure his grandmother's care. For the first time in his life, he didn't have a plan. He sat poised atop the trail's tallest hill, helmet strapped, bike in gear, ready to fly down and let gravity take him where it would.

Maybe he'd soar. Maybe he'd crash.

But he was in for the ride of his life. And ultimately, regardless of what bumps and bruises he incurred along the trail, he'd come to a safe stop. What that looked like or where it would be, he had no idea, but he was riding behind Someone who knew the trail intimately. Who had a map of the best possible route. He didn't have to plan or fret or obsess anymore.

All he had to do was follow.

It was terrifying. It was exhilarating.

At long last, it was right.

# CHAPTER TWENTY-SIX

GARRETT COULDN'T ASK for a better Saturday morning on his favorite trail. Sunny and humid, but with enough predawn crispness lingering in the air to make it tolerable. Quiet, with only the rustling of leaves, the whiz of tires on pavement, his own breathing, and the twittering of birds.

Not too busy either. Just a few other cyclists, to whom he tossed a friendly wave, and a group of dedicated-looking runners clad in T-shirts emblazoned with the logo of a local shoe store. Was it his imagination or did a couple of them look slightly envious when he glided past?

He didn't blame them. Four years of high school cross-country and he'd never once experienced the famed "runner's high." But a few miles on the bike always left him awash in endorphins and ready to take on the world.

He was counting on that today. Because two dilemmas loomed, each as puzzling and pressing as the other. The first was Grandma. She loved it at Plaza de Paz, but her stay there would be short unless he could summon some serious cash.

And his heart—Sloane's too, probably—still lay in shards from their breakup. Plan B? Ha. Couldn't be further from the truth. But could he convince her? Could anything he said or did penetrate the fortress she'd doubtless built around her shattered soul?

On his own, he would make thousands of plans. But now, rather than tumbling his problems over and over in his head, depending on his own ability to solve them, he'd brought God into the mix. Asked him, time and again, to provide his solutions in his way. Though not having a plan felt strange, that strangeness was underpinned with a peace Garrett hadn't known in months. Emboldened, he increased the intensity of both his pedaling and his prayers and started up the final series of hills leading back to the trailhead.

Halfway up the second hill, amid the rapid, rhythmic thudding of his heartbeat, came a name, more strong impression than actual sound.

Kimberly.

The trail grew steeper, and he shifted gears and stood up on the pedals.

Kimberly.

His legs burned with effort. Was this the guidance he'd prayed for? Or was it just coincidence, grasping at straws, trying to assemble something—anything—resembling a plan?

Kimberly.

*So . . . you want me to list the house?* He'd need to talk to Lauren, of course. She'd jump at the chance to sell it to hipster homesteaders if it meant the house would be spared. But then he was back to the work it needed and the time it would take to sell. Grandma's savings might run out before then, and then what?

*Kimberly.*

All right. He'd prayed for guidance, and maybe this was the answer. It would've been nice to have additional instructions. A detailed, multistep plan.

But God didn't provide those. Just a name.

So Garrett would go with it.

Besides, in this section of the trail? He couldn't spare the energy to argue.

A few minutes later, he arrived back at the parking lot, shaky and sore, but satisfied. After loading his bike onto the back of his car, he pulled off his helmet and enjoyed the cool breeze through sweat-soaked hair as he guzzled some Gatorade.

Hydrated enough to know he hadn't been hallucinating on the trail, he fetched his phone and scrolled through his contacts until he reached the name that had bounced around his head for the last four miles and umpteen hills.

Kimberly.

"Are you sure?" he said aloud. An older couple walking a golden retriever glanced his way, and he offered what he hoped was a reassuring, I'm-not-really-talking-to-myself smile.

Then his phone buzzed in his hand. He glanced down.

Kimberly.

*Well played.* He lifted the phone to his ear.

"Garrett. Hi. Kimberly Walsh. Listen, I'm sorry to call so early, but I'm booked solid today, and if I didn't call now, I probably wouldn't."

"No worries. I was about to call you anyway. How can I help?"

"I heard through the grapevine that you and Warren Williams reached a deal on your grandparents' land. Is that true?"

He pulled his right foot up for a quad stretch. "We did have a deal. A verbal one anyway. But I chose not to proceed."

"Really?" Kimberly seemed to be weighing her words carefully. "So Warren Williams won't be buying the property?"

"Nope." Garrett shook out his right leg, then reached for his left.

"Well, I can't say I'm entirely unbiased," Kimberly replied. "But in my humble—and biased—opinion, I'm glad."

"Thank you." He spoke both to Kimberly and to God, and his loosened, limbered muscles echoed the release in his heart. Not a day would pass when he wouldn't be glad God had yanked him off the disastrous path of his own planning.

"So have you made any other plans regarding the property?"

A robin hopped along the asphalt and stopped in front of him. It cocked its head and peered at Garrett, as though it too were interested in his answer.

"Nothing definite, although I'm leaning toward an auction. I had one set up with McCue's that I canceled when I made the deal with Williams. I'm not sure when their next available date is." He propped his right foot on the bumper of the Camry and bent forward to stretch his calf. "Mostly I'm just praying for direction."

"I see." Another thoughtful pause. "Maybe I can help with that. Because I'd like to throw my hat into the ring."

He straightened and switched legs. "I appreciate that, but we had to move my grandmother to a care facility sooner than we thought. Time is of the essence now, and we can't afford to have the place sit on the market for months—"

"I'm sorry, I wasn't clear. I'm not interested in listing the house. I want to buy it."

Garrett froze. "Like, for a flip?" If she wanted to flip it, they could sell it as is. The sale price would be lower, of course, but they wouldn't have to wait.

"No, not a flip."

"Wait, you're the hipster homesteader with the chickens?"

Kimberly's laughter bubbled through the phone. "Nope. No chickens. My husband's allergic to feathers. I've just . . . come to appreciate the home's legacy. Something that's been there that long, that means so much to so many, deserves to stay standing. I'm all for development, obviously—wouldn't have much work if I wasn't—but this place is special. I want to make sure it's preserved."

Garrett leaned for a torso stretch. "Sounds like you've been talking to Sloane."

The pause on the other end stretched far longer than his offhand comment warranted.

"Yes." Her voice sounded odd. "I have been talking to Sloane."

⇥⇤

Birds trilled in the trees over Sloane's head, their melodies floating on the warm, summery breeze buffeting Jamesville Park Cemetery. A curious cottontail paused beneath a shrub to chew a blade of grass, studying Sloane through round, wary eyes. Gossamer tufts of white fluff drifted like fat snowflakes from a stately cottonwood, illuminated by golden sunshine.

It was so peaceful. So serene.

Totally at odds with the chaos churning inside.

Sloane's footsteps punctuated the birdsong, the crinkle of the plastic around the flowers she'd brought the only other sound. Perhaps it was weird, meeting the woman who gave her birth at a place for burying the dead. But this little country cemetery, nestled among the wheat fields just outside town, was where Jack and Annabelle were laid to rest. Where, according to her research, several other relatives were buried as well.

The Brennan family. *Her* family. Her origins.

So what better place to meet her connection to those origins? If her mother thought the location strange, she hadn't said a word. She'd simply agreed on the time and place.

Score a point for Marinera.

Sloane glanced at her watch, terror and exhilaration competing for supremacy. She'd purposely arrived early to see the Brennans' graves. Marinera wasn't due for another few minutes.

Though photos of the monuments were available online, viewing them digitally couldn't hold a candle to being here. Walking where her ancestors had walked. Standing where her bereaved family once stood, comforting one another with fond memories and reassurances of a glorious eternity.

Paying her own respects to the foremother she knew only through faded ink on yellowed pages, yet to whom she was indelibly linked.

She had to be close to the Brennans' stones, because here were the Maxwells, memorialized with a large white obelisk. With her finger she traced the engraved birth and death dates of Annabelle's Uncle Stephen and Aunt Katherine. So much life encompassed by those years and the simple dashes between them. So much adventure. So much love. So many contributions to this county and its history.

A yellow butterfly flitted past Sloane, fluttered off to the left, and— *there.* There they were.

With a last reverent glance at the Maxwells' monument, she hastily crossed to another granite obelisk, this one in reddish stone, the name *Brennan* etched prominently along the top.

The side facing her featured Jack's information, and tears stung her eyes as she took it in. The dates of birth and death. The forty-six short years God had given him. Regimental information from his Civil War service, mentioned only briefly in Annabelle's diaries. He never spoke much about that time in his life, she said.

Sloane traced the rough stone etching with a fingertip, then walked around to the next side. *Sarah E., wife of J. F. Brennan*, it read. Below it, *J. H., son of J. F. and S. E. Brennan.*

Sloane swallowed around a lump in her throat. Though only a fortunate few knew Sarah Brennan's true burial site, it was comforting to know she'd been immortalized here. Especially given the likely fate of the original graves.

Anger welled, but Sloane ordered it into silence. This was a place of peace. Besides, what she was looking for was likely just around the corner of the stone . . .

There.

*Annabelle M.*
*Wife of J. F. Brennan*
*b. Mar. 14, 1852*
*d. May 22, 1936*
*Aged 84 years*

She hadn't gone to California after all. Tears fell at the confirmation. And what a life. What a legacy. The girl who'd come to Kansas in a covered wagon in 1870 had lived to see automobiles. Radios. Airplanes.

Her heart overflowing with a thousand emotions, Sloane knelt in the cool grass before Annabelle's grave and laid the cellophane-wrapped spring bouquet amid bright yellow dandelions and puffy purple-and-white clover. How long had it been since anyone laid flowers here? Far too long.

After a moment, she stood, kissed her fingertips, and pressed them to the stone's cool, lichen-covered surface, then walked around to the fourth side. Etched there were Emmaline's name and dates, along with those of Jack and Annabelle's son Stephen, gone in 1905 at the tender age of twenty-two.

Sloane gazed at the dates, at the dash of another life cut short. What tragedy had befallen him? They'd yet to find any diaries from that era, so she could only guess. An illness perhaps? An accident? She made a mental note to check newspaper archives for more information.

Sloane laid a hand on the rough edge of the obelisk. Poor Annabelle. How had she coped with the loss of yet another child, another precious loved one?

But the question had a simple answer. Annabelle had doubtless coped the same way she always did.

By running to the arms of her heavenly Father.

Footsteps crunched through the grass behind her, and Sloane's breath caught.

Her mother was here.

This was it. The moment she'd waited three decades for.

She was so ready.

And so not ready.

Heart somersaulting into her throat, mouth cottony, she turned.

A familiar flash of red hair, brushed back with a pale hand. A wobbly smile as the woman walked toward her.

Sloane stared. "Kimberly? What are you . . . ?"

Kimberly slipped off her sunglasses to reveal eyes shining with unshed tears.

Brown eyes, flecked with gold.

Eyes that suddenly looked all too familiar.

The wobbly smile widened. "Hi, Sloane."

# CHAPTER TWENTY-SEVEN

SLOANE'S MOUTH OPENED, but no words came out. Tingling heat flooded her body. Darkness danced at the edges of her vision. A bird chirped from what seemed like the end of a long tunnel. She wanted to run, but her feet had taken root right here next to the Brennan family plot. All she could do was stand and watch Kimberly—Marinera72, her mother—advance slowly toward her.

She stopped a few paces away, sunglasses in hand. "My word, you look so much like Nonna."

Nonna. Domenica Brennan.

Sloane's link to Annabelle.

Kimberly's link to Annabelle.

Her birth mother was Kimberly.

Was this some bizarre cosmic prank? Was God laughing in her face right now? Or was it a dream? Was she about to wake up in a cold sweat, glance at her phone to find some ridiculous hour, and be relieved—or maybe disappointed—it wasn't real?

A squirrel's chatter pierced the stillness. A spring breeze kissed her face. Another tuft of cotton wafted past her.

She was wide awake.

But was Kimberly for real? How had she found out? When?

And why hadn't she said anything?

Questions condensed into a single, monosyllabic squeak. "How . . . ?"

"That day Garrett had me come out and look at the house, remember? You were there. That's why I was so confused, because there was just something so familiar about you. Your dark hair, your heart-shaped face, the way you carry yourself . . . it was so much like Nonna it gave me chills." The wobbly smile returned. "I thought I was losing it."

The faded scene replayed in her mind. Sloane had been so focused on Garrett, on the Carter and Macy Realty logo on Kimberly's SUV, that she hadn't taken a close look at Kimberly herself.

Her mother. Sharing space with her for the first time in thirty years.

"My mind's always played tricks on me," she said. "Lots of times I'd see someone about the right age and I'd wonder if she was my daughter. So I tried to convince myself it was all in my head. But then Garrett took me inside. I saw those family photos his sister had all over the table . . ."

The photos Sloane had come over to see just moments before. The whole reason she was at the house when Kimberly arrived.

"And one of them made me do a triple take. Because I'd grown up with a picture just like it on the living room wall."

Words. Words. They buzzed around Sloane's head like pesky flies. Bounced off the surface of her confusion.

Kimberly dug in an ivory Coach purse and withdrew her phone. With a manicured fingertip, she scrolled through some photos, then held the phone out. Sloane took it, and her fingers brushed Kimberly's pale ones.

Her mother's fingers.

Their first physical contact in thirty years.

Her heartbeat jackhammering, she cupped her right hand above the screen to better view the grainy black-and-white image.

It was one she vaguely recalled seeing on the table, though at the time it hadn't registered since she'd focused on the photo of the woman she now knew was Annabelle. In this picture, two women in flapper-era dresses and headbands smiled at the camera. One of them, fair-skinned and blonde, resembled a young Rosie.

But the other one, with more olive-toned skin and darker hair . . . Sloane's breath hung suspended between inhale and exhale. Because that woman had her nose. Her chin. Her cheekbones. The same dimple on the left side of her smile.

Goosebumps pricked her arms despite the day's warmth.

"And here's the one I grew up with." Her voice tremulous, Kimberly pulled a faded black-and-white picture from her purse. "Meet my Nonna. Domenica Brennan."

Sloane took the photo with a shaking hand. The same two women, a few years older, now joined by two men. The one beside Domenica stood with his hand on her waist, his dark hair slicked back. From the nose down, he resembled Jack, but his eyes looked just like Annabelle's.

"John Patrick." Sloane caressed the man's face with her fingertip.

"I never met him." Kimberly's voice barely registered, so focused was Sloane on the photograph. "He was a few years older than Nonna. I think he died in the '60s sometime. Nonna lived until 1978."

Sloane's gaze moved to the other couple in the photo. The Rosie look-alike had added glasses since the previous photo and held a chubby baby boy on one hip. "Who's this?"

"That's Grampy's second cousin Pearl and her husband. I didn't know her well, but she and Nonna were close. They became friends at a family wedding—that's the story I heard anyway. They wrote letters back and forth and were practically inseparable whenever Grampy and Nonna visited Kansas."

Kimberly kept talking, no doubt sharing valuable family information, but the words dulled. Because behind the couple stood shining white clapboards, fresh and clean. A porch Sloane knew well—a porch she'd always seen listing to the left—stood straight and tall.

"Do you know where this picture was taken?" she asked.

"At Rosie Spencer's house." Kimberly's voice wavered. "I didn't recognize it when I went out there because I'd never been, and I hadn't paid much attention to the house in the photo. But Nonna always spoke fondly of coming to Kansas for Granny Annie's eightieth birthday. Once you made the Brennan connection, I put two and two together."

Sloane's gaze fell on the name on the Brennan family obelisk. On the bouquet she'd laid there minutes before.

Granny Annie.

Annabelle.

Kimberly gave a soft chuckle. "There's a family story that Nonna's nickname in Grampy's family was Betty Boop. Nonna experimented with a short haircut right after that cartoon came out. I guess one of the littler cousins started the nickname, and that's what they all called her until the day she died."

The truth slammed into Sloane's midsection. Auntie Boop. No wonder Rosie had called her that from the beginning. She doubtless would have remembered Domenica. Would have seen the resemblance.

Sloane handed the phone back to Kimberly, wide-eyed.

It was all true.

Kimberly was her mother.

"I found another letter." Kimberly tucked her phone into her purse and pulled out a plastic bag containing a worn, yellowed envelope. "It's to Nonna from her mother-in-law. Since you've been reading those diaries, I thought you might like to have this."

Hands trembling, Sloane took the envelope. It was covered with Annabelle's handwriting. The same scrolls and loops. The same faded ink.

"I knew you'd been . . . looking for me." Kimberly's hesitant words yanked Sloane's attention from the envelope. "And I thought I wasn't ready to know you. To admit what I did."

Sloane took a step back. "Wait. You knew I was looking? The whole time?"

"No, I only got on that website last fall. Thirty years after I found out I was pregnant." Kimberly wrapped her arms around her midsection. "I knew you had to be out there somewhere, but once I set up the account, I only had the guts to look a couple of times. I . . . didn't feel like I had the right to look. That you wouldn't want anything to do with me, and I certainly didn't deserve to find you. And I thought I was fine with that."

Last fall. Her mother had been on the site since *last fall*.

Kimberly's gaze skimmed Sloane's face, and her smile widened. "But then I saw you, and I figured out who you were, and you were looking for me, you wanted to know me, even after what I did . . . and it gave me the courage to try. To risk it. Because I wanted to know you."

Her mother. Wanted to know her. After thirty years of silence, her mother wanted to know her.

"And I want you to know me." Kimberly moved toward a bench beneath a big, shimmering cottonwood. She sat down and patted the surface next to her, her rings clinking against the concrete. "So . . . here I am. Any question you have, I'm ready to answer."

Any question? The question that had been the drumbeat of Sloane's entire existence? Surely Kimberly didn't mean she could ask that. Not after a handful of emails and a few minutes of in-person contact.

She was bracing herself for it, though. Her guarded expression as Sloane drew closer suggested she expected the question. Dreaded it.

Sloane sat with a sigh and folded her hands in her lap. A whiff of Kimberly's perfume cut through the fragrance of flowers and freshly mown grass.

"In all the time I looked for my mother, I never expected her to be . . . here. In Wichita." She studied Kimberly's face. "Especially when you led me to believe you live somewhere else."

Kimberly's gaze fell. "It was a little misleading, I'll admit. Although technically not a lie. We live in Andover."

A suburb in the next county. Semantics. Sloane wasn't going to get distracted arguing finer points of the map. "So why do you live here?"

"My second husband got transferred. I wasn't thrilled—I thought it'd be flat and boring with nothing to do. That's what everyone said about it anyway. But I remembered all the things Nonna would say about beautiful sunsets and kindhearted, salt-of-the-earth people, and I decided to give it a chance. And Nonna was right. Wichita's not flashy. It's not the kind of place that shouts from the rooftops about all it has to offer. You have to look beneath the surface. And Greg hated it here. He never looked. But I did. And I loved it. So I stayed."

Simple as that. For an untold number of years, Kimberly had been right under Sloane's nose. Making the same city home. Eating at the same restaurants perhaps. Visiting the same museums and libraries.

Watching the same sunsets.

"You said in your emails you grew up in Cleveland." Sloane glanced up. "Is that true?"

"Born and raised. My whole family lived there at the time. I was the first one to leave. For college. In Seattle. I got a full ride to a private liberal arts school there. I wanted to study English literature. Become a college professor and spend my career in academia." Kimberly's eyes fixed on her lap; her fingers laced together. "And I thought I was ready. I was a straight-A student after all. Valedictorian. On top of the world. But I had no idea how that world really works."

Sloane picked at a loose cuticle. Her whole body tensed, her stomach knotted. Answers loomed like storm clouds on the horizon. Answers she'd sought her whole life.

Was she ready to hear them?

Kimberly's attention shifted toward the flapping flag at the cemetery's entrance. "So when my lit professor said he wanted to tutor me after hours . . . I thought that was exactly what he meant."

A gust of wind clanked the flag's metal rings against the eagle-topped pole.

"When he told me it was okay to act on our feelings, that they were normal and natural . . . I believed him."

Sloane's breathing grew shallow. Her legs itched to run. Had she really wanted answers? Was it too late to change her mind?

"When he told me he loved me, that he wanted to be with me forever . . . I thought that meant he'd leave his wife for me."

Sloane's hands balled into fists. A naive college student and a lecherous lit professor. That was her DNA. That was how she came into the world.

Kimberly gave a dry chuckle. "He didn't, of course. Not even when I showed up with the baby."

A scream welled inside. Sloane bit it back, but it filled her chest and throat and demanded escape. Maybe if she gave in, if she screamed and screamed and screamed, she wouldn't have to hear the rest.

"I thought once he saw what we made together, he'd realize what a fool he'd been. But I was the fool. For so, so many reasons." Kimberly's voice was robotic. As though she were relating the story to a brick wall rather than the child she'd abandoned.

"He threw me out of his office. Told me he never wanted to see me again. Threatened to file a restraining order. So I got on a bus, my life in pieces . . ."

"And you left me." The words were a dull thud.

"Yes."

The screaming stopped. The storm fizzled. The answers she'd sought for so long lay quiet in her lap.

She expected to feel angry. Relieved. All the things, all at once.

But she felt nothing. Nothing except a sad resignation.

She wasn't a baby to her mother. Not a person. Not really.

She was a last-ditch effort to save a doomed relationship.

And, true to form, she hadn't been enough.

"I found out later I had severe postpartum depression. Not that that's an excuse for what I did. There is no excuse, and I'm sorry, Sloane." Kimberly was crying. "I'm so sorry, and I—"

Sloane held up a hand. "Can we . . . not do this? At least not right now? I need some time."

Kimberly sniffled and dabbed her tears with a tissue. "Of course."

Sloane crossed her legs and stared at the sky. Brilliant blue, with white cotton-ball clouds. Oblivious to the miserable woman and her miserable daughter below, trying to make some sense of their miserable beginning.

An ache welled in her chest. If only Garrett were here. He always knew how to smooth things over. He'd pull her close and stretch out those long legs and let her be a mess for a bit.

But he wasn't here.

She hadn't been enough to save that relationship either.

"So what's your life like now?" Sloane searched her memory for fragments of her mother's emails in hopes of steering the conversation to safer territory. "You're married, right?"

Kimberly stashed the tissue in her purse. "Yes. Third time was the charm. Todd's a heart surgeon. He and I are going on twenty-two years."

Third? And that didn't count her birth father. Sloane's mind spun. "Do I have siblings?"

"You have a brother and a sister. Well, half."

Still, people who shared half her DNA.

Yet they had nothing in common with her at all.

"Do your kids know about me?"

"No." Kimberly's voice was small. She seemed to shrink in on herself. "I'm sorry. I couldn't."

Sloane felt like a boxer who'd suffered so many blows she'd grown numb to them. "It's fine."

"This is Ethan." Kimberly held out her phone. "He's a sophomore. Plays football at Collegiate."

Sloane blinked, stunned, at the dark-haired young man clad in the blue and gold of one of Wichita's private high schools. This stranger bore some resemblance to her. Same hair color. Same nose. But how could anyone with athletic ability be related to her?

"And this is Siobhan. She's my daughter with Greg." Kimberly's finger slid left to display a breathtakingly gorgeous brunette. Slender and willowy, with the same high cheekbones as her mother—*their* mother. But she also bore a more than passing resemblance to Annabelle.

"She studied music in college and works at a church now, plays violin, sings on the worship team."

Sloane's head jerked up. "She sings?"

"She has a beautiful voice." The words were rich with pride. The kind of pride Sloane would have heard had Kimberly kept her. And she'd have a sister. A sister who sang, who grew up right here in Wichita. She could've run into them dozens of times. The library. Cowtown. Riverfest. She nearly choked. Ethan and Siobhan—her brother, her sister, her blood—had likely been some of those field trip kids shuffling through the exhibits. Probably before she worked there, but still. And she'd never known.

Because Kimberly chose not to allow it.

"She gets that from my father," Kimberly was saying. "He had a voice to die for, God rest his soul—"

"He's dead?"

Kimberly crossed herself. "Three years next month."

It was too much. It was all too much.

"You took that from me."

"I'm sorry?" Kimberly paused, her phone halfway back into her purse.

"I sing. For fun. At a jazz club. I said that in one of my emails."

"You did, and I—"

"No." Sloane stood. "*I sing.* I sing because I can't not sing, and I never knew anyone else like that—except, hey, I've got a sister who's the same way. And a grandpa. Only he's dead, and I'll never know him because you took that chance away from me. You took my family from me because you were a naive teenager who used me to try to patch up your doomed affair. And when that didn't work? You left me on a bus."

Kimberly's mouth opened, but no sound came out.

"And I would have been happy with you."

Kimberly got to her feet. "No, Sloane. You wouldn't. You have to trust me on that."

"Why?" She flung out her hand. "Sounds like Ethan and Siobhan are doing just fine."

"They have adults for parents. Not a heartbroken, messed-up, mentally ill teenage single mom."

"But they know you love them. They know you're proud of them. They know they're not just some bargain-basement plan B." Sloane paced the grass in front of the little concrete bench. "Did you know my parents wanted to have a little girl more than anything else in the world? So they adopted me. And I tried so hard to be everything they wanted. But I couldn't, because I wasn't theirs." Tears welled, but she held them back. "I could have grown up knowing who I was and where I came from. That I look just like my Italian great-great-grandmother. That the big old house up in Jamesville belonged to my family. All that, I could have known. But I didn't. Because you took it from me."

"Sloane—"

"No." She gathered her purse. "I'm sorry, but no. I just can't."

Blinded by tears, she stumbled to the shady spot where she'd parked her car, flung her purse in the passenger seat, and pulled out of the cemetery, her tires kicking up clouds of white gravel dust.

Finally, after decades of searching, she had what she wanted. Answers to her life's core questions. Information she thought would make her complete.

Instead, she felt emptier than ever.

## Chapter Twenty-Eight

GARRETT REACHED FOR his coffee and flew through another email. Though his inbox this Monday morning was predictably full, it was a comfortable, manageable full. Inbox Double Digits, once a pipe dream, was now the norm. And given a few more minutes of quiet, there was at least a snowball's chance he'd reach Inbox Zero.

Such was life in a more settled state.

He and Kimberly Walsh had agreed to terms on the house last week. After Friday's closing, it would no longer be his burden. Lauren, relieved that the deal with Williams had fallen through, was thrilled to sell to Kimberly. As for Grandma, it seemed Plaza de Paz was treating her so well she barely even remembered the house. Whether that was due to her disease or to how happy she was in her new digs, he wasn't sure. But he'd take it.

And yet. As quickly and easily as God gave him direction regarding the house, he'd been curiously silent on the issue of Sloane. Garrett's heart still bled at her absence, but he hesitated to call her. To hop in the car and drive down, as had occurred to him more than once while passing the exit for I-35 South on his way to work.

But he'd seen what happened when he charged ahead, and he dared not risk doing that with the woman he wanted to spend the rest of his life with. She was too precious. Too important. So he'd vowed to wait for complete assurance from God as to his next steps. Thus far, that assurance had yet to be given.

Garrett clicked to the next email. "Quick question," the subject line read. He had to smile. "Quick questions," as a rule, were never quick. Especially when they came from clients like Gilda Roberts.

But a knock came at the door before he dove in, and Joseph Sterling leaned against the doorjamb.

"Garrett. Good morning." Sterling's expression was unreadable. "Could I steal a moment of your time?"

"Sure." Garrett turned from his computer as the boss settled into the chair opposite him. Sterling leaned back and studied him, fingers interlaced.

Garrett's stomach tightened. He wasn't about to get fired, was he?

No. That was ridiculous. Maybe in the thick of things with Grandma, Sterling would've had cause. But not now. Garrett wasn't behind anymore. He didn't take hours to return phone calls. He was close to Inbox Zero.

"I'll get right to it," Sterling said. "You've no doubt heard buzz about us possibly opening a satellite office. Somewhere outside the KC metro."

"I've heard rumors, yes." Garrett's shoulders relaxed slightly. This didn't sound like a pink-slip conversation.

"Well, it's happening." Sterling's smile lit his face. "And the suits have asked me for a couple guys to start it up. Given the administrative duties, it'd mean a promotion. Pay raise. Your name was the first to come to mind."

Garrett's eyebrows shot up. "It was?"

"Naturally, since the satellite office will be in Wichita."

The name hit him square in the solar plexus.

"Somewhere on the west side. One of those newer office parks. Can't remember exactly where. Anyway, I think you'd be a perfect fit for it. You're young. A go-getter. Plus, it'd be more convenient for you, what with your grandmother, your sister, that girlfriend of yours . . ."

*Girlfriend.* The word stung like lemon juice on a paper cut. "Oh, we're not—I'm not, ah . . ."

"Never thought I'd see Garrett Anderson speechless." Sterling gave a quiet chuckle, then eyed Garrett over the rims of his glasses. "So how's this strike you? Think we could persuade you to pack your bags and head south?"

Garrett blew out a breath. "I'd have to give it some thought."

"Of course." Sterling stood. "But we want to get moving on this, so if you're out, I'll need to find someone else."

"Absolutely. I understand."

Sterling slipped out, and Garrett tapped his pen against his desk, the emails in his inbox blurring as his contacts dried out from staring.

He could be moving to Wichita.

What about his clients? Who else would be so patient with Geraldine Krantz's weekly stock market panic? Who would take the time to answer Gilda Roberts's "quick questions"?

And what about him? Wichita was never part of the plan. An idyllic slice of childhood, sure, but his real life was here. Royals games. Arguments over which restaurant had the best barbecue. Great jazz. Rolling hills, thick groves of trees, and the wide Missouri River. He'd grown up here. His family was here.

Except they weren't here. Not anymore. With Mom in heaven, Dad in Florida . . . and what were Lauren's plans exactly? Did she even have any? Would she stay near Grandma, or chuck it all and backpack across Europe? Either was plausible.

He needed to talk to her.

And Sloane.

His heart thudded.

This move wouldn't be like the one he made for Jenny Hickok. It wouldn't be a hasty abandoning of his lifelong plans, but a surrendering of them to the God who'd had a better plan all along. And the move wouldn't be for Sloane, necessarily. For all he knew, he'd already torched his chance with her. Even so, Wichita was big enough that awkward run-ins at the corner coffee shop would be the exception, not the rule. The two of them could doubtless coexist peaceably.

Never mind that he ached for so much more.

His coveted quasi-settled feeling evaporated like mist in the face of yet another huge decision. One that would lead to another. And another. And another.

Yes, he needed to talk to Sloane. And Lauren. And his colleagues.

But before he did any of that, he needed to talk to God.

*Lord? Hey. It's me. I've got a quick question . . .*

>‹

The rough bark of a cottonwood dug into the back of Sloane's shirt. Damp soil seeped through her pants. And she was probably trespassing, since

Garrett's family didn't own this land anymore. The "sale pending" sign out front was proof. Heck, Warren Williams's bulldozer could come along at any moment.

But for now she was here. At Annabelle's spot. Or as close to Annabelle's spot as she could reasonably guess. Her foremother found such peace beside these rippling waters.

Maybe she could too.

Her head fell back against the tree and she closed her eyes, enjoying the warm breeze on her face and trying to make sense of this morning. Her whole life, she'd wondered who she was. Where she came from. Why her mother abandoned her. And now she had the answers.

But rather than salve the wound, those answers ripped it wide open. And through its jagged, bleeding edges stormed the words she'd always believed about herself. The silent shrieks that had defined her.

Unwanted.

Unloved.

Not enough.

A gust of wind stirred the leaves overhead and tugged at the soft, weathered envelope between her fingers. She'd almost forgotten Kimberly gave her Annabelle's letter to Nonna. Before today, she'd have dug into its contents as eagerly as the fragile paper would allow. Now, she eyed the familiar handwriting with abundant caution. Would Annabelle's words soothe her troubled soul? Or would they pour more salt into that ripped-open wound?

Curiosity won out, and Sloane carefully pulled the yellowed paper from the envelope, unfolded it, and scanned the faded handwriting. A bit wobbly now—the date indicated Annabelle was in her seventies—but still familiar.

The letter was mostly updates on relatives. Some of the names registered, others didn't. But toward the end of the second page, a few lines caught Sloane's eye. Made her slow in her skimming and drink in the words.

*My dear Domenica, it is always difficult for a mother when her last chick flies the nest. I remember how hollowed out I felt when Maggie Ann married Daniel and moved to Oklahoma. I missed her laugh, her sparkling wit, those gray eyes so like her father's. Children leave, and it is as it should be, but oh how bittersweet!*

*Rest assured that the God who blessed you with those beautiful children loves them even more than you do. And the Lord loves you too, Domenica. He never leaves you. He alone is sufficient.*

*It took me many years and many trials to learn this. When my mama passed, God cared for me. My papa left, but God never did. I lost Emmaline, but the Lord held me in my grief. He shepherded me through losing Jack. And yet, when Oliver and Kate planned to move to California, I fought God tooth and nail. I couldn't bear the thought of losing the only place I'd truly called home. Of giving up on Jack's dream and being torn from the last bit of him I had.*

*But the Lord convicted me of my sin. My idolatry—for that is what it was. I had depended on my identity as a daughter, a mother, a wife, a resident of Sedgwick County. But in reality none of those things are my true identity, nor are they yours. We are daughters of the most high God. He alone can satisfy. Even though I still miss Jack dearly and look forward to that day when we are together in glory, I have grown closer to the Lord in ways I never knew I could. He has filled all my empty places and indeed given me the peace that passeth all understanding.*

*Give my love to John Patrick and the children. You are all in my prayers daily.*

*Ever yours,*
*Mama Brennan*

As Sloane lowered the letter, a fresh sense of loss gripped her. Something far beyond not getting what she wanted. The sheer emptiness of gazing into the chasm at the core of her being and knowing that all her efforts to fill it had failed.

Trying to please her parents, to be the little girl they wanted so desperately, hadn't worked.

Meeting her birth mother, getting answers . . . that hadn't filled the hole.

Even finding Annabelle, connecting to her birth family, her blood, felt hollow. She was grateful beyond measure to have found her roots, but they still weren't really what she sought.

But now Sloane walked around the chasm's edges with a new perspective. The thing she truly wanted, Annabelle had found. The answer was both further away and closer at hand than she ever could have imagined.

Though Sloane had been a believer all her life, God always felt somewhat distant. A vaguely judgmental presence more than a person who could fill her. Her sins were forgiven, she was destined for heaven, but she'd always sort of thought divine involvement in her life stopped there. This utter dependence on God that Annabelle painted such a beautiful picture of . . . that was foreign. And Sloane wanted it more than anything.

Could it be she held God at arm's length? Hadn't truly surrendered to him because she feared she wasn't enough for him either?

Could it be that she already was enough? That the peace she so desperately sought everywhere but its true source was right here, shimmering in the sunlight, waiting for her to reach out and take hold?

Slowly, Sloane sat up and pulled out her phone. Opened her Bible app and scrolled through the promises that had always flitted in one ear and out the other. Promises she'd never truly absorbed as being meant for her.

She was loved. Chosen. Knit together, fearfully and wonderfully, in her mother's womb.

And even though her birth parents viewed her as an unwelcome surprise, even though the Kelleys saw her as a befuddlement, to God she was neither. He'd created her. He knew her. He gave his life for her. And through that sacrifice, she'd been adopted into his family. Not in a plan B, *she'll do* sort of way, but as a cherished, beloved daughter of the King.

Since before time began, he'd planned for her. Wanted her. And he'd always, always loved her.

Cleansing tears dampening a tissue, Sloane bowed her head and basked in those promises. In that love.

God was enough. His love was enough.

And because of that infinite, unfathomable love . . . so was she.

# Chapter Twenty-Nine

"You're looking for what?" Garrett frowned at his phone, as though its flat silvery surface could interpret his sister's confusing request.

"The Christmas relish recipe." A touch of impatience edged Lauren's voice. "It's in the church cookbook, I think."

Amid all the turkeys and hams and sides of every description that had always graced the family holiday table, he couldn't conjure up anything befitting the name. "Did we have relish at Christmas?"

"No, Mr. Literal," Lauren huffed. "It's made with red peppers and green tomatoes. Red and green?"

"Christmas colors."

"I knew you'd figure it out eventually." Lauren's smirk was evident even through the phone. "Grandma used to make it with all her end-of-summer produce. I'm figuring out my fall blog posts and that'd be a great feature."

"Look at you, planning ahead." Garrett rose from the sofa and made his way to the pile of plastic crates along his otherwise nondescript living room wall. "You're coming along nicely."

The raspberry Lauren blew would've made their grandmother proud.

Garrett ran a fingertip along the tower of crates from the farmhouse, each labeled with a strip of Sharpie-scribbled packing tape. "A church cookbook, you said?"

"It's got a sketch of a church on the front. Light blue cover maybe?"

"If it's here, it should be in this one. Let me put you on speaker." Garrett set the phone on an end table and hoisted a crate marked "Kitchen" from atop the pile. "How's the apartment hunt coming?"

"I think I found a place."

The crate thumped on the sofa. "Really?"

"It's *adorable*." Lauren's voice went tinny over the phone. "It's in this ancient elementary school building that's been converted into apartments. Mine's got a chalkboard along one wall and everything. Hardwood floors, tons of natural light, and the kitchen is ah-mazing."

"That's great, Lo. I'm happy for you." Plastic popped as Garrett unlidded the crate and flipped past the red-and-black plaid cover of an ancient *Better Homes and Gardens Cookbook*, relishing the release of another weight from his shoulders. Not that Lauren's living arrangements were his responsibility, of course, but it was still a relief to know she'd found a place she liked. "I may be apartment hunting myself soon."

"What? Why? You bought your house practically the second you graduated from college. Said it was a sensible investment. Are you feeling all right?"

"It'd just be temporary. A month or two. And it's not definite yet." He fingered a book of cookie recipes. "My firm's opening a branch in Wichita, and my boss thinks I should be the one to get it off the ground."

"Harassing me from three hours away isn't enough anymore? You have to do it in person?"

He quirked a grin toward the phone. "That would be a perk."

"So are you going to take it?"

"I don't know. It depends on a lot of things."

"Like patching things up with Sloane?"

"If only it were that easy."

"You guys broke up because of the house and the distance, right? Kimberly's buying the house, and if you take this job, the distance thing goes away too. What are you waiting for?"

"It wasn't just that, Lo. You remember how things ended with Jenny. How much it messed me up."

"I believe it was my all-knowing big brother who said Sloane is nothing like Jenny Hickok. And as usual, he's right. Jenny was a flutterhead. She was silly and immature and she didn't deserve you. But Sloane just fits. She's nerdy in the same ways you are, she puts up with all your weirdness, and . . . Garrett, I've never seen you as happy as you were with her."

"But meeting her was never part of the plan, and I—"

"Oh, come on." Lauren's exasperation rattled the phone against the end table. "You're turning your back on the best thing that's ever happened to you because she doesn't fit in your plan? Then revise the plan, jerk face. Grand Master Life Plan, section 5, paragraph 3A, revision 12B: 'Meet the woman of my dreams, fall madly in love with her, and do whatever it takes to win her heart.'"

Bittersweet amusement tugged his lips. "We said some things last time we were together. Things I'm not sure can be fixed."

"Don't you want them to be?"

Pain pressed against the walls of his heart. "Of course I do."

"Seems like maybe you should make a phone call then. Apologize for whatever dumb thing you said. Because it was obviously you."

"You're right. I should."

"Whoa. Did you just say I'm right?"

"Yeah, yeah. Don't let it go to your head." *Jackpot.* A light blue spiral-bound cookbook peeked up at him from the crate. "I think I found what you're looking for. *Hearth and Home: Recipes from the First Christian Church of Jamesville, Kansas.*"

"That's it. Thank you."

"I'll text you a pic."

"That'll work." She gave a thoughtful pause. "There might be some other things in that cookbook I could make over, health-food style. Could you bring it next time you visit? Y'know, when you come to look for an apartment? The one next to mine is available."

He chuckled. "Let's not get nuts, Lo."

After they ended the call, he flipped through the little cookbook. Sure enough, page four featured a recipe for Christmas relish. He snapped a photo and texted it to Lauren. When she replied with a string of heart-eyed emojis, he slid the little cookbook back into the crate.

Why had he brought all these cookbooks here anyway? It made far more sense for Lauren to have them, especially with—

Wait.

That little brown book wasn't a cookbook.

Adrenaline zinging through him, he carefully lifted the book from its nest. He didn't carry archival gloves in his back pocket the way Sloane always seemed to, but he'd do his best.

His heart ached at the sight of the familiar, faded scrawl. *Dear God, I miss Sloane.* He missed the eager gleam in her eyes, the excited flush in her cheeks. The voracious reverence with which she'd dive into the diary and devour its century-old contents. The adorable enthusiasm when she made a new discovery.

The first date in the diary squeezed his heart.

April 23, 1894.

Sloane's birthday.

→←

### April 23, 1894

Shiny wet ink transformed to matte black under the gentle spring breeze. Annabelle blew on the ink to speed the drying process, then closed the diary, set it on the corner of her worn quilt, and leaned back against the tree.

Mercy, the creek was lively today, chattering and bubbling its joy at spring's arrival. Tentative green leaves unfurled from branches; wildflowers stretched toward the sun. The apple and cherry trees along the drive perfumed the air with subtle sweetness.

But instead of joy at the signs of new life, sorrow weighed on her soul. Because unless plans changed, she'd never again see spring bloom on Jack's beloved land. Come summer, she'd leave all this behind. The creek. The flowers.

The dream.

It was for the best, of course. If staying was too painful for Oliver, then as a widow with limited options, she needed to go with him. Submit to God's plan, as she had years ago when Uncle Stephen's bumpy wagon brought her here. Oliver was God's provision for her, for her other children. His invitation was gracious. Necessary. And she would accept.

But that didn't mean it wouldn't hurt.

Footsteps swished through the grass, drawing her attention from the burbling creek. Her breath hung suspended at the sight of the dark-haired man approaching.

It wasn't Jack, of course. It was Oliver.

Time and again, Oliver's resemblance to his uncle stunned her. Not even blood relatives, they nonetheless had the same inky hair, the same sharp cheekbones. But while Jack's eyes had been a deep, stormy gray, Oliver's were a brilliant blue. A gift from his mam, Jack always said.

Oliver's shadow fell across her quilt. "May I join you?"

"Certainly." Smiling, she scooted to her left.

He lowered himself to the corner of the coverlet, and Annabelle filled with love for this boy turned man she adored as much as the ones she'd birthed herself. They shared a love for reading, for writing. As soon as Oliver learned penmanship, he'd begun scribbling in his own diaries. Though she'd not seen him write in one for years, she suspected he kept up the habit.

A cottonwood branch floated by in the creek, and nostalgia tugged her heart. "The first time I laid eyes on you, you were in that water."

Oliver chuckled. "I thought you were an angel. My mother had a painting of an angel back in Wisconsin. It's one of my earliest memories." He plucked a blade of grass, twirled it between thumb and forefinger. "I'm not sure what happened to that painting. I never saw it here. But to my eyes, at that moment . . . you looked exactly like her."

Annabelle covered his hand with hers. "You never told me that."

"You always treated me like your own child. And you made Uncle Jack so happy. What you did for him, for us . . ." One corner of his mouth quirked. "I'm not certain you aren't an angel after all."

Emotion thickened her throat and stung her eyes.

"I called him Uncle Jack because that's how I'd always known him. But he was every bit my father." Oliver blew the blade of grass toward the rippling waters of the creek. "I hope and pray I'm as good a father as he was."

Was he saying . . . ? Annabelle squeezed his hand.

A smile split his face.

"Oh, Oliver." Joy bubbled up in a laugh. "When?"

"Early November, Kate thinks."

"Is she feeling all right?"

"Mercifully, yes. She's a bit queasy in the mornings, but it passes as soon as she eats."

Annabelle smiled in relief. "Then she is a blessed woman indeed."

"And so are you." Mischief gleamed in deep blue eyes. "You'll be a grandmother, after all."

Annabelle pulled up short. "That makes me sound frightfully old."

"What about Granny?"

"That's even worse."

"Granny it is then." Oliver's eyes crinkled at the corners. "Or maybe even Granny Annie. It rhymes."

She gave him a playful shove. "You will *not* call me Granny Annie."

"You'll get used to it in time." Oliver put his arm around her shoulders and pulled her close.

"Perhaps it's good that babies take months to arrive then." She shuddered. "Granny Annie."

"It suits you."

She studied her eldest, her feelings so chaotic she couldn't even pluck one out to examine, let alone name. "You're going to be a wonderful father. Jack would be so proud."

Oliver bowed his head. "I miss him."

"I miss him too."

"I keep thinking . . . what if I'd been there? What if I'd gone fishing with him instead of for a drive with Kate? What if I'd repaired the roof myself when I found the fallen shingles?"

She leaned her head against her son's broad shoulder. "It wasn't your fault."

"I know. But I don't always feel it." His chest rose and fell with a heavy sigh. "I can't look at that corner of the house where he fell without seeing him."

"Oliver." Tears blurred his image. "I understand why you need to leave. Which is why I've decided to come with you and Kate."

He pulled back. "You have?"

"The Lord showed me my error in thinking this place is all I have of Jack. Far from it. He lives on in Thomas's determination and John Patrick's smile and Maggie Ann's eyes. He lives in the hearts and memories of those who love him. I don't need the land, the house, to feel close to him, especially not when I know we'll be together in glory one day." She smiled at Oliver. "Besides, you'll need the extra hands, with the baby and all."

"Well, that muddles things up a bit."

"How so?"

"You're not the only one who's been talking with God. I've been praying for guidance, and he's provided it through Kate."

Annabelle examined her son for clues as to what he was about to say, but with Oliver she couldn't push. He needed time to gather his thoughts. So she waited and watched as he plucked another blade of grass.

"Kate's quiet. She seems delicate. But she's as tough as they come. When she makes up her mind about something, I'm learning, fast, that it's nigh impossible to change it. And she told me that if she were in your shoes, she'd want to stay. Even if she had to go it alone. And she wouldn't be thrilled if her child were so far away." His eyes twinkled. "That's how she told me about the baby."

Annabelle beamed. She knew she liked Kate.

A shadow crossed Oliver's face. "One of my earliest memories is of my parents arguing, late one night when they thought I was asleep. My mother was expecting again."

Annabelle blinked. Jack had never told her that. Perhaps he hadn't known.

"Pa wanted to abandon the trip and go back to Wisconsin. But Ma wanted to press on. She said they'd come too far, sacrificed too much, to give up. Within a week, they were both gone." He cleared his throat. "I know we'd be taking the train, and the trip would be easier. But still. I won't subject Kate to such a journey. Not in her condition."

Annabelle stared, slack-jawed. Could he possibly be saying what she thought he was saying?

"Now, my feelings on the house have not changed. I still don't want to go anywhere near it. But what would you say to Kate and me purchasing some of your acreage? We'd farm it all, work out some rent . . ."

He kept talking, but Annabelle couldn't hear anything beyond *they're staying* and *that means I can stay too.* How wondrous God was! How beautifully he had worked out every last detail to redeem the dream she'd surrendered to his care.

"Oh, Oliver," was all she could say. He wrapped one arm around her, and her heart burst into song.

She could stay. In her house, on her land, by her creek. By God's providence, she could live out the rest of her days making Jack's dream come true. The dream the Lord had given him.

The dream he'd given her too.

✦

"You kept the house."

Garrett shook his head. Now *he* was talking to Annabelle? He must be certifiable.

But what he'd said aloud to his empty living room was true. Annabelle had never left the house. The land. And if Oliver kept the property, there was a decent chance it had been in the family for its entire existence.

He closed the diary and studied its dusty cover with bone-deep certainty. He needed to tell Sloane.

Of course, this was Sloane Kelley, researcher extraordinaire. She probably already knew. The minute she read of the potential move to California, she'd have dug through land records or census films or whatever other resources she had access to.

But there was one thing she didn't know. One thing she needed to know.

The house she'd fallen in love with, the house that stood at the center of this mess, wouldn't fall victim to Warren Williams's wrecking ball. It wouldn't stay in the family, not with Kimberly buying it, but it would stay standing.

Whether it made any difference, whether he could win her back, he had no idea. But even if it couldn't heal things between them, it might heal her.

He pulled his phone from his pocket. Heart thumping, he scrolled through his contacts to the number he used to call all the time. To the little picture of her, the one he'd snapped while she was reading one of Annabelle's diaries, the one that had caught her off guard and made her look up with that bemused "what in the world are you doing?" expression.

It would be so good to hear her voice. Even the thought was like rainfall on parched land.

But a mere phone call would be like a two-minute thundershower on ground that hadn't seen a drop in weeks. Wonderful and welcome, but nothing close to enough.

He needed to see her. To be with her. Even if it was the last time, even if there was no hope for a future, he needed to see her face. Touch her. Hold her.

And the diary in his hand was the perfect excuse.

She had all the others. She needed this one too.

Before he could talk himself out of it, he grabbed his keys off the counter, stepped into a pair of sneakers, and headed for the garage.

He was going to Wichita.

# CHAPTER THIRTY

"A WOMAN HAPPILY in love, she burns the soufflé. But a woman unhappily in love, she forgets to turn on the oven."

Sloane dug her toes further into the navy microfiber of the sofa, her fuzzy orange blanket draped over shorts-clad legs. Though she'd seen *Sabrina* countless times before, the lines had never hit home quite like this.

She reached for the remote. Maybe this wasn't the lighthearted escape she'd thought it'd be.

A knock came at the door, and she glanced at the clock. 9:48. The Chinese delivery guy must've flown here, as recently as she'd ordered.

Cool air hit her legs as she threw off the blanket. "Coming." Bare feet thudding on the wooden floor, she fumbled through her wallet, found a crumpled ten, hurried to the door, and—

Garrett.

In the hallway. Right outside her door.

He had on that KU Final Four T-shirt he liked so much, red basketball shorts, sneakers with no socks, and a plastic grocery sack draped over one arm. Stubble shadowed his jaw, and his hair was longer than she remembered. Wide-eyed, he looked as astonished to see her as she was to see him.

This despite the fact that he was the one who'd driven here.

He'd driven here.

He was here.

"I should've called," he said.

Sloane glanced down at her worn Wichita flag tank top and striped lounge shorts. Her hair was still damp from a shower, her face devoid of makeup. Not how she'd have looked if she'd known he was coming, but it could always be worse.

A dawning expression crossed his face, like he'd suddenly realized where he was and what he was doing. "Right. I'm sorry. I should've called."

He stepped back. Was he about to leave? No, he couldn't leave. Not when he was here.

"It's fine. You're fine. I just wasn't . . ." Whatever bare-bones train of thought she'd managed to assemble slid clean off the track at the sight of those crinkled-at-the-corner eyes. "Hi."

He smiled, and her stomach fluttered. "Hi."

Those blue, blue eyes. Eyes she could fall into and lose herself forever. She'd missed those eyes.

He rummaged in the bag around his wrist. The scent of warm car mixed with traces of his morning cologne teasing her nostrils. "I found this."

She tore her gaze from his face to his hand. To the little brown book he held out to her.

"I thought you had them all, but this one hitched a ride with me to KC. In a crate of cookbooks, believe it or not. I thought you should have it."

Her heart sank. Of course. The diary. That was the sole reason he stood on her doorstep. He was probably in town anyway, visiting Rosie or something, and this was the last stop on his itinerary.

Sloane took the worn leather volume from his outstretched hand. "Thanks."

"She kept the house, y'know."

The huskiness in his voice drew her eyes upward. "What?"

"Annabelle stayed. She didn't move to California. Neither did Oliver. They all stayed." Stuffing the empty bag into his pocket, he scanned her face. "But I'm guessing you know that already."

She nodded.

"Of course." His mouth flexed. "But do you know why they stayed?"

"No. The diaries I had didn't go that far."

"Kate got pregnant. Oliver didn't want to risk her health. It's all in there." Garrett gestured to the diary.

A smile bloomed despite everything. "Spoiler alert." She set the diary on the little table inside the door and laid her crumpled cash next to it.

Garrett shifted his weight and leaned an arm against the doorframe. "Sloane, about the house—"

"Forget it. I don't care."

Surprise flared in his eyes.

"Okay. That's not true." She folded her arms across her chest. "I care a lot. But it's just a house. Bricks and plywood. I thought it would fulfill me, that meeting my mother would fulfill me, but they won't. Nothing will except God himself, and he has. So . . . no hard feelings, okay? You needed to do right by your grandma, and if Warren Williams has to bulldoze the place for that to happen, then I shouldn't . . ."

At Garrett's odd smile, she trailed off. "What? Do I have something on my face?" She gave a self-conscious swipe to the end of her nose.

His dimples deepened. "No. It's just . . . I didn't sell the house to Warren Williams."

"Wait, what?"

"I came close. A deal was in place. But when I saw his plans for the land . . . I couldn't do that to you."

*To you.* She savored the words. "Do I want to know what those plans were?"

"Probably not."

"I have to admit, I'm curious."

"Of course you are." His gaze caressed her. "That's one of the things I love most about you."

She froze. Had Garrett really said that word? Had he meant to say it?

Those deep indigo pools almost crackled with the electricity that hovered between them. The word wasn't a slip. It was one-hundred-percent intentional.

"What did he want to do?" It didn't matter really. Nothing mattered. Nothing except that Garrett was here and saying things and looking at her in that sizzling way.

"He wanted to dig the whole thing up. Turn it into a ski lake."

The words would've devastated her had they not been delivered in the past tense, and in that adorably flirty tone. Garrett let his hand drop from the doorframe and stepped closer with that intense, heavy-lidded gaze. Goose bumps broke out over her arms.

"A ski lake?" She smiled. "That's appalling."

"I thought so too. So I backed out." His eyes darkened. "Like I said, I couldn't do that to you."

She stared at him.

He'd altered his plan.

For her.

Before she could think better of it, she stepped toward him, cupped the back of his neck, and pressed her lips to his in a quick, fierce kiss. But at his lack of response, she pulled back. Had she misinterpreted? Done something wrong?

"I'm sorry," she said.

"You don't need to apologize. Not for that. Never for that. It's just . . ." He drew a shuddery breath that spoke of restraint rather than reluctance. "Before I let myself kiss you, I need to tell you what I came all the way down here to tell you. Because I didn't come just to give you the diary. I came because you're not plan B, Sloane. You were never ever plan B. You've been God's plan all along."

His voice faltered. Was it nerves? Emotion? Either way, it turned her heart to liquid.

"Unexpected?" he continued. "Yes. A surprise? Most definitely. But I love you. And you are someone who is—without question—worth chucking all my old plans and making new ones. So many new ones. All of which feature you in a very prominent role."

Her knees wobbled. Her breath stopped.

Garrett was here. And he loved her. Like that.

Her gaze never leaving his, she led him inside. Shut the door. Grasped his face in her hands and captured his mouth.

This time, he responded. This time, he tangled his fingers in her hair and whispered words of love against her lips. This time, he spun them around, pinning her between the heated wall of his chest and the cool, smooth surface of her apartment door.

When he finally released her, she opened her eyes to find him breathless and beaming, his hair disheveled, his cheeks flushed.

"I take it this means maybe you love me too?" he asked.

A smile sprang to tingling lips. Her fingertips traced the contours of his face. "Yes, smart guy. That's exactly what it means."

Their lips met and mingled once more.

"So what do we do?" she asked when he freed her mouth and moved to her cheek.

"About what?" His lips trailed past her ear to the corner of her jaw, and she shivered.

"About the distance."

"What distance?" He had a point. She was so close to him she could feel his rapid heartbeat, syncopated against her own.

But that wasn't normal. Normal meant three hours on the turnpike. FaceTime and texting and other forms of communication that didn't involve her pulse pounding against his scorching lips.

"We don't exactly live next door, y'know." The words struggled out.

"True." His lips tickled her neck with his response. With the kiss he feathered to tender flesh. "Although we could."

Wait. "What?"

"That was something else I needed to tell you." He pulled back to look at her. "I got a job offer. Here in Wichita. One I'm thinking about maybe . . . absolutely definitely taking." The words rushed out on a heady exhale, a split second before he returned to her mouth with a happy groan.

She allowed a moment of bliss before studying his expression. "You're serious? You're moving here?"

"Yes. I just decided." His fingers combed through her hair. "I want us to work, Sloane. But even more than that, I wanted to make sure I was following God's plan and not my own. I've prayed about us more than I've ever prayed about anything. And he's removed the obstacles between us one by one. The distance . . ."

"The house . . ."

"Oh, man. I forgot to tell you the best part."

"Better than you moving here?"

"I don't know about better. But it's really good. Can't believe I forgot all about it. Must've been distracted." He planted kisses down the side of her neck. "Very, very distracted . . ."

*"Garrett."* She took his face between her hands. "What is it? What's the best part?"

He looked blank for a moment, and if the stakes hadn't been so high she'd have giggled. "Oh. Right. The house. I sold it."

"You did?" Emotions tumbled in her chest.

"We close Friday." Apology flitted across his face. "I know you wanted it, and I'm sorry we couldn't—"

She cut him off with a kiss. "It's all right. That house led me to Annabelle. To my mother. To God even. And to you. I don't need to own it for all those things to still be true." She stroked his cheek with her thumb. "I just hope you sold it to someone who'll take care of it. Who'll appreciate its history."

Capturing her hand in his, he brought it to his lips. "That was my number one stipulation. More than any dollar amount. That Jack and Annabelle's house be preserved. And Kimberly said that's exactly why she's buying it. So its history can—"

Sloane's eyes flew open. "Kimberly's buying the house? The real estate agent?" A shiver coursed through her frame, one that had almost nothing to do with the kisses Garrett pressed to her fingertips.

He glanced up. "I know that look. Your mind's going a mile a minute. Why's that?"

"Because . . ." She wrapped her hand around his, her heart in her throat. "Kimberly is my mother. My birth mother."

Garrett's mouth fell open. His brows fluttered together, then apart. He tried to speak, but no words came out. Bless him, he looked so adorably confused that she couldn't help but want to kiss him again.

So she did.

⊰⊱

It felt odd, this Wednesday morning breakfast date. After waking up half convinced she'd dreamed Garrett's impromptu late-night arrival—and his kisses—Sloane had answered another unexpected knock at her door. Again, it was Garrett, flowers in his hand and a smile on his face. Right there in her living room, radiating assurance, he'd called his boss to accept the position in Wichita—and to take a personal day. Heart filled with joy, Sloane reached for her phone to cash in the same privilege.

After a leisurely breakfast at a cute little café in Riverside, they slid into Garrett's car, Plaza de Paz their intended destination. But just before the highway on-ramp, Sloane spied the red-and-white Carter and Macy Realty logo on a glass office door.

"Do you mind if we stop for a minute?" She gestured toward the office building. "I want to see if Kimberly's in."

Garrett slowed the car and cut her a glance. "Are you sure?"

Despite the churning tightness in her gut, Sloane nodded. "Things didn't end well between us, and I want to apologize. Especially since she's buying the house."

"Of course." Garrett's turn signal clicked on, and he pulled into the lot. And there was Kimberly's big white SUV. Her mother's SUV.

Her mother was right inside.

"Want me to come in with you?" Garrett asked.

*No. I can handle this.* The instinctive answer welled inside her. She always had before. But at the concern etched on his face, at the compassion in the hand stroking the nape of her neck, she bit it back. He loved her. Even this raw, wounded, confusing mess at her core. His quiet, steady confidence proved he could handle it. He could handle her.

Her initial resistance faded to a river of gratitude for this wonderful man. Despite her nerves, despite her tangled-up insides, she flashed him a smile and unbuckled her seat belt. "Sure. What's a Wednesday morning without a little mama drama?"

Chuckling, he pulled the keys from the ignition. "Drama is like second breakfast."

They piled out of the car onto a warm, sun-drenched sidewalk, and she laced her fingers with his. But they were still a few feet from the door when it opened, and there was Kimberly.

"Sloane." Her clicking heels stopped in a patch of shade. "Hi."

"Hi . . ." What was she supposed to call her? Kimberly? Mother? Mom? Nothing sounded right. "Hi," she repeated dully.

An uncertain smile hovered at the corners of red lips. "I wasn't sure you'd ever want to talk to me again."

"I wasn't sure I would either."

"That's fair." Kimberly slipped off her sunglasses and nested them in her hair. "Garrett. I wasn't expecting you until Friday." Her gaze fell to Sloane's hand in his.

Sloane smiled into the awkwardness. "It's okay. He knows about . . ."

"Oh." Kimberly shifted uncomfortably.

"I was already grateful to you for buying the house and preserving its legacy." Garrett flashed a reassuring grin. "But now that I know just how personal it is to you, that you're Sloane's mom—Jack and Annabelle's descendant—I'm even more grateful. You're keeping it in the family."

"Which is why I'm here." Sloane tightened her grip on Garrett's hand. "This house, this whole journey of discovery I've been on . . . it means the world to me that you're buying it. I'm glad it'll be cared for."

"I'll say it will." Kimberly's voice caught. "Knowing you, you'll restore it to its former glory. There might even be a historical plaque."

"Knowing me?" Sloane's brow creased. "I mean, I can find out what period paint and wallpaper would've looked like, but I don't have a lot of experience with actual historical restoration."

"Well, restore, redecorate, hire it out—whatever you like. You'll be the one living there, Sloane." Kimberly's eyes shone. "I'm buying the house for you."

Sloane's jaw unhinged. "What? No. You can't be serious. It's too much—"

"I am serious. And it's not too much. It's something I want to do. For you."

A sob caught in her throat. "Why?"

"Because." Kimberly stepped closer. "You can't undo the past. Much as you might want to. But you can do whatever it takes to make the future as bright as possible."

Sloane stood, speechless. It was too much. It was all too much.

"I'm not trying to buy your affection." Her voice thick, Kimberly gripped the strap of another expensive-looking handbag. She looked at the ground, lips trembling, then fixed wet eyes on Sloane. "I don't expect this in any way to make up for thirty years of absence. I'm not doing it with the expectation of forgiveness, or reconciliation, or anything like that. If you never want to see me again, that's your choice, and I'll respect it. No strings. No guilt. I just wanted to buy the house. For you. Because when you were born, I couldn't give you a home. And now I can."

"I—I can't let you do this."

Kimberly blinked and dabbed at a fallen tear. "You can't?"

"No. I mean yes. Of course. But not unless you let me put some money in it too." At her mother's quizzical expression, she hastened to explain. "My parents—my adoptive parents—gave me a little nest egg, and I can't think of a more perfect way to spend it. Because you gave me life. And they gave me my life. And this house is where all that comes together."

The house. She was getting the house.

Kimberly's hand fluttered through the air. "Use it for renovations. Last I checked, the place needed a little work." One corner of her mouth tipped up as she glanced at Garrett. "Take Jack and Annabelle's house, Sloane, and make it your house. Your home."

Slowly, Sloane turned loose of Garrett's hand and walked toward her mother. Feeling poised over the edge of a great chasm, she opened her arms. With a teary smile, Kimberly stepped into them, and Sloane relaxed into the embrace she hadn't felt for three decades. Her mother's chunky necklace pressed into her chest. Complex floral perfume tickled her nostrils. It was all so strange. So unfamiliar. And yet . . . right.

There would doubtless be bumps in the road ahead. Awkwardness. Discomfort. More wounds to uncover, to heal, as a result of lost years and poor decisions. But the one who'd brought them together would guide them through this messy, figuring-it-out stage.

If God had used a dusty satchel and an old diary to answer her deepest prayer, then there wasn't a thing in the world he couldn't do.

⊱⊰

Garrett stood astonished on the sun-dappled sidewalk, watching Kimberly walk inside the office.

Kimberly was Sloane's mother.

She was buying the house for Sloane.

No wonder he'd never felt right about selling the place to Warren

Williams. No wonder he'd felt such a strong urge to call Kimberly that Saturday morning a few weeks back.

No wonder none of his plans had worked out. God had a different plan. One that was immeasurably better.

Sloane's adoring gaze snapped him out of his trance. "This can't be real. None of this. I'm going to wake up any minute."

Inspiration struck at the amazement on her face. "Y'know, I've got something that might help with that." He dug in his pocket for his keys. Found the little round silver one that had been on his key ring for as long as he could remember. "Closing's not until Friday—which you'll probably want to be there, since your name's going on the deed—"

A squeal from Sloane interrupted him. Man, he thought he couldn't love her any more than he already did, but the sparkle in her eyes, the flush in her cheeks, the heart-melting smile all proved him wrong.

"Anyway, since the house is staying in the family"—he wedged a thumbnail into the key ring—"I figure I can give you this a little early." The key popped free, and he held it out to her. "Warning you, it's a little old."

"Too late, Anderson." She flashed him that snarky grin he'd come to love. "I'm already head over heels. Warts and all, whatever issues it has, it's a treasure. And I'm going to love it and care for it the rest of my life." The husky tone of her voice, the sheen in her eyes, made it clear she wasn't just talking about the house.

"Well then. There's no one in the world I'd rather give this to." The house? His heart? The answer was the same for both.

Clearing the emotion from his throat, he placed the key in her palm, tucked her fingers around it, and wrapped his hand around hers.

"Welcome home."

# CHAPTER THIRTY-ONE

*One Year Later*

FOR GARRETT, EARLY summer evenings didn't get much better than this: sitting on the farmhouse's porch swing, cell phone off, his arm around Sloane. An uncharacteristically cool evening breeze caressed his face and teased tufts of cottonwood fluff from rustling leaves. Winking pinpoints of neon green light hovered above the grass, marking the presence of fireflies. Occasional flickers of lightning illuminated a distant thunderhead to the west, but it'd still be a while before they needed to go inside.

Over the months since Sloane had moved in, wide-eyed and giddy, she'd done much to improve the place. Floral wallpaper had given way to a fresh coat of creamy paint that enlarged and brightened the space. Brass light fixtures were donated to charity in favor of antique bronze ones that looked right at home. She had hired landscapers to restore the grounds, worked out an arrangement with a nearby farmer to ensure the continued prosperity of the land, and was even trying her hand at resurrecting Grandma's beloved garden. Under Sloane's care, the house was flourishing.

She was flourishing too. Reconnecting with her mother, answering the questions that had dogged her all her life, had awakened a quiet contentment Garrett hadn't seen before. Though her budding relationship with Kimberly had its rough patches, they'd forged a fragile peace that had even enabled Sloane to meet her half siblings. After the predictable period of shock following the discovery of their long-lost half sister, they'd welcomed her—and Garrett—with open arms. They were all coming for Thanksgiving this year, which Sloane planned to host in the newly renovated Brennan farmhouse. He couldn't be more proud of her.

He was pretty proud of himself too. The Wichita branch of Mitchell and Graves Financial had hit the ground running. He was busy, but it was a good busy. A busy that fulfilled rather than drained. And being in close proximity to Sloane, being able to meet for lunch or take in some jazz or just hang out on her front porch . . . nothing in the world could compare to that.

With a contented sigh, he pulled Sloane close and inhaled the sweet fragrance of her hair. Freshly repaired porch beams gleamed in the flickering light of citronella candles. No contractors required here. Hours of Google searches and YouTube videos had given him the courage to tackle it himself. Install the porch swing and everything. And he'd done it. Amazing what some elbow grease, a few basic tools, and a lot of sweat could accomplish. It had unlocked a handyman side of him he didn't know he possessed.

Yes, it was a perfect evening. The kind that, any other night, would melt tension from his muscles and lull him into heavy-lidded relaxation.

But the ring he carried wouldn't let him relax. Not yet. Its electric presence in his shirt pocket, next to his heart, buzzed with hopes. Dreams. Plans. Everything he wanted in life, everything he wanted to promise Sloane, was captured in that little circle of garnet and gold. He'd just been waiting for the perfect moment to give it to her.

And sitting on the porch with Sloane snuggled close, her head on his shoulder . . . no moment could be more perfect than right now.

"Sloane?" His voice almost didn't sound like his, as dry as his mouth was.

"Mmm?" She raised her head, and his hammering heart nearly tripped and fell over itself.

"I've been thinking . . ."

She gave a good-natured roll of her eyes. "Oh, brother. What grand plan are you cooking up now, Mr. Handyman?"

He chuckled. "Nothing to do with the house. At least not directly."

Her keen gaze swept over his face.

But when he slid from the swing to kneel in front of her, her confused expression melted into astonishment, then pure joy. Her hand flew to her mouth. Her eyes filled with shimmering tears.

"My plan is pretty simple, actually." He wrapped her hand in his. "I love you, more than I ever thought it was possible to love someone. You came into my life when I wasn't looking, but you're the one who makes everything make sense. You shake me loose when I get too stiff. You make me feel alive in ways I never knew I wasn't. And if there's even a chance I can do the same for you, then my plan is to try. For the rest of my life."

Where had all those words come from? He hadn't planned them.

Oh well. The best things often went unplanned.

"Sloane . . ." He swallowed hard and looked up at her, memorizing this magical moment. "Will you marry me?"

She nodded and made an adorable squeaking sound. Was that a yes?

It sure didn't feel like a no. Not with the way she flung her arms around his neck and smothered his lips with kisses.

Finally, she pulled back, her arms still locked around him. "Yes, Garrett. Absolutely. Yes."

She moved in for another kiss, but he held up one finger and fished in his shirt pocket for the little velvet box.

"What's that?" She dabbed below one eye with a fingertip.

"You said yes. It comes with jewelry." His smile a flimsy cover for his racing heart and trembling fingers, he popped the box open.

She stared, her mouth forming a little O of surprise.

"Wow." Taking the box from his hands, she tilted it back and forth. "That looks old."

"It is."

She slipped the ring from the box and turned it in her fingertips. "It's beautiful. I've never seen a ring like this."

Garrett bit his lower lip to contain the excitement that longed to burst forth. Of all the scenarios he'd envisioned, this one—where she didn't immediately place the ring and was in fact utterly clueless as to its significance—hadn't occurred to him.

No matter. He'd roll with it. Because now he got to unwrap the rest of it for her.

She studied the ring as she would any other historical artifact. Her sharp eyes peeked inside the band. Checking for an inscription, no doubt.

Maybe she wasn't in love with the ring. Not yet.

But she would be.

Of that he was certain.

>←

There was a story behind this ring. Had to be.

Because this didn't look like the kind of ring Garrett Anderson would pick out. Though they'd discussed marriage, talked about rings even, the classic diamond solitaire was what she'd expected from him. What she'd always pictured receiving in those rare moments she allowed herself to imagine someone choosing her for the rest of his life.

But this ring was unique. Quirky. Breathtaking in its simplicity. The deep red stone glittered in the candlelight. The delicate gold band seemed lit from within. It wasn't the ring she'd have chosen for herself, and it only fit her pinky, not her ring finger . . . but it had a sense of destiny about it. A feeling of perfection. Of rightness.

As though it was somehow always meant to be hers.

She pressed a kiss to his stubbled cheek. "This ring is incredible."

"I'm glad you like it," he said as he resumed his seat on the swing. "Sorry it's a little small."

"We can get it resized. Or not." She held out her hand to admire the stone. "I kinda like it on this finger."

"Up to you."

She beamed up at Garrett. Her fiancé. The man who wanted to spend his life with her. "So tell me the story."

Mischief gleamed in his eyes. "What story?"

"Come on. A ring like this? There has to be a story."

"Okay, twist my arm." His voice was light but held a nervous undercurrent. "It actually took quite a bit of research. Colleen even helped."

Sloane's eyes widened. "Really?"

"She's the one who found Anita."

Sloane stared. Garrett had been in cahoots with Colleen, and now there was a new name she'd never heard, and it was somehow connected with the ring?

She'd never felt so out of the loop in all her life.

"Who's Anita?"

"Anita Morgan. She's sixty-three. Elementary school librarian in Norman, Oklahoma. I went down to see her last weekend."

"In Sooner country?"

"Don't worry, I wore my KU shirt the whole time." Crossing his legs in front of him, he leaned back in the swing and draped his arm over her shoulders, but his shaky voice belied the relaxed posture. "Anyway, Anita's had this ring forever. Wanted to give it to her daughter, but she ended up raising goldendoodles, not kids. The ring was her grandma's, though, so she held on to it. Said God would tell her when it was time to let it go."

"Hmm." The richness of the gold and garnet deepened with new information. What could Garrett have possibly said to convince Anita Morgan to let go of a family heirloom? She almost felt bad for the woman. Maybe she should return the ring. Explain the well-meaning mix-up. It should stay in her family, not go to a stranger.

"I guess I should tell you her grandma's name." Garrett's gaze slid toward her with elaborate casualness. "Maggie Ann."

"As in *Annabelle's* Maggie Ann?" If Anita Morgan was sixty-three, then Maggie Ann Brennan was well within range to be her grandmother.

"One and the same. But Maggie Ann wasn't the original owner of the ring either." A smile crept across his face, and he took her hands in his. "It belonged to her mother."

Recollection slammed into Sloane. Annabelle's diary. The wedding day. Jack. Her garnet ring on a band of gold filigree.

"Garrett." Her voice shook. "Are you telling me . . . Is this Annabelle's ring?"

"There it is." His eyes shone. "I knew you'd catch on eventually."

The tears that had threatened since the moment he knelt in front of her spilled forth. Joy burst out in strange, laughing sobs as she threw her arms around his neck and buried her face in his shoulder. She was so overcome—with the ring, with his proposal, with his desire to spend the rest of his life with her and be her family—that speech deserted her.

Finally, his name slipped out. Over and over she said it. He held her close, kissing her hair. Chuckling softly.

"I can't believe you went to all that work for a ring." She pulled back to look at him. "You could've just gone to a jewelry store."

"Now where's the fun in that? This took a lot of planning. And you know how I feel about planning."

She laughed, and another tear spilled out. He thumbed it away, then slipped his hand beneath her hair and kissed her forehead.

"I knew coming up with Annabelle's ring might be a long shot, so plan B was to have a replica made. Colleen was willing to help me with that too." His fingers whispered over her cheekbone. "But I'm really glad I didn't have to go with plan B. Because you're a plan A girl, Sloane Kelley. You are—forever and always—my plan A."

# AUTHOR'S NOTES

FAMILY IS AT the heart of this book, and without my particular family, this book wouldn't be here. While the contemporary characters are entirely fictional, my historical characters are inspired by three of my ancestors, painstakingly discovered and researched by my genealogist mom.

Annabelle Collins's inspiration is Antoinette Patrick Peterson, a paternal ancestor of mine whose father, Chauncey, fought for the Union as a member of the 19th Indiana Infantry in the famed Iron Brigade. After losing his wife and baby daughter in a fire, he left nine-year-old Antoinette with her aunt and uncle, Stephen and Katherine Cooper, who raised her. Around 1860, the Coopers, along with Antoinette, moved to Jefferson County, Kansas. Although being sent to live with relatives was a common practice at the time, I couldn't imagine it not being painful for a child, and I wanted to explore the theme of healing from parental abandonment in both the contemporary and the historical story lines.

Jack Brennan was inspired by two ancestors on my mother's side, William Fletcher Stevens and Francis Thomas Little. A native of Kentucky, William Stevens moved in 1870 to a section of land in Sedgwick County near what is now the town of Maize, becoming one of the area's earliest settlers. His first years as a homesteader were marked by tragedy, as he lost his wife, Sarah, and infant son, George, shortly after arrival. In fact, my great-great-great-grandfather would lose a total of eight of his fourteen children, six of whom died before the age of seven. His perseverance and steadfast faith in the face of unimaginable hardship are an inspiration to me, and something I wanted to honor in this book.

The rest of Jack's backstory, including his birthplace of Aghadrumsee,

Northern Ireland, his immigration to the United States as a young boy, and his stops in Wisconsin and Illinois before reaching Sedgwick County, are all real-life details of Francis Thomas Little, my great-great-grandfather. Much of the research for this book came directly from his memoir, *A Kansas Farmer*, which he wrote in 1934. Grandpa Little, as he's known in my family, settled not far from William Stevens's homestead and married William's daughter, Mattie. After homesteading in nearby Harper County for several years, the Littles returned to Sedgwick County in 1901, living in a big white farmhouse not far from where I live now. That house, which remained in the family for decades, is the inspiration for this book. At the time of this writing, it still stands, but the land where it sits has been sold for development. Though its days on earth are numbered, the Littles' house will live on in the pages of this book.

Most of the story takes place in the fictional town of Jamesville, a nod to an early and short-lived frontier settlement called Jamesburg, which sat where my neighborhood is now. Blackledge Creek is fictional, but Cowskin Creek, which meanders through the western part of Wichita, is its real-life inspiration. The museum where Sloane works is based on the Wichita-Sedgwick County Historical Museum in downtown Wichita, but enough aspects are fictionalized that it needed its own name. Other Wichita locations mentioned in the book, such as the Keeper of the Plains, the Arkansas River, and the downtown park where Garrett and Sloane have dinner, are real, but the names of specific restaurants, churches, and other establishments are creations of my imagination.

Garrett's and Lauren's memories of weekend visits with their grandparents are inspired by my own trips to Ulysses, Kansas, to visit my grandparents, Wilbur and Opal Miller. Although many details of the visits were changed for the story, the soul-deep memories imprinted during formative years are the same for both. In fact, it was a recollection of these weekends that I wrote for a high school assignment that prompted my English teacher to look me in the eye and say, "You need to get this published." Twenty-odd years later, in a much different form than either of us imagined, here it is.

Although I endeavored to keep real historical details as factual as possible, there may be unintentional oversights or inaccuracies. These are entirely my fault, and I apologize sincerely for anything I happen to get wrong.

# ACKNOWLEDGMENTS

ALTHOUGH I ALWAYS entertained the notion that writing books was a solitary endeavor, I now know it's the exact opposite. From the spark of an idea to the fully finished book, God has brought some amazing people along the way, whose assistance, support, prayers, and love during this process have been invaluable. From the bottom of my heart, I want to thank:

My wonderful husband, Cheech, and my hilarious and adorable Wenlets, for putting up with my distraction and absentmindedness when I'm in Creative Mode and the roller coaster of emotions when I'm in Submission Mode, and above all for loving me, believing in me, and always, always making me laugh.

My parents, Jim and Deanna Peterson, for decades of research into our family history, for their enthusiastic support of all my endeavors, writing and otherwise, for teaching me the true meaning of family, for underpinning even the craziest notions with a cheerful "we can do that" attitude, for giving me some truly memorable childhood vacations, and for introducing me to Jesus. None of who I am today would've happened without your love and guidance.

My pioneer ancestors, William and Sarah Stevens, Francis and Mattie Little, and Antoinette Patrick, whose adventurous and inspiring lives are woven into the fabric of this story. I'm especially grateful to my great-great-grandfather, Francis Little, for penning his memoir. My book would not exist without his.

My delightful agent, Tamela Hancock Murray, for her expertise, her enthusiasm, her prayers, and her unflagging confidence in me (along with the occasional edgy Demi Lovato song when I really needed it). I'm so glad God brought us together, and I'm thrilled to have you in my corner!

My dear friend and editor Janyre Tromp, for falling in love with and championing my story, and for her brilliant and inspirational guidance to shape it into more than I ever thought it could be. I am endlessly grateful to you for suggesting I write one more Jack and Annabelle scene. That scene is my absolute favorite.

My copy editor, Joel Armstrong, for taking a hatchet to my weasel words, pointing out some embarrassingly overused verbal tics, and in general working your magic. The changes I've made in the copy-editing stage seem small, but I'm blown away by how much stronger the story is for having incorporated them.

The team at Kregel Publications, for being simply amazing to work with. I couldn't have asked for a better start to my writing career or a better group of people to help bring my dream to life. I love you all, and I deeply appreciate all you do.

Theresa Romain, my middle school BFF turned writing coach (and still BFF), for taking my earliest attempts at stories and gently pointing out all my newbie-writer bad habits, but also for reassuring me that my stories had promise. Thank you for your expertise, your enduring friendship, and your commitment to helping me maintain my sanity.

Linda Fletcher, Rebekah Millet, and Rachel Scott McDaniel, my critique partners, cheerleaders, and copresidents of the Jack Brennan Fan Club. You guys always know just what to say and how to say it to keep my spirits up. Y'all are the bestest.

Heidi Chiavaroli, Susie Finkbeiner, Joanna Davidson Politano, and Deborah Raney, for your encouragement and advice from the trenches. Thank you for being there; you talked me off the ledge more times than you know.

My distant cousin Bruce Nicholson, for giving me a tour of the house that inspired this book. After so many years of driving by that old white farmhouse, knowing it belonged to my family but never seeing the inside, it was wonderful to get a glimpse.

Rev. Dr. Jeff Slater, for his church history expertise (and geekiness), and

AMANDA WEN

Matt Webber, for clearing up some last-minute questions. Details matter, and you both helped me with a couple important ones.

The Quotidians, for keeping me endlessly entertained, informed, and prayed up throughout this whole process. I'm so glad God brought us together.

My family at Riverlawn Christian Church, my mom's prayer group, and several years' worth of Bible Study Fellowship groups and church small groups, for praying this book into existence. Thank you specifically to That Group, for your support, your prayers, and your snark.

My Lord, Savior, and dearest friend, Jesus Christ. Thank you for giving me the gift of words. I pray this book blesses all who read it and helps them get to know you a little bit more. Thank you for choosing me, saving me, loving me, and bringing beauty from my ashes. I love you.

And last but not least, Libby Eaton, Andrew Davis, and all the other teachers and friends who've told me for decades, "Hey, you should write a book." I finally did.